The Actuary in Trouble

The Calculated Risk

K T BOWES

Join Me

♥

I have a reading group which you're very welcome to join.
You can do that by signing up on my website ktbowes.com
In return, you'll receive four free eBooks sent to your inbox and an
email from me once a month.
I'd love for you to join us.

Love from Kate x

Acknowledgement

♥

This novel is dedicated to a lady who had a massive influence on my thirties and prayed for me every morning at nine o'clock. I underestimated the power of those prayers and felt the lack of them when she died and interceded for me no longer.

Peggy Rapps taught me what grace and goodness looked like in the flesh and if I conjure up her face in my memory; everything else is eclipsed by her beautiful smile. She was one of the very best things about living in Market Harborough and I hope she won't be too mortified about my fictional renovations of her apartment on Northampton Road.

I suspect right now that she's sorting out heaven from the comfort of her armchair and laying place cards bearing the names of her family, ready for the wedding feast at the coming of the King.

She loved intrigue and excitement and had a wonderful view of the world. I wish I could tell her I'd finally written it all down.

Chapter 1

❤

"Why won't you tell me?" Emma postured, hands on hips and full lips pulled taut across her mouth. "You looked desperate to spill the gossip yesterday. What's different today?"

The tall Irishman screwed up his face and turned his body sideways, deflecting Emma's perceptive gaze. "That was yesterday. And besides, the cop was right der in da kitchen. It isn't easy having him showing up all the time."

Emma's eyes narrowed. "He's my manager's son and he can visit at any time." She jabbed a finger at the Irishman. "And you won't be doing anything likely to pique his interest, will you, Christopher? So it won't matter."

"Er, no, I don't think so." His weak smile was unconvincing.

"So, tell me the big news," Emma demanded, leaning her butt against the Aga. The warmth filtered through her maternity jeans like a sunburst and she shivered at the instant comfort. "What made you run along the hallway like a fishwife with a juicy piece of gossip."

"Aw, nuthin' really," Christopher said, dismissing her with a wave of his hand. "There's doves nestin' in da roof of da folly is all. I thought you'd want to know." He ran a hand through the dark waves which surged across his head, a speckling of stubble beginning along his jawline and joining up on his chin.

Mischievous brown eyes sparkled in his handsome face and a vein ticked just above his shirt collar.

"Liar!" Emma spat. "Something's going on and I will find out." Fear crossed her expression like a scudding cloud. "It's Rohan, isn't it? He's taken another job as The Actuary." She chewed her bottom lip and anxiety filled her breast. "He promised he wouldn't."

"No!" Christopher exclaimed. "Yer husband's word is his bond. He said he'd punch my lights out and he did. Left me for dead, so he did. See, he means what he says."

"So what's the big secret?" Emma begged. "You have to tell me."

"No, I don't." Christopher crossed the room in three strides and fixed his strong arms around her. He pressed his lips to her forehead with a fraternal kiss and then let go. "Stop worrying." He opened the fridge door and pushed his face inside, rustling wrappers and poking at tubs balanced on the shelves. Emerging with a chicken wing he closed the stainless steel door with his shapely bum and winked at Emma. "There's nothin' to fear. Promise."

The kitchen door closed behind him and Emma forced herself to relax. Shaking fingers stroked the budding pregnancy which rose from her pelvis in a gentle arc and forced her into maternity jeans. "What are those men up to now?" she sighed. The warmth from the Aga soothed the backs of her legs and worked its magic into the aching small of her spine. Emma leaned her head back on her shoulders and closed tired eyes as her mind sifted through recent events. The scar on her neck from a knife attack smarted, reminding her how Rohan's last job ended and she strengthened her resolve. He promised he'd be satisfied with a desk job as an actuary, but Christopher's excitement the day before made her doubt. "I'll bloody kill you," she whispered. "There's more at stake than just you now."

Strong fingers snaked around her hips and she smelled the familiar masculine scent which made her heart race. "Da?" he asked, his voice husky as his lips grazed the exposed underside of

Emma's jaw and a smooth, shaved cheek brushed against her soft skin. "Who will you kill?"

"You." Emma turned and fixed her gaze on the brilliant blue eyes which widened in surprise. Rohan Andreyev blinked once and then his pupils dilated, making his irises dance and sparkle as his eyes darkened.

"Do it slowly then, comrade," he whispered, bowing his blond head to let his lips cover hers. "Slow and painful, with lots of screaming." His breath felt hot on her face and Emma's anxiety melted against her husband's obvious desire. "Come upstairs with me. We can die together." He pulled Emma's hands away from the warm Aga and fixed them around his waist, pushing his body against hers. His hands got to work massaging her neck and the back of her head, his heavily accented whispers an aphrodisiac in their own league. "Syn is out for the night with friends, bloody Irishman just left and Ray went to town to see family. Come." He ceased his ministrations and tugged at Emma's hand, urgency in his face.

Her lips twitched with the unasked question but then relaxed into a smile. "Ok."

The old house creaked and shuddered in the last of the winter storms as Rohan Andreyev clutched his wife's hand and led her through the darkening corridors of the old mansion. Predating the Norman Conquest in 1066, it enfolded the Andreyevs in its bosom, thousands of square metres of living space being painstakingly renovated room by room. Emma smiled at her Russian husband in the gathering dusk, his haste masked by a limp which hindered his stride, despite his efforts to hide it.

At the bottom of the stairs he pushed her up ahead, maintaining his grasp on her fingers so she turned to face him on the first step. "Ladies first," he whispered, fixing his long arms around Emma's waist. He dragged her into him and she smiled, pressing her lips over his and enjoying matching his extreme height.

Her mouth tantalised Rohan's senses, making him gasp for breath as she slipped her tongue between his full lips and let it dance with his. Soft fingers caressed the skin around the collar of his shirt and Emma deepened the kiss, feeling Rohan's body tighten against hers. Once she possessed him she drew back, feeling his disappointment and confusion. Slipping her fingers through the buttons of her blouse, she popped the first five open, exposing a lacy bra which barely contained breasts that swelled daily with pregnancy induced hormones. His lips parted and pleasure turned his blue eyes to a stormy grey in the poor light.

"Nyet!" Rohan jumped in alarm and swore, staring at his left trouser pocket in betrayal.

"No!" Emma lurched for his phone and battled to yank it from his pocket, holding it between finger and thumb and backing up the stairs. She peered at the buttons as the screen flashed and an English sounding name beginning with 'W' scrolled across the screen. "Not now." She dangled it over the bannister, watching Rohan's face change from regret to annoyance.

"Don't, Em."

"I will," she threatened. "Call them back later or I'll drop it."

Something flitted across Rohan's face, an almost imperceptible emotion which Emma failed to read. It came and went, a threat of foreboding and she halted three steps away from him, fear beginning its familiar flutter in her breast. She held the phone out and he clasped it, strong fingers belonging to a tanned hand with blue veins standing out beneath blond hairs. Emma held her breath, searching Rohan's face as he pressed buttons until the screen went dark, shoving the device back into his front trouser pocket.

He inhaled and Emma watched him replace the mask of indifference before looking up, his eyes regaining their sultry anticipation. Emma shook her head, the mood ruined but Rohan raised an eyebrow in challenge. He began the climb up to the first floor, gripping the bannister in his left hand and stepping with his left leg, bringing up the unwilling right side with an expertise born of practice. On the step below Emma's he drew level, their faces close. She felt his soft breath against her skin, peppermint and warm. He leaned in, administering a soft nip to her lower lip while snaking his right arm around her waist. "Stop doubting me, devotchka," he whispered. "I love you."

Emma nodded and swallowed the panic in her throat. She closed her eyes against the soft kisses on her cheeks and the whispers of promise in her ear, allowing her husband to herd her to the four poster bed in the opulent master bedroom. Rohan undressed her, his fingers kind as they breached clasps and buttons until her full breasts spilled into his palms and her burgeoning pregnancy pressed against the scratchy zipper of his trousers. His eyes never left her face, reading her and processing her inner fears like a mathematical formula being run through a computer program. The answer was always the same.

Emma didn't trust him.

Chapter 2

♥

The fire in the huge grate cast a dusky glow over the furniture, turning the dark oak black and giving the room an ethereal hue. Emma shifted her head on Rohan's chest, feeling his body shiver as her long curls caressed his flesh. With a lazy finger she traced the outline of a shrapnel scar on his stomach, knowing by heart its jagged, winding route but tracing it through an innate compulsion.

"I regret so many things." Rohan's low, gravelly accent broke the silence, fracturing Emma's peace like a hatchet blow.

"What?" Alarmed, she raised her head and sought his vibrant blue eyes in the flickering light. "What do you regret? Us? Me?" Self-preservation dictated the pitch and tone of her question and Rohan brushed her rebellious fringe away from her forehead.

"No, dorogaya. Not you. I regret my conduct only."

Emma moved so she could study his face, searching for the threat of rejection in his strong jawline or the glittering diamond blue of his irises. Her sitting distracted Rohan, his eyes roving over the silky smooth skin of her breasts and stomach as she sat between his arm and ribs and faced him. The firelight played across her nakedness and Rohan sighed and fixed his gaze on the ceiling high above his head. Emma nudged his hip with hers and the sheet slithered away from both of them.

"Relax, devotchka," he soothed, tugging at the soft fabric. When Emma kept hold of her end he relented and lay in the half light, his muscular chest like a brick wall against the mattress. She lifted her hand and traced a line from his hip to his navel, feeling the lumps and bumps of the scars which almost killed him.

"What do you regret?" she demanded, her voice gritty with fear.

"I regret lying to Mama about falling in love with my step-sister," he replied and Emma inhaled, his answer unexpected. "So much of my life has been intrigue and deceit and I wonder if it could've been different."

Emma shrugged. "I don't know, Rohan. We were children thrust together in a blended family by adults who didn't know what the hell they were doing. I don't regret the secrecy but I'm amazed it never blew up in our faces."

Rohan nodded. "Didn't it? I think sometimes that Mama knew."

Emma stroked the line of hair below Rohan's navel, smoothing her palm across his flat stomach. A smile touched her lips. "She didn't. We fell in love, eloped to Gretna Green and married, all without interference. Even when you were deployed to Afghanistan and she discovered my pregnancy, she still didn't realise you were Nicky's father."

"Da, and that's why I feel guilty." Rohan's exhale shook the bed. "She had a grandson and didn't know until it was too late."

Emma winced. "Ro, I didn't have a choice. She wanted to force me to abort my son. What did you expect me to do?"

"Nyet, no blame." Rohan sat up using his stomach muscles and Emma turned, dangling her foot over the bed. Coldness seeped up her leg, the heat from the fire leaving a void outside the range of its glow. His long arms reached out to pull her into an awkward embrace which bent her spine sideways. "Der was nothing we could do. I torture myself with the hope she might have accepted my syn if she'd known. It's just fantasy, Em. My regret is not giving her the opportunity."

Emma shook her head and rolled her eyes against Rohan's collarbone. It seemed pointless reminding him that Alanya's medicinal herbs ended the lives of children and husbands alike. Her brand of maternalism involved poisoning and death. "I don't want to go over it again," Emma sighed. "We can't change anything. Anton rescued me and made me promise to keep my baby away from his mother, which also meant no contact with you. You have us now, Ro. We need to look forward, not back." Emma ran her palm across the growing mound below her belly button. "You can watch this baby be born and take its first smile and steps. It has to be good enough, Ro. I can't give you back six years of Nicky's life, so it's this, or nothing." The veiled threat hung over them both and Emma registered it at the same time it exited her lips.

Rohan's eyes became hard like ice, his expression changing as he pushed Emma upright, holding her shoulders in his strong hands. "Don't say that," he said, his voice shaking. He released her left shoulder and ran his index finger down her cheek, following her jaw line to brush across her bottom lip. "Never say that. You're all I have left."

Emma nodded and swallowed, seeing the heartbreak behind Rohan's curved eyelashes. "You're grieving," she whispered. "It's normal, Ro. Your mother's death was unexpected and after losing Anton too, it's hit you doubly hard." Emma wrapped her arms around his neck and inhaled the familiar scent of him, aftershave and male. She scooted closer, pressing her breasts against his bare chest and sensing him relax.

"But she died in prison," Rohan said, his voice bitter. "A murderess."

Emma squeezed him harder, her own fears pushed aside. "I know, baby. I know."

Rohan Andreyev wouldn't cry. Emma doubted he knew how. Watching their families grafted together without skill from the age of six, Emma grew up with the Russian brothers in her life and never saw Rohan cry. His younger brother, effeminate and tender, cried like a girl over anything which tugged his heart strings; movies, sad stories, death. But he laughed with abandon also, his acting ability making it difficult for Emma to know when it was truth or charade.

Thinking of Anton felt like picking at a loose scab, the wound underneath still fragile. Her saviour, gone without warning. Emma struggled with her own emotions, hiding her face in Rohan's blond hair and waiting for her equilibrium to right itself. Her husband's emotional candidness flashed warnings in her brain and wariness replaced grief.

"Is everything ok?" she asked, her tone guarded. "Is there something I need to know?"

"Da," Rohan replied, pushing her upright. His vulnerability back under control, he smiled at her, his blond hair tickling her cheek as he nibbled the soft flesh beneath her ear lobe and nuzzled the ligament in her neck. "Ya lyublyu tebya."

Emma sighed, recognising the Russian phonetics as she stroked a soft blond curl at the back of Rohan's neck. "I love you too," she replied, meaning it and hoping it was enough to get her through the storm she sensed rolling across the horizon.

Chapter 3

♥

"Mummy! I'm home!" The front door closed and there was a scuffling sound before running feet padded down the hallway to the kitchen. Emma lifted her face, the smile already brightening her persona and she half stood to greet her son.

"Hey, baby," she said, her voice soft and lilting. He ran around the table, his coat flapping over his hips and pushed his face into Emma's stomach. Nicky's slender arms wrapped around her waist in his usual excited greeting and Emma breathed in the outdoor chill which rose from his clothing. "Where're Allaine and Kaylee?"

"Coming." Nicky's voice sounded muffled against Emma's fleece. "But I wanted you first." He gave a final squeeze and turned, trotting back to the kitchen door. Yanking it open, he yelled down the echoing corridor, "I'm in the kitchen."

Emma heard a faint reply and then the light patter of a female tread. "Nicky," she hissed, coupling her rebuke with a look of sympathy. "Please don't leave guests at the front door, sweetheart. It's rude."

Her son's brow furrowed as he processed her words before nodding. "Ok. I just wanted to see you first and make sure you was happy."

"Why wouldn't I be?" Emma asked, resting her fingers on the dimpled wood and feeling wrong-footed.

"Coz you sometimes get sad," Nicky replied and Emma swallowed, forcing a stupid grin on her face as a little girl with swinging pigtails danced into the room. Purple swinging pigtails.

"We lost you," she announced with a giggle and Nicky glanced towards Emma with a look of guilt on his face. "This house is massive."

"Where's Mummy?" Emma asked, staring at the door in expectation of her friend's arrival and sneaking a sideways look at the purple hair.

"I'm here." Allaine breezed through the kitchen door, closing it behind her. The heat from the Aga hit her like a humid wall and she shrugged out of her winter coat, revealing a slender body and gentle face with the inner beauty gifted by her Swedish forebears. She jerked her head towards Kaylee's purple pigtails and waggled her eyebrows. "Don't ask," she whispered. "Wash-in-wash-out hair dye which apparently doesn't wash out."

Emma stifled a giggle. "Tea or coffee?"

"I would say vodka, but I'm driving. Coffee should be fine."

Emma moved towards the counter and flicked the kettle on to boil. "Ro's got some vodka somewhere, but it's the genuine Russian stuff. It would probably blow a normal person's head off."

Allaine sank into a chair and ran a hand through her blonde bobbed hair. "A few hours of oblivion sound perfect." She peered over the table at the two children squatted in front of the Aga. Seeing them stroking the black spaniel butted up to the heat, she relaxed. Their six-year-old style conversation involved Barbie dolls and the merits of bungee jumping and Allaine rolled her eyes.

"What's with the you-know-what?" Emma asked, clanking mugs on the counter and stabbing a spoon into a jar of coffee. She halted, staring at the brown granules nestled in the bowl of the spoon and wrinkled her nose. Allaine rose and seized her hand, tipping the coffee back in the pot.

"Tea will be fine," she said, her tone soothing. "Just as you think you're over morning sickness, back it comes."

Emma nodded and sank into Allaine's vacated chair. "Thanks. I'll be ok." She breathed out through pursed lips and Allaine sought to distract her, speaking in an ancient maternal code learned by instinct.

"Somebody wanted something in their you-know-what and I thought it'd be ok seeing as it's holidays. Now the something won't come out of the you-know-what and is making the somebody distressed at the thought of you-know-where starting next week."

Emma glanced at Nicky and caught his eye. His father's blue eyes sparkled back at her, filled with amusement and the threat of a giggle explosion. Emma gave him a look which straightened his lips into a line, but she could see he struggled. Alone with Emma for almost all his six years of life gave them a bond far stronger than the hypothetical umbilical cord. Surviving on the wretched council estate made him wily and perceptive. Analytical like Rohan, code was wasted on him, reduced to comfort for the speaker while Nicky eaves dropped like a spy.

"The fire's on in the sitting room," Emma said, staring at her son until he got the message. "Take Kaylee in there to watch TV but behave." She raised an eyebrow in warning and Nicky twisted his face in disappointment.

"Can I just...?"

"No!" Emma replied.

"Yeah!" Kaylee sat up like a meerkat, resting her delicate knees on the hard tiles. "Can I see the secret passage?"

Nicky's eyes glinted with mischief, fading to dismay as Emma hardened her resolve. "No. Daddy's locked it. You don't go down there."

Kaylee postured as though shaping up for a tantrum and Allaine shook her head. "Do as you're told or we'll go home right now."

Both children allowed their shoulders to slump, slouching through the kitchen door and slip sliding along the hallway floor boards in their socks. Allaine walked the ten steps to the kitchen door and closed it behind them. "They can't get down there, can they?" she asked, concerned.

Emma shook her head. "Rohan's jammed it closed. It needs to be opened from the inside and Nicky doesn't know where the other entrances are. He's spent most of the holiday trying to find them."

Allaine flipped tea bags into the dustbin and plonked a mug in front of Emma, sinking into an adjacent seat with a sigh. "What am I gonna do? School starts on Tuesday and I can't get that dye out of her hair. I can't send a purple headed child to a Year 2 class; Dalton will send her home. And then what will I do?"

"Did you take her to a hairdresser?" Emma asked, sipping the tea and feeling a wave of nausea clench her throat.

"Yeah, already tried that. They wanted eighty quid to sort it out and reckon they need to dye it blonde. I'd have to sign a waiver to allow them to use bleach and it might all fall out."

"Oh." Emma pushed her mug away. "I remember a neighbour in Wales doing something similar. She had the loveliest auburn hair and dyed it blue for a Halloween party with one of those temporary dyes and then couldn't get it out. Lucya helped her because she had a job interview the next day." Emma's eyes grew dull as another grief bit at her soul. Allaine laid a gentle hand over hers.

"Lucya sounds amazing."

"She was." Emma smiled, but the expression held pain. "How many people would take in a pregnant sixteen-year-old running away from home? She opened her front door and Anton said, 'You don't know me, but I'm your grandson. This is Rohan's wife and she's pregnant.' Then he passed out on the doormat from driving for eight hours with chronic Glandular Fever." Emma chewed her bottom lip and ran a hand over her burgeoning stomach. "Pity Rohan doesn't remember her."

Allaine's blue eyes were gentle and attentive, fixed on Emma's lips as they moved making no sound. She grew anxious in the moments of silence as Emma struggled with her memories, both women startled by the sound of childish giggling in the corridor outside. The dog barked and the front door slammed. "TV must be boring," Allaine said. "Sounds like they've gone outside."

Emma's brow knitted and she stood and left the room, tracing the children's steps to the front door. Nicky clutched his skateboard under his arm and strode along the driveway, Kaylee bouncing along next to him. "Hey, guys. Where're you going?" she called.

Nicky squeezed his eyes tight shut and grimaced. "Sorry, Mummy. We should've asked."

Emma folded her arms and leaned against the door frame, her face stern. "Yes, you should. You don't just disappear without telling a grown up."

"We did!" Injustice flared in Kaylee's eyes as she folded her arms and mimicked Emma.

"Yeah, not the right one though," Nicky said, his stage whisper carrying across the distance. "We asked Ray and he said we could skate in front of the stables. He's over there with Christopher."

"What?" Emma disappeared inside the house for a moment, wrenching her ankle boots from the cupboard in the lobby. She hopped onto the front steps, shoving her feet into them. "What's going on?"

"Wait." Allaine caught her up, pushing her toes into Emma's wellingtons. "Gosh, your feet are small." She walked like a penguin, complaining. "Kaylee, are you misbehaving?"

"No!" The child looked shocked. "We asked the man!"

With a huge sigh, Emma dragged her cardigan tighter around her breasts and hugged herself to keep warm. She strode after the children and saw the confusion in Nicky's face as she approached. "You ask me, Nicky, not Ray, not Christopher, me!"

"What about Daddy?" he asked facetiously. "Can I ask him?"

Emma gritted her teeth, feeling her son testing the boundaries. "What do you think?" she replied.

Nicky picked at a stone in the wheel of his skateboard and nodded, not daring to meet his mother's eye. "I think yes, I can ask Daddy," he concluded.

Emma strode through the archway into the stable yard and stopped, her boots sliding on the concrete. Ray supervised a crew of workmen as they navigated the stairs from Christopher's apartment, bearing huge sheets of glass between them. "Stay there!" she called to Nicky, who halted under the arch. "It's not safe here, especially for you zinging around on a skateboard."

"Zinging," Nicky sniggered, sounding out the word for his audience and punctuating each repetition with a snort. "Zinging."

Ray heard Emma's boots tapping across the rutted surface and whipped around, his face relaxing as he saw it was her. "Hey, miss," he said, his tone casual.

"What's going on?" Frustration gilded Emma's voice and Ray's forehead creased in confusion.

"Christopher's moving into the folly, miss, like you said he could."

Emma watched the workmen struggle across the cobbles closest to the Tudor style buildings, their boots slipping and sliding on the surface. "Who are they?" she demanded, pointing her index finger in their direction.

"Oh, just some local guys but they won't spread gossip, miss. I know the bloke on the left from the army and he'll keep his mouth shut about the stuff they shift."

Emma's hands reached her hips and she glanced back at Allaine and the children, their outlines back-lit by the watery sun, casting them into silhouettes. Nicky stood on his skateboard gyrating his hips back and forth and holding onto Kaylee's shoulders. His blue eyes studied his mother with veiled interest. "Why did nobody tell me what was happening?" she hissed. "Don't I have a right to know what's going on in my own home?"

Ray swallowed. "I just do what I'm told, miss." He licked his lips and his eyes darted everywhere but at Emma's face.

Anger tugged at her sensibility and she descended into rich bitch mode, unfamiliar territory which made her afraid of the words that spewed from her pretty mouth. "I gave you a list of jobs at the start of the week and you've chosen to do this instead?" Emma waved her arm towards the workmen as they struggled to fix the glass into the bed of their truck. "I didn't write that list for fun."

"I'll get to it, miss." Ray licked his lips again and a vein pulsed in his neck, thrumming blood past his jaw line and into a face which flushed red. "Christopher asked me to..."

"Christopher." Emma said the name with distaste, the Irishman's influence on her home and life acting like a hidden fissure in a rock face, undermining everything from the inside. She turned glassy eyes on Ray's embarrassment. "I didn't realise you worked for Christopher. My apologies." She backed away, the damage done as Ray registered the threat and opened his mouth to protest. Emma's boots sounded loud and clunky as she switched from cobbles to concrete, striding away in fury. Ray's eyes widened as she stopped and skidded, turning to face him. "Oh, and Ray. Don't tell my son what he can and can't do in future. He checks with me, not you."

"I'm sorry, miss can we talk about this?" Ray called after her as Emma strode away from the stable yard. He sounded distressed, caught between a rock and a hard place and faring badly under the pressure. To her shame, Emma ignored him, intersecting with the little knot under the archway who stared at her in surprise.

"Are you ok?" Allaine asked, her blue eyes troubled. "Is there anything I can do to help?"

Emma shook her head, noticing Nicky's scowl. "No. I own this massive house and acres of property and not one person on it does what I ask." Petulance forced a shrieking quality into the sentence and Emma winced.

"We just wanted to skate!" Nicky retorted. "Ya didn't have to be mean to Ray!"

Emma rounded on him, her eyes flashing. Her blood pushed into her brain at a furious rate, making her chest feel like a pressure cooker. The scar on the soft flesh of her neck throbbed, a reminder of Ray's skill as an army medic as he stitched her up on the kitchen table. Anger dissipated quicker than it bloomed and Emma's eyes glittered with tears. "I'm sorry," she said and Nicky's brows knitted.

"I love you, Mummy," he said, his magic key to the world's suffering, doled out like candy. He carried his skateboard under one arm and used the other to wrap around her waist; reminiscent of the old days when they co-existed in starvation and solidarity on the council estate. "It'll be ok," he affirmed in his childish optimism. "I don't have to skate today."

The group walked back to the house in silence and kicked off their outer clothing in the lobby. The house felt luke warm despite the gravity fed radiators pumping out hot air and running through cash like a London stockbroker. Emma forced a smile onto her lips and turned to Nicky. "Go into the basement and ride your skateboard on the tiles down there in the corridor. Don't go into the rooms, though."

The boy's eyes lit up. "Yeah! Thanks, Mummy." He disappeared off to the left, past the kitchen door, trailing Kaylee behind him.

"What's downstairs?" Allaine asked, curiosity making her tilt her body to watch the running children.

"A cellar." Emma placed her boots on a shelf in the cupboard and pushed the wellingtons Allaine handed her, into the bottom next to a man's pair and a child's. "There's a set of stairs in the old boot room past the kitchen. The floors down there are quarry tiled and the corridor runs parallel to this one." She jerked her head to the left, encompassing the ornate archway and passage beyond. "But the skateboard makes a terrific noise on the tiles so I don't usually let him." She exhaled in annoyance. "I didn't remind him not to go into the wine cellar." Emma chewed her bottom lip. "He can't resist things like that. The darkness and dust act like a little boy magnet. Go back into the kitchen where it's warm and I'll nip down and see if Ray's managed to mend the lock on the door. It was one of his jobs this week." She stopped herself mid eye roll and forced a smile onto her face. "See you in a minute," she said.

Emma gripped the hand rail as she descended into the old servants' quarters, the ghosts of former service staff seeming to still as the mistress of the house deigned to visit. The steps were worn into a groove in the centre of each tread, the scurrying of countless feet over the centuries leaving their mark as they fetched and carried for the gentry upstairs. The archivist in Emma delighted in the history of Wingate Hall but the pregnant mother felt unnerved by the potential treachery of the stairs.

Two rooms downstairs made up the wine cellar, mostly empty but filled with hopeful racks of shelving, biding their time before a restock. The other two made up a series of boiler rooms, visited only when the heating system failed to crank out hot air or someone received a cold douse mid shower. Other vacant alcoves in the huge area represented the servants' dining room, accessed through an archway and some form of workroom. "Nicky?" Emma called, hearing no sounds of skating. Her heart sank. "Nicky!" she shouted, her voice echoing in the cavernous space. The dull light bulb probed the first of the boiler rooms as the stairs terminated on the western side of the room, its glow pathetically inadequate.

"What?" Her son's face appeared, a cobweb adorning his blond hair. "I was just showing Kaylee around."

The little girl's eyes resembled glassy saucers and Emma detected a frisson of fear in the brown orbs. "It's amazin' down 'ere," the child gushed.

Emma crooked an index finger and the children skittered towards her, the skateboard abandoned in lieu of other, more promising adventures. "This is the list of rules," she stated, glaring at her son's look of annoyance. "I'll repeat them for Kaylee so you both know. You do not go into the wine cellars because the shelves are unstable and might fall on you. You do not touch the boiler equipment because it has the potential to blow up you and the rest of this house. If I find you doing either..." Emma fixed her brown-eyed gaze on Nicky, "and I will be checking when you least expect it, you will never come down here again. Do you understand?"

The children nodded, Nicky producing the requisite, "Yes, Mummy." The cobweb dangling over his left ear said otherwise.

"I mean it," Emma reaffirmed. "You've already been in the wine cellar when you know it's naughty. That's your last warning."

Nicky swallowed and his eyes bugged. Emma hid the smirk, maintaining her hard line against the only person in her life who was still amenable to her control. "I know everything," she stressed, wagging her finger. "So don't make the mistake of thinking I don't."

"Ok." Nicky looked contrite and padded through the far door of the boiler room, aiming for the corridor and wide spaces on the other side of the wine cellar.

Kaylee turned, her eyes sparkling with excitement. "Can we look for the secret passages?" she begged.

"Yep, sure," Emma said. "There aren't any down here so go for it. Just don't go in the places I asked you not to."

"See, told you," Nicky griped. "There's none down here."

Emma faced the stairs again, pausing at the dog leg half way up to listen. The sound of the skateboard wheels began on the quarry tiles, dull and rumbling, guaranteed to be heard from the kitchen above and annoying after a few hours. She smirked, pushing away guilt at her lie. The locked door outside the wine cellar led to another set of stairs which terminated in the butler's pantry. If Nicky found access to that, she figured they'd never see him again. The Lords and their offspring might have owned Wingate Hall through centuries of English turmoil and changes of guard, but a sequence of capable butlers ruled it with an iron fist. It made perfect sense that the butler's pantry would be the epicentre of everything, including the series of passages which ran behind walls and under floors, stretching as far as the ancient chapel a few miles away in the grounds of the house and the folly on the edge of the property, the folly into which the troublesome Irishman currently moved his belongings.

Chapter 4

♥

E mma reached the kitchen chewing her lip, the misgivings making tracks into her brain. She'd offered the folly to the Irishman hoping to move him away from the house, a strategy which looked set to backfire. Pushing the door open she found Allaine warming her bum on the Aga and sipping cold tea.

"They're fine," Emma said, slumping at the table and seizing her drink. She pulled a face of disgust at the tepid liquid and pushed it away. "I'll make some more."

"Don't worry, I need to get home," her friend said, watching Emma through experienced eyes. "Right after you explain why you're so stressed and snapping at anyone who gets in the way."

"It's nothing," Emma lied. She flicked at a toast crumb on the wooden surface and winced as in her peripheral vision, Allaine raised a sceptical eyebrow.

"That was more than nothing," she scoffed. "Your poor manager looked like he wanted the ground to open up and swallow him. The poor guys with the glass almost dropped that big pane on the cobbles."

"Well, he's taking advantage!" Emma snapped, the fire of her anger restored.

"Ray?" Allaine asked in confusion.

"No. Bloody Christopher, the Irish git!" Emma spat. "I give him an inch and he takes a mile, every damn time. He and Rohan put their differences behind them with that last job and everything seemed ok. I don't want Christopher living over the stables so I said he could have the folly. It's over three miles away and I thought it would provide a bolt hole whilst being away from us."

"So what's the problem?" Allaine asked. "It sounds perfect."

Emma shook her head. She glanced at the closed kitchen door and lowered her voice to a whisper. "Rohan's discovered that one of the passages goes right to the basement of the folly. I wrongly thought the building dated from the 1800s, some foppish construction by one of the former Lord Ayers but apparently not. The foundations date back another three hundred years and Freda Ayers has studied the area. She thinks priests used them to move between the old chapel, the house and the folly during times of unrest and persecution. I've given Christopher a route straight to the house again."

"Oh." Allaine pursed her lips. "You must trust him, otherwise you'd have made him leave altogether."

Emma shrugged. "I have this misguided loyalty towards him and it clouds my judgement. Anton trusted Christopher and my stepbrother didn't suffer fools. He spent his whole life acting and knew a scam when he saw one. I wish he was here, then I could ask him myself." The bite of Anton's premature death bit at Emma's insides until her chest ached. She missed the Russian with the effervescent personality like craving the kiss of sunshine during a long winter.

"I can't really help you," Allaine said with regret. "The few times I've met Christopher, he's appeared charming and debonair." She smirked and Emma groaned.

"Just stay away from him," she warned. "He'll have you stripped and wrapped around him in seconds if you give him the slightest encouragement. That man's got no moral compass!"

Allaine narrowed her eyes, the smirk dropping from her face at speed. "Em, I hope that's not experience talking."

Emma tutted and shook her head. "No. I resisted his charms before I knew who he was. Now he just irritates me." She wrinkled her nose. "I think I wanted Rohan to pull rank and veto it; to throw Christopher out of our lives for good but he didn't. He's said very little." Emma attacked the crumb again, concern etched into her face. "He's keeping a secret and I'm scared."

Allaine exhaled, the root of Emma's problem laid bare at last. She sat on the nearest chair and drew Emma's writhing fingers into hers. "Then that's easy, isn't it? You ask him."

Emma snorted and threw her head back. "Ask Rohan? I could torture him for a week and get nowhere. He's a safe that can't be cracked, Allaine. I tried asking and ended up going round in circles, which only made it more frightening. I thought at first he felt miserable over Alanya's death but I see now that was what he led me to think."

"Like a cover?" Allaine asked, her fingers stroking Emma's in a steady, comforting rhythm.

"Exactly," Emma sighed, her mind retracing their passionate lovemaking and struggling not to see only betrayal as her husband distracted her from a quest to tap his mind and emotions. "And what makes it worse is that Christopher knows what's going on. He rushed into the kitchen to tell me something and stopped because Ray's son was here."

"Ah, so you're assuming because he's a cop, that it's illegal?"

Emma gave a noisy exhale. "Everything they do seems illegal. You'd think an actuary was just a really clever person who spent their life looking at numbers and data and forecasting financial losses related to risk. My husband travels the world eliminating the risks and trying hard not to die in the process." Emma leaned back in her chair. "It's as though losing his leg in Afghanistan gave him something to prove and he won't stop until he feels equal to every other male on the planet."

"That won't be hard," Allaine scoffed, a sharp edge to her tone. "Most of them are losers."

Emma sat forward, making the rear chair legs lift and clatter on the tiles. "What's wrong." She gripped Allaine's fingers resting over her hand and squeezed, comforted turned comforter. "I've never heard you say something like that. Are you fighting with Will?"

Allaine's eyes widened and her face shuttered behind an unfamiliar mask. "I don't want to talk about it." She pursed her lips but her face softened at Emma's expression of hurt. "Sorry, Em. I know it doesn't feel fair when I'm probing your heart for wounds so I can fix your problems, but won't tell you mine." She pressed the fingers of her free hand over her chest. "I'm feeling a little raw at the moment."

Emma shrugged. "It's ok. I know what that's like." She fixed a watery smile on her lips. "We're a right pair, aren't we?"

Allaine gave a quick succession of blinks and swallowed. "Yeah. Not forgetting my purple headed child."

"About that." Mischief flooded into Emma's eyes. "I remember what Lucya did, but I don't think you'll approve."

Chapter 5

♥

"Hahaha!" Nicky's giggles echoed in the cavernous basement, interspersed by the sound of his skateboard wheels running across the quarry tiles.

"Nicky, be quiet!" Emma snapped, watching as Kaylee's small mouth gaped and her eyes grew wide in her pretty face.

"Do you want the purple out, or don't you?" Allaine asked, tugging on her daughter's hand, her tone ragged and her body language more fraught than usual.

"Don't," Kaylee replied. "I like purple hair."

Emma watched her friend flounder and stepped in to help. "That's a shame," she said. "Nicky will miss you."

"What?" Her son stopped the board with his foot, abandoning it on tiles marked with the scrape of servants' chair legs over centuries of wear. "What you sayin'?" Nicky's blue eyes reflected his horror, understanding Emma's inference even while his purple headed friend admired the end of a pigtail with a pleased smile. He strode towards the knot of women, his face moving fluidly through dismay to irritation.

"I like it," Kaylee declared, primping a purple curl.

"But we won't see each other!" Nicky raised his voice. "Don't you care?"

"Yeah, we will." Doubt crept into Kaylee's voice. "You said you liked it, Nick. You promised."

Nicky's face crumpled and his shoulders slumped. "I do like it. But Mr Dalton won't like it. I don't want you to leave school. Please don't leave me by myself." Nicky pressed his face into Emma's stomach and his chest heaved. "Mo's already gone and now I'm gonna be by myself."

"I'll be there," Kaylee maintained, stubbornness fading from tight lips which wavered in fear. "I'm not moving schools!"

Emma winced, the veiled threat taken too far by highly strung children. She watched as Allaine shook her head. "It's true, Kaylee. It's in the school rules."

"No purple hair?" Dark eyes peered up into her mother's face.

"No dyed hair at all," Emma conceded. "I'm sorry. It's beautiful but Mummy didn't know it'd stick to your hair and not come out. She believed it would be gone before term started."

Kaylee gulped. "One more day," she begged. "You can wash it out tomorrow, I promise."

Allaine rubbed at a headache starting in her temples and nodded. "Fine. But tomorrow it comes out or you'll be standing in front of Mr Dalton on Monday with an embarrassed face."

"Why don't we have a tea party here tomorrow?" Emma suggested.

"It's a bit dark," Nicky piped up, looking around the dull space. "Can't we do it upstairs, where it's nice?"

Emma fought the urge to roll her eyes and nodded. "What a good idea. How about the sitting room?"

"Yeah!" the children shrieked, their voices colliding into a cacophony of noise. "A party. A hair washing party."

"Fantastic." Emma's voice sounded flat as Nicky listed party foods he might like. She tried not to dampen his enthusiasm.

Allaine pursed her lips and thanked Emma with her eyes, leaving the children to their party planning and retreating to the warmth of the kitchen. "Sorry," she said, slumping in her chair. "You didn't have to do that, but it helped."

"It's fine." Emma boiled the kettle again and poured more tea, her energy sapping as she wondered how long Rohan would be at the office. "I've got a recipe book somewhere. I could do some baking and try not to poison you."

"Don't be silly." Allaine gave her a smile and accompanied it with a sigh. "I'll provide the food and even bring the washing up liquid."

Emma plonked both mugs on the table and laughed. "Ooh, what flavour?"

Allaine rolled her eyes. "Something pink and floral. I guess I'll be washing Kaylee's hair in it a lot in the next few days."

"Yep. I hoped she'd cave and let us start today," Emma conceded. "That's why I pushed, but I'm sorry I upset them both."

"But you're right," Allaine stressed, clasping her fingers around the mug. "It's written in the school rules; no hair dye. Dalton sticks to the rules like a drunk on a painted line."

"What does that mean?" Emma frowned.

"It means he weaves all around it but somehow manages to stay on it. You know when the cops stop you for driving under the influence, they make you walk a sobriety line?"

Emma shook her head. "Never been stopped by one. I wonder how Ro manages with his limp. Would they take that into account?"

Allaine exhaled and pulled a face and Emma apologised. Yet her friend seemed listless and preoccupied still. Forcing herself not to ask, Emma changed the subject. "Sergei and his wife arrived back home in Russia." She chewed her bottom lip. "I'm not sure how I feel about them leaving yet."

Given the opportunity to probe Emma's fascinating problems instead of her own, Allaine zeroed in, just as her friend knew she would. "Didn't they enjoy Britain?"

"Not really. They fled here to get away from a threat which no longer exists. Mikhail's death mean's he can't hurt them anymore. Sergei and Rohan grew up apart, not knowing they were brothers and despite how much like Anton he looks, Sergei's completely different. There's no bond there and Rohan felt awkward around him. They're happy to be home and they were over here illegally anyway."

"Were they?" Allaine raised her eyebrows.

Emma winced. "Yeah. Forget you heard that."

"Dodgy passports?" Allaine whispered and Emma rolled her eyes and grinned.

"I'll refer my honourable friend to the previous answer. Please forget you heard that."

Allaine laughed. "Very politically correct, Em. It's not easy being married to a police officer. Nobody tells me anything."

"Fibber! I tell you way too much," Emma muttered. "Not that I know half as much as I'd like."

"Is Rohan at work?" Allaine asked, sipping her tea.

Emma nodded. "Yeah. He went to London on the fast train early this morning." Her tone sounded flat. "Something's going on, I know it."

"Maybe we'd both be better on our own," Allaine sighed.

"No, thanks, I'll pass," Emma replied. "Been there, done that. I'd rather have a tiny piece of Rohan than nothing at all."

Chapter 6

B y the time Rohan's car pulled up in front of the house, darkness shrouded the country, the last throes of winter hurling icy rain at the country in a miserable meteorological low. Emma met her husband at the front door, forcing a smile onto her lips.

"Zdravstvuyte, dorogaya," he said with a sigh.

"Hey," she said in reply, closing the outer door and waiting while he sat on the chair and stripped off his shoes, socks covering the prosthetic and slender toes of his other foot. Rohan pulled indoor plimsolls on to aid his grip on the shiny floorboards. "You look tired." Emma ran a gentle hand through his blond hair, feeling the softness of the waves and loving the way the short layers hugged the back of his neck. "How was the train ride?"

"Da, ok," Rohan mused, rubbing his eyes. He smiled up at Emma and caught her around the waist, pulling her onto his lap and taking her weight on his good leg. "I missed you though. Where is Nikolai? It's still holidays, da?"

"He's in bed. Wore himself out with Kaylee downstairs on the skateboard."

Rohan nodded. "How did Ray manage with the shelves in the wine cellar and the lock? I set up the floodlight for him to plug in. It made a big difference for drilling and using the ladder. I said he could get help from a tradesman and I'd pay for it."

Rohan wrinkled his nose. "I was meant to help him today but got called away." He kissed Emma's neck. "At least with the door locked, Nikolai can use the area without his mama worrying about him being buried under a mountain of shelving." Rohan's lips twitched.

Emma pressed her lips to his temple, smelling aftershave and the scent of the train carriage. "You told Ray to get a tradesman in?" Emma asked, wondering if Christopher had hijacked all their help.

Rohan nodded. "Da. It's not a job for one man."

Emma smiled. "I love it when you're tired. Your speech gets lazy and you sound so Russian."

"I am Russian," Rohan smirked. "Do you not remember problems at registry office because I was not a British citizen?"

Emma bobbed her head to touch his lips with hers. "Not really. I focussed on other matters at the time." Her fingers worked their way between the buttons of his shirt and she contacted the downy hair which formed a crown over his firm pectorals. "Yet they let you in the army?"

"I became a British citizen, remember? You want to show me the wine cellar?" Rohan asked, halting the steady intrusion of Emma's fingers.

She shook her head and pulled his hand over her breast. "No," she whispered. "I want to show you the bedroom."

The tiredness left Rohan's face and he bit his lower lip, his irises twinkling in the light reflecting through from the chandelier in the reception hall. "I'd like that," he breathed.

They negotiated the stairs and Rohan undressed while Emma lay on the bed and watched, propped up on one elbow. As Rohan shucked the last of his clothing and strode towards the four poster bed, Emma smiled and inhaled with satisfaction. Ray's disobedience, Christopher's arrogance, Rohan's secrecy and even Kaylee's purple hair lost significance against the chance to savour her husband's body and she made the most of it, smiling as he slipped her nightdress up over her thighs.

Satiated, they lay in a tangled heap beneath the sheets, Emma's head on Rohan's breast. She felt his heart pounding in its chamber and counted her blessings. "I love you, comrade," she murmured, hearing him snuff with amusement.

"Do the women in your office fancy you?" she asked, the random question surprising her once it was out in the open.

Rohan turned his head to meet her eyes, his brow knitted in confusion. "Ya nyeh ZNA-yoo!"

"What does that mean?" Emma mouthed the unfamiliar words and Rohan stroked her fringe back from her forehead.

"I said, I don't know. How am I supposed to tell?"

Emma rolled onto her stomach and bit her lip. "Do they stare at you and smile lots?"

Rohan frowned. "Da. They smile. Don't you smile at your headmaster?"

"Yeah!" Emma scoffed. "But not like I want to undress him."

Rohan's eyes widened and a spark of anger flitted across his angular face. "Bloody hope not, devotchka! I'd have to kill him."

Emma giggled and traced a fingernail around Rohan's nipple. The dilation of his pupils betrayed the blazing trail it left on his skin. "Can I see your office sometime?" she asked. "I'd like to view the pretty girls and weigh up my competition."

Rohan threw his head back and laughed. "You'd be very disappointed. It's mainly men in our industry."

"Really? What about equal opportunities?" Emma feigned mock horror on behalf of her sex and her husband winked.

"What of it?" He teased her and Emma relished the lightness of the mood, reluctant to blight it.

"So, how many women are there?" She batted her eyelids, cloaking her sense of inadequacy and terror of losing him to a better candidate.

"None like you." Rohan turned on his side, his perception heightened by the flicker of fear in her eyes. "There is my receptionist." He dragged his index finger down her cheek causing her to shiver in anticipation. "But I don't like blondes."

Emma opened her mouth to contradict him and Rohan lifted an eyebrow and silenced her with a kiss. "Don't even go there." He smirked. "Stalkers don't count. You can come to my office, Emma Andreyev. I have nothing to hide."

"Yes, you do." Emma cupped Rohan's chin in her palm and studied his eyes, recognising the signs of his defences rising. "Tell me," she whispered.

His brow knitted and he lay back on the pillows, cradling her in one arm while the other supported his head. "I'm being investigated," he said with a sigh. "I could lose my licence to practice."

"As The Actuary?" Emma asked, part of her hoping he could never break out that persona again. But Rohan shook his head.

"Nyet, Emma. Rohan Andreyev, the actuary, the legitimate businessman with the office in London."

"Oh, no!" Emma sat up and faced him, hauling the sheet up and holding it between her breasts. Realisation forced a dark cloud of doom over her head. "But when you retired The Actuary, you said you'd work in the office and earn a living that way. Does this mean you can't?"

"Nyet, dorogaya. It's just an inquiry. It happens."

"Who's investigating?" Emma's voice sounded tiny in the huge room.

Rohan squeezed her shoulder. "The Financial Reporting Council. Every report I write must comply with Technical Actuarial Standards. A few months ago, I submitted a report and followed best practice. As far as I was concerned, overall compliance was assured but now there's an alleged irregularity within the body of the aggregate report and the client has made a complaint."

"But you believed it to be ok?" Emma asked. "Did someone else not do their job properly further down the line?"

Rohan shrugged. "I don't know, Emma." He stroked her cheek with the back of his hand, tugging the sheet away and moving his fingers down between her breasts, letting them rest on the small mound of her abdomen. The baby inside gave a series of small twists and Emma's brow knitted at the strange, butterfly movements. Rohan's face softened and his blue eyes flicked upwards to meet her gaze. "I'm not worrying about it. I triple checked everything today at the office and can't find anything wrong with my data or the component report I put together. My communications are clear and can't be taken out of context. I'm not convinced there's a problem." His brow knitted for a split second and Emma seized on the loose thread of doubt.

"What do you mean?"

Rohan shook his head. "I think this is about something else."

"Someone who doesn't like you?" Her eyes widened.

"Da," Rohan replied. "Maybe someone trying to cause problems for me."

"I bet Christopher Dolan's at the heart of it somehow!" Emma spat, rolling her eyes in anger. "First, he couldn't wait to tell me there was a problem and then he played coy. All our troubles stem from that damned Irishman."

Rohan cocked his head and laid his palm fully across Emma's stomach, her rising blood pressure causing her child to fret. "Why do you say that?"

Emma's eyes narrowed. "Because it's true! And you know what? He rerouted Ray into helping him move across to the folly today, so the wine cellar isn't done and the front lawns look like a jungle. For all we know, Christopher's had Ray moving furniture for him all week. I think the tradesmen I saw moving his glass were meant to be helping Ray in the wine cellar, which means we paid for that too. Who does that bloody Irishman think he is?"

Rohan snorted, a low sound like a stallion crying an alert to his herd. "He kidnaps you, lures me into a trap which almost kills us all; yet you stand by him and favour him despite my warnings. Now he's overstepped the mark by diverting your property manager and you're livid." Rohan lay back against his pillows, both hands behind his head as he stared at the canopy above the bed and smiled to himself.

Emma sulked. "Well, did he? Did he betray you again?"

Rohan turned vibrant blue eyes onto Emma's face, his long lashes sweeping across his cheek. She chewed her lip and waited for him to reply, uncomfortable in the silence. Stubble graced Rohan's cheeks and chin, masking high cheekbones and the dimple on the right side of his mouth when he smiled. The march towards thirty marked his face with fine lines and her influence wrought crows' feet in the corners of his eyes from smiling more.

"Nyet," he replied, his voice soft. "He didn't, Em. Not this time." Rohan reached for her, the moment filled with heady tension and Emma felt his need to dispel all thoughts of Christopher Dolan and his treacherous brand of trouble, satiating her with him and him alone.

Chapter 7

♥

Emma groaned at the sudden shaft of light which played across her face like an irritating feather. It jarred her from sleep and the first words onto her lips proved unsavoury for the audience.

"Mum!" Nicky rebuked. "No swearing, not on Saturdays."

"Close the curtains," Emma grumbled, shielding her face with her hand and yanking the sheet up over her exposed breasts. She nudged Rohan in the ribs and he gave her a sideways smile, the soldier in him already disturbed by their son's feet padding along the wide hallway moments ago.

"Sit up," Nicky instructed and Emma covered her face with the sheet. Rohan said something in Russian to Nicky and the boy sniggered and responded with a word which sent Emma into orbit. "Lenivý!"

"Really?" she shouted. "You both think that?" Her tone held an instant edge of hysteria and she felt the pressure building in her chest.

"Emma!" Rohan's blue eyes stared at her in shock, brow knitted and confusion working his full lips into a straight line. "It was a joke. We don't think you're lazy."

Emma swallowed, but it wouldn't leave her, the sense of judgement as Alanya's words cut through the years, upbraiding her for some omission in her chores. Emma remembered the sting of the cane on the backs of her legs and nausea locked up her chest and stomach.

A sense of being trapped sent her into a panic and she floundered, snatching the nightdress from beside the bed and shoving it over her head. "Toilet," she muttered, making a run for the bathroom. She cut through solid swathes of tension as she fled, knowing it followed her into the room as she closed the door behind her.

"Mum?" Nicky's gentle knock on the door startled her and Emma ran the tap, washing her hands in freezing water and splashing her face.

"I'm coming now," she called, scrubbing her face on a towel.

The atmosphere in the bedroom seemed to clatter against the silence as the males eyed each other with a knowing look. Emma ignored their unanimity, refusing to sacrifice any more of her dignity. "You're not lazy, Mummy," Nicky implored, following her to the bed. "You do heaps. There's the driving and then the working and the washing and..."

"Ok, syn," Rohan warned. "Where's my breakfast? I'm excited to see it and eat it all up."

Nicky's eyes twinkled, widening to occupy most of the space beneath his eyebrows. "It's coming," he announced. His small feet pattered to the bedroom door and he squatted and reached out. Two glasses of filmy water entered in his outstretched hands, slopping over his wrists and soaking his pyjama sleeve. "There ya go." He handed one to Rohan, who spared him the wet journey around the huge bed by giving it to Emma. Nicky spilled most of the second one on the bedspread, wincing in apology before bouncing out of the room leaving Rohan with a dripping arm and a soaked crotch.

"Sorry," Emma said, sipping the fetid water and pulling a face. "That word has so much violence attached to it; I can't bear it."

Rohan nodded. "Ok. I didn't remember."

Emma stared at the grey sky through the half opened curtains. "You wouldn't," she said, her jaw tight. She stopped herself uttering the words *golden boy*, just in time. Rohan raised a blond eyebrow but wisdom convinced him to leave the matter alone.

"He means well," Emma said, jerking her head towards the remains of Rohan's water. "You should drink it before he comes back."

Rohan sniffed the rim of the glass and screwed his face up. "It smells weird," he said. "What is it?"

Emma sniffed hers and took another slug, draining the glass as Nicky's footsteps mounted the stairs. "It smells like the stuff I sprayed on the skirting boards in the kitchen to stop the dog chewing them."

Rohan's eyes widened and he made a lurch for Emma's empty glass. "You drank poison!"

"Course I didn't!" She elbowed him. "It's herbal stuff. Farrell hates it. Drink up, he's coming."

Rohan swigged the liquid and swallowed, giving a hearty shudder as it slipped into his throat. "I'm nervous about breakfast now," he whispered.

Emma grinned. "You should be. He made muffins for me once."

"What happened?" Rohan's blue eyes rounded in horror and he turned his torso to face her.

Emma shrugged. "I ate them but they were weird."

"How weird?" Rohan asked, swallowing in anticipation.

"We didn't have an oven," Emma said. "But that wasn't the worst part."

Rohan closed his eyes and pressed his head back against the headboard. "Tell me?"

Emma waited until he squinted sideways at her, Nicky's feet thundering across the landing. "We didn't own a mixing bowl. I think he stirred it on the floor."

Rohan's jaw gaped. "You didn't eat it?"

"Of course I did!" Emma scoffed. "I couldn't hurt his feelings, could I? He scrounged the ingredients from Fat Brian's wife and it was my birthday present." She balanced the empty glass between them and rubbed her eyes. "I daren't risk it today if it's dodgy though. Not with being pregnant. You'll have to eat mine."

Rohan said a Russian word which Emma refused to translate, even in her head. She got her best smile ready for the child's entrance, keen to remedy her earlier behaviour.

"This one's yours, Mum," Nicky announced, pride in his voice. He strutted around the bed bearing a knife and fork and balancing a dinner plate in his small hands. "It's fried egg on toast," he said. The oval-shaped face scowled. "Ray said you can't have runny egg and he smushed it in the frying pan." Nicky looked cross, his brow furrowed as he handed over the plate.

Emma settled it on her thighs and smiled. "Oh, my favourite!" she exclaimed. She picked up the cutlery. "I'm glad Ray helped you, baby. I wouldn't be pleased if you cooked by yourself."

"Yeah, I know," Nicky conceded. "I asked him last night and he said he wanted to help."

"Lovely, darling," Emma said, cutting off a piece and shoving it into her mouth.

Nicky skipped from the room, halting at the door to eyeball his father. "Yours is next, Dad. Ray's just doin' it."

"Spasibo, syn," Rohan answered with a smile.

"Yeah, he might be a few minutes." Nicky looked wistful. "He's just on his way back from Shit Creek." Nicky slipped away leaving his parents aghast.

"I thought we'd sorted the language issue!" Emma exclaimed.

"Ha!" Rohan snorted. "You turned the air blue when your eyes first opened."

Emma groaned. "Sorry." She sighed and pushed another square of toast and hard yolk into her mouth. Swallowing, she darted a mischievous look at Rohan. "I'm guessing Ray's worried about yesterday. He could see I was upset with him."

"Da." Rohan leaned across and snatched the next square of toast Emma sliced for herself, popping it into his mouth. "Want me to deal with him?"

Emma eyed her husband with suspicion. "When you say deal...what exactly do you mean?"

Rohan snorted as Nicky jogged through the door bearing the second plate. The toast was in the same hand as the cutlery and the egg slithered around leaving a snot trail. Rohan accepted the offering with a show of feigned gratitude and stared at the plate. He held out his hand for the slice of toast and Nicky slapped it on top of the egg, detonating the yolk with the downward force.

Rohan stared at it hard before raising his cutlery. Observing the first bite with intensity, Nicky relaxed as Rohan chewed and then turned to leave. "Ray's makin' me one now and..." He turned and squinted at Emma. "And...nobody," he said. He twisted his lips and winced. "But Mummy, nobody says you need to get more eggs." Nicky skipped from the room and his heels thudded on the floorboards of the landing.

"What?" Rohan pushed the slime around the top of his egg. "Does that mean we need eggs or we don't need eggs?"

Emma rolled her eyes. "It means Christopher's downstairs eating our food and lording it around again. Mr Bloody Nobody!"

Rohan raised his eyebrow at Emma's expletive and she sighed and finished her breakfast with a scowl on her pretty face.

Chapter 8

♥

"Mummy," Nicky said, sitting with his back to Emma while she pulled a tee shirt over her wet hair.

"Mmnnn?" she replied, sitting on the bed to fit her feet into socks.

"What happens at a party?" He turned around, his eyes narrowed and fearful. "I've never been to one."

"Oh, baby." Emma held her arms out and Nicky bounded across the bed, seeking the safety of her body in his confusion. "We've always been too poor to have one, but the friends we had were in the same position, so didn't have them either."

"You shouldn't have said it," Nicky groaned, his voice muffled into Emma's chest. "I wish you hadn't."

"It's fine," Emma reassured him. "I had a tea party for my fifth birthday and enjoyed it." She closed her eyes and remembered a woman with dark, curly hair which coiled around her shoulders. The hazy memory wore a feeling of pleasantness and joviality. Emma swallowed as the puzzle fell into place, her mother's face the only absent piece of the jigsaw. "My friends from school came and we played games in the garden. My mother made cakes and there was lots of laughter."

"Your mother?" Nicky's upturned face showed a splodge of egg yolk on his forehead and Emma smoothed it off with her fingernail. "Is she dead?" He lowered his voice to a whisper and Emma nodded.

"Yes. She died shortly after."

"How?" Nicky flexed his lips until they shaped a duck beak, not really wanting to know the answer.

"Car accident," Emma replied, putting a false brightness into her voice. She smiled to reassure him she was ok.

"Everyone's dead," her son said, pushing his face into her shoulder. "I've got no grandparents left. It's not fair."

"I know." Emma sounded matter-of-fact. "Can't be helped."

"I don't want a party," Nicky sighed. "Not without grandparents. Other people have grandparents at their parties. It's not right."

"But it's not your party." Emma felt her irritation rise, Nicky's self-pity fuelling some reactionary thread in her defences. "It's a getting-rid-of-purple-hair tea party and only to stop Kaylee feeling so upset about washing it out."

"I don't want purple hair!" Nicky's eyes widened. "I don't want to have to get it so that I can wash it out, just to come to the party." His mouth hung open in horror. "I'll stay in me room."

Emma groaned and flopped back on the bed, her day's allocation of energy already spent. Nicky pursued her, laying on his stomach alongside and pressing his fingers over her lips. "I don't want purple hair!" he wailed. "I'm a national blond." He pressed Emma's lips into a beak, missing the warning signs of an explosion in his self-absorption. Fortunately for him, Rohan didn't.

"Off!" he snapped, pointing at the boy's hand. He stood in the doorway, naked from the waistband up, the scarring on his stomach and torso ugly in the half light. "What's the problem?"

Nicky slithered off the bed backwards and strutted to the door. He edged past Rohan with wariness in his eyes, affecting an exaggerated sigh as he marched to the stop of the stairs. Emma heard him chuntering to himself and put her hands over her eyes.

"What's wrong?" Rohan stood by the bed and undid his jeans. Emma tipped her head back to watch as he slithered them down over firm buttocks and smooth, tight underwear. He sat behind her on the bed and she felt the movement of the mattress. She rolled on her stomach and watched him disconnect his stump from the prosthetic sleeve and adjust the sock covering it. "Bloody thing!" he said, irritation evident in his voice. He glanced backwards at her. "Why was he...?" Rohan lifted his fingers and patted them to his lips, demonstrating Nicky's actions.

Emma rolled onto her back. "He was getting himself upset about nothing. He does that sometimes."

Rohan frowned and stood to pull his jeans up. "Da, but not erm..." He waved his hand at his mouth again.

It seemed impossible to explain. Emma sensed Rohan's struggle to fit into an existing family in which Nicky had taken a role way beyond his years, expected to relinquish it once his father appeared. She exhaled slowly and let her hand rest on her abdomen, hoping her baby knew only peace in a family with a mother and father, security and enough food to eat. She thanked Anton in her mind for the legacy of the house and money to last her into old age. '*From Russia, with love,*' his will said, a tender kiss from a man who began as a child imposed on her as a step brother, finishing life as brother-in-law and cherished friend.

"It's fine," Emma sighed. "You stopped me blowing up at him and I'm grateful." She sat up and saw the nervous twitch of Rohan's lips, seeing how much he wanted to be a decent father embodied in that single stress tell. "It's good having you on the team. Being on my own wore me down and I felt so embattled most of the time, I had no energy for disciplining him or stopping him crossing boundaries." Her efforts went into feeding and clothing him and Emma stopped short of the statement, knowing Rohan would see only criticism for his absence.

"He'll cool off," she said. "Where have you been? Aren't you cold?" She grabbed the stretchy jeans from the bed next to her and shoved her feet into the legs.

"Siberian genetics," Rohan said with a smile, watching Emma dress. He walked around to her side of the bed and ran his fingers along the oak pillar supporting the bed canopy, sensing the history in the century old wood. "What do I say? Do I rebuke Nikolai or leave it to you, or what?" Rohan's blue eyes searched her face for clarity.

"Do it," Emma replied, asserting her husband's authority. "He needs to get used to it and I'm grateful for your support. I always knew if we stayed on the council estate, he'd end up influenced by what went on, but there seemed no way out. Now we've gone from one extreme to the other and I'm confused, so there's no wonder a six-year-old is struggling to orient himself."

"You don't want to raise a brat?" Rohan stated, his perception creating a sense of relief in Emma's chest.

"No," she breathed. "I want him to remember what hunger felt like and the excitement of owning a bicycle with a pedal missing. I don't want him to lose touch with where we've come from, but I can't take him back there either." Emma shook her head. "It's hard." She licked her lips. "We said we'd have a hair washing party here to help Allaine get the purple dye out of Kaylee's hair before school. Yesterday Nicky felt excited but today, he's afraid."

Rohan's blue eyes never moved from Emma's face, listening to every syllable as though she held the key to a fortune. She lowered her voice and glanced at the door before continuing. "He thinks he's never been to a party before but he has." Sighing, she ran a hand across her face. "It was so horrible, we both put it out of our minds. Because I worked at the National Library of Wales, his day care was nearby in a nicer area than we lived. I managed to get by on my salary, paying the rent, feeding us and Lucya and maintaining her old car. Nobody knew we weren't from round there. Then he came home with an envelope and I hoped I could decline the invitation and forget it. But the children hyped it up and Nicky knew all about it. I had no choice and Lucya dropped him off at a big house on the outskirts of Aberystwyth one afternoon. I finished work and went to fetch him and he was a mess. He couldn't tell me why, but he still had the present with him. It was unwrapped and stuffed back inside, a skipping rope I'd gone without food to buy and they sent it back with him."

Emma swallowed. "I don't think the invite was for him. A woman used to drop off a girl called Nicola in a flash BMW and they called her Nicky. I think the invite went astray. They wanted the rich kid and the kind of present she would've given, not some little boy who wore the same clothes every day with his cheap skipping rope and a handmade card."

Rohan sat on the bed next to her, not touching her but there. "You think he doesn't remember?" he asked, his voice soft.

"I think he doesn't want to remember," Emma whispered. "He was four."

"So," Rohan said, gentle blue eyes staring into Emma's. "Without making my syn into a brat, I must give him good party memories?"

Emma nodded, swallowing memories of humiliation and poverty. "Yes," she replied.

"Ok." Rohan leaned in and imprinted her lips with the taste of his, pulling away as she craved more. He stroked her cheek and stood, yanking the tee shirt from the chair over his head and leaving the room.

Chapter 9

♥

Emma smiled as Kaylee sat in her dressing gown in the kitchen, swinging her legs under the table. Her long blonde hair, safely ensconced in a towel and piled upon her head, had assumed a shade of pale lilac.

"Washing up liquid," Allaine whispered, leaning sideways. "Who'd have guessed it would work?" She sipped lemonade from a plastic cup and watched Rohan limp around the table bearing a plate of sandwiches. He wore black dress pants and a white ruffled shirt, a neat black bow tie at his neck. "Scrubs up well, doesn't he?" Allaine added, tilting her head and peering at the Russian beneath hooded lids.

Emma smiled at her husband, offering a lascivious wink of promise as he glanced over. His jaw tightened and he buried the smirk, directing Nicky to offer Kaylee more lemonade. Nicky flounced towards the bottle, tiny hands around its huge neck as he wrestled with the lid. His school pants looked crisp against the white tee shirt, the hand drawn bow tie looking inky black against the fabric. "I'm your waitress for today," he said to a beaming Kaylee and grinned at his father, who winced.

"She looks like the queen," Allaine snorted, observing her daughter's look of snooty superiority in the face of male devotion. "She'll be here every Saturday."

Emma shook her head and sipped iced water. "One time only offer," she said with a smile. Her husband moved into view again, wielding Allaine's tin of muffins and speaking to the little girl in a formal, Russian accent. "Cake, madam?" he asked, sending Nicky into a fit of uncontrolled giggles.

Emma felt the heat move up through her chest and into her head at the outworking of her husband's wisdom. To cure her son from the trauma of being a bad experience receiver, Rohan opted to show him the value of being a fantastic experience giver. Emma watched Nicky as he copied every movement his father made, vibrant blue eyes studying face expression and body language, every nuance and quality of Rohan's personality reflected in his own. Emma swallowed and rested her fingers over her stomach, isolated by the male bond, yet at the same time wrapped in its strength.

"You ok?" Allaine asked and Emma nodded.

"Yeah, you?"

"Just relieved about the hair thing," Allaine sighed. "It's one less thing to deal with."

Emma's brow knitted. "There's something wrong between you and Will, isn't there?" She watched her friend's reaction, guilt pricking at her heart in case it spurned a huge revelation which would jeopardise the good feelings induced by the party. Emma chastised herself inwardly for her probing. "Sorry." She raised her hand. "Not the time or the place. It's fine. You don't have to tell me but I'm here when you want to."

Allaine swallowed and nodded, seizing the get-out-of-jail-free-card and playing it. "Everything will be ok," she said, as much to herself as to Emma.

Chapter 10

♥

"I like you in those dress pants," Emma said to Rohan with a smile, running her fingers over the fabric which clung to his neat bum.

"Would you like to see them some more?" he asked, leaning back against the Aga as Emma reached for the dirty tea plates.

"Less of the pants and more of you." Emma smirked and watched Rohan's blue eyes twinkle.

"I meant, would you like to come out with me to somewhere I have to wear them?"

Confusion shrouded Emma's face as she stared at her husband. "Don't you have to wear pants everywhere?" Her eyes sparkled. "Unless you're inviting me on a foreign holiday somewhere hot. Somewhere pants are not required." She inhaled at the delightful thought, realising Rohan looked confused.

"Nyet. Not holiday." He pointed at her stomach. "After the baby we can go on holiday. Maybe to Russia."

Emma swallowed and bit back her sarcasm, forcing a wooden smile onto her face. "Where then?"

"The partners of a big client have asked me to attend an event in London on Monday night. I always say no but this time, I feel I should go." His eyes flickered with a trace of midnight blue until he got the veiled irritation under control. He pointed at his smart dress pants. "Come with me. See these trousers again."

Emma opened her mouth to object, hearing something altogether different come out. "Ok," she said. "I'd like to see where you work."

They finished clearing up and spent a quiet evening in the sitting room, watching a brainless movie with Nicky snuggled between them. The vivid black bow tie leeched into the skin on his chest, but he kept it on like a talisman. He seemed fine with the plan to sleep at Allaine's house while Emma travelled to London with Rohan.

"I'm borrowing a dress from Allaine," Emma whispered over his head and Rohan's brow knitted.

"Not the same one you wore before," he said, sulkiness in his tone.

Emma shook her head. "Don't be silly. I'll borrow a green one she thinks will fit. My belly's too big for that other one."

"Good!" Rohan mouthed, not wanting a reminder of Emma's date with Christopher Dolan back in the early days of their reunion. As he watched animated characters move about on the TV screen, his face creased into a smirk.

"Stop it!" Emma mouthed, feeling Nicky tense in irritation next to her. He snuggled in closer and Emma's eyes lit with mischief, glaring at her husband. She watched his brain working as he processed the memory of popping the buttons open at her breast, his temper flaring with pent up desire. Emma saw him glance at her stomach, their first union in six years producing a baby. She observed Rohan's lips as they twitched and swallowed, pushing the memory to the back of her brain and concentrating on loving her son instead.

Rohan sent lascivious looks over the top of Nicky's blond head, his hair flipped over one eye and his lips twisted into a smile. He raised his eyebrows and Emma read the promise there. Her handsome Russian intended to work his way into any dress she wore.

As Rohan put Nicky to bed in Anton's old bedroom upstairs, Emma emptied the dishwasher and boiled the kettle for a drink. A pair of hands settled either side of her hips as she bent to retrieve a teaspoon in the bottom of the machine and she froze, knowing they didn't belong to Rohan. "Get your hands off me or I'll break your face," she threatened, her tone icy.

Christopher Dolan chuckled, a throaty sound filled with lust. "Too bad," he said, raising a dark eyebrow. "Yer don't know what yer missing."

"And I don't want to," Emma replied, shoving the rest of the cutlery into the drawer. She turned to face him. "Why are you in my kitchen?"

"There's no food in mine," he said, as though his answer might be reasonable.

Emma gritted her teeth, feeling temper flare beneath the surface. A flush rose from her neck into her cheeks, increasing at the amusement in the Irishman's eyes. "You're renting the folly," she said, her lips showing only the barest movement. "That makes you a tenant with a rental agreement. You don't walk in and out of my home without invitation."

"Now, now, Em." He brushed her off with ease, sitting at the kitchen table as though he owned it. "Don't be like that."

"You've got no respect!" Emma raised her voice, her eyes blazing coals. "You made Ray help you move your gear and hijacked tradesmen meant to work on my property. I bet you haven't paid them yet. You're hoping I'll just pay their invoice amongst all the rest, like the power bill for the last few months which you made astronomical through running electronics I didn't even know about." Her words tumbled out, weakening her case against the cocky male and she swallowed before delivering her final line. "I'm revoking the rental agreement. I want you out, Christopher. You've been nothing but trouble for me since the moment I met you. Leave before the end of the coming week and I won't tell Rohan you just touched my bum. If you're still here next Friday night, I'll tell him and watch him tear your bloody head off."

"I did not touch your bum!" Christopher said, indignation screwing up his features. "I put my hands on your hips."

Emma's eyes narrowed. "Same difference, Irish. I'm another man's wife and you said you were happy with that. I'm not leaving Rohan and running away with you. There's no point hanging around in hope."

"Look at you, up yerself!" Christopher exclaimed. "You think that's why I'm still here?"

"I've no idea why you're still here," Emma replied, the flush creeping up as far as her forehead. She took a step forward and held out her hand. "Give me Anton's keys," she demanded.

Christopher swallowed, his eyes closing in exasperation. "You don't mean it, Em," he said, shaking his head.

"I do mean it!" She gave his rock hard shoulder a shove. "Give me Anton's keys. Now!"

With a sigh, Christopher stood, thrusting his groin forwards so it bumped against Emma's thigh. He pushed his long fingers deep into his jeans pocket and pulled out a bunch of keys. It looked smaller than Emma remembered, the last time he'd pretended to hand them over. "Where's the rest?" she asked, her voice sharp. Christopher opened his mouth to speak and Emma shook her head. "Don't bother lying, Christopher. I want them all back by Friday morning. Don't waste your time making copies either. I'll make sure they don't fit."

"You think I need keys to get in here?" Christopher asked. He stood, towering above Emma and infusing threat into his stance. His hand was lightning quick as his fingers fixed around the back of Emma's neck. Before she could speak, he hauled her face towards him and pressed their lips together.

Emma shoved his chest hard and as he took a step backwards, swung her palm at his face, contacting his cheek with a ringing slap which hurt her hand and sent shock waves up her arm. Christopher hid his surprise and resisted the urge to put his hand up to touch the burgeoning red mark that spread out into a handprint on his flesh. "I'm going nowhere, Em," he said, his voice low. "Anton told me to look after yer and that's what I'm gonna do." He strode towards the door, his footsteps hard as he channelled his temper into the tiles. He stopped with his hand on the handle. "You think you don't need me, Em," he said, turning his dark gaze onto her face. "There's a storm comin', sweetheart, whipped up by a very persistent lady. Don't say you weren't warned."

"What lady?" Emma snapped. "You're so full of crap."

Christopher turned, the slap encompassing half his face as a red welt. "So, your perfect husband's not told you about his wee problem with the Financial Reporting Council then?"

"Of course he has!" Emma sneered, twisting her face into an ugly mask.

"Aye." Christopher smirked. "Has he told ya that the auditor for the Panel is a woman? A woman he turned down?"

Emma swallowed. "It's a man investigating." As she uttered the words her mind sifted through their conversation. She assumed the auditor would be male. Rohan neither confirmed, nor denied it. Wrong footed, she lost ground and Christopher descended on her weakness, hammering his advantage home.

"She's a woman, Em. A very beautiful, accomplished woman who always gets what she wants."

Emma dropped her eyes to the red quarry tiles, noticing every blemish acquired over centuries of wear and tear. Her lips moved with silent words, none suitable for broadcasting.

"Wear your best dress on Monday night, Em," Christopher said, his eyes softening. "You've got competition."

Emma opened her mouth to speak, wondering how he knew about their stay in London. The click of the kitchen door revealed the Irishman's neat exit, effected after playing his ace card. "He's bugged the bloody telephone again," she hissed in annoyance her eyes narrowing. "No, the sitting room. He's bugged that."

But his words remained behind like a portend of doom, threatening her relationship and hard won security. Doubt filled Emma's mind and spread to her heart, poisoning her trust in Rohan. She collapsed into a kitchen chair wringing her hands and second guessing her husband's every word. He knew the investigator's name and sex, yet said nothing, letting her believe he was targeted by a male wanting dots and crosses in the right place, not a woman scorned.

Emma heaved out a sigh as she realised the Irishman's cruel trick had worked, distracting her from the issues surrounding his presence on her property and in her life. "Well played, Irish," she breathed. "But you're still leaving on Friday."

Chapter 11

♥

"Well, children. Did we all have a wonderful Easter break?" Mr Dalton's lilting accent washed over the assembled children as they sat crossed legged on the hall floor, scratching shoe buckles against the parquet and fiddling with themselves and each other. Emma perched on a tiny chair at the back of the hall behind the four hundred small people, aged between five and eleven. They increased towards the back of the room in order of size like a human ramp. "Did anyone do anything very special?" Mr Dalton asked, mesmerised by the immediate show of hands.

"I wet myself!" A tiny wail went up from the front row and Mr Dalton darted an urgent look at the reception class teacher. "Already?" he said in consternation. "It's not nine o'clock yet."

A classroom assistant darted forward and removed the miscreant, holding hands with the damp child in shared guilt as they traipsed towards the exit doors at the back of the room. A flurry of paper towels appeared on the puddle as if by magic. Nicky's teacher leaned across to Emma and whispered. "It's so hard for them. They're just babies."

Emma nodded and watched as Nicky raised his hand high, keen to tell a tale of his Easter holidays. She cringed, fearing what array of things might come out. Mr Dalton's pointing finger moved past Nicky, generating a look of disappointment. It rested on Kaylee, a fairly safe bet. "And what did you do, my love?" he asked, his bouncy Welsh accent lulling everyone into a false sense of security.

Kaylee stood up, brave and proud, a smile on her face. Emma's colour rose as she prayed the child would keep quiet about the only thing guaranteed to create a fuss in her tiny world. "I dyed my hair purple," she announced. "It's a bit faded, but it's still lilac." Mr Dalton eyed her blonde head, noticing then the faint blackberry hue. He raised an eyebrow at the Year 2 teacher and Emma felt her colleague slump into her seat with a sigh.

"And so it begins," Mrs Clark muttered under her breath as the rest of the assembled children broke into a hum of chatter, stretching and craning their necks to best see Kaylee's head.

"Very nice, sit yourself down then, Kaylee," Mr Dalton said, moving past her at speed. But Kaylee hadn't finished.

"And my mum and dad are getting a divorce."

"What?" Emma's voice sounded loud in the melee and she saw Nicky dart his head around and stare at her. He opened his mouth and she shook her head at him, telling him to stay seated.

"Well, I didn't see that coming," Mrs Clark muttered. "But I guess you can't really tell what goes on behind closed doors."

"No. You can't." Emma gritted her teeth and wondered how Allaine would feel, her private life spattered around the Arden community before she felt able to deal with it.

After assembly, Nicky broke file to run to Emma, burying his face in her shoulder. "You need to go back to class, Nicky," Emma whispered into his ear. "Mrs Clark's in charge of you at school, not me."

"I know." His voice sounded small. "But I was wondering something."

Emma swallowed and rolled her eyes. "What a surprise, baby."

Nicky looked up, his blue eyes wide with apprehension. "If Kaylee shares my daddy, do you think I could share her grandparents?"

"She's still got a daddy," Emma said, standing and pushing him towards his exiting class members. "He just might live somewhere else."

Nicky opened his mouth to protest and Emma pointed towards Mrs Clark's expectant face and gave the order. "Go to class right now, or I won't work here anymore."

"Ok, Mummy." Nicky scooted to the back of the line and Mrs Clark smiled and nodded at Emma.

"I might not have a job anyway," Emma muttered to herself. "Now the celebration's a farce, there's not much call for an archivist."

"It's not that bad, is it?" The Year 4 teacher's voice made Emma jump and she bit her lip, looking guilty.

"Sorry, Annabel, you weren't meant to hear that. I'm just feeling sorry for myself."

The Year 4 teacher walked next to her, trailing a line of older, more obedient children. She held the hand of the one nearest, the little girl trotting along sucking her thumb. "I heard the police found evidence which suggests the school is five years older than previously thought," Annabel whispered. "But they're still going ahead with the 150th celebration. Why don't you think you're needed?"

"Because I got everything ready," Emma said. "There isn't much left to do."

They reached the door through which Annabel and her train would depart and the teacher turned and stared at her as the children walked into one another's backs. "You haven't got all the photos."

"Well, I've got what there was," Emma replied. "Sam pulled them down from the mezzanine floor for me and I've catalogued, digitised and stored them. The only thing left to do are the displays and Mr Dalton said each class would take a decade or two and use the copies from the school server. You don't need me for that."

"You haven't got them all," Annabel said, emphasising the sentence with a jab of her finger. "Five years ago when the builders put up the mezzanine floor, each member of staff took two boxes from the original loft space home for safekeeping. Over the years as they've left, I've ended up with them all in my spare bedroom. I want them out now. My husband has plans for the room."

Emma gaped, opening and closing her mouth in surprise. Annabel leaned close and dragged the child with her. The sound of sucking filled the air between them. "You remember that old lady who prayed for me a few weeks ago," Annabel hissed and Emma nodded.

"Freda, yes."

"She prayed I'd be pregnant soon?"

Emma nodded and her lips parted, wanting to defend Freda's godly eccentricities. "Yes, but..."

"It worked!" Annabel's eyes lit up like Christmas tree bulbs. "I checked in the holidays and it worked. I'm pregnant." She hissed the last word and stared down at the thumb sucker. "I want that room as a nursery, so tell Sam to get his lazy you-know-what round to my house and fetch all those boxes."

"Oh. Congratulations!" Emma gave a weak thumbs up and watched as Annabel strutted across the rainy courtyard towards her mobile classroom. The human snake followed in a weaving line and Emma closed the door behind them, blocking out the gust of wind bringing rain with it onto the doormat.

Emma caught up with the headmaster in his office. He saw as she raised her hand to knock and jumped to his feet, waving his arm like an orchestra conductor. "Ah, Mrs Andreyev," he boomed, the timbre of his Welsh accent wobbling the cups and saucers on the shelving unit. "I was just coming to look for you."

"Really?" Emma sat down in response to the flick of his wrist as he waved at the squashy visitor's chair. She waited for him to sit and then broached the knotty subject uppermost in her mind. "I understand there're more photos to be sorted which a teacher stored on behalf of the school." Emma swallowed. "I'm not sure what you want to do. My position seemed unclear at the end of last term and I didn't know whether to come back today, or not."

"Not come back?" Spit leapt from Mr Dalton's lips as he emphasised the last word in his sentence. "Why would you not come back?"

Emma shook her head. "Everything's ready for your celebration, should you choose to continue with it. You were unhappy with my findings relating to the age of the school and I understood you were approaching the board of governors for a resolution."

"I did!" Mr Dalton replied, folding his arms across his chest. "I certainly did."

Emma moved to the edge of her seat. "But you didn't contact me, so I felt unsure of your intentions regarding my contract."

"Oh." His eyes bulged in his round face, intense and comical. "Oh, I'm so sorry. I remember now, yes." He ran a hand across his eyes and shook his head. "I've had the strangest holiday, Mrs Andreyev. There was a murder in St Dionysius over the holiday. The police contacted me because they found our plaque right in the epicentre of all the killing! How could it have got there? I couldn't believe it!"

"Yeah." Emma's smile looked wooden. "Thanks for sending them to me. I told you it was missing, if you remember. I also told you where the copies were stored on the school server."

"Oh, I know, I know." Mr Dalton sat up and leaned forward, shaking his head. "It was very remiss of me not to get in touch with you and I'm glad you've come in today, because I need to speak to you about many things."

Emma's eyes narrowed, not liking the idea of many things requiring her attention.

"Well," Mr Dalton began. "Annabel spoke to me this morning about the artifacts stored in her spare room and I must admit I'd completely forgotten. I've asked Sam to nip round after school and bring the boxes back here on the trailer. I understand there's another term's work there, at the very least. Would you be keen to finish the job?" He leaned forward in his chair, his eyes widening at the doubt which roved across Emma's face. "I'd be very grateful and I am sorry for not ringing you over the holiday."

Emma nodded. "Ok. I'll work this term but I definitely need to finish at the start of the summer holidays in July." She swallowed. "I'm expecting a baby in August." Her cheeks reddened as Mr Dalton leapt to his feet and scurried around the table.

"Congratulations!" he beamed. "I like Captain Andreyev very much and that young man Nicky is one of our most gifted and talented." He pumped her hand as though attempting to draw water. "I hope that means you're staying here in Market Harborough."

Emma nodded and released a smile. "Yes, Mr Dalton, we're staying right here."

"Oh, that's wonderful news!" he gushed, moving his head like a bobble head dolly. "I hoped Captain Andreyev might be willing to come in and speak to the Year 6 class about Afghanistan and his experiences."

Emma's face dropped. "I don't know," she stammered. "You'll have to ask him; I can't answer that, sorry."

Mr Dalton looked disappointed. "I understand," he said. "Losing a limb is a massive thing and I imagine it's very difficult to talk about."

"Yes." Emma nodded. Eager to change the subject, she steered the conversation back to archival matters. "I'll go and tidy the office today, but tomorrow I'll come back and begin work on the other boxes. Do you have an idea how many there are?" Emma asked. "A whole term seems like more time than I need."

"There's apparently a few," Mr Dalton winced and strutted back to his seat. "But I also wanted to speak to you regarding another matter."

Chapter 12

♥

Kaylee cried the whole way round the supermarket, bawling even louder as Emma browsed the shelf stocked with hair dye. "Stand still," Emma said, her tone sharp as other customers stared and whispered to each other behind their hands.

Kaylee hurled herself on the floor and pressed her face to the tiles, her screams echoing off like a claxon. "I don't wanna dye my hair," she wailed. "I wanna be lilac!"

Emma squatted down close to her face and made a pretence of checking out the freaky colours on the bottom shelf. "Kaylee," she hissed. "If you don't get up and stop behaving like a baby, I'll make sure the only hair left on your head is your eyebrows!"

There was a silence of only a few sacred heartbeats before Kaylee launched on a different tack. "I want my mummy!"

"You have no idea how much I share that sentiment!" Emma snapped. "And believe me, I wish Mr Dalton could have contacted her and then I wouldn't be standing here trying to pick hair dye for a silly little girl who seems far too big to be laying on a supermarket floor throwing a paddy!" Emma stalked to a nearby shelf and let Kaylee drag herself off the tiles and catch up.

"Excuse me, is that for her?" The uniformed shop assistant pointed at the box of hair dye in Emma's hand and then at the lilac head bobbing up and down next to her.

Emma nodded. "Yeah, wash-in-wash-out didn't wash out. We did our best to get rid of it and to be fair, it isn't that noticeable." Emma glared at Kaylee. "Unless you stand up in assembly and announce that you have purple hair. Until then I think the teachers assumed it was a trick of the light. Now she's been stood down from school until we can correct it."

"Hairdressers?" the assistant asked, looking at Kaylee's head as though she might catch her own personal dose of purple.

Emma shook her head. "Her mother tried and she'll need to sign a piece of paper denying the hairdresser's liability if her daughter walks out bald."

"Bald!" Kaylee clutched her head in her hands and hit the floor again, legs making swimming actions.

"Or blue," Emma added, watching the floor show. "Apparently blue is also an option."

"Ah, well, I'd try this one if it was my kid," the woman said, giving Emma a look of sympathy. She reached forward and seized a box from the middle shelf. "It's a bit dearer but it might bleach the stuff out without making a mess. It's got quite a lot of natural ingredients to negate the harm." She leaned in closer to Emma. "My daughter once coloured her brother's entire head in using a blue marker pen. She thought I might not notice he'd lost his swimming hat if I thought he was still wearing it. They think we're dead thick, don't they?"

Emma nodded. "Is this what you used?"

The assistant winked. "Yep. Leave it on three times longer than the instructions say and you might have this blondie back to her usual self. Natural blondes don't know how lucky they are." She patted a whitened hairdo showing exposed roots.

"I'm a national blonde!" Kaylee screamed at the top of her lungs. "A national blonde!"

"I'm so sorry," Emma said to the poor woman on the checkout.

"Sorry, sorry," she called to the man wheeling his trolley through the front doors. She kept her hand clamped over Kaylee's mouth as she hustled the wailing child towards her car. At the vehicle the child became apoplectic, hurling herself on the concrete and crying herself sick. Emma sat sideways on the driver's chair and watched, stroking her abdomen and fearing for the temperament of her new baby. Nicky's odd bout of hysterics rarely reached the kind of decibel level which Kaylee seemed apt to achieve and Emma concluded it must be a female thing.

When Kaylee took a veiled swipe at the paintwork of the rear passenger door with her head, Emma stood and yanked her upwards by her shoulders. "Enough!" she shouted into the child's face.

Shocked, Kaylee stilled, her little body heaving and blowing and her eyes narrowed by exhaustion. A line of sweat graced her upper lip and forehead and her face looked shocked back into sanity.

"No more!" Emma said. "Now, get in the car."

Kaylee moved like an automaton, shifting with robotic obedience. Emma fastened her seat belt and then leaned across, concern in her face. "Can you tell me what that was all about?" she asked, stroking the damp cheek.

Kaylee shook her head, eyes filling with tears. She released a hiccough with each exhale.

"How about we go to my house and sort your hair out?" Emma said, her voice soft. "Then maybe we can see if there are other things to be made better too."

Kaylee nodded and remained silent for the ride back to Wingate Hall, although Emma studied her in the rear-view mirror, knowing it ceased to become about the purple hair sometime between the start of the tantrum and the end of it.

Ray met Emma on the front steps, his hair covered in a film of dust and builders' debris. He raised dirty eyebrows as Emma helped Kaylee out of the car. "You swapped Nicky for a girl?" he asked, the humour wasted on both females.

"Something like that," Emma replied, without smiling. She gathered purse and child and skipped up the front steps, halted by Ray's call.

"Miss!"

Emma turned with tiredness in her face. Kaylee stopped on the top step and opened her mouth, the sound muffled by Emma's palm. "I'm busy at the moment," she said without apology. "We'll talk later."

Ray watched as Emma pushed the little girl onto a seat in the lobby and disgorged her from her school shoes, steering her to the left towards the corridor. "Nice one, big man," he muttered to himself. "Upset the only person who gave you a fair go. Sounds like a plan to get fired."

Emma heard the last few words and ignored him, hating herself for appearing so mean. The almost healed scar on her neck nestled under a floral scarf and it prickled in discomfort. Ray's hasty stitches, removed a week after his ministrations, left tiny holes and a strange puckering of the skin. Emma sent Kaylee ahead of her as she caught her breath at the bottom of the stairs and heaved a sigh. "It's not his fault you stumbled into Rohan's last job and got knifed!" Emma appealed to herself through gritted teeth. "It's yours." Emma tackled the stairs with all the finesse of an elephant, wishing the image of Ray's face that night would disappear from her memory. It hung over her, ghostlike and afraid, wielding a needle and thread like he'd rather be anywhere else but there. "It's not his fault," Emma reiterated at the top of the stairs. "Get over it."

"Whose fault?" Kaylee asked, her chest heaving with every alternate breath. "Daddy's?"

"No, sweetie, I was talking to myself," Emma answered. She wondered what Allaine's mild mannered policeman could have done but refrained from asking.

"I don't wanna be lilac anymore," Kaylee said, tears spilling from her huge blue eyes and tumbling over pale cheeks. "I don't want Mummy and Daddy to get divorced." She hiccoughed and Emma feared the histrionics cranking up for another display.

"Let's fix one thing at a time," she said in a matter-of-fact voice. "I think we'll use the family bathroom."

Chapter 13

♥

Kaylee splashed around in the massive cast iron bath in her knickers, enjoying the bubbles Emma added with liberal abandon. Emma sat on the closed toilet lid and supervised, relieved the operation was over.

"How does your baby come out of there?" Kaylee asked, creating a bubble beard with tiny fingers. She paused to point at Emma's stomach. The plastic bag knotted atop her head rustled with the movement, giving her white petals like a daisy.

"Ask Mummy," Emma replied, deferring responsibility to Allaine.

"But how did it get in there?" Kaylee persisted and Emma stood.

"Definitely ask Mummy," she replied, fixing a no-nonsense look on her face. "You're getting wrinkly." She smiled and pointed at Kaylee's skinny toes. "I can't send you back as a blonde frog. It's time to pop you in the shower and wash it out now."

"It's been ages," Kaylee sighed. "Do you think it's worked?"

"We're about to find out, but I really hope so." Emma flapped her hand and Kaylee stood, allowing Emma to help her over the huge white side. "I'll ring Mummy again in a minute."

"You don't think she's run away, do you?" Kaylee's face channelled fear; the real root of the tantrum and Emma shook her head.

"Definitely not. If she ran anywhere, she'd take you, so get that thought out of your head right now."

"But what if she couldn't find me?" Kaylee tottered across the slippery tiles, clinging onto Emma's hand.

"You're not hard to find, Kaylee," Emma said, leaning into the shower to turn on the hot water. "She'd go to school and Mr Dalton would tell her I'd got you. Simple."

Kaylee nodded, the Band Aid of adult reassurance temporarily applied. "Ok."

Emma tested the water and adjusted it to the right temperature. She affixed Nicky's swimming goggles over Kaylee's eyes, tightening the rubber band as far under the child's hairline as she dared. Then she issued last minute instructions. "The goggles will protect your eyes but I want you to keep your head back under the water for the first few minutes to let the chemicals wash away. When we think they're gone, I'll take the goggles off so you can do the back where the band is. Ok?"

Kaylee nodded with enthusiasm, her eyeballs huge under the raised plastic. "Do I look like a froggie now?" She grinned and splayed her fingers. Emma rolled her eyes.

"Like Mr Kermit himself. Now, let me whip the plastic bag off and in you go. I'll wait here behind the curtain." Emma fought to detach the plastic bag from where they'd caught on the goggles, the rubber gloves on her hands making it harder.

"You should've put the goggles on after you taked the bag off, shouldn't ya?" Kaylee said and Emma fought frustration.

"No, actually. As soon as I take the bag off your head, all that lovely blonde hair will tumble down and get everywhere so I'm happy with the way it's gone."

Once released, the blonde hair resembled a ball of tangled barbed wire, covered in white foam which was alarmingly tinged lilac. Emma groaned.

"What?" Kaylee asked, her froggy eyes widened further.

"It's fine," Emma answered. "I think it's stripped it out."

"And I'm not bald?" Kaylee raised a hand and Emma batted it away.

"Don't touch the chemicals," she warned. "I've got the gloves, remember?"

Kaylee moved towards the water, placing her feet with care on the sloping wet-room floor and pushing her head back under the stream, as instructed. Tones of lilac increased in intensity, washing down the plughole. "I hope you're praying hard," Emma told the child who closed her eyes against the heaviness of the water.

"Yep," Kaylee replied. "About my hair and about Mummy."

"Why Mummy and not Daddy?" Emma asked. "Doesn't he deserve prayers too?"

"No." Kaylee shook her head. "Can I take the goggles off now? They're biting me."

Emma leaned into the shower space and flicked the mechanism to stem the water. She released the child's face from the plastic, wincing at the tracks evident in the pale skin. Darker when wet, Kaylee's hair looked more blonde than lilac, although a peculiar hint of ginger replaced the blueish hues. Emma kept quiet. "Has it worked?" Kaylee asked, her face eager.

"Yep," Emma lied. She forced a smile onto her face. "Definitely no purple left."

Kaylee exhaled, her skinny, naked shoulders slumping. "Thank God!" she exclaimed. Emma winced, not knowing if the sentiment represented blasphemy or relief and deciding to let Allaine sort out the spiritual welfare of her own child. Bloody Allaine, wherever she was.

"Go and wash the back of your head now," Emma instructed. "Then we'll put this aftercare conditioner on." She snapped the tiny lid and sniffed the contents. "It smells lovely."

Kaylee stood with her head forward while the shower pounded the back of her skull with warm water. She looked like a sleepwalker, head bowed and face immobile, eyes closed against the dancing droplets. She jumped as Emma halted the flow. "Better now?" Emma asked and Kaylee held onto the wall as

Emma ventured behind the curtain barefoot and rubbed the conditioner into her hair. The gloves swished against the foam they created.

"Daddy took money from a man," Kaylee said, the suddenness of her revelation making Emma drop the tube of conditioner. She bent to pick it up.

"What do you mean?" she asked, nervous about the reply.

"A man gave him thousands of pounds," Kaylee added and Emma swallowed.

"What for?" she asked, regretting the trespass into Allaine's life but feeling the tug of curiosity far stronger. "That's a lot of money. For a policeman." Emma winced, the magnitude of Will's misdemeanour sounding worse out loud.

"He said," Kaylee stopped while she lowered her chin and attempted to mimic her father's deep voice. "He said, 'It's nothing to do with my job. I've never taken a bribe in my life.' Then Mummy said, 'But it's wrong. Why would someone give you money for a friend's address?' Then Daddy said, 'He just bloody did!' Then Daddy stormed off and Mummy cried."

"When was this?" Emma asked, resuming the massage of Kaylee's head, kneading the red strands of hair in the faint hope they would disgorge their strange gingerness into the foam.

"Last week," Kaylee said. "But they've not done speaking since then and Mummy cries a lot."

"Oh, dear," Emma said, understanding Allaine's quiet reticence over her marital issues.

"But Daddy took the money weeks ago," Kaylee said, her head a giant snowflake. "He put it towards his new car and Mummy just found out."

Emma chewed her bottom lip, the mystery deepening. She retreated behind the curtain after restarting the water and snapped the gloves from her hands, stuffing them into the box left over from the hair dye. A quick peek at Kaylee showed her running her fingers through her hair and washing out fruity conditioner. The water ran clear. Emma's phone rang in her jacket which she'd hung on the back of the door and she grimaced and flicked the extractor fan off. The screen looked condensated as she dug it out of her pocket. "Where the hell are you?" she bit at the caller, aiming a nervous glance at the basking seal in the shower. "Get round here now."

The caller replied and Emma shot another look at the child. "Just bring a few and hurry up! Ro's due back home soon and he expects me to be ready to leave." In answer to another question, Emma replied, "Of course you can. You didn't need to ask."

Kaylee sat on Lady Celia's dressing table stool at the far end of the hallway while Emma attempted to comb the dust bunny on top of the child's head. "Why are we in here?" she asked, swinging her legs and looking in the mirror. "And why is it so tangly?"

"It's the hair dye," Emma stated, running another handful of baby oil through it. "It'll come right, don't worry."

"So, why are we in here?" Kaylee repeated.

Emma frowned at a knot which wouldn't release. "You and Mummy will stay here while I'm away. She's bringing your things over and then she'll get Nicky from school."

"Where are you going?" Kaylee demanded.

"To London with my husband." Emma reached for the scissors as Kaylee admired her nose in the mirror. She didn't hear the quick snip or see the tatty blonde knot fall to the floorboards and Emma heaved a sigh of relief. Another one.

"Do you like your husband a lot?" Kaylee asked and watched Emma's reflection in the mirror as the woman smiled.

"Yes, I love him," she replied, meeting Kaylee's gaze. "Very much."

"Does the man love him too?" the child demanded, her face sincere.

"What man?" Emma asked, pulling the final lock of hair into place with relief. "Sergei? He lived in Rohan's old house up the street from you for a few weeks. Remember?"

"Not him," Kaylee said, swinging her legs. "The other one. The one who paid Daddy for your address."

Chapter 14

♥

"Do you think it was Mikhail?" Emma asked, her hand resting on Rohan's thigh as they huddled together on the long seat. The Intercity 125 train hurtled towards St Pancreas Station at breakneck speed. Emma's overnight bag nestled at her feet, the hastily chosen green gown squashed into it.

Rohan raised blonde eyebrows. "Do we have a time frame?" he asked, his face close to Emma's like a co-conspirator.

She sighed. "It doesn't make sense. Allaine said the man paid Will weeks before any of that started. Your Uncle Mikhail would've been in England but the first time he came to the house was the night Christopher brought him to talk to you. Remember? He seemed surprised to find you in a manor house and said so. He knew nothing about me or us or where you lived. If he paid Will weeks before for the address, wouldn't he have checked it out?"

Rohan shook his head. "Uncle Mikhail never paid for information. He extracted it. He didn't care where I lived because he could get to me whenever he liked." Rohan tapped his top pocket. "On the phone. Physical placement is irrelevant." Rohan stroked his arm across Emma's shoulder. "Don't worry, dorogaya. I'll look into it."

Emma shook her head. "I have a bad feeling about this, Ro. Allaine admitted the man sought Will out when we went for dinner after New Year, remember? Their daughter-in-law minded the children and we walked into town. Apparently the man approached Will at the bar that night and he told him to get lost when he started asking about you." Emma's mind went into overdrive. "I remember now. Will acted weird and insisted we walk home this really odd way. We cut through the alleys and he made out he was drunk. What if he suspected someone followed in a car and that was his attempt to fool them?" Emma sat up straight. "This stranger knows where we live, Ro! Nicky's at home and we're swanning off on the train for a night out." Her eyes glistened with emotions ranging from terror to guilt and Rohan ran his hand over her cheek, aware of the interest they gathered in the crowded carriage.

"Em, stop," he warned. He leaned close to her ear in a pretence of kissing her cheek. "Ray and Christopher are on duty, devotchka. Nobody gets in or out tonight."

Emma swallowed, trusting the skill of the ex-soldiers, one of them at least. "Will told Allaine the man approached him four times and in the end he gave in and told him what he wanted to know. Allaine's freaking out and blaming herself for what happened with Mikhail and now Kaylee's convinced they're getting a divorce because of all the arguing." Emma bit her lip. "Allaine sobbed her heart out when I told her I knew about the money. I bought the Girly Car from Will but he'd set his heart on a big, expensive car and didn't quite have enough. Allaine said he turned up with the car one night, even though she knew they didn't have the right amount saved yet. Will acted weird about it and they had a few blazing rows before the truth came out. She wanted Will to come and tell you but he refused on the grounds that you'd get him fired from the police force."

Rohan raised his eyebrows and looked at Emma sideways. He lowered his voice to a whisper so the man opposite couldn't hear over the hammering of the runners on the tracks below. "What kind of cop tells a friend's address for money, Em? There's more to this than just a car, dorogaya."

Emma nodded. "That's what I'm afraid of. What other information has he sold?" She sighed. "I told Allaine too much in the first place because I had nobody else and I needed a safety valve. She promised not to tell Will and I shouldn't have expected her to keep her word on that." Emma stroked Rohan's hand. "I tell you things."

"Not everything." His light kiss on her cheek made Emma shiver and she acknowledged the truth of his words with a guilty twist of her lips. Rohan's soft laugh made her want to lift his expensively tailored shirt and rest her face against his chest, extracting a fragile sliver of the merriment contained there beneath the sarcasm. "It will be fine," he whispered, his breath soft on her face. Passion hung like a thread above them as time halted for a millisecond, the promise of a night away in a hotel overriding good sense and safety.

The commuter opposite cleared his throat and rustled an open newspaper and Rohan bit his lower lip in amusement before kissing the end of Emma's nose and sitting up. "How was work?" he asked, his tone casual.

Emma shrugged and let him slide his fingers through hers under the table. "Ok. Mr Dalton says I've got another term's work and he's spoken to Freda. She'll come in a few mornings a week but he'll pay her this time."

Rohan's lips lifted into a smirk at the antics of the ninety-year-old woman who graced their lives with hilarity and history. Freda Ayers represented all pensioners whose teenage minds found themselves trapped in the bodies of old people. "That should be fun," he remarked, the smile staying on his lips.

Emma let the fingers of her other hand slide across Rohan's thigh, teasing him with promise and watching the tell-tale vein tick in his neck alongside the collar of his crisp white shirt. "Fun's something very different," she breathed, forcing her fears to the back of her mind. Wingate Hall's fortifications would repel an intruder without difficulty, she reminded herself. *Unless they have a key.*

Rohan coughed and moved her fingers away from his inner thigh, sliding her hand to a safer destination and keeping his clamped over it. His brow knitted at the distant look on her face. "Stop worrying, Em," Rohan whispered beneath his breath. "I promise, everything's fine."

Emma nodded and studied her husband's face from the side, savouring the angular jaw and long, Slavic features. His blonde hair behaved, slicked back from his face and sitting neatly above his ears. She longed to run her hands through it, dragging his fringe over his eyes as she kissed the full, pink lips beneath the day's rough stubble. Emma fidgeted in her seat, focussing on lust to distract her from Will's betrayal. Mikhail's face swam before her as it often did, ghoulish and terrifying as he lay slumped on the floor of St Dionysius' Church, the handle of the knife protruding from his throat.

"Clarissa Jameson Arden is still on the board of governors," Emma blurted, drawing a startled glance from her husband. "I thought she'd quit after her brother's death in the church and the cops finding the plaque." Emma chewed her lip. "But she didn't. She's still there, lording it around and pretending nothing's wrong."

"Nothing is wrong," Rohan said, a look of warning in his eyes.

Emma ignored it. "Of course there is!" she replied, struggling to keep her voice down. "Her family spent the best part of a century covering up a murder and pretending the school was five years younger than everyone believed." The archivist in her rose up in indignation. "They altered precious historical artifacts to make their case watertight. It's wrong and she shouldn't be allowed to continue as chairwoman."

Rohan squeezed her fingers in a strong grip and Emma bridled under the silent rebuke. She opened her mouth to speak and found his tongue flickering between her lips in a kiss designed to silence her for good. "Not now," he breathed, "not here." He transferred his lips to her ear and whispered, "The cops found the plaque, Em, but nobody else has done the research yet. Be careful what you say out loud, da?" Rohan sat upright and shot a curious glance at the man opposite, his eyes narrowing in suspicion as the newspaper rustled again, the owner hidden behind it. Emma felt him stiffen and then relax as though dismissing his overreaction. She relented, squeezing his fingers and offering a smile of contrition.

"I'll behave," she whispered and saw the dimple appear in his right cheek. Rohan narrowed his eyes in a mock grimace and Emma grinned.

London overwhelmed the rural girl, thrusting her into panic mode as Rohan navigated the underground and led her from one platform to another. The location maps flew past as Emma jogged to keep up, her overnight bag banging her legs as Rohan spun her from train to train. "Stop!" Emma groaned, yanking on his hand as the flagstones of King's Cross surged up to meet her.

"Em!" Rohan squatted down next to her, his face concerned as Emma shifted from her knees to her bum. People milled past like water parting to avoid an island, unconcerned for the woman on the ground. "What's wrong?" His eyes glinted with fear and he glanced at her stomach.

"Not the baby!" Emma snapped. "Me! You're hauling me along like a small trailer. I hate it." She stared back towards the semi-circular departures concourse with its complicated grid ceiling formed from steel. It glittered in a strange purple glow and Emma swallowed. "I don't like this. I want to go home." She sounded like Nicky, stroppy and uncooperative and a flicker of shame divided her heart between protest and regret.

"Emma, get up!" Rohan hissed, holding out his hand and glancing around him. She focussed on the passing legs, noticing shoes and ducking as handbags and holdalls whipped past her face. "Emma!" Rohan gritted his teeth and Emma heard the tension in his voice, surprised at his lack of compassion. She opened her mouth to protest and he shook his head, his eyes intense.

Emma clambered back onto her knees and used Rohan's outstretched hand to help her stand. He reached for her luggage and fitted the handle into his large palm, next to his own, carrying both bags together. "I need to walk slower," Emma grumbled. "Please?"

Rohan looked behind them and pulled Emma onwards to the platform which would take them to their hotel. The rush-hour crowd milled around them and Emma fingered her phone, tucked safely in her jacket but not immune to pickpockets. She tugged on Rohan's arm as he stole furtive glances around them. "Are you worried about robbers?" she asked, her face filled with an innocence which made his heart clench, the after effects evident in the wince on his face.

"Nyet, devotchka," he replied, switching to Russian and imploring her to understand. "Sposleduyushchim…" The inbound train obliterated the end of his sentence and Emma mouthed the words to herself.

She tugged on Rohan's hand. "Followed by who?" she asked, her eyes wide. Her hand found its way to her stomach, shock overriding her usual fearlessness.

"Man on the train," he hissed and Emma glanced around her, seeing only shoulders and chests. "Stop looking," Rohan said and yanked on her hand. "Stay close and walk onto the train."

"This train?" Emma asked, her voice faltering.

"Da, this train," Rohan replied.

Brakes squealed as the train came to rest and the doors opened on their automated loop. The hiss filled the space as Rohan tugged Emma onto the tube and pushed her to the right of the door. His eyes raked the following crowds as London's workforce filed on like zombies and Emma felt his fingers shift up to grip her wrist in a vice hold.

The train gave a shudder as the last footstep crossed the gap and the crowd of commuters lined up on the platform in obedience to an unspoken code of conduct, readying themselves to assault the next one.

"Off!" Rohan hissed and pulled at Emma, yanking her through the doors and only just making it onto the platform before they closed. Emma let out a piercing scream as her jacket caught in the doors, her body hauled backwards. Rohan's eyes widened and he kept hold of her wrist, struggling not to overbalance as she pinged against him at speed.

"It ate my button!" she wailed, examining the bite out of her jacket. "Look, it's made a hole."

Rohan's face changed from deathly white to pink and back again. "Der'mo!" he swore, his breath coming in quick gasps.

"Stupid foreigners!" a Cockney voice intoned, drawing nods of silent agreement from the waiting zombies. A uniformed transport cop made a beeline for them and Rohan galvanised himself, tugging Emma towards another platform, a short walk away. He limped, the pace not ideal for a prosthetic leg, no matter how wonderfully engineered.

Emma felt her resolve sapping, desperate for the sedate pace of Market Harborough against the faceless cruelty of the metropolis. "I don't wanna be here," she grumbled as Rohan pulled her inside the doors of another tube train. She tensed her body in case he chose to jump trains again but he crushed her face into his chest and kissed the top of her head. "We're good, now," he whispered in her ear. "We'll get out and find our taxi at the next stop." He pulled out his phone and pressed buttons while Emma's body shuddered against his.

"Ok." Emma nodded, adrenaline filling her lungs with tainted air. Her chest pounded and she cast her eyes around the carriage, searching for signs of familiar faces. Nothing. "I don't see him." She sought to reassure her husband but his confused look caused her cheeks to flame pink. "The man with the newspaper," she whispered, urgency in her eyes.

Rohan's brow knitted into a line and he shook his head. "Relax," he ordered, but she saw the tension in the set of his jaw. He stroked Emma's hair and she accepted the soothing motion with gratitude. She poked her finger into the hole left by the button and fretted. At Warren Street, Emma readied herself to exit but Rohan shook his head and stilled her with an arm around her shoulder. At Oxford Circus, he switched tubes, taking them from the Victoria Line to the Central Line, leaving the Underground altogether at Bond Street.

Outside in the fresh air, Emma calmed her panicked heart and forced herself to take regular breaths. Rohan hailed a black cab and gave instructions for an address in Kensington, pushing Emma into the vehicle ahead of him. He glanced around with watchful attentiveness, his head turning at regular intervals, his eyes searching from behind long lashes. Emma gripped the seat of the taxi in one hand and clung to her lap belt with the other, wishing she'd remained at home. The thought of home brought a precariousness of its own. "Who are we hiding from?" Emma asked, watching as Rohan spun in his seat again.

"Not sure," he answered, his tone serious.

"Is it the man with the newspaper? The one opposite us on the train? I though he was just embarrassed by you kissing me. I saw him again on the platform but he didn't look interested in us."

"Nyet, not him!" Rohan snorted. "He was just a regular commuter. It was the other man, the one with the umbrella."

"I didn't see a man with an umbrella!" Emma exclaimed, casting her mind back to the crowded train and equally crowded station.

"That's why you have me," Rohan replied with smug satisfaction. He leaned forward and tapped the window behind the driver, tipping forward to speak through the row of holes in the glass. "I have a man following me," he stated with admirable calm. "In the taxi two cars behind. Please can you lose him?"

"Sure thing, Captain Andreyev," the driver replied and Emma's eyes bugged. She leaned in close to Rohan.

"How does he know you?" she demanded. "You just hailed the nearest cab."

Rohan shook his head. "Nyet. I texted him from the tube train and asked him to meet us here instead."

Emma peered at the back of the driver's head, noting the crew cut and a scar in his skull which ran from crown to behind his left ear. "You're ex-army," she said to him and the man winked over his shoulder.

"Yes, ma'am," he replied, raising his voice to be heard. "Served alongside this gentleman until an explosion took his leg and half my brain."

"Half your brain?" Emma said glancing at the steady hands resting on the steering wheel, her tone concerned. "I'm so sorry."

"Don't be," he replied, "and don't worry, I've been cleared to drive." Brown eyes smirked back at her through the rear-view mirror and Emma pursed her lips and forced a smile onto her face. Her shaking fingers found Rohan's hand on the seat between them and she gave it a squeeze and counted her blessings. Rohan leaned forward and pressed his lips against her temple.

"He's fine," he whispered. "He exaggerates."

"Where are we going?" she hissed, her voice sounding hoarse against the cab driver's radio as he turned it up to cover their conversation, flooding the vehicle with 1980s tunes.

Rohan smiled as though pleased with himself, lifting Emma's hand and kissing her wedding band. "Somewhere you'll like," he replied. Emma caught a flash of apprehension in the vibrant blue eyes as though he doubted himself for an instant.

The cab pulled to a sudden stop on Clareville Street after negotiating the busy Gloucester Road. "Thanks, matey," the driver barked as Rohan tossed him a wad of notes. The car sped away as soon as the rear door clicked closed and Emma stood before the white frontage of a semi-detached Kensington property with her lips parted in surprise. "You said we could stay at a hotel," Emma muttered, the observation emerging as complaint.

"No point," Rohan remarked. "Not when I have a house right here."

"You own this?" Emma said, staring up at the iron railings which bordered the front garden like black sentries. The house towered above her, pristine white and twinned with the semi next to it.

"Da," Rohan replied, hefting both overnight bags through the gate and up the stairs to the front door.

A long corridor met them inside, the floors original and stripped bare. A clear varnish showed the wood to its best advantage. Rohan took Emma's ripped jacket and hung it on a coat rail to the left of the front door and then waited while she kicked her boots off on the mat. He kept his shoes on and moved into a wide room with a seating area. "This is the drawing room," he said, his tone bashful. Emma nodded. She walked around the large room, taking in every detail of the immaculate furniture and recognising some old pieces.

"You don't like it." Rohan's voice sounded dull as the late afternoon sun kissed Emma's hair with highlights of red and gold, fluttering through the darker browns as she moved in front of the bay window, her hand resting on the back of the white sofa. "Is it ok?" He sounded disappointed.

Emma ran a finger across a dark bureau, finding less dust than at home. "You visit often?" she said in resignation. "This is where you go when you come to London."

"Da." Rohan shrugged. "Did you not expect me to have a house?"

"No." Emma turned, her expression sad. "I pictured you in a soulless hotel somewhere." Her fingers caressed a fat Russian doll on a beech side table. It looked crude and unpainted, projecting an old world look in the distress of its wooden surface as though a child once held it and disgorged the family of replicas who clunked against the inside as Emma tipped it. Distracted, she twisted it across the fat middle, hearing the satisfying grind of wooden surfaces. Then she stopped. Rohan cocked his head.

"You can look. It was my father's."

Emma shook her head and sat it back on the shiny table. "No, thanks."

Rohan took a step towards her and Emma shied away. "What's wrong, Emma?"

She swallowed and pointed to the doll, its hollowed eyes watching her every move. "You're like that doll." Her eyes darted around the opulence of the town house, fighting disappointment. "Every time I twist a layer, I find another and another." Emma closed her eyes. "I don't want to know anymore."

Rohan's jaw worked beneath the flesh, a day's growth of stubble softening his angular, Russian looks. "Anton said you would like this house," he said, his fingers flexing and balling by his sides.

"Like Newcombe Street?" Emma replied, her voice soft. "I do. They're both beautiful houses."

"I don't understand." Rohan slumped into a white four seater sofa, angled on to the vast open plan room. He bent his good leg and clumped the heel of his shoe on the coffee table, disturbing a white runner placed with care in the centre. The Russian shook his head and rubbed the backs of his fists into his eyes.

"Another secret." Emma stared out at the sumptuous yard surrounded by houses worth upwards of ten million pounds each. The gardens looked immaculate, the pristine windows glinting with the reflected rays of the London sun as it ploughed downwards in a game of hide and seek it played with the creator. "Something else I didn't know about you."

Rohan observed her through narrowed eyes. "It's not a secret, dorogaya. I have a house. Nyet, I have a nice house. What's secret?"

"You never told me!" Emma snapped, her voice lifting at the end of the sentence and revealing her fear. "I don't know who you are. You could live this whole other life down here and I wouldn't know, you come and go like a hotel guest sometimes and I feel out of my depth."

"Should I take you to a hotel?" Rohan growled. "You'd rather I lied and hid the house?"

"No!" Frustrated, Emma slumped into the seat opposite, putting her head in her hands. "I'm glad you've shown me but I wish you'd mentioned it before."

"Why?" Rohan's eyes flashed with warning and Emma heaved a sigh as he launched, his tone veiling latent anger. "It never came up in conversation." The words were on the tip of his tongue and Emma heard them as though he'd spoken them out loud.

"And it's none of my business!" she said for him. "You tell me what you want me to know and I'm supposed to be satisfied."

"Fine! What do you want to know?" Rohan hauled himself to his feet, righting his balance on the prosthetic limb as he turned. "Ask me!" He held his arms out by his sides, palms upwards and his face showed anger and frustration. "Ask and I'll tell you!"

"I don't want to know now," Emma replied, disappointed with her own pettiness but buying time so she could create a mental list of questions. "You'd probably lie anyway!"

With a sound like a snort, Rohan left the drawing room and Emma watched him stride to the stairs, metres away. She closed her eyes and listened to his slow descent, imagining the house in its Victorian state, large reception rooms boasting wide windows and dark coloured walls. Women in wide, sweeping frocks would watch the street for entertainment, acknowledged by men who tipped top hats in response to giggles and painted lips hidden behind splayed fans. She opened her eyes to the wide living space, stark white walls and minimalist themes; a show home, not often lived in and a far cry from the house's history.

Emma stood, exploring with her fingers as she stroked the furniture. Bleached and faded by age, some of the pieces bore Russian emblems and Emma's palms stroked the wood reclaimed from snowy Siberian forests far away. She heard Rohan battle the stairs again and felt his eyes boring into her back as she touched the furniture with gentle fingers. "My father's," he said, swinging his right leg wider than usual as he stepped across the expensive rug in the centre of the drawing room.

Emma nodded. "I remember." She examined a dent in the corner of a tall cabinet, pushing her fingers into the tiny concave space and then touching them to a spot above her temple, beneath her hair.

"Emma, don't," Rohan said, his voice husky. "Mama's dead. Her sins went with her."

"I agree," she replied. "But the marks are still here in the world."

Rohan crossed the crisp white rug and wrapped Emma in his arms, pressing his face into her neck and snuffing in her floral scent. He gave her no chance to react before he crushed her to his chest and feeling the momentary shudder of his body, she accepted the embrace, sensing desperation beneath her husband's veneer of courage and emotional nonchalance. "I'm sorry," he breathed, the sinews and tendons in his arms running thickly across Emma's shoulders and back. "I don't want to fight, devotchka, please. This was meant to be a surprise, not an argument."

Emma nodded. "I don't want any more of your surprises, Ro. Just the truth. I need to know everything. We promised."

Rohan's head nodded against the side of her face. "Ok," he replied in his sexy drawl. "Are you ready to meet my other wife and deti now?"

Chapter 15

♥

Emma gaped, her face whitening with shock. She swallowed. "You have another wife and children?" Her voice came out as a squeak.

Rohan jerked his head back and looked at her, examining the horror on her face. Then he laughed. "You really don't trust me," he said, a statement not a question. He squeezed the end of her nose in an annoying older brother gesture which guaranteed a sparky reaction. "Bigamy is illegal even in Russia. You're safe. I'm not a bigamist."

Emma swallowed, reddening at her own ridiculous overreaction. "I hate you!" she said.

Rohan smiled and released her. "Nyet. You don't." He waved his arm. "Come, I'll show you the house."

Four floors made up the semi-detached house on Clareville Street, London, SW7. Emma hadn't noticed the garage door at the front of the house, hidden behind wrought iron railings which slid aside to allow entry for a single vehicle. The front steps ran up to the floor she'd already seen, comprising the drawing room and staircase. On the upstairs level were two bedrooms, two sumptuous bathrooms, a storage closet and the stairs. The rooms looked stark, painted in white with neutral browns and creams forming the base tones. Neither of them bore personal items, the furniture placed with show home precision. "I don't come up here much," Rohan said, glancing around. "Not much point."

"Who keeps it clean?" Emma asked. "I can't imagine you popping to London for a business meeting and taking a detour so you can scrub the bath on the way through."

"I have a cleaning lady," Rohan said.

"When did you buy the house?" Emma asked, admiring a painting of a deserted beach scene in one of the bedrooms.

"Five years ago," Rohan replied. "The stairs proved difficult at first with my prosthesis but were good exercise. It's around the corner from my original office and the hospital I attended as an outpatient, so it was convenient on the underground. I moved office two years ago but it's still only twenty minutes on the tube."

"When did Anton see it?" Emma asked, closing her eyes to search for an imprint of her stepbrother in the fabric of the house.

"He stayed often," Rohan said. "When he visited London we spent time together. There was a restaurant nearby which he loved and we walked there. I can take you sometime." Rohan stood at the top of the stairs, his right hand gripping the bannister. Close enough to touch his arm, Emma kept her hands to herself, a canyon of deceit opening up between them. "This place was a shell," Rohan said, turning and beginning his awkward descent. "A house fire destroyed the internal structure and the insurer paid out to the owner. He didn't wish to rebuild, so I made him an offer and commissioned it myself. The architect opened out the living spaces and added the garage beneath. The house next door required modifications, gutted in the same fire so the builders did both under the same contract."

"Who owns next door?" Emma asked, reaching the upper ground floor.

"Me," Rohan answered, his brow knitted. "I just said that."

Emma bridled. "No, you didn't."

"Did," he said, shooting the comment over his shoulder. "Both houses were destroyed by the fire so I buy them."

"Bought," Emma corrected his English, usually so perfect. "You bought them both."

Rohan turned at the bottom of the next flight of stairs, catching Emma in his arms. Her socks rested on the first step, putting her face level with his. "You're a pest, woman," he breathed. "You pick on my grammar and twist my sentences. I'll take you to the basement and punish you."

Emma's lips quirked into a reluctant smile. "Promise?" she whispered.

"Da, I promise," Rohan grinned. He accepted the tender kiss she pressed to his lips and let her go, turning to show her the kitchen at the bottom of the stairs.

The kitchen formed the centre third of the floor, a bench and appliance station covering the back wall. A centre island gave additional workspace and the room seemed light and bright for something below street level. A dining area graced the space nearest the stairs and fronted onto a small back yard overlooked by the Georgian houses in the street behind. Emma gulped, feeling like a fish in a goldfish bowl and dug her heels in, not wanting to be spied upon. Rohan tugged at her hand and noticed her gazing towards the enormous patio door beyond the table. "It's mirrored glass," he reassured her.

"Are you sure?" Emma stared at the glass, half expecting another homeowner in a far off window to wave at her.

"Want me to prove it?" Rohan asked, a twinkle in his eye.

Emma shook her head, but he ignored her, striding over to the window and turning his back on the outside view. "Pull the curtains!" Emma squeaked as he removed his outer jacket and flipped it carelessly over the back of a dining chair.

"There are none," he replied, undoing his tie and adding it to the jacket.

"Rohan, please!" Emma's eyes darted to the tiny rear garden and the overlooking windows. "Just show me the rest of the house. There's another floor below, isn't there?"

"Da," he said, his tone nonchalant as he stripped his shirt from his waistband and began undoing the buttons. "But you don't trust me." The shirt fluttered from his bulging pectorals, added to the growing pile on the chair. Rohan's fingers fumbled with the catch of his trousers and Emma inhaled in disbelief and covered her eyes as the zipper made its familiar metal on metal sound. "Do you believe me yet?" Rohan asked, his trousers in the process of sliding past his hips.

"Yes! Yes, I believe you!" Emma gushed. She ran towards her husband, banging herself on a dining chair as she sought to stem his exhibitionism. It skittered across the floor with a dull clatter. Emma seized Rohan's fingers and stilled them on his waistband, wresting the material from his hands. "You crazy man!" she giggled, hauling his pants up over firm buttocks and allowing her fingers to stray against the tight muscles.

Rohan's angular jaw flexed in defiance, denying the smirk which touched the corners of his lips. Emma's busy hands clasped the trouser fabric but Rohan's free hands pushed into the hair at the back of her neck. He nipped the underside of her jaw and felt Emma groan and press against him. "Want to see my bedroom?" he whispered. "It's in a sub-basement. Nyet windows."

Emma giggled. "Ok, but do your pants up, otherwise you'll break your neck on the stairs."

Rohan fixed his fly closed and pushed her towards the stairs behind the kitchen and let her go ahead of him down to the basement. Emma halted in a wide lobby flanked by built in storage cupboards and waited for Rohan to direct her. He followed slowly and nodded to the right, "My room," he said with pride, stepping over the threshold and revealing a smart bedroom which reflected his personality more than any other room in the house. Dark covers adorned the king size bed and a black headboard butted up to the white wall. Emma smelled his familiar aftershave and heaved a sigh of relief.

"No windows," she said, staring at the overhead skylights above the bed. "That's so clever."

"Ah, so you believe me now!" Rohan exclaimed. He sat on the edge of the bed to remove the shoes from his feet, edging off the one on his prosthetic leg. Then he stood up and dropped his trousers, grinning at the look of pleasure of Emma's face. Tight, silky shorts left nothing to the imagination and Emma nibbled on her lower lip, her body tensing with desire. Her eyes roved her husband's fantastic body, caressing the metal shin of the leg which replaced the gentle swell of absent flesh. Used to its robotic appearance, Emma felt only grateful for the mobility it afforded Rohan and bore no grudge for the loss of his real leg which lay smashed into bone shards and shredded flesh in the Helmand Province of Afghanistan. Everything remaining was in perfect working order and Emma licked her lips.

"Are you ok?" Concern flitted across Rohan's face as his excitement waned and he glanced at Emma's stomach. "You fell before. Do you need a doctor?"

Emma crossed the space between them and pressed herself up against his naked body. "I need you," she whispered. "Hold me, Ro."

He made love to her beneath the last vestiges of a London Monday, the sky above disappearing in a haze of flitting clouds as day gave way to evening.

Emma sat astride Rohan, her hands splayed across his chest. "Can't someone see in when the lights are on?" she worried, looking up at the skylight overhead. Street lamps cast a yellow dome over the city and stars speckled in the distance.

"Nyet," Rohan replied, flexing his stomach muscles and displacing her weight to his hips. His hands smoothed the skin over her waist and moved upwards, resting under her swollen breasts. Emma pouted as he bit his bottom lip, seeing the sparkle in his blue eyes.

"Mirrored glass?" she said, her tone teasing. "Do you know because you've done a strip under it?"

"Nyet," Rohan replied with a smile. "You did."

Emma's eyes widened in horror and she glared at him, accusing him of betrayal in her expression. "You'd better not be serious!" she snapped, shoving his hands away and covering her breasts by folding her arms. "Otherwise what we just did verged on indecency! We'll be arrested." She peered at the overhead sky with the pleasure spoiled.

Rohan's body shook with his low chuckle as Emma slapped his chest. "Don't do that, devotchka!" He feigned shock and placed his large palm over her exposed breast. "Everyone just saw you abuse me." He glanced upwards into the dusky sky and grinned. "You sit there and I'll help you cover up."

Emma peeled her gaze from the stars and saw them reflected in Rohan's glittering eyes. "I don't trust you!" she whined.

Rohan sat up using his stomach muscles and wrapped his arms around Emma's back. His skin felt warm from his exertions and his lips were soft as he kissed her. "I love you, Emma Andreyev," he said with a smile. "Nobody makes me laugh like you do."

"I'm not sure that's a good thing," she admitted, pushing her face into his neck. "It kinda sounds like an insult."

Rohan shook his head, his eyes sultry and full of a different agenda. His hands moved up her spine and into her hair. Emma groaned and peeled her focus from the evening sky.

Chapter 16

♥

"You recognise this?" Rohan jerked his head towards the aged piece of furniture in the corner of the other downstairs bedroom, the towel from his shower trailing from his hand. He navigated the room on his crutches. Emma wore the bedsheet like a shroud as she trailed behind him, staring at the bureau in disbelief.

"Yes." Her hand shook, her fingers kneading the sheet and she chewed on her bottom lip. "Why is it here?" Her voice sounded dull and flat.

"I saved it for you," Rohan said. He turned, the movement laboured and awkward.

Emma reached out a hand and touched her father's bureau, the sinking sensation filling her chest cavity. "Thanks."

Rohan cocked his head. "You don't want it?" His eyelashes fluttered and he reached out to Emma, almost overbalancing himself.

Emma glanced down at Rohan's knees, readying herself for the shock of his missing shin and the scarred, pink stump. The sight wasn't hideous or ugly but she forgot with surprising frequency he was no longer the teenage soldier she married. If she didn't catch herself, a horror reaction crossed her eyes and it diminished Rohan's confidence although he said nothing. He stood before her, his knuckles raised as he gripped the crutches, a beautiful naked Adonis of perfect physical stature. But it was as though a hidden artist had erased his lower right leg below the knee, leaving only background in its place. Her eyes sent the message to her brain about what they saw and her brain told them they were wrong.

Letting go of the bureau and clutching the sheet, Emma moved across the floor with her billowy wedding train. She pushed her face into Rohan's chest and inhaled his safe, masculine scent. "I do want it," she said. "Thank you for keeping it safe."

Rohan kissed the top of her head and she felt him relax. "Sit," he said, backing up towards the double bed behind him. He sank onto the mattress and Emma followed, waiting while he laid his crutches on the wooden floor. "I should tell you why I have it, da?" His blue eyes were questioning and Emma nodded, focussing on the vibrant blue pools with intense interest to stave off the feelings running riot in her chest. Rohan's fingers picked at a thread on the mattress cover and watched Emma's face. "When Mama wanted to go into the apartment in the seniors' home, she sold your father's possessions. I listed the house she lived in and it wasn't on the market for long."

Emma's eyes flashed as though she'd caught him in a lie. "How could you sell it? She rented it. I lost my home after she killed my father, remember? You can't live in a vicarage when there's no vicar."

Rohan raised his hand to silence her, letting gentle fingers caress her lined brow. The darkness stayed in her eyes and he cast no judgement over her. The poisons of Alanya Harrington were given as medicinal cures for ailments which didn't exist and while the dust of his mother's body frequented the four winds, nothing could excuse the damage her illness had wrought on the children in her care. "I received compensation for my accident, Em. I used it to purchase her house and give her security. The rest I put into shares which tripled my investment. During my convalescence I played the stock market and raised enough to buy this house. The apartment hasn't sold yet, but when it does I'll do something good with the money." His stroking fingers calmed Emma's soul and her eyes lost their haunted look.

"Good luck selling it," she said with an edge of sarcasm. "I can imagine why nobody wants to live there. It's one thing calling an old folks' home a 'waiting room for God' and quite another having someone helping you there early."

"It will sell," he said with surety. "Need always trumps bias."

Emma shrugged and the sheet slid a little, exposing the soft flesh of her left breast. "Thanks for saving Dad's bureau," she said. She glanced towards the weathered oak with its myriad fascinating drawers and spaces for storing stationery. "Is it empty?" she asked, her eyes hopeful.

"I don't know." Rohan followed her gaze. "I paid a company to courier it here. They put it in place and I haven't looked at it since. Anton probably poked around in it; he was the nosiest person I've ever known."

"Well, thanks." Emma placed a gentle kiss on the end of Rohan's prominent nose. "I'd like to take it home to Wingate Hall sometime." She jerked her head towards his leg and her protruding stomach. "But probably not at the moment."

Rohan smiled. "I gift it to you," he said, placing one hand over his breast. "With my heart."

Emma smirked and pushed at his thigh. "Idiot!" she laughed. Her eyes strayed towards an ornate dressing table, bare but for the mirror and a brown leather wallet. They opened wide with surprise. "Anton's wallet?" she asked.

"Da," Rohan said, his blue eyes seeking it with naked hunger. "It was given to me at the hospital after his death. Nobody knew where he lived and this was his room when he stayed with me." Rohan's speech sounded stilted and he lapsed into Russian before correcting himself with an apology and beginning again. "He liked this room. That armchair under the skylight was his favourite sitting place." Rohan ran his hand over his chin, an obvious stress tell. "He said you'd love this place one day and I held onto it." He swallowed.

"I do like it," Emma said, running her hand over his hairy thigh. "Anton's right. I love it."

Rohan sighed. "He must have known you'd love Wingate Hall, he knew you'd love Newcombe Street and this house and yet, I feel I don't know you at all."

Emma smiled. "You know what I love in bed," she whispered and watched the flush bleed into Rohan's cheeks. "You know who I am and where I've come from. The rest will take a little longer."

"Will we be ok?" Rohan asked, his eyes intense and his face serious. The doubt in his eyes sent Emma's brain into a panic.

"Of course we will," she stated, adopting the uncharacteristic role of cheerleader in their tortured, complicated marriage. She dropped another kiss onto the end of his nose. "We're not children anymore and we've had six long years apart. Let's keep getting to know each other but Rohan, for goodness sake, don't keep secrets from me." Emma's brow knitted. "I can't stand it."

Rohan nodded and his lips felt hot as he kissed Emma's neck from her collar bone to below her ear. She groaned and then rose from the bed, allowing the sheet to puddle around her feet. Rohan drank in the beautiful skin tones as her flesh curved over her hips and across the gentle swell of her belly. He reached for her and sighed as Emma danced out of reach. "Behave, Rohan Andreyev," she giggled. "I need a shower and then we have a party to attend."

Her eyes strayed to the bureau as she glided from the room, praying in her heart for some coded message from her dead father. Her fingers itched to search the drawers and press themselves into the nooks and crannies of the wood, needing to make a connection with the man who thrust his only daughter into the hands of a murderess. "There'll be nothing," she told herself as she climbed into the clinical white shower. "You'll get your hopes up and be disappointed."

But the feeling wouldn't leave, a strange sense of foreboding hanging over Emma as she dressed for the dinner engagement. Rohan stayed silent as he fixed safety pins into the waist of the dress to haul it tighter to Emma's figure, not losing patience when she fidgeted and complained. She piled her hair onto her head and used a clip Allaine lent to fasten it. Then she used the time it took Rohan to finish getting ready to speak to Nicky.

"Hey, baby," she said, forcing a lightness into her tone which she didn't feel.

"Mum!" he cried with enthusiasm at the sound of her voice. "Is London scary?"

"It's big," Emma admitted. "Too big for me. I can't wait to come home."

"Good! I miss you." There was a crackling sound in the background. "We're toasting marshmallows over the sitting room fire."

"That sounds like fun." Emma imagined the peaceful domestic scene with longing.

"Oh, that nasty lady came in today and had an argument with Mrs Clark."

Emma's body stiffened. "What nasty lady?"

The sounds through the handset became muffled as Nicky licked a marshmallow off a stick, huffing at the delicious hot goo which coated his tongue. His first answer sounded unintelligible and Emma groaned. "Tell me tomorrow when I get home," she said.

"Her what's got the same name as the school," Nicky repeated and Emma's body slumped.

"Clarissa Jameson-Arden," she sighed.

"Yeah. She wanted to take me off somewhere and Mrs Clark said absolutely not. I love maths and I didn't wanna go, so I'm glad."

"What did she want you for?" Emma demanded, trying to keep the angst from her voice. "You don't go anywhere with her, do you understand?"

"Yep," Nicky replied, his tone bright. "She's a stranger. I don't go wiv strangers."

"Good boy," Emma said, her brain turning cartwheels. "I'll be back in the morning. Pass me onto Allaine and behave. Remember I love you."

Emma's chest felt tight as her friend came onto the line. Allaine sounded brighter than before. "Don't worry about Clarissa," Allaine said. "She just wanted to borrow a cute kid for a photo. They're making the big posters for the celebration at the moment but she used another child instead. She's harmless, Emma, don't worry."

Emma shook her head. The woman was a liar who'd do anything to protect her family names; both of them. Her ancestors falsified the age of the school to cover up the Jameson's role in a murder and Clarissa was embedded in the centre of the scandal. "I don't want her near Nicky," Emma said, her tone blunt.

Allaine faltered and then recovered. "Ok. They both had a nice day at school. Mr Dalton took them out on the field for rugby practice in PE so they needed baths. Kaylee wasn't sure if a ball was involved but she apparently enjoyed rolling around in the mud."

"How are you?" Emma asked, relieved to hear Allaine's more upbeat tone.

"Yeah, good," her friend replied. "Ray and Christopher are entertaining the children so I'm chilling really. I'm halfway through a romance novel already. Your library's pretty well stocked."

"What're you reading?" Emma asked out of interest, smiling when Allaine admitted to a hearty Jane Austen.

"Christopher was in the library when I went in so he helped me find something."

"What was he doing in there?" Emma asked, fearing for the safe hidden behind a set of book shelves. She didn't trust the Irishman as far as she could throw him, which given their respective body types, wouldn't be far.

"Dunno," Allaine replied. "But he's really sweet." She lowered her voice. "I didn't think I'd like him after all the stuff you said, but I do. He's charming and he listens to everything I say as though I'm really important."

"Allaine, grow up!" Emma snapped. "He's playing you. Christopher Dolan will have you in bed before you can turn out the light. Do not trust that man!"

Allaine sighed. "Will hasn't even bothered to try to find us," she said, her tone acerbic. "He owes both of us an apology, so where is he? I realised something today; we've been married twenty-five years and I've never heard him say he's sorry."

"You must have," Emma interjected. "Or you'd have noticed before now. It's a glitch and you're letting your brain make it worse. Stay away from Christopher, I'm warning you. He'll make you forget your own name and before you know it, you'll have messed everything up."

"Is that the voice of experience?" Rohan muttered, standing to button his fly. Emma raised her hand and offered a rude gesture in response, not appreciating his allusion to her aborted date with the seductive Irishman.

"Do not spend time on your own with him," Emma warned. "Just remember why you're there."

"I'm looking after your son!" Allaine exclaimed. Emma heard the children's giggling in the background cease and Kaylee murmured something in a concerned tone.

"Yes, exactly," Emma replied. "And your daughter. "But you could've done both those things at your house. You're there because you need time and space to think. So don't you dare jump into bed with Christopher Dolan!"

The awkward silence cut across the miles between London and Market Harborough like a high tensile buzz. "Ok," Allaine conceded. "I'm disappointed you think I'd do that. I'll see you tomorrow evening."

Emma stared at the dead phone in her hand and pursed her lips. Then she rounded on her husband. "Are you going to hold that over me for the rest of our lives?" she demanded. "I went on a date with Christopher when I thought he was an acquaintance of yours. If you remember rightly, I had your little stalker girlfriend in my ear telling me you were out of bounds. And I never slept with Christopher Dolan!" Emma hurled herself backwards on the bed, forgetting the hair piled on her head and wedged in its precarious place with a spikey clip.

Rohan's eyes flashed and Emma tasted the danger. "I don't want to talk about Hack," he spat, using Christopher's call name. "Tonight is about us, Mr and Mrs Andreyev going out to dinner." He looked pleased with himself as he finished fixing a neat bow tie to his neck and folded his collar properly. "Are you ready, devotchka?"

Emma nodded and stood, repairing her hair in the long mirror near the door. She eyed the high-heeled shoes which matched her green dress with disdain. "How far do we need to walk?" she asked, wrinkling her nose.

Rohan shrugged a dinner jacket over his broad shoulders and caught her reflected eye. "I called a taxi," he said. "We were going to walk, but that was before we were followed."

"Oh." The thought of venturing outside didn't seem so attractive and Emma reached for her shoes with reluctance. "Who knows you're in London?" she asked. "Or did they follow us from home?"

"Nyet. Not from Harborough," Rohan stated with certainty. "He picked us up at King's Cross."

"So, what does that mean?" Emma asked, pushing her toes into the shoes and feeling grateful the weather had improved enough for her to avoid taking a coat.

Rohan eyed her with approval, his blue eyes moving over her lithe body, taking in the way the dress pushed out from the tight waist and covered her budding pregnancy. It plunged at the neckline revealing smooth, youthful skin and his eyes roved down to the gentle swell of Emma's breasts beneath the bottle green fabric. He forced himself back to her question. "It means that unless his job is to sit at King's Cross every day waiting for me, someone told him I was coming."

Emma swallowed. "Who knew?" she asked.

"I only returned my acceptance by email yesterday," Rohan replied and raised his eyes. He held out his hand and bowed like a Russian Tsar. "So, let's go and find out, shall we?"

Chapter 17

♥

"Keep the change," Rohan said as he flicked a fifty pound note through the window towards his friend. The taxi driver winked at Emma and he and Rohan did a peculiar handshake before the man flicked on the indicator and eased his black cab into passing traffic.

Emma's heels scraped against the pavement as she shifted from foot to foot, her face creased with nerves. "How do you know nobody followed us here?" she asked, chewing on her bottom lip. Rohan stroked a finger across her chin, his eyes smiling.

"Don't chew your pretty lips," he whispered. "You're putting the red stuff on your teeth."

"Lipstick?" Emma's eyes widened. "Damn!" She ran her tongue over her teeth and then offered a fake smile. "Is it gone?"

Rohan's eyes narrowed. "You make me want to kiss you." His jaw hardened as he fought to control his desire. Emma stamped her foot in impatience and he laughed. "Yes, dorogaya, it's gone."

"You didn't answer my question." Emma glanced around the darkened street, lit by the yellow glow of overhead lamps which resembled a throwback from the Victorian era. "Should we be standing outside here? The man might see us."

"I want him to." Rohan's face set into a look of determination. "I don't care if he sees me attend work functions but there's no need for him to know where I live when I'm here."

"But he can look at the electoral register or anything else where you've given your name. He could go through your mail or your bins."

"Come." Rohan turned and led Emma towards an ornate set of steps leading into a hotel. An awning covered the space before the front doors and light spilled from the entrance. Rohan glanced over his shoulder. "That would only be possible if I used my real name, devotchka," he said with an expression of awkwardness.

A white gloved attendant stepped forward and greeted the couple, pulling the door open so they could step through into the warmth. "Good evening sir," he said with a smile.

Rohan nodded and shook the man's hand. Emma watched as the attendant pursed his lips, let go and slipped a thumb and fore finger into his smart front pocket. The movement was so fluid she almost missed it as the door closed on silky hinges. Rohan's hand in the small of her back propelled her forward into a lobby with crystal chandeliers and polished floors. She looked up sideways at her husband and he narrowed his eyes and shook his head. It was a miniscule movement which contained a world of understanding and Emma closed her lips, swallowing the unasked questions.

A reception room to the left of the lobby buzzed with the sound of human interaction and Emma took a deep breath and steeled herself to endure the evening. A white board in the doorway declared the event as a line of initials which Emma didn't recognise and she pressed close to Rohan as they entered the throng of bodies.

The windows on all sides faced darkened gardens and were condensated from the heat of people breathing and moving around. The room seemed dominated by dark suited males and Emma's lithe figure and form fitting green dress raised eyebrows as she slithered past on Rohan's arm. He walked towards the bar, straight backed and stern faced and Emma tripped along next to him on her heels, feeling the burden of eyes burning into her face and neck. It took five long minutes to greet the people in their path and Emma's face grew tired of smiling. The gathered group of mainly males eyed her with open curiosity although they addressed their questions to Rohan.

"You must be Mrs Harrington." A stout man with a large grey moustache pushed through the group and stepped into Emma's path, sticking out a pudgy hand. "He always said he had a wife, but we'd started to think you were a figment of his imagination." He laughed, a low belly induced sound which rocked his frame. Emma gaped like a fish and grasped the sweaty hand.

"I'm Emma," she said, "Just Emma." Her cheeks flushed with shock at the confusing use of her maiden name and she stared at the little man, wondering how he knew it.

"Jolly good," the man said, appearing satisfied. "I'm Jed. Smith's the last name, not very exciting, I know. Rodney and I work in offices opposite each other, not that he's here very much." Jed eyed Emma from top to toe, lingering on her breasts. "Mind you, I can see what keeps him away from the office." His eyes flicked up towards Rohan's face and he blanched at what he saw there. "I'll leave you to it," he said, his brown eyes watering behind hooded lids. "Have a great night. Catch you later."

Emma nodded and watched him lope away. Nobody leaned across to slow his progress with congratulations or meaningless party chatter and Emma pegged him as a loner. She spoke to her husband out of the side of her mouth. "Rodney Harrington?" Exhaling slowly hurt her chest, especially when she wanted to knee him in the balls with everything she had.

"Da." Rohan looked unrepentant and Emma forced her lungs to work on demand. She gritted her teeth.

"Forget to mention you were using the name of my dead father, did you?"

Rohan's grip on her upper arm started to pinch as they navigated groups of chatting people. Emma wriggled her arm but found it futile against her husband's strength. She noticed odd smatterings of cocktail dresses like pops of colour on a dull canvas as she sped past, eyeing the flute glasses filled with bubbly champagne. The desire for alcohol overpowered her and Emma's fingers itched to seize the numbing liquid from one of the trays touted by smart waitresses dotted around the room. The crush in the bar area meant Rohan cut her loose long enough for him to order drinks for them both. His height advantage got him instant service and Emma accepted the tumbler filled with orange juice.

"So much for no more secrets!" she snapped, sipping the drink with lips which trembled on the edge of the glass.

"It's not a secret," Rohan said, observing the room with flickering eyes and leaving no corner unexamined. "You know now."

Emma raised her voice. "You don't think a warning would've been kinder?"

"Em," he hissed in reply. "He was my father too."

She swallowed, emotion rising in her chest and constricting her breathing. "Step. Father." She kept the words apart, alienating Rohan by separating the two roles of her father. A memory flashed into her mind of the vicar playing soccer in the back garden. Anton rolled on the grass like an imbecile but Rohan passed the ball, his ten-year-old face serious as he worked on his skills. He kicked the ball and it shot through the vicar's legs and into the goal. Rohan's tiny smile betrayed his pleasure and Emma held her breath, the flimsy nightdress hindering her legs as Alanya's footsteps sounded on the stairs, ensuring a slapped bottom for being at the window past her bedtime.

"He was my father," Rohan asserted, nodding at a passing colleague.

Emma swallowed more of her drink and pushed away the memories. She ground her teeth and suppressed anger and grief, a far more damaging cocktail for her unborn child than any alcohol.

"So, the famous Mrs Harrington." The female voice sounded light and tremulous, but the blue eyes darted from Rohan's face to Emma's. A giggle punctuated the statement, offering an effect of silliness. "We didn't think you were real."

Emma forced a smile onto her face, her heart sinking into the pointed toes of her shoes as she recognised the signs of another admirer. Her oblivious husband chuckled, a low, melodious sound. "Em, this is Stephanie," he said, indicating the blonde with a flick of his champagne flute. The woman swallowed and batted her eyelids at the sound of her name on his Russian tongue. "She works in admin and produces our reports."

Stephanie simpered and fixed piercing blue eyes on Emma's face, as though in challenge. "Mr Harrington and I work very closely," she said, leaning in close and breathing alcohol into Emma's nostrils. There was enough liquor on her breath to suggest she'd been partying a while.

"Fascinating," Emma replied, flashing a warning at her competitor. "A typist." She let out a grating laugh. "A valuable function, I'm sure."

The woman bridled as Emma intended. Rohan's brow knitted in surprise at his wife's denigration of a worthy role and he shifted on his feet, the oestrogen spat sending him into unfamiliar territory. Taking a sip of her champagne, the blonde took a step forward, the toes of her shoes touching Emma's. "How long have you been married? Rodney never mentions you."

"He must have done," Emma retorted. "Otherwise you wouldn't have called me, the famous Mrs Harrington, would you?"

Stephanie swallowed her mouthful of booze with a loud, unattractive gulp and Emma pressed home her advantage. "We've been married seven years and our son is six." She ran a hand over her abdomen and gave a smile which showed her teeth. "And this one's due in August."

Stephanie looked down and gaped, her jaw flapping like a fish out of water. "Oh," she said. "I didn't know." Her eyes shot towards Rohan and then down at the floor. "Congratulations."

"Pasibki," Emma replied and Rohan's eyes bugged at her cute use of the colloquial Russian word for thank you.

Wrong footed, Stephanie nodded, an awkward bob of her head which made the blonde hair swish around her face, before moving away on her stilettos. Emma glared at Rohan and sipped her orange juice. She caught the tail end of his smirk and knew she'd been used like a fly swat, to dispense with his latest problem. "I wish I'd said I was your step sister now," she grumbled. "Then she'd be all over you like a rash. It would serve you right!"

Rohan turned to face her, his back masking her from view of the room. His eyes smirked and his lips quirked upwards in mirth. "Then you'd suffer such pangs of debilitating jealousy, it would eat you up every time I worked in London."

Emma snorted. "Steady on mate. You can love yourself too much, you know?"

Rohan grinned and pressed his lips to her forehead. "I have no energy left for loving myself; you consume me."

"And you're full of..." Emma's insult ceased as another female arrived to pay court. Rohan's reaction at the presence of the tiny woman seemed entirely different and left Emma floundering.

"Ah, you made it," he said, adopting a puppy dog look which hung awkwardly on his strong frame.

"Yes, thank you for sending the taxi," she replied, turning to hold out a hand to Emma. The handshake was firm although the fingers and palm were tiny, the owner standing just shy of five feet tall. Short dark hair lay neatly on the woman's head and a dark business suit contrasted with the smattering of cocktail dresses in the room. Delicate flat shoes dressed her feet, exuding a confidence which said she was comfortable with her stature. Something about her bearing suggested a personality larger than most of the average height females in the room. "It's great to finally meet you," she said to Emma, her eyes crinkling at the corners. The hazel brown irises spoke wisdom and Emma knew in her heart; this was her, the conductor in Rohan's strange and confusing orchestra of deceit.

"This is Maureen Allen," Rohan said, a peculiar pride in his tone. "She's my assistant." A look of knowing passed between Rohan and the woman and Emma watched unspoken communication run across a veiled thread. "She manages my administration and office work." He bobbed his head once, in acknowledgement of a superior competence and Emma watched, transfixed by his deference to someone who barely saw much above his collar bone without craning her neck.

The woman smiled with satisfaction and Emma allowed her mind to run over all the times Rohan referred to encrypted communications relating to his role as The Actuary. He spoke often to an assistant or secretary in London who fielded enquiries, information and covert instructions. Emma felt herself relax in the presence of massive competence projected from such a tiny transmitter. Rohan's assistant was all business and Emma put her age somewhere in the fifties.

Without looking at Rohan, Emma made her own assessment and put Maureen on the spot. "Do you know everything?" she asked, assuming the astute woman would understand the question.

Attractive brown eyes fixed on Emma's face and Maureen gave a tiny nod. "Yes," she replied with honesty.

"Thank goodness for that!" Emma exclaimed. "Because right now, I feel like I'm in an alternate reality."

Rohan's jaw dropped and he looked hurt but Maureen cracked a smile. "I can imagine. But you'll be fine." She glanced at Rohan and shrugged. "Will I get my own drink?" she asked with a cheeky down turned smile.

"Nyet, sorry." He turned back towards the bar and Emma heaved a sigh of gratitude. She'd finally met someone who could put the big Russian in his place and some of her misgivings retreated in the unfamiliar environment. The gathering might actually be fun.

Jed Smith bounced back into Emma's eye line with a question on his lips and she quailed. "Stephanie said you can speak Russian," he stated, wobbling a little as the alcohol took effect. He glanced back at the group which set him up for the awkward task and they turned away, leaving him an outcast in his mission. "So what kind of name is Rodney Harrington? That's not Russian."

Emma set her jaw and channelled cold, hard eyes into the little man's face. "It's his name," she replied, her tone of indignation cutting through his drunkenness like a knife.

Rohan turned from the bar wielding a tumbler of what looked like whiskey for Maureen and his eyes rolled heavenwards in disdain at the sight of Jed's lumpy body standing with the women. He opened his mouth to speak but found it unnecessary.

Maureen tipped forward, her lips speaking to Jed's chin. "Go away, little man," she said, in a tone which would have put an army squadron back into formation during a bar fight.

Jed leapt backwards and tipped his wavering glass of champagne down his shirt front. Emma watched the sparkling liquid drip from his quirky red bow tie. "Ok," he said, hot footing it back to the tight circle of accomplices who seemed reluctant to reabsorb him.

Rohan handed the tumbler to Maureen who nodded in thanks. "As you were, Sergeant," he said.

Chapter 18

♥

Emma stared at Rohan and Maureen in turn, her eyes moving from one to the other with a look of profound disbelief. "No way!" she exclaimed.

Maureen kept a straight face which rivalled Rohan's deadpan expression. But Emma knew her husband's every nuance and spotted the tiny quirk in the right side of his lip. She rolled her eyes and relaxed. "Idiot!" she said, taking a sip of her juice.

"No, really. I was in the Air Force," Maureen said, bristling at Emma's lack of belief. "I made sergeant before leaving to get married. We weren't allowed to stay in as married women." She slugged a mouthful of the whiskey and savoured the expensive taste. Then she handed the glass back to Rohan. "Nice," she said, "but please can you exchange that for some decent water?"

Rohan smirked and nodded, turning back towards the bar. Maureen opened her mouth to speak and he huffed in exasperation and interrupted. "Yeah, yeah, not that tap stuff. The tap stuff is horrible."

Maureen looked pleased. "He's learning," she jibed, knowing Rohan heard.

Emma watched his back stiffen and admired the woman's courage. "I've never met someone with quite such a big death wish," she remarked, studying Maureen with keen interest. "I hope you sleep with one eye open."

Maureen snorted. "He wouldn't dare touch me," she said and something in her tone told Emma she believed it. "I know far too much," she concluded and her smile looked sunshine bright.

Emma laughed. "Oh dear. I'd pay good money to watch you two working together in a confined space." She watched her husband's back as he stretched over the heads of smaller men to retrieve Maureen's drink. "Why'd he bring you whiskey?"

"I told him once I liked it." Maureen straightened and watched him walk across the shiny parquet floor. "And I do. It's all we drank in London in the 1960s, but I need a clear head tonight." She raised her eyebrows as Rohan navigated a group of men discussing something in loud voices. One of them roped him into the conversation and he shot a look of annoyance at the man before answering his question. "And I wanted a moment to speak with you."

Emma swallowed and fixed her eyes on Maureen's face, suspecting the older woman wanted the discussion over by the time Rohan returned. "Ok," she said.

Maureen made the covert conversation appear casual, leaning in with a smile of collusion fixed on her face. She pointed to Emma's shoes and to an observer, it might appear they discussed the smart heels strapped to her delicate feet but in reality, Maureen rapped out a series of questions. "Has Rohan ever mentioned the name, Myles Oskar?"

Emma shook her head. "No. I'd remember a name like that."

"Are you sure?" Maureen seemed insistent, keeping one eye on Rohan as he progressed towards them. "He hasn't appeared on your doorstep or sent letters?"

"No." Emma's eyes narrowed. "What's going on? Who is he?"

"I'm not sure yet." Maureen chewed on her lower lip and readied her smile to greet Rohan as he arrived with the tall glass of water. "Say nothing and if he turns up, don't speak to him."

A gong sounded and a door opened onto a formal dining room. Maureen offered Emma a look of warning before joining the crowd surging in towards the food. The seating was allocated and mapped out using small name cards. Emma found her name nestled next to Rohan's and heaved a sigh of relief. The seats beside Emma bore the names, Jed Smith and Matthew Kranz. Maureen humphed and picked up the nearest card in her small fingers. Gold rings glittered in the light of the chandeliers and an emerald stone winked at Emma from the centre of an ornate heart as Maureen moved Matthew's seat card away from them. She reached out for Jed's name but a sharp shout halted her activity.

"Leave that alone!" Jed's voice rang out and the group gathering at the next table stopped to stare at them. "I'm sitting here!" He pulled out the chair next to Emma and sank his large bottom into it with a grunt of defiance. He patted Emma's seat and she glared at him, refusing to sit until he'd removed his pudgy hand. "Isn't this nice?" he crooned, squinting up at her. "All friends together."

After a shudder of disgust, Maureen adopted the finesse of a West End actress and sat, pulling her chair up closer to Jed. "I'm enjoying it already," she said, her voice as sugary as a bucket of treacle. "I think it might be the best night of my life." She looked so thrilled, had Emma not watched the mask slip down over her slight features, she may have been fooled. With a smirk, Emma flicked the napkin from its neat fan and slipped it across her thighs.

"I'm starving," she said, leaning around Jed to speak to Maureen. "I wonder what we'll have."

"Nothing with a face, I hope," Maureen answered. "I don't eat things with faces." Her eyes strayed to Jed's wide eyed expression. "Although sometimes there're exceptions."

Emma snorted at the interloper's expression of horror and wondered if he'd switch name cards with someone else and bolt. "Where's Matthew?" Jed asked, his tone petulant as he searched for an ally.

"Sick," Maureen answered. "He sent his apologies." She reached for Matthew's name card and fingered it lightly, before balling it up in the palm of her delicate hand. Dropping it into Jed's glass of champagne she bugged her eyes wide and pushed her face into his. "Some people can't stand the pressure of lying on legal documents; it makes them ill." Her smile resembled a grimace. "Does it make you unwell, Jed? Does the thought of getting caught create that gnawing sensation in the pit of your stomach?"

Jed's chair shot back, squealing on the parquet floor. He stood, his cheeks red and his fists balling at his sides. "Stupid granny!" he hissed and moved away backwards until he felt it safe to turn.

Rohan ceased conversing with the man to his right and swivelled his head to look at Jed, bending his knees and rising in the same fluid movement. "Who do you think you're talking to?" he demanded, raising his voice.

"You are all in so much trouble!" Jed spat, spray from his lips coating his chin. High pink spots spread out from his cheekbones and engulfed the rest of his face. Rohan's expression looked impassive as he raised his hand and pointed towards the exit, his lips giving the smallest upwards quirk. Jed clattered away, stumbling past chairs and people as he lurched towards the doors, going against the flow of people coming in for dinner.

"Is he drunk?" The man next to Rohan leaned forward to question Emma and she shrugged. "He seemed it. I've never met him before."

Maureen gave her a smile of approval before reseating herself on Emma's left. She moved Jed's champagne flute out of her eye line and nodded in thanks as a waitress leaned in to scoop it up onto a tray. "This is much better," she mused, reaching for her water glass with a satisfied sigh.

"What's he lied about?" Emma whispered, reaching for Rohan's hand as he sat back down next to her. He squeezed her fingers and resumed the conversation with his neighbour, a discussion which involved complicated mathematical formulae and seemed to excite both men in ludicrous proportions.

"Oh, I wasn't sure he'd lied." Maureen smiled, watching an ice cube bob around in her drink.

"But you said he did," Emma replied, sounding confused. A waiter passed by with a tray of champagne balanced on his hand with dubious skill and Emma winced and waved him away with a polite smile and shake of her head.

"No, I didn't," Maureen said. She leaned forward and peered into a basket of bread, reaching out a tentative hand and then pulling it back again. "Don't give in to temptation," she recited with a smile and Emma wondered who she referred to, herself or Emma. The tiny child in her belly danced a jig and she sighed at the sight of the delicious, hand twisted loaves. Rohan's companion snagged a small loaf in the shape of one of Kaylee's hair plaits and ripped it apart. He slapped a knob of butter into the soft, moist centre and Emma watched it collapse into the bread like a gorgeous yellow landslide.

Rohan avoided the bread. He always ate with care, evading fatty foods and carbohydrate laden junk, although he called it a rude Russian name. Emma wanted a loaf so badly she contemplated crawling across the table to grab one. "They're full of crap," Maureen added, seeing Emma's eyes pining. "But go ahead. Do you want me to pass you one?"

Emma nodded like a naughty child and as Maureen half rose from her seat, a hand snatched up the basket and sent it down the other end of the rectangular table. Emma fought the urge to wail and stamp. Her tantrum was averted by the sudden arrival of the soup. Maureen rattled off a list of ingredients she couldn't have and the server assured her they were absent from the delicacy staining the edges of the white bowls. Emma fell upon hers and demolished the vegetable soup with enthusiasm. The bread didn't return, so she concentrated her efforts on interrogating Maureen. "You did say Jed Smith was a liar," she asserted, watching the other woman's face.

Keeping her composure under fire, Maureen laid her spoon in the bowl at right angles to her body. "I didn't," she maintained. "I only asked if lying made him sick. And if you recall, I also asked if getting caught made him even sicker."

Emma shrugged. "Why? I know he's irritating but I could've put up with him for an hour. Why scare him off?"

Maureen fixed perceptive brown eyes on Emma's face and exposed the extent of her superior knowledge. "Because someone's trying to frame your husband and I believe I just outed one of their puppets."

Chapter 19

♥

Emma's jaw dropped, exposing the last of her soup. She swallowed and covered her mouth with her hand, making a hasty apology. "You need to tell Ro," she hissed and Maureen shook her head with a long, slow movement.

"Don't be ridiculous," she replied, nudging her spoon a few degrees north. "I'm just getting started. He'll spoil my fun."

Emma took a quick peek at Rohan and found him scribbling on a paper napkin with a ball point pen. Strange mathematical language spewed from the nib and the man next to him nodded like a donkey, his nose millimetres from Rohan's hand. She turned back to Maureen. "Someone's been asking around Harborough, trying to find out where we live. They paid off a cop and he told them. Then when we got to King's Cross, Rohan made me change trains because he said there was someone tailing us."

"Do you think it's the same person?" Maureen lowered her voice and turned her back on the man to her left, an elderly gent who looked like he struggled not to nod off in the remains of his soup. His body tipped sideways and he righted himself with a hand on the empty chair at his other side.

"I don't know," Emma whispered. "Ro said he didn't care if the man knew where he worked but he didn't need to know where the London house was."

"Were those his exact words?"

Emma blanched. "No, I can't remember those. But we ran from him at the tube station and lost him, yet when we got here, Rohan said he wasn't bothered if he saw us at a work function."

"Hmmmn." Maureen adopted a thoughtful pose which scared the gentleman opposite. Emma wondered if she realised she possessed a resting bitch face.

"I'll just ask Ro," Emma concluded as the severe expression seemed set in concrete. But as she turned towards her husband, Maureen grabbed her hand.

"No!" she insisted. "The less he knows about this, the better."

"I can't keep any more secrets," Emma groaned. "It's a disaster and we promised."

"A few days," Maureen begged. "Let me find out what's going on in the office with these auditors and give me a chance to identify the groups tracking you."

"Groups?" Emma's voice raised to a squeak and Rohan turned sideways, his face drawing into a frown. "Sorry, I'm fine," Emma said, adopting a guileless look. "Go back to your er...maths." She pulled a disgusted face and Rohan grinned. His momentary distraction lost him the pen and the satisfaction of finishing the calculation as his companion took over with obvious glee.

"Fine!" Emma grumbled. "But you must work fast. I've got a house full of people at the moment and someone bad knows the address. I feel like they're all my responsibility."

"They're not," Maureen said with certainty. "I take it Hack's still living with you?"

"Not with us." Emma wrinkled her nose. "I've exiled him to the folly at the edge of the property in the hope he'll get into less trouble there."

Maureen snorted. "Don't bank on it. That guy could find trouble in a broom cupboard with only himself in it."

"You're not helping." Emma eyed a waiter as he leaned over people to collect crockery, balancing the dirties on his arm like a circus performer. His antics transfixed her and she missed the appearance of an arm sliding between her and Maureen.

"Excuse me, madam," a male voice said and Emma jumped. She raised her eyes, temper flaring in her chest as she rounded on the newcomer. A handsome waiter stood before her with his hand outstretched. Dark hair was slicked back from a high forehead and a smirk stretched from ear to ear. As Maureen turned towards him, Christopher Dolan wiped his face clear and reached for Emma's empty soup bowl. He dipped forward to collect it and grunted as Maureen stuck a sharp elbow into his ribs.

"You're supposed to stay with the little boy!" she hissed.

"Change of plan," Christopher replied, keeping his head down and voice low.

"I'm going to kill you," Emma said, her voice calm and certainty conveyed in her tone.

"I'll look forward to dat," he whispered in her ear and withdrew the bowl and cutlery.

"You're supposed to be looking after Nicky!" Emma's eyes filled with tears and she half rose, anxiety creating a knot in her stomach which reacted against the delicious hot soup.

Christopher rested his right hand on her shoulder, balancing bowls in his left. "Ray's stayin' in da house and I'm checkin' in every few hours. It's all locked up like a nun's knickers, so it is. Don't be worrying."

The whites of Maureen's eyes showed at the mention of nun's knickers and Emma figured she didn't know Christopher as well as she claimed. He'd know all about underwear, even the clerical brand. He collected the plate and limped away, surviving a jab in the balls from Emma's elbow and a swift kick to the shins from Maureen's tiny court shoe. "Bloody idiot!" Emma groaned, watching the neat Irish backside shimmy away towards a swing door into the kitchen. Both women looked at Rohan in the same instant, heaving a collective breath at his oblivion.

"At least he's not trying to seduce Allaine," Emma whispered. "I was worried about that. She's hit a speed bump in her marriage and Christopher Dolan could make that little bump into Kilimanjaro."

Maureen nodded. "And some!"

"Why are you whispering about Dolan?" Rohan looked suspicious and Emma looked to Maureen for guidance.

"He's got a nice bum," she said, keeping her face as straight as the M1 motorway. Rohan narrowed his eyes and looked from one woman to the other.

"Yours is nicer," Emma said, forcing her face into a smile. "I promise."

Rohan shook his head and heaved out a sigh. "Why did I not think putting you two together would be a terrible idea?"

Chapter 20

♥

"**I** wanted bread," Emma grumbled as Rohan said his goodbyes and led her outside to the street.

"You should've got some," he replied, helping her down the steps and watching his own footing. The sky looked jet black above the glow of the city and stars speckled high above the ozone. Emma looked up, searching for Orion's Belt and smiling as she found it. Her father's astronomy lessons returned along with his gentle, coaxing voice.

"What?" Rohan looked up and followed the line of her eyes, brushing a dark curl from her forehead. "He was a good man, da?"

"Yeah." Emma nodded. She reached for his fingers in the darkness and squeezed. "It's ok. You can use his name. Dad would've enjoyed the notoriety but I wish you'd warned me."

Rohan nodded and tugged Emma's hand, moving her aside from a throng of loud men who emerged onto the top step, laughing and shouting to each other. "I should've told you; I apologise." He looked down at his shoes and narrowed his brow. "I transition from one persona to another easily and forget others might not be up to speed."

"How can you operate under another name?" Emma asked, lowering her voice. "Your qualifications, everything, it must all be in your own name if you studied in the army."

"Da." Rohan nodded. "I sign as Andreyev but the others I work with assume he's my supervisor."

"Where did the Rodney Harrington thing come from then?"

Rohan shrugged. "It's the name of my company."

Emma gaped and took a moment to process the revelation. "You named your company after Dad?"

"Da. He was my papa too for a while." Rohan cleared his throat and worked at keeping his face neutral. "After I left hospital and qualified, I needed to set up a limited company and couldn't think of a name. Your father was on my mind a lot and it helped to keep him near. He had a massive influence on my life and I owe him much."

"So who do the financial people think they're investigating?" Emma asked. "Rohan or Rodney?"

Rohan looked at Emma, the mask shifting back over his face. "Ahhh," he said. "Me."

"So whoever complained, knows you as Rohan Andreyev, not Rodney Harrington?"

"Da. It's fine, Emma. It's nothing; please don't worry. These things happen all the time."

Emma registered the brush off and gave up, knowing she'd get nothing further from her closed husband. "I still wish I'd eaten some bread," she grumbled. "The food looked incredible."

Rohan nodded with enthusiasm. "It was good."

"Not if you're pregnant!" Emma rubbed her stomach, imagining the luscious taste of the pate on her tongue or the chilled delicacies she daren't try for fear of introducing her child to botulism or salmonella. "I wanted that mousse like I've never wanted anything."

"Anything?" Rohan tucked her arm beneath his elbow and smirked sideways. "It's nearly midnight but I know somewhere we can get hot bread."

"Take me there!" Emma begged.

Rohan laughed and raised his arm, standing with one foot overhanging the kerb. Lights flicked on across the road, illuminating the cab interior and a familiar face. The driver pulled in next to them and a nearby group raised their voices in complaint. "We were 'ere first, mate," a young man with red hair petitioned Rohan. "You need to take yer turn, boy."

Rohan ignored him but Emma felt the atmosphere take a nasty hike. Her eyes darted from the taxi driver to her husband and back again and Rohan slid the door open for her to get in first.

"Hey! I'm talking to you!" The man's red hair stood out in spectacular highlights against the glare from the street lamps and he approached, a bottle of beer in his hand. Still Rohan ignored him, turning his back and indicating that Emma should get into the vehicle. She stood her ground as irrational thoughts powered through her brain, anticipating the worst. The man would touch Rohan to get his attention and her husband would hurt him. Enter the police, all kinds of complications and a world of trouble guaranteed to follow Emma back to Market Harborough and disturb Nicky's safe place.

As Rohan turned with his fists balled and a thin pulse ticking in his neck, Emma glided past on her high heels. "Go away!" she said, her voice icy calm.

The man sneered and swayed on his feet, slopping beer from the open bottle down his trouser leg. "Who's gonna make me?" he slurred. His eyes strayed to the soft swell of her breasts sequestered behind the silky green fabric and a lecherous grin spread across his freckled face. "Hey baby, come with us. Leave the dirty Russian conman on his own." A foolish hand snaked around Emma's waist and hauled her in towards his groin. Emma heard Rohan snort behind her like an angry Arab stallion and acted without thinking.

Her open-handed slap sounded loud in the dark street and the man stepped back in shock. "Bitch!" he exclaimed. Rohan yanked Emma's arm to move her to safety but her overwhelming focus was the arrogant male who dared besmirch her husband's good name and by association, her father's. As Emma tipped backwards under the force of Rohan's grip, her right leg lifted off the pavement. She saw a flash of movement from her left eye and saw the taxi driver bolt from the car and move around behind her. It was all academic. Her right leg continued its momentum skywards and the pointy toe of her stiletto made adequate contact with the target. The redhead let out a bellow of pain and bent like an envelope before crumpling to the ground.

"What happened?" The doorman of the hotel rushed forward, joined by the raucous crowd on the pavement.

Emma stood up straight and more for effect than genuine distress, shouted in the man's general direction. "I told you no, you bloody sexual predator. I'm pregnant! Do you not understand what no means?"

With looks of distaste and surprise, the advancing group halted and then filtered backwards at a slower rate. Emma's accusation seemed to echo amongst their number and they detached themselves and their reputations from the drunk man rolling on the ground clutching his nuts, appearing to have forced himself on a pregnant woman. Emma felt her husband explode into action next to her and lurch for the prone male, no doubt intending to put him out of his misery with a humane but deadly sleight of hand. The taxi driver grabbed him around the waist and held on with an iron grip. "Captain, he's not worth it," he implored. When Rohan ignored him, lurching forward and taking the smaller man with him, Emma heard the driver hiss the magic words. "The cops will be on their way. Don't you have enough trouble yet?"

Rohan ceased, his body rigid as he shrugged the other man's grip away. The look he gave the redhead was enough to turn him into a pile of ash on the pavement, his lips wrenched into a straight line of pure frustration. Emma spun her body and pressed her face into Rohan's chest, clutching his lapels and crying, "Just take me home!" like an Oscar winner.

Rohan and the taxi driver hustled the distraught woman into the vehicle and sped off up the road. Rohan patted Emma's back and whispered hushed endearments into her ear. At the end of the street she sat up, brushing her hair back from her face. "I want bread," she said.

The taxi driver roared with laughter at Rohan's look of incredulity. "Where'd you find her, Captain? She's bloody priceless."

Rohan gaped, his eyes narrowed in disbelief. Car headlights moved their beams across his hair, turning it into highlighted roads of gold and white. "You kicked him in the balls!"

Emma shrugged. "Do I get bread now or will I have to scream?"

"You kicked him in the balls."

Emma pressed her back against the seat, feeling the cold leather against her skin through the plunging back line of her dress. "He called you a dirty Russian conman."

"You kicked him for that?" Rohan sounded surprised. "You shouted that he'd touched you." His fists balled and released as fury channelled through his eyes. "I should kill him."

Emma heaved out a sigh. "He pulled me into him and I slapped him so he let go. I shouted what I did because I needed the crowd to turn on him and it worked. If you kill him, the cops will lock you up and you'll never be able to prove your innocence in this actuarial investigation." Emma glared at him. "And seeing as you're using Dad's name; I don't want his character dragged through the mud either. He can't defend himself."

"Where to, Captain?" the driver called through the partition as they joined a main road.

"I want freshly baked bread," Emma replied. "And I want it now."

"Leicester Square it is then," the driver replied with a smile. "Now, do you want it with the guys tailing you from three cars back or should I lose them?"

Chapter 21

♥

"Stop turning round." Rohan covered Emma's lips with his, calming her with his surety that everything would be ok.

"Who are they?" Emma asked, rubbing at the crick in her neck.

"They're persistent," the taxi driver called back. "And I'm guessing they want you to know they're there. They've had multiple opportunities to hide but stayed in plain sight. What do you want me to do?"

"Pull over here," Rohan said as Leicester Square loomed in the distance. "We'll walk the rest of the way."

"You sure, guv?" the driver asked, wincing.

"Da," Rohan replied. "It's fine."

He paid the fare by the roadside and Emma twitched, needing to be around the other hundreds of people still walking around London in the dead of night. She felt exposed, the cold air biting her shoulders and bare arms. Rohan saw her shiver and slipped off his jacket. "Here, dorogaya," he said, gently laying the coarse fabric over her light dress. "You look beautiful." He pressed his lips to hers again, savouring the boutique scent of lipstick and perfume.

"Are they following?" Emma asked, her voice tight with fear. Rohan nodded without looking around.

"Da."

"Do we need to go down an alleyway so you can bump them off?" Emma asked.

Rohan looked horrified, his eyes widening in disbelief. "I'm not an amateur!" he protested. "Nyet. We'll go somewhere public and if they want to, they'll approach us."

The shop buzzed with activity as the midnight feasters of London dined on Subway sandwiches the size of small logs. Despite wanting warm bread, Emma succumbed to a toasted baguette filled with cheese and salad. She ripped the paper off before Rohan's bum touched his seat, inhaling the fresh bread aromas accompanied by melting cheese. "I want this so bad," she sighed, tucking in.

Crumbs littered the Formica table between them as she licked her lips and chewed, eyes closed and taste buds craving more. Rohan grinned and sipped their shared soft drink. "You'll be awake all night with indigestion," he joked and Emma winced, suspecting he was right. She jumped as the two men stood next to the table and indicated the vacant seats.

"Can we sit?" one asked and Rohan nodded.

"You might as well. You tail like jokers."

Emma squirmed as one of the men trapped her up against the wall, placing his backside into the seat next to her with care. Rohan shook his head and gave her a smile which only touched one side of his lips as the other man slumped into the chair next to him. She watched as his hand went to his left hip and wondered what his weapon of choice might be. Gun? Knife?

"Careless, Mr Andreyev," the man next to Rohan said. He turned in his seat to face Emma's husband, his cropped hair showing scalp in the harsh overhead strip lights. "Wouldn't it make more sense to leave the space near the wall for strangers? You might get trapped in your seat."

Rohan snorted. "Unlikely. Stab you or shoot you, the choice is mine. You'll die whichever seat you pick."

The man smirked and turned dark brown eyes onto Emma. "That might have been true once, but you have more to lose nowadays."

Emma felt her heart flip flop into her stomach and all enjoyment of the soft bread disappear. Swallowing her mouthful, she picked up a plastic fork and examined the white tips.

"Don't, Em," Rohan said, his tone soft. "I think they want to talk, not fight."

Emma took a sideways glance at the man next to her. His sleeve touched her arm and she shrank back, pulling Rohan's jacket tighter around her slender frame. "Then why don't they get on with it?" she asked, fear making her rude. "I'm hungry and tired and have already performed one vasectomy tonight." She flicked a nail across the fork prongs and listened to the dull musical note they made.

"We saw." The man next to Emma had longer hair. Blonde with blue eyes he wasn't bad looking but his stocky build ruined the effect. More testosterone than sense. They looked older than Rohan and he seemed familiar with them.

"So talk fast," Emma said, turning in her seat and jabbing the prongs into her seat companion's thigh.

To his credit, the man held in his squeal as the plastic snapped and the fork skittered under the table. Emma reached for another and Rohan rested his fingers over hers. "Bored now," he said to the men. "We're leaving in one minute and if you try to stop us, I'll give your fondest wishes to your wives and children." Emma baulked at the seriousness of his tone and ripped off a large piece of her sandwich, not wanting to forgo it in a bloody battle for her life.

"Mr Wright wishes to speak to you," the man next to Rohan said and Emma snorted.

"Mr Right doesn't exist," she said, drunk on fear and exhausted by the never ending evening. "A million women can tell you that."

The man turned cold, blue eyes on her face and grimaced. "Mr Winston Wright wishes to speak to your husband," he reiterated. "He didn't mention you."

"Is he invisible to women?" Emma giggled, the word pun incongruous with the two men bearing the message.

"Why?" Rohan asked and Emma used the change of focus onto him to collect herself.

This is not a joke, she repeated to herself. *This is not funny.*

"We're not privy to Mr Wright's personal business," the man replied. His accent sounded extreme south, verging on coastal. Dover, Folkestone, Emma guessed. "We're just the messengers," the man continued. "Would you be amenable to a meet?"

"Not without knowing why," Rohan countered.

Emma cocked her head. Something in her husband's tone told her he knew exactly why this Mr Wright wanted to see him. Her mind leapt to the problem at hand and imminent investigation. Experiencing a flash of anger, she stuck another fork into the beefy thigh to her left. "Tell him to sod off!" she snapped, the fork collapsing in her fingers.

The man let out a grunt of discomfort and squeezed Emma's fingers in his giant hand. "Bloody hell!" he complained. "Quit it with the forks, lady." He let go and Emma gave him a look of pure hatred.

"Maybe if you tell us who you are, my husband might find it easier to decide whether to put a bullet in you or send you for a swim in the Thames," she gloated, Rohan's skills inflated to the level of invincible in her mind.

"Em, I know who they are." Rohan's voice sounded soothing but his eyes channelled a clear message. *Shut the hell up!*

She swallowed and glared at the thickset man next to her, his bulk encroaching onto her seat and making the process of eating her giant sandwich uncomfortable. Emma elbowed him in the ribs and he moved his chair aside. When she glanced at him, he stuck his tongue out in a childish expression of enjoyment at her position of being out of the information loop.

"Tell him he's too late," Rohan said, his accent sharpening with tiredness and some other emotion Emma didn't recognise. He swept up the soft drink and held his hand out to his wife. "Come, Em," he said.

Not wanting to abandon her sandwich, Emma balled it up into the many wrappers and followed, elbowing the man next to her in the back of the head as she slid behind his chair. They exited the shop, Rohan's palm gently in Emma's back as she clutched wrapper and sandwich to her chest.

"What was that about?" she asked as Rohan led her away from the shop and into the packed street. A juggler pushed a sword down his throat and juggled fiery glass jars filled with flaming oil, drawing a crowd of London visitors. Emma spotted a pick pocket using the distraction to his advantage but Rohan led her on before she could call out a warning.

"They were just the messengers, like they said," Rohan announced as they navigated a crowd of late night ice cream eaters. "Wanna see my office?"

"Yes please." Emma perked up as Rohan threw her crumbs of information, wondering if the feeling of being in the dark with him would ever recede.

Rohan hailed a cab and Emma didn't recognise the stern faced driver. He took them to a glass fronted building near Canary Wharf and Rohan paid the man to park down a side street nearby. Then he led Emma to the front doors and used a key and an alarm code to gain access. "Aren't there cameras?" Emma whispered as they used the elevator and rose through the deserted building.

"Da," Rohan replied, pointing upwards in the lift at a small beaded eyeball in the ceiling. He waved and then raised his middle finger, sending Emma into a paroxysm of nervous giggles.

On the seventh floor, the lift stopped and opened, dumping them in a lobby surrounded by doors. To the left, the words Rodney Harrington Associates sparkled like gold against the night lights and the London glow through a window next to a seating area. "These are rented." Rohan waved his hand towards four other doors in the space. "I've been up here longest."

"You own the building, don't you?" Emma said, disbelieving her own logic and Rohan allowed himself a smirk.

"Nyet, devotchka. You do."

Chapter 22

♥

"What?" Emma wondered if the parallel universe she sometimes felt at hand had somehow overlapped and swallowed her up. "I don't own an office building in Canary Wharf. Don't be silly."

Rohan shrugged. "Whatever," he replied. "But you've owned it for two years. I thought you might have noticed."

"Is there anyone's name you haven't used?" Emma asked in disgust. She rolled her eyes and then halted, staring at the gold lettering on the office door. "Wait! You haven't used Nicky's name, have you?"

Rohan grinned. "Not yet." He raised his hands in supplication, his eyes smiling. "And I won't."

"Yeah, but you used mine," Emma grumbled. "Is that even legal?"

Rohan raised an eyebrow. "There are loop holes for most things." He flicked on a desk lamp.

"I've seen no rent!" Emma exclaimed as the realisation struck her.

Her husband snickered. "I used it to repair my Mercedes after you dinged it most days over a three-month period."

"Oh." Emma stared around the lobby of the office, seeing the neat seating area beneath a long window. "They shouldn't make cars that big. It's ridiculous. It was asking for it with that massive bonnet." She patted the big table forming a reception desk. "Is this Maureen's?"

Rohan nodded. "Da."

Emma leaned back against the desk, admiring her husband's strong shoulders as he pushed paper around in Maureen's in tray. He leaned forward and the low lights from the city caught the chiselled line of his jaw as he concentrated. Emma sat the sandwich on the desk next to her, the wrapper crinkling in the silence. She inspected the slit up the side of the dress, dismayed to spot a tear in the seam where she'd kicked the redhead in the balls. Emma pulled the dress up to examine the rip, chewing her lower lip and groaning at yet another of Allaine's cocktail garments she'd managed to ruin. Her shapely legs looked pale in the lighting and the black pointed shoes stuck out from under the folds of fabric.

"You ok?" Rohan's voice broke her reverie and Emma jumped and dropped the tresses, watching as they shimmied down her thighs.

"Yeah," she said, her voice sounding flat. "I thought you wanted to show me the office, not work in it."

Rohan crossed the small space around Maureen's desk, wrapping his arms around her. "You looked beautiful tonight," he whispered, his stubble scratching along her cheek. His hands sought the top of the slit and tentative fingers pushed upwards towards her thigh.

"You said there were cameras," Emma breathed, enjoying the persistence of his fingers as they sought the fragile lace of her underwear.

"Not in here," Rohan said. His lips found hers and he ran his tongue across the seam, sighing as they parted for him.

"You're a liar!" Emma broke away. "This is exactly the place where you'd have cameras, capturing every bloody angle. You're such an exhibitionist!"

"There isn't." Rohan protested his innocence. "They turn off when the alarm is deactivated."

"I don't believe you." Emma's voice ended in a whoosh as Rohan's expert fingers found their mark and his lips grazed her neck. He parted her knees and pressed his body against her, supporting her neck as he laid her back, ignoring the crinkle of paper beneath her.

A whirr trembled the floor beneath their feet and Rohan started, jerking away from Emma at the same time as clamping a hand over her mouth. He yanked her dress back around her thighs and leaned across to switch off the desk lamp, tugging Emma's hand and leading her towards another office. A wide glass window was back-lit by lamp posts at street level and cast an eerie glow over the space. Rohan stalked towards a long cupboard at the back of the room and tugged Emma behind him. She fell over a chair and coffee table, sending a stack of leaflets scattering across the rug. Rohan paused for an instant and then led her on, shoving her into the cupboard ahead of him and then closing them in.

"Your jacket," Emma hissed, anxiety in her voice. "It fell off my shoulders when we were...it's on Maureen's desk."

Rohan swore and shook his head. "Too late," he said. He patted his pockets in the darkness and Emma heard the clink of keys. "I've got the important stuff," he whispered. He turned sideways and pulled a pen from his trouser pocket. Emma rolled her eyes, wondering if he'd decided to graffiti the wall prior to their demise.

"The rumble was the lift, wasn't it?" she asked, her eyes wide in the light emerging from the end of the pen.

Rohan nodded. "Da." He pushed against the back of the cupboard and Emma heard a dull click. In the tiny glow she watched as the panel slid sideways to reveal a cavity. "Get in," Rohan said and Emma shook her head, her eyes wide and round as he used the glow to illuminate the cavity.

"No!" She dug her heels into the floor of the cupboard, feeling the stiletto spikes catching on the carpet. Shelves cut into her back and a metal file on the floor scratched her leg as she pressed backwards.

"Em! In!" Rohan picked her up bodily and shoved her into the small space. Before Emma could right herself he closed the panel on her, sealing her off from the world.

The hiding place felt airless and Emma bent double to calm herself and force oxygen into her lungs. Alanya's child abuse included stints in an outdoor toilet adjoining the coal shed and Emma concentrated on not remembering the hanging spider webs and the scent of mice. Rohan put her in the back of the cupboard, not Alanya and Emma worked hard to summon gratitude instead of hatred at his attempt to keep her safe. She squeezed her eyes tight shut and lowered her heart rate by force, tuning in to the surrounding sounds.

The swish of fabric against the panel alerted her to Rohan's continued presence in the cupboard, accompanied by the sound of the safety disengaging on a handgun. She held her breath and waited, hearing her heart pound in her breast. The dress stuck to her back and belly as the space grew hotter.

Keys clanked against the main office door as several were tried and failed. Emma heard muffled voices coming through the back panel and pressed her face against it.

"He must've changed the locks." The voice sounded irritated, the other muffled as it replied; a woman's timbre. Emma exhaled. They couldn't get in.

"You said it was a master key," the woman replied and Emma closed her eyes and fixed on the owner of the voice, recognising something in the tone. "Then again, you were meant to talk to him tonight."

"So were you!" the male retorted. "Now we have to do it the hard way."

There was more jangling of metal keys against the door and then silence. "This isn't working. He's changed the locks since he and that secretary of his moved up here. You're not allowed to change the locks; it says so in the rental agreement."

"Let's report him to the landlord." The woman sounded keen.

"Yeah, right," the man said. "We were trying to break in using a master key and found he's broken the rules and changed the locks. That'd be perfect."

"Anonymously, I meant!" the woman snapped and Emma heard a hiss of anger from the male.

"What do we do now?"

"Break the window," the woman said and Emma pulled her face away from the wall as it shook with the pounding of a fist.

"No!" The voice sounded hysterical and familiar. "We're putting documents into his room not stealing anything. You're giving him a reason to deny having them. You must do it tomorrow when he's out to lunch or something."

"He doesn't go out to lunch." The woman sounded sullen. "I've tried, remember. I've just about propositioned him and he isn't interested."

The man snorted. "Don't take it so personally; he'll be gay."

"He's not gay. You saw her tonight. Married and pregnant." Sourness dripped from the woman's words and Emma fought the urge to break out through the wall in temper and slap the woman who'd evidently attempted to seduce her husband. She experienced a flicker of satisfaction that Rohan had rebuffed her. Emma pictured his look of disinterest as a colleague propositioned him, imagining his angular face fixed in a look of blandness. As soon as the expression gained traction in her mind, Emma knew the identity of the woman.

Frustration budded in her chest. Why didn't Rohan move? She'd seen her husband in action, undeterred by blood and death, so why was he hiding in a cupboard a few centimetres away?

"We'll think of something else." The woman sounded defeated. "But that document needs to be in there somewhere for them to find before Wednesday, otherwise we're screwed."

"I think we're screwed anyway. Those signatures don't look exactly like his and if he gets a good legal team, they'll prove it."

"We can't help it if he signs nothing like his name!" the woman said. "They'll have to understand we did our best. This is a mess and he's our way out of it."

There was a clunk against the wall as the woman turned and clattered it. "Are you sure you turned those cameras off on the main switch?" Her voice betrayed a layer of panic.

"Yes!" Impatience met it. "Give me credit for something. Let's get back to the others and sort this out tomorrow. It'll be fine."

Footsteps moved away towards the lift and after a slight delay, Emma heard the whoosh of the doors opening and closing. The floorboards rumbled again as the lift descended. Claustrophobia re-entered her psyche and lit a fire of panic in her stomach, bubbling upwards like indigestion. "Rohan!" She sounded desperate as she pushed on the panel, the space seeming to close in on her. "Ro, please!"

The panel slid back on precision bearings, making little more than a muffled slithering sound. The gun was nowhere in sight and Emma wondered where on his body Rohan kept it. He led her through the cupboard and out into the office before wrapping his arms around her. Emma felt hot and sticky, her fringe sticking to her face and the short breaths coming in gasps. Rohan kissed her forehead. "You were afraid," he said, his voice tender. "I'm sorry."

Emma broke away and brushed her hair back with a frustrated action. "Not afraid. Hot! Why didn't you do something? They're trying to frame you, just like Maureen thought."

Rohan raised an eyebrow, quirking his face in the ghoulish light from the street. "She thinks that? Clever girl."

Emma rolled her eyes. "She's in her fifties. That's past the girl stage and yes, she told me that's what she thought."

Rohan snorted. "She's in her sixties, Em, but still a girl in her head. I'm glad she's on my side, put it that way."

"But why didn't you do something?" Emma balled up her fists and shook her head. The clip holding up her curls let go and bounced to the floor. Rohan bent to retrieve it and turned it in his fingers, his face thoughtful.

"What can I do? I open the door and they ask me an inane question and leave. Or would you have me fight them and be arrested for assault or murder? How do these actions help?"

"Because they're trying to frame you for something!"

Emma threw her head back in exasperation as Rohan lifted a finger to his lips as though she was a child who needed to be quietened. "They're still in the building, Emma." He crossed the carpet between them and turned her with pressure against her shoulders. Scooping her hair in his big hands, he re-fixed the clip, hissing in annoyance as the disobedient curls looped around his fingers and tumbled down Emma's back in rebellion.

His fingers felt feather light as he stroked her shoulders, dragging his nails gently down her flesh to sensitive elbows. Emma shivered. "They're trying to hurt you. I want to kill them."

Rohan smiled, a slow, lazy expression which offered reassurance. "Everything they said is on camera and I'll choose when to share it with the investigators. I'll warn Maureen that nobody is to come into my office and she is to watch visitors like a hawk. She does that anyway." He smirked. "Which is probably why they're scrambling now."

"It's Stephanie," Emma blurted. "And I think Jed."

Rohan grinned. "Beautiful and a detective." He ran his thumb under her lower lip. "Now I know why I love you."

"But what are they doing?" Emma worried at her lower lip, holding her breath as Rohan kissed her. She pulled away. "Do they work for this Mr Wright? They must do."

"Doesn't matter." Rohan took Emma's face in his hands and persuaded her to look at him. "It will be ok. I promise." His kisses became insistent, wiping the mystery from Emma's mind as he loosened his shirt from his dress pants. Emma discovered his bow tie was real as she snagged the loop and it came undone in her fingers, keeping hold of it as Rohan pushed her backwards over his desk and raised her dress above her hips. He reached for the desk lamp and Emma clamped her fingers over his hand, fearful the intruders may be drawn back by light streaming through the high window. Emma heard the dress give another rip in protest at the same time as she raised her arms above her head and sent a tub of stationery tumbling to the carpet with a dull thump.

Rohan's fingers seemed tantalisingly slow as he fumbled with his buttons, his face grey in the semi darkness. In frustration, Emma sent the keyboard after the pens and paperclips, acknowledging the heavier thud with a smirk of satisfaction. Abandoning the buttons behind the dressy frills, Rohan pushed Emma's knees up, his fingers running down her legs and caressing the lethal shoes. He fingered her knickers to one side and she sighed and closed her eyes against the reflection of car lights on the ceiling. She'd wanted to see his office for so long and now she had. Emma smiled at the tiny victory as she took over yet another place in Rohan's complicated life.

Chapter 23

♥

Emma sighed and rubbed her hand across Rohan's bare chest. "Do you think they'll complain to the landlord?"

"Who?" Rohan ran his fingers along Emma's spine and she shuddered in his big double bed.

"Laurel and Hardy."

"What?"

"Stephanie and Jed," Emma said with a sigh. "Do you think they'll put in an anonymous complaint about you changing the locks?"

Rohan chuckled, a low, tantalising sound. "You'll have to let me know. You're my landlord."

"Oh, yeah." Emma rolled onto her stomach and shot a quirky look in her husband's direction. "I'm putting the rent up."

"Go for it." Rohan sat up using his stomach muscles. He stretched and yawned and Emma picked at a loose thread on the pillowcase.

"Was your taxi driver in your squadron in Afghanistan?" she asked, recalling the man's limp as he leapt from the taxi to assist Rohan against the drunken redhead. He took a military fighting stance she'd seen both Rohan and Christopher use. "Did he serve under you?"

Rohan leaned on his elbows and Emma watched as he shook his head. "Nyet. He was with another squadron who alternated shifts with mine and lost both legs at the same time as shrapnel embedded itself in his head. He was kidding when he said he lost half his brain, but a few centimetres either way and he wouldn't have been joking about much at all."

"In a bomb blast?" she pressed and Rohan winced.

"Kind of. A hand grenade was thrown into his truck and a friend covered Dan's body with his and took the blast. Dan lost his legs and gained a head injury but his friend died."

Emma hissed out a breath, sorry she knew something about the man which he would be able to see in her face. "You stayed in touch after hospital?"

"Da. We became drinking buddies and rode the pity train together for a while. Then we wised up."

"You make it sound so casual," Emma remarked. "I think you're both entitled to feel hard done by."

"But not to become alcoholics," Rohan said, his voice quiet. "Veteran drunks filled with self-pity and hatred for being left behind. I finished my qualifications and he learned The Knowledge and became a London hackney carriage driver."

"The Knowledge?" Emma asked and Rohan nodded, his hair shushing against the pillow as he laid back down.

"It's extensive training for hackney drivers. They can be hailed from the street and don't need to be booked like the others. But he needed to learn every road, street and cul-de-sac. He earned a green badge which means he learned the whole of London and is a musher because he owns his own cab."

"What are the others called, the ones who don't own their cabs?"

"Butter boys."

"Aw, cute," Emma sighed and rested her chin on the pillow. "Did you loan him the money to buy the cab?"

"No. I pointed him at a good investment and it paid off. He has a wife and children now and makes a decent living."

"He's a good friend if he always comes when you call," Emma remarked, thinking of Allaine who did the same.

"Da, he is. And I also do his tax returns for free." Rohan smirked. "Brothers stick together; it's army law. Fight together and if you don't die together, you remain linked in spirit forever." Rohan sighed and bent his arms behind his head. "Sometimes even when they do die, you stay linked."

"What did he do in the army?" Emma asked, curiosity forcing her closer to Rohan's boundaries of confession.

"Does it matter?" he asked, seeking her eyes in the semi darkness. Sunrise blinked above the skylight, breaking through the fluffy grey clouds above.

"Don't you want to tell me?" Rebuffed, Emma hated the feeling of being chastised.

"If I said he was in the catering corps or a squaddy who painted grass green for a command inspection, would it change your view of him?"

"I dunno," Emma mused. "Maybe."

"It shouldn't," Rohan said. "He left his legs in Helmand Province but has more balls than most of the men I meet daily. People judge others by their trade or the amount of money they have in the bank. They should look into a man's eyes and judge by what they see there. That's all there is."

Emma buried the instant sense of rebellion and turned on her side, letting the sheet slither down to her waist. Rohan looked pensive and she fought to break the heavy mood threatening to settle. "You're my hero," she whispered and he glanced sideways and smiled.

"Good," he replied. "I need to be someone's. And Dan was a driver."

After a romp and a shower, Rohan led Emma to the nearest cafe for breakfast. The bread she craved the night before sat in her gullet in a hard lump, causing a bout of indigestion which didn't want to leave. Despite the emptiness in her stomach, thinking of food made her want to gag. She settled for warm milk while Rohan ordered toast and coffee.

"Have you spoken to Maureen and warned her about the visitors she's likely to get today?" Emma asked.

Rohan nodded and buttered his toast. Emma watched his capable fingers as they wielded the knife, loving each knuckle joint and the small scars on the underside of his left hand. She fought the urge to reach out and touch him, knowing he wouldn't understand. She watched him eat, careful and meticulous just as he was as a teenager, concentrating on his food but aware of everything around him. He appeared engrossed, a clever way of observing a room without drawing attention. Rohan glanced up at Emma, offering her a bite of the toast. She screwed up her nose and shook her head. "No, thanks. I feel a bit off today; probably tired."

"I downloaded the camera footage while you slept," Rohan said, keeping his voice low.

Emma widened her eyes. "From the corridor? Wow, that's amazing. I didn't know you could do that." She frowned. "I guess Christopher installed it. What on earth was he doing waiting tables last night?"

"Working," Rohan replied. "Something of his own perhaps."

"Why so secretive then?" Emma demanded. "I spent the journey down worrying about keeping him away from Allaine and all the time he was in London. Why let me think he'd be at Wingate Hall?"

"We'll ask him when we get home," Rohan said. He leaned across and stroked Emma's fingers as her hands writhed on the tablecloth. "I'm glad you've seen where I work, Em. I feel like things are more in the open. No secrets."

Emma's nod appeared in slow motion, sensing her husband had called Christopher himself and tasked him with finding out who Mr Wright could be. "Maybe," she concluded. "I bet if I started asking you certain questions, you'd clam up like an oyster and pitch a fit." She sighed and linked her fingers through his. "But for now, I'm happy with what I know."

Rohan seemed satisfied with her answer and they set off back to the house on Clareville Street. The sky looked azure blue and Emma's happiness hiked in the sunshine. Mr Dalton's relaxing of her working hours took the pressure away and she felt settled for the first time in her life, able to come and go as long as she filled in a time-sheet. "I love you, Rohan Andreyev," she said with a smile.

He reached down and kissed her. "Good." He smiled, a lazy, sexy quirk of the lips and then his face grew serious. "Emma, there's something I need to tell you."

She saw the dark car pull up next to them in her peripheral vision. Thinking it was the taxi driver, she readied her face to how it would be if she knew nothing about him; didn't know he'd been blown up beneath a friend who sacrificed his life for him, didn't know he'd toyed with alcoholism or despair. She turned with a smile and found herself face to face with the two men from the previous evening. They exited together in a fluid dance of determination, another darker skinned man gripping the steering wheel and revving the engine enough to make a fast getaway. Off guard because of Emma's presence between him and the men, Rohan wasn't quick enough to defend himself. She watched defeat enter his face as the nozzle of the revolver poked into his ribcage from behind. Emma's eyes narrowed in frustration and a look of anger crossed her face.

"Don't, Em." Rohan's voice sounded commanding as he jerked his head towards her. A crowd of school children trotted past on the other side of the road as a bell tolled in the distance. Another group approached, rucksacks bouncing on their backs and cute striped caps on their small heads. Their grey and white striped blazers looked large on their tiny shoulders and they ploughed on, giggling and chatting amongst themselves. Emma knew Rohan could get out of trouble easily but he wouldn't, knowing the consequences of a discharged round hitting a child. She gaped and felt her chest tighten, realising she'd forgotten to breathe.

"Do we want her?" one man asked the other. The one with the gun in Rohan's ribs scooted closer as the children passed, making a pretence of conversation.

"No," he replied. "There's no need. Unless she kicks off. Then we'll take her."

"Don't take her," Rohan said, his voice icy. "Let her walk away or you'll get nothing from me."

"Why does Mr Wright want him?" Emma begged, her voice rising to a wail. "He's done nothing wrong."

The man next to her laughed and lifted his fingers in a rude gesture. Emma remembered the plastic fork from the night before and wished she'd stuck it into his leg much harder. As the fingers shaped a 'V' sign in front of her face, she dipped her mouth and lay hold of them with her teeth, biting down until she felt bone.

To his credit, the man kept his roar of pain inward, although Emma's odd behaviour attracted the attention of another passing group of children pushing bicycles. The little boys stared as the man squeezed her nose between the fingers of his other hand to cut off her oxygen and make her let go. "We're taking her!" he hissed, anger mixing with misery as he stared at his bulbous fingers.

"No!" Rohan asserted, one eye on Emma and the other on the man with the gun pressed into his side. "Let her go home."

"Does she know not to call the cops?" the gun wielder said and Rohan nodded and looked at Emma.

"Yes, you know that, don't you, devotchka? No police."

Emma's wide frightened eyes greeted her husband with disbelief. Surely he didn't mean that. The man she'd bitten balled his fingers together in a wince and opened his jacket, showing her another holstered gun under his left arm and Emma felt her resolve weaken. "You call the police and we'll send him back to you in little pieces." He sounded so certain, Emma gulped, finding it hard to remove her eyes from Rohan's face. He looked pale, his blank face in position but his eyes held a peculiar fire behind the flashing blue irises.

"She can't get into the house," Rohan said, his voice soft. He held his hands out by his sides and jerked his head towards his jacket pocket. "Inside front right," he said. "Door keys. Let her take them."

The man next to Emma kept his painful finger aloft as he reached into Rohan's jacket. Emma waited for something to happen; a mouse trap to bite him so Rohan could knock him to the ground; anything. The keys emerged from her husband's jacket in the pudgy palm and Emma grasped them as they were offered. Still Rohan did nothing.

Emma watched, feeling helpless as the men bundled him into the dark sedan and closed the door. They sandwiched him in the middle with the third man driving and Emma knew then it was over. They'd given him no room to manoeuvre, understanding his capabilities better than his own wife. Rohan afforded her one last look through the tinted window as the driver indicated and pulled out into the traffic. He gave her no last clue or instruction in his eyes but the expression was unmistakable. He looked like a man about to meet his maker.

Chapter 24

♥

Emma stood alone in the street as the dark car powered away in the traffic. People moved around her as though she was an island in an estuary, negotiating her body whilst avoiding the bubble of black misery surrounding her. She examined the keys in her hand, recognising the ignition key for Rohan's Mercedes but nothing else. The direction of Rohan's house eluded her like a dose of brain freeze and Emma panicked. "Please, can you help me?" She appealed to a woman pushing a buggy and felt relieved as she stopped.

"Here, now leave us alone. Get a job!" the woman snapped, throwing a pound coin onto the ground at Emma's feet.

"But..." Emma began, ignored as the mother pulled her other two uniformed children closer into the arc of protection around the pram.

"Go away!" the woman repeated. "We don't want your sort around here."

Emma put her hand up to her mouth, surprised by how deathly cold her fingers felt against her face. Seconds ago, Rohan's warmth covered her lips and she missed it with a dreadful ache. Gone. He was gone.

She left the gold coin lying on the pavement for another heartless Londoner to find and pocket, setting off in the direction Rohan had led her. At the end of the road she agonised, not knowing whether to go left or right and starting to cry as she reached the tube station entrance and realised she'd gone the wrong way even before that. Emma backtracked, picking up the road leading to Clareville by accident rather than design, climbing the steps up to the house on tired feet. The key worked like a knife in butter but as the burglar alarm bleeped, it dawned on her she didn't know the code.

"No, no, no," she begged, punching numbers into the keypad only to hear the alarm beep faster and louder in her head. Emma stopped. She dug her nails into her palm and tried to think like Rohan, going back to how he might reason out codes and numbers. Her fingers flew over the keypad, punching in six familiar digits as her heart stopped in her breast. She held her breath and with a last, dying bleep, the noise stopped. Anton's birthday. He used his brother's birthday.

Emma closed the front door behind her and sank onto the ground, slipping down the white wooden surface like a rivulet of water. She pressed her head onto her knees, willing the faintness and nausea to leave her alone and desiring a clear head more than anything. She pictured her fancy mobile phone still charging on the dressing table at Wingate Hall where she left it and rued her inability to accept a life of comfort after such abject poverty. This time her stubbornness would cost her.

Emma hauled herself to her feet, feeling shaky. She cleaned her teeth in the bathroom to rid herself of the taste of the man's blood and began to look around for something that might help her. On the ground floor she found a landline running across the skirting board and traced it to a telephone unit in the kitchen below. Dialling the number for Wingate Hall, she held her breath.

"Hello." Ray's voice sounded sharp and Emma sank into a kitchen chair as the faintness got a secure grip. "Hello?" he said again, sounding irritated.

"It's me, Emma." Her voice sounded crackly and shaken, even to her and Ray missed nothing.

"What's up? What's happened, miss?"

"It's Rohan," she said, hysteria near the surface. "They took him off the street right in front of me. I couldn't do anything."

"Where are you?" Ever practical, Ray reverted to soldier mode.

"I'm at Rohan's house in London. He gave me the key, but they drove off with him." Emma thought about the mother with the pram, a sister who should have shown solidarity. "Nobody would help me," she sniffed. "They let it happen and didn't care. I don't like London."

"It's ok, it'll be ok. Give me the number of where you are."

Emma looked at the handset and the unit on the counter, seeing nothing written there. "I don't know it!" she wailed. "It doesn't say."

"Do you know the address?" Ray asked, keeping his voice light and factual. When Emma failed to answer, he pushed her. "What's the street called?"

"Clareville." Emma ran a hand over her tight forehead and closed her eyes against the pounding headache beginning. "Yes, Clareville. SW7."

"Ok. Well done. Do you know the number, miss?"

"Wait a minute." Keeping the keys in her hand, Emma stumbled to the front door and let herself out, running down the stairs and looking back up at the house. The black numbers stood out on the frosted glass and she slammed the front door behind her and ran back downstairs to the kitchen.

"Good girl," Ray said as she spluttered out the number. "Sit tight. Allaine took the kids to school already so I'll ask her to stay here longer. I'll ride over to the folly and talk to Christopher. He'll have a way of finding the phone number. Then I'll either call you back, or someone will come for you."

"No!" Emma shrieked. "I'm staying here. I need to wait for Rohan to come back." The desperation in her own voice made her sick and she lowered herself back onto the kitchen chair, no longer able to control the wobble in her legs.

"Ok, we'll take care of everything," Ray soothed. "Don't go outside or answer the door. Just stay there in the house and we'll contact you somehow."

Emma nodded as the line went dead, the sickness gripping her insides and choking the life out of them. She sank to the floor and lay still, wishing away the debilitating weakness. The child stirred in her womb and she cried then, fearing Rohan might be gone for good.

Chapter 25

Emma heard nothing for hours. She sat by the telephone until she realised it was wireless and tucked the handset into her jacket pocket. Wandering the house without Rohan lost its excitement and mystery and she ached for him. She walked from room to room, killing time and wishing back the morning so they could start again. She would refuse breakfast and stay in bed with her husband, pleasuring him until it was time for the train ride back to their son. Then they would leave, hop into his friend's taxi and be gone.

In the downstairs bedroom opposite Rohan's, Emma sensed Anton and sought his essence. She found it in the shape of a tiny die cast fire engine he'd loved. The red paint looked chipped and worn and she closed her eyes and remembered his fingers clutching the metal surface. He carried it everywhere until it ceased to be a toy and became an ornament, gracing every surface of his bedroom in turn. Emma sat on the bed and grieved afresh, wishing she'd known how near death he hovered the last time he'd visited her on the council estate. He'd promised to visit at Christmas, knowing he never would. Emma kissed the fire engine and put it back, noticing her father's bureau reflected in the mirror.

The phone rang in her pocket and Emma fumbled it and dropped it on the floorboards. The casing came away from the back and a battery skittered across the floor and buried itself underneath the bed. Emma needed a coat hanger from the wardrobe to retrieve it and then discovered once reunited with the handset, it needed to be married with the unit upstairs to reset itself. Five minutes later she stood with the phone in her hand, staring at it with hope and expectation.

She answered it on the first ring. "Rohan?"

"Na, sweetheart, it's me." Christopher's voice sounded tinny and Emma heard car sounds in the background as he changed gear. "How're you holding up?"

"Did you find him?" Emma closed her eyes and let her head fall back on her shoulders at Christopher's negative reply.

"I'd enough trouble finding you," he said, clicking the indicator on and then off. "I didn't know about that London house because he's got it in a different name. He's a cheeky bastard." Christopher's Irish brogue seemed to make everything sound like a joke and Emma experienced a flash of desperation mixed with annoyance.

"Just find Rohan," she pleaded.

"Look, I'm an hour away. Sit tight and don't leave that house. I'll call again when I'm around the corner. We'll brain storm when I get there. It'll be all right."

Christopher disconnected and Emma stared at the handset. Why did all the men in her life insist on telling her it would all be ok when they couldn't possibly know that? She dialled Wingate Hall again and got Ray. "I want to talk to Allaine," she demanded, regretting her rudeness in shoving him aside. Allaine came on the phone and Emma struggled not to fall apart and slither onto the floorboards as a puddle of goo.

"Oh, Em, I'm so sorry. You poor baby." Allaine's sympathy unhooked the last of her resolve and Emma felt the tears lodge in her throat.

"I just want Rohan," she sniffed. "They took him off the street from right in front of me."

"Ray said," Allaine soothed. "Christopher's on his way down to you."

"I know. He's an hour away," Emma said, her voice thick with tears. "I don't know what to do here." She looked around at the pristine house, freshly cleaned by an anonymous woman for her arrival.

"Do nothing," Allaine said. "And don't worry about Nicky. He's fine. Mr Dalton collared me when I dropped the children at school. Apparently the water tank burst in the loft and flooded Sam's office. He asked if you could stay away until next week as there's nowhere for you to work. Oh, he also said everything in the mezzanine roof is fine. The water went down, not sideways so all the stored artifacts and photos are fine."

Emma nodded and then forced herself to speak. "Ok," she said.

"Make a drink, sit down and wait for Christopher," Allaine instructed. "Ray's orders."

Emma nodded again. "Ok," she agreed.

Allaine rang off and Emma watched the dots flash on the digital dashboard, signifying passing seconds. Then she galvanised herself and went downstairs to Anton's room. She stroked the leather wallet, feeling the smoothness of its worn surface. Inside the front flap his driving licence faced upwards, blonde hair tousled as he gazed from the photograph, suppressing a smile to conform with the regulations. His lips quirked upwards and Emma raised his one dimensional face to her lips and kissed it through the plastic window. "I miss you, Anton Andreyev," she sighed. The pockets and zippers contained bank cards for accounts no longer in existence and a five pound note sat crumpled in the section at the back of the wallet. Emma touched the money, imagining Anton's long fingers shoving it in there. She folded the wallet and sat it where she found it, an ache in the pit of her stomach. Picking up the fire engine again, she wandered across to her father's bureau and began opening drawers.

The scent of her father's aftershave assaulted Emma's nostrils and forced her into a sitting position on the bed with her head between her knees. "Oh, Daddy," she groaned. "I miss you so much."

The drawers were all empty, apart from two coloured headed drawing pins and a paper clip in the tiny rectangular crevices either side of the pull down desk. Emma remembered her father's gentle hands pulling open drawers to retrieve colouring pencils and focussed on the memory of his fingers helping to fill shapes in her book. He had a peculiar way of colouring which fascinated her; colouring in the air before allowing the pencil to touch the paper. In her mind's eye she reached out and touched the fluffy hair covering his large hands and bent to kiss the olive flesh. When she thought of him, it was always in his cassock, the dark robe reaching his shiny shoes. Even in the soccer memory she saw him scoring goals in his vestments although it wasn't possible.

Emma stared at the middle drawer beneath the writing hatch and a sense of something strange bit at the back of her mind. She saw Rodney Harrington's fingers as they pulled on another drawer and he looked back at her and spoke. *'I'll show you this, one day,'* he said. *'When you're a big girl, I'll show you.'* Child-Emma nodded, not prompted to insist he showed her right then. She trusted him to reveal the secret when it was time and a memory surfaced from the fog of her brain, of knowing there was something her father promised to say, but hadn't managed to. Emma pulled out the middle drawer and ran her fingers over the surface above, finding nothing. She sighed, knowing her efforts to distract herself would only foster more grief and misery.

She bobbed down onto her knees and peered upwards, searching the old wooden surface with keen eyes. "What did you want to show me, Daddy?" she asked, wiping her nose on the back of her hand. "Show me now."

There was nothing there. The surface felt smooth and glossy and in frustration, Emma smacked her hand upwards, seeking to punish her father's bureau for his abandonment and disappointment of her. A click sounded in the silent bedroom and a flap appeared, moving downwards from the level above. It disgorged a small wooden box, but then refused to close upwards again.

Kneeling up and stretching her arm into the small space, Emma wrestled the box past the flap and once the obstacle pulled free, the flap closed. She clambered back up onto the bed and handled the smooth, wooden surface, turning it round and around in her hands. Hinged at the back, a groove ran the full circumference of the box, deeper at the bottom than the top. Hard as she tried, Emma found no opening. Exasperated, she closed the bureau and put the fire engine in her jacket pocket for comfort and plodded upstairs to the kitchen.

The box sat on the table while she made a cup of herbal tea, drinking and staring at the object before her. Something about it nagged at a memory deeply buried and Emma felt exhausted with the effort of digging for it. She spun it with her fingers, watching as the box skated on the glass table. The clock on the wall ticked a slow passage of time and the silence grated like nails on a blackboard. In temper, Emma gave the box a shove and winced as it flew across the slippery surface and clattered to the floor with a loud thud and the clunk of something inside falling over. With its unvarnished bottom pointing skywards, Emma peered at the dark hole on its surface. No bigger than a pin hole, it was centred beneath the front, on the opposite side of the hinge. Pushing the mug of tea away, Emma searched in the kitchen drawers and located a metal skewer. She hefted the box one handed and shoved the pointed end into the hole, holding her breath as the satisfying click filled the kitchen.

Chapter 26

The hammering on the front door accompanied the ringing of the bell and Emma wiped her nose on the back of her hand. She sniffed and rose, shoving the chair back with a loud scrape on the floorboards. The stairs to the ground floor felt endless, her feet heavy and her body leaden. Without checking the peep hole, Emma flung open the front door, no longer caring what greeted her.

"Geez, sweetheart!" Christopher exclaimed at the look of thunder Emma faced him with. He closed the door with his heel and gathered her into his arms. "You didn't disconnect the phone properly. I couldn't warn you I was near."

Emma said nothing, closing her eyes and drawing in the Irishman's familiar scent. He smelled earthy and of home, with the faint tang of spray deodorant and she pushed her face into his armpit. Christopher rubbed her back and kissed the top of her head. "We'll find him, sweetheart," he promised, his biceps firm against Emma's temple. She sniffed and he pulled her face up, his palms cupping her cheeks so he could look at her.

His dark eyes narrowed in sympathy and he placed soft lips against her forehead. "Let's sit down and you can tell me everything they said." He looked around him as though unsure where to go.

Emma set off ahead, stumbling her way down the staircase to the kitchen, her shoulders hunched over in defeat. Christopher followed, not stopping to remove his shoes. Emma's psyche linked in with his safe male presence, forcing a chink in her armour. As she stepped off the bottom stair into the kitchen, Christopher looked around him at the mess. Shards of wood covered the floor, the remains of her father's box nothing but smithereens and the meat tenderiser laid in the middle of the damage. "What the hell?" Christopher narrowed his eyes and stared at Emma. "Did they do this? I thought they took him off the street."

"I did it." Emma swallowed, the lump in her throat still there, threatening her with its painful exit. She slumped into a kitchen chair, defeat etching her slender frame into a twisted branch of hopelessness. There were wood shards in her hair and Christopher shifted on his feet, filling the room with nervousness and uncertainty.

"Talk to me, Em," he said, keeping his voice soft. "Help me find him."

She lifted her face to him, her eyes filled with tears. "It's all a lie. I don't know anything anymore."

Christopher squatted next to her as Emma writhed in the chair, rocking it back on its rear legs. "Is this about Rohan, sweetheart?" he asked, his voice caressing her soul. "Or somethin' else?"

"He's not here!" Emma balled her small hands into fists. "He should be here for this but he never is."

Emma took a gulp of air and covered her face with her hands. Christopher pulled her forwards until her forehead rested against his shoulder and he balanced there, holding her as she sobbed. "It's ok," he soothed into her madness and Emma shook her head, not believing him anymore.

When her noisy crying slowed, Christopher risked the question he dreaded most. "Did you lose the baby?"

It shocked her, the crassness of his question until she took stock of her dishevelled state and the level of misery she exuded.

That would be worse; worse than this for sure. Chastened, Emma gathered herself and shook her head. "No, not that."

She stood, drying her eyes on a tea towel she found in a drawer under the draining board. Christopher stood and rubbed the blood into his thighs. "What then. Rohan?"

"They said if I called the cops, they'd send him back to me in bits. Will they?" Her expression implored Christopher to negate the threat.

"I don't know," he replied. "I don't know who they are."

He spent the next hour coaxing from Emma everything she knew and even more she didn't realise she knew. "When they asked Rohan to see this Mr Wright, what did they call him, Em? Did they say Andreyev or Harrington?"

Emma squeezed her eyes tight shut and put herself back in the sandwich shop. If she hadn't demanded bread, they might have been safely tucked up in bed and never seen the men. "Andreyev," she replied. "Rohan said he knew them. He said they wanted to talk, not fight."

"Talk about what?" Back he came to the crux of the problem and Emma drew a blank again.

"I don't know. Just before they arrived this morning, Rohan said he had something to tell me and then it was too late. They got out and held a gun to his side, here." She lifted her jacket and touched the spot on her ribs, imagining what a bullet there would do to her already scarred husband. Emotion roiled around in her chest and made her breathing tight. The hand over her stomach alerted Christopher to her distress.

"This is too much for you. We need to think of the baby," he said, his tone serious. "I'll drive you back to Harborough; there's nothing you can do here."

"No!" Emma stood. "I'm not leaving. I want my husband!"

Christopher sighed. "I don't know how to help you this time, Em. I've never heard of a Mr Wright and all the checks I did on the way down turned up nothing. He's a ghost; he doesn't exist."

"He must do," Emma wailed. "He must do. What will I tell Nicky?" She balled up the bottom of her blouse in writhing fingers and compassion lit Christopher's face.

"Find me something to eat," he said. "I'll do some more digging. Does Rohan have an internet connection here?" He cast around the room looking for something and coming up empty. At Emma's blank look he absolved her from responsibility and shook his head. "I'll sort it out, don't worry."

Chapter 27

♥

Emma found bread in the freezer above the fridge and defrosted a few slices. She toasted them in a toaster from a cupboard, burning the edges in her distraction. She discovered an opened pot of blackcurrant jam in the pantry and plastered it over the bread, suspecting Christopher wasn't really hungry, but searching for a useful task to keep her out of his way.

The Irishman tapped away on his laptop, plugging in other devices and watching something move on the screen. Emma laid black coffee next to the toast. "What's that?" She saw the cursor on the screen spinning and spinning.

"I'm seeing if he wore one of our trackers," Christopher muttered, unplugging one device and switching it with another. "If he thought this might happen, he may have used one." The screen showed a solid blue image and then began the whirling again, making Emma feel sick.

"Why would he do that?" she asked. "Why allow himself to be willingly tracked?"

"Why not? It would be sensible." Christopher looked at the salt tracks on Emma's cheeks. "But he wouldn't risk you, no matter what. So he must have assumed it was safe to come to London."

"Stephanie and Jed took him by surprise," Emma said, her voice wistful. "He wasn't expecting them to show up at the office."

Christopher nodded. "Aye, he did. Working as The Actuary made him tight on security, but he had me ride down last week and change some codes and add a few cameras. I don't think he expected them to visit and confess all in the hallway while you listened though. That probably came as a surprise. Amateurs!" he spat.

"Did you talk to Rohan this morning?" Emma asked. "Didn't he say anything about Mr Wright?"

"No, nothin', Em. I promise you, he didn't. You know more than any of us."

Emma sighed and watched the cursor on the screen swirl in neat, frustrating circles. "I need him here," she said, her voice quiet and sad. "I need to talk to him."

"Will I do?" Christopher cocked his head, masking his hurt as she shook hers.

"I can't." The words pained her and Emma gritted her teeth, refusing to let any more tears fall. "I need Ro." Her fingers writhed in her lap and Christopher reached across and stopped their movement, crushing her hands beneath his palm.

"Trust me," he said, his eyes full of promise. "I won't let you down."

The laptop pinged and the spinner stopped. Christopher removed his hand and punched letters into the keyboard. "Bingo!" He grinned.

"You found him?" Emma demanded, her eyes wide. "Where is he?" She stood and zipped her jacket, ready to leave. "Is the Merc outside or did you borrow my car?"

"Steady on!" Christopher sounded irritated by Emma's impatience and she sat, scooting her chair next to his so their shoulders touched, her chin almost on his forearms as she peered at the screen. They watched in confusion as a blue blip moved across the screen, causing the map to refresh every couple of seconds.

"That's not possible," Christopher said, his brow knitted as the landmass below the blip changed over and over. "Unless he's bloody Superman."

Emma sat up. "That's it! They're flying him somewhere." She stood in panic and then sat down in defeat. "He could be headed anywhere. We need a plane." She rose again, the chair scraping the boards behind her. "I've got money; we'll charter one."

"And do what?" Christopher asked.

"Call Frederik and the other soldiers. They can break him out."

Christopher sighed and chewed at his thumbnail. "Could do, but only Rohan knows how to get in touch with them."

"Frederik's married to my friend! I'll call her." Emma forced Christopher to stand while she yanked the mobile phone from his front jeans pocket. He shook his head, letting her ramble and plan until she'd fought the screen lock four times and looked ready to throw it.

"It doesn't work like that, sweetheart. There are ways of calling them into a job and I don't know how he does it. They won't come." Christopher prised the phone from Emma's fingers and stroked her cheek. "Why don't you go for a lie down and let me think?"

"No!" Emma protested. "You can't make me."

"Yeah, I can." Christopher's tone was firm, overriding Emma's rebellion. "I made a promise to Rohan a few days ago; if anything happens to him, I step in and take care of you and the wee man."

"Why?" Emma's huge irises glittered like coals. "Why would he ask that a few days ago? He knew this was going to happen? Why bring me here?" She chewed her bottom lip, hysteria getting a good hold on her and threatening to pitch her over the edge. A life without her soul mate stretched in front of her and the adoration in Christopher's face made her want to scream. She'd never loved anyone but Rohan and doubted she ever could.

"I can't do this." She sank into the kitchen chair and rested her head against her forearms. "This is messed up."

Christopher rubbed her back, trying to infuse her with love but only accentuating Rohan's absence and the presence of an apparent handing over which she wasn't privy to. "Please find him?" Emma begged, wondering if her usually perceptive husband had for once, made a fatal error of judgement.

Chapter 28

♥

Exhaustion drove Emma to sleep, cancelling out all pretence at bravery. She woke up in the wide double bed, her boots missing and a blanket pulled up over her shoulders. Rohan's scent shrouded her, fooling her into believing he was within arm's length. His musky maleness and the aftershave he wore permeated her consciousness and Emma heaved a sigh of relief.

Daylight scattered her with dappled kisses through the skylight and she screwed up her eyes and turned sideways. Rohan's empty pillow drove her into a sitting position so fast, it made her head spin. She stumbled to the bathroom and sat on the floor tiles, pushed between the toilet and shower cubicle. Rohan's towel hung over the rail, still damp from his early shower and Emma threaded it off and let it fall into her lap. His soapy scent assailed her nostrils and she pushed away the misguided promise he'd extracted from Christopher. If her husband didn't return, she'd manage alone, just like last time.

"Em?" Christopher pushed open the bathroom door and nosed his way in. He glanced at Emma's legs, the dark woolly tights encasing her limbs and feet like the ones children wore to school. Her tartan skirt bunched up around her thighs and she suspected he could see her knickers through the tights. Nothing seemed able to make her care anymore and she hugged her knees and wished herself at home with her son. And her husband.

"How do you feel now?" He tested her as though she might bite, venturing further into the room and squatting in front of her. He fingered the hem of her skirt near the knee and Emma remembered it was an Irish tartan, maybe reminding Christopher of home.

"You carried me downstairs?" she asked, her head empty of anything since the conversation in the kitchen.

Christopher nodded. "Eventually. You cried yourself to sleep. I disturbed you; probably should've left you where you were. Sorry."

"Why were you in London last night?" she asked, the question popping from her mouth before she'd processed it.

"Seeing what I could find out about that crowd Rohan shares an office building with." Christopher sat on the end of the bed. "They're definitely up to something, but from what I overheard when the senior guys got drunk towards midnight, it's something they're about to do and not something they've already done."

Emma shook her head. "No, the two outside the office wanted to hide something which would trip Rohan. That means it's something they've already done, doesn't it?"

"What if it's an ongoing fraud they keep repeating?"

"Oh, I don't know," Emma sighed. "I can't pretend to understand any of his actuarial job."

Christopher screwed up his nose. "Me neither. That kind of maths is way beyond me. Whatever it is though, it's big and starts from the top. The two clowns outside the office were obeying orders and they'll try again." Christopher shifted in position and shook his head at Emma. "You look awful."

"Thanks." Emma's face pressed in her legs muffled her speech. "You didn't find Rohan, did you?"

"I did actually." Christopher raised a hand in caution. "But it's too far, we can't get there. They must have flown."

"Where is he?" Emma asked and Christopher chewed his lip before replying.

"Falkirk. Remember that house I tried to flood but accidentally torched?"

Emma nodded, already knitting her brow at the unexpected location. "Yeah. Why did they take him there?"

Christopher shrugged. "I don't know Em. He owns it; maybe that's why."

"He owns the Falkirk house?" Emma's voice sounded flat. "I know absolutely nothing about my own husband."

"Makes both of us," Christopher replied. "I never knew he owned this." He glanced around the sumptuous ensuite, his expression pensive. "He keeps buying stuff and hiding it under different names."

"Whose is this?" Emma poked her face up and studied Christopher, wondering if he'd bother lying.

"A guy named Clarence Clutterbuck. Sounds like a made-up name."

Emma buried her face in her knees and smirked. "He was a boy at school in Anton's year. Sometimes he waited for me after school to beat me up."

Christopher winced. "Nice. And Rohan thought he'd buy a title in that name?"

"It means something to us. The first time Rohan kissed me was after he'd pulled me off Clarence Clutterbuck. I'd just bust his nose and was about to stomp on his balls when Ro waded in and dragged me home. I'd loved him my whole life but he never let on that he felt the same." Emma sighed. "We have to go and get him, Chris."

"We'll leave now and head north," Christopher promised. "Grab your gear but you might as well leave his."

Emma protested she'd rather Rohan returned to find no clean underwear than his belongings abandoned. She stuffed everything into one bag and hauled it upstairs to find Christopher looking out of the front window and swearing. "What's happened?"

"Traffic warden," he spat. "It must be residents' parking because he just ticketed the car."

"But Ro's car must be registered here," Emma complained. "It's his house."

"Not on paper," Christopher conceded, letting the blind fall into place. "He probably puts the car in the garage under the house. There's a remote in the glove box but I didn't think about it. I was more interested in getting to you."

"At least he'll have something to complain about when he gets back," Emma said, adding certainty into her voice. "He won't pass up a chance to make your life hell." She rinsed the plate and cups they'd used under hot water and detergent and left them on the drainer to dry, before pushing her feet into her boots. "How far's Falkirk from here?" she asked.

Christopher's silence made her turn to face him, half way through zipping up her left boot. His complexion looked pale and his body had a defeated stance as he peered close at the laptop screen. When he shook his head, Emma stood up, panic already blighting her face. "The transmitter's stopped, Em. It's disappeared."

"No!" Emma wailed. "It can't have. It's fallen off or they've found it and broken it. We have to go up there and find him."

Christopher shook his head, his face setting in determined lines. "No, Em. I'm sorry. We're not driving for eight hours to find he's either not there, or put ourselves in the same mess he's in. It's foolish, I'm not doing it."

"Please, please!" Emma rushed him, thumping his chest with her fists and begging. Christopher refused each hysterical demand and plea, spinning Emma and holding her wrists behind her in one strong hand while she thrashed and kicked. Her tantrum alternated between desperation and pure rage.

"I hate you!" she screamed, standing with her back against the front door and her face streaked with salty tears. Her fringe stuck to her face in sweaty ringlets and her chest hitched like a hysterical toddler.

"Yeah, well I love you so I'm not taking you on a dangerous wild goose chase!" Christopher shouted back, the veins standing out on his neck.

Emma groaned and turned to face the door, resting her forehead against the glossy wood and crying without shame. Christopher gathered his gear and attacked her face with wads of toilet roll, refusing to look her in the eye as he mopped up her distress and readied her for the street outside. Emma's lungs heaved and she sounded incoherent as she begged him one last time to take her to Falkirk.

"No!" Christopher snapped. "Set the burglar alarm and then get in the car. Don't even think about doing a runner with the keys or the car. I swear, Em, I'll call the cops and report it stolen. If the guys who took Rohan are watching for cops, you'll have signed his death warrant."

Emma obeyed, stung by Christopher's cruelty, working on automatic to close up the house and climb into the car. Rohan's presence assailed her senses, his scent, his CDs and the neatness of the vehicle's interior. Unable to bear it, she curled up into a ball on the passenger seat and pressed her cheek against the window. Christopher loaded the car and buckled himself in. "Belt up," he said, his tone firm. Emma closed her eyes and ignored him and he leaned across the centre console, pulling her head sideways and yanking the seatbelt around her. His forearm moved dangerously close to her mouth and for the second time that day, Emma considered taking a bite out of a man's flesh. "Don't you dare!" Christopher warned and the moment passed with the click of the seatbelt.

Christopher navigated London using an app on his mobile phone. He pushed the device into the holder on the dashboard and Emma leaned forward, snatching it and throwing it on the floor, not wanting anything of Rohan's disturbed. "Childish!" Christopher exclaimed, stopping at traffic lights and grovelling on the floor for his phone. "Never thought I'd be so grateful for fully tinted windows."

Emma squeezed her eyes closed and refused to engage with him, so he balanced his phone in front of the gear lever and drove out of the metropolis. Two hours saw them driving through Market Harborough, Christopher swerving to avoid the pot holes on Northampton Road. Ten minutes later they slid through the gates of Wingate Hall and rounded the sweeping drive up to the manor house. The front doors snapped open before Christopher applied the foot brake and Allaine and Ray emerged at a run. Christopher deactivated the central locking so Ray could open the passenger door, almost pitching Emma onto the gravel. The seat belt saved her and Christopher leaned in and undid it. Emma heard him speaking to the other adults as though she wasn't there, her catatonic state having permeated every brain cell she possessed.

"I had to lock the doors," he muttered to Ray, who sent a nervous glance across at Emma. "Thought she was gonna jump out every time I stopped."

"Hey, babe." Allaine's voice sounded soft and her face showed pure compassion as she helped Emma stand. After two hours under her bum, her legs felt like jelly and she wobbled around, disoriented and unsteady. In her peripheral vision Emma saw Christopher and Ray with their heads together and mistrust burgeoned in her heart. The memory of Rohan's stealthy soldier sedating her rose to the fore and she wasn't prepared to take the risk of leaving the Irishman to find ways to quieten her. As the clock tower struck two o'clock, Emma pushed Allaine's helpful hands away and bolted for the house. She slammed the outer door behind her to buy time and clambered up the stairs. Across the hall she sped to her bedroom, locking the door behind her and leaning against it.

Rohan's favourite watch glittered from his nightstand, the mechanisms whirring in a ceaseless display of precision timekeeping. Emma left her guard post and stole across the floorboards, lifting the watch into her hand. The gold face blinked back at her on its tan leather strap and she imagined it gracing

Rohan's strong wrist. The thought induced physical pain and Emma pushed up the sleeve of her jacket, strapping the watch to her left wrist. Even on its tightest setting it dangled and she covered it up with the sleeve, hiding it from damage and view.

"Emma, I'll go and fetch the kids soon," Allaine called through the door. She sounded anxious and Emma shrugged off her guilt. "Let me come in, sweetie. I need to see you're ok."

Emma sat on the bed and pushed her face into Rohan's pillow, bargaining with God for his life whilst expecting to lose.

Allaine cleared her throat. "Em, unless you let me in, Christopher's threatening to break down the door."

Emma eyed the solid oak and wrinkled her nose. She'd like to see him try. The sound of muffled whispering drifted through the wood and a hearty click followed. The door handle moved and Allaine poked her face through. "Change of plan," she said by way of apology. Emma watched Christopher put the long metal spike back on his key ring and fought the urge to poke her tongue out at him.

"Go away," she said, pressing her nose back into the pillow. "Bring me my husband or go away."

The door closed and Emma heaved a sigh of relief. It lasted only until the bed sank down next to her. "I'm so sorry, Em," Allaine whispered. "I don't know what to say."

"He's not dead." Emma sat up and swiped at her eyes with her sleeve. The watch poked through and left a painful scratch across her cheek. "I know he's not dead."

Allaine rubbed her back. "What're you gonna do?" she asked and Emma shrugged.

"Find him and bring him home." Her bottom lip trembled as self-doubt vied with determination. The doubt gained the upper hand. "I don't know how but I'm gonna."

"What do you want me to do with the kids? Should I take them to mine or bring them here?"

Emma exhaled and cast her eyes around. Her body stiffened and she sat up straight. "Where's Will? Is he at your place?"

"I don't know." Allaine looked unnerved. "I haven't spoken to him for days and I don't want to. He's moving his stuff out and I'm going back to the house." Pain filled her face and her lips twitched.

Emma jumped up. "We're going to yours," she said, her jaw determined. "If my husband's hurt because of him, I'll make him sorry!"

Chapter 29

♥

"Hey, Alli." Will looked pleased to see his wife as she unlocked the front door and slipped inside, leaving it open for Emma to follow. He balanced the suitcase against the bottom step and stood up straight, rubbing his palms against his thighs. Emma stepped into the hallway and stood with her hands on her hips, her face grim.

Will's eyes darted to his wife and back to Emma's face and he swallowed. "Hey, look, I'm really sorry for what happened," he began. "It was a stupid error of judgement and I have no reasonable explanation for what I did. The guy pestered me for days and in the end I couldn't see the harm. It's not like Rohan's a master criminal or an MI6 agent. He said he was a friend and we got talking about cars. Before I knew it, he'd handed me a wad of cash and I was too far down the line to get out of it. I only gave him the Newcombe Street address though, not Wingate Hall. You have no idea how sorry I am, Emma." His eyes roved towards Allaine as she stood in the corner of the hallway. "I've lost my family and if you make a formal complaint, I'll lose my job too." He licked his lips and leaned on first one foot and then the other. "I took the car back to the garage. They didn't refund all the money, but I'll find the guy and return the cash." His eyes sought Allaine's, but she ignored him. "I want everything to go back to how it was before," he implored. He waved a hand towards the suitcase. "Don't make me leave, Alli. I know I was stupid; let me make good. Give me another chance? Please, Alli."

"You want everything to go back the way it was, do you?" Emma said, her voice slick with fury.

Will's eyes studied her face growing wary at the emotion he saw in her eyes. "Yeah." He nodded.

Emma crossed the distance between them in four strides, her brown eyes flashing and her boots clicking on the wooden floor. She raised her hand and slapped him around the face hard. Will recoiled and took a step back, lifting his hands to protect his head as Emma loaded in on him, purging herself of hopelessness and despair. "My husband's missing because of you!" she screeched into his face. "How do you suggest I go back to normal, if it's so bloody easy?" Emma choked on her own words, feeling Allaine's hands on her shoulders tugging her backwards. "What do I tell our son?" Emma wailed and Allaine turned and enfolded her into a tight embrace.

"It's ok, Em," she soothed, her voice tearful. "It'll be ok."

"Rohan's missing?" Will's tanned face paled to a deathly pallor and he plopped backwards onto the third step. He ran a hand across his eyes and shook his head. "Shit. I'm so sorry."

"As you can see, sorry doesn't count for much," Allaine replied, her voice acidic. Will winced.

"I'll call it in," he sighed, digging in his jeans pocket for a phone. "I'll tell them everything. Please forgive me; I'll make this right."

"Don't you dare!" Allaine snapped. "Don't you dare make it all about you. The men said no cops or they'll kill Rohan. Do you want that on your conscience too?"

"No! Of course not. But there's no alternative, is there?"

Allaine's phone sounded in her coat pocket and she reached in, examining the screen with wide eyed apprehension. "It's Christopher," she said.

"Christopher who?" Will took a step forward, jealousy reddening his cheeks. The women ignored him.

"Answer it," Emma demanded, sniffing and brushing a hand across her face.

Allaine allowed the call to connect and listened, nodding in silence. "Ok, I'll tell her," she said, turning back to Emma. The screen darkened as Christopher disconnected and Allaine's face lit up in hope. "He sent a message to Frederik asking for help. He found out how Rohan contacted them."

Emma stared at her in expectation. "And?"

"And they responded." Allaine's excitement permeated to Emma and she put her hands up to her mouth, stifling the groan of relief as her friend continued to speak. "They're en route," she said. "Christopher said to get back to the house. We'll go for the kids and take them to your place." She jerked her head towards Will. "He said to bring him. He's got questions to ask." Her eyes narrowed. "And he will be answering them."

Chapter 30

♥

Allaine fed the children and took them to the sitting room to watch TV. Nicky hugged Emma around the stomach, believing her tale that Rohan was called away to work. As her friend led him from the kitchen, Emma saw the doubt in his eyes and he kicked up a fuss, insisting he wanted to show her his homework.

"I'll come soon, baby," she promised. "We'll have a cuddle; I've missed you so much." She gave him a reassuring smile and waved as Allaine closed the door behind them. Emma waited until the children's noise chirped along the hallway and then she leaned over Will's shoulder. "I hope you enjoyed your tea," she said, her voice like razor blades in his ear. "Because if I have anything to do with it, it's gonna be the last meal you eat without using a straw. How does it feel hearing Kaylee tell you she loves you while Nicky's dad's out there somewhere?"

"Ok, Em," Christopher warned, his voice low. He glanced towards the kitchen door and jerked his head at Emma. "Lock it," he said.

Emma stepped across to the door and turned the key, leaning back against the wall. Will shifted in his seat, fear lighting up his face in a grimace. "I'm a serving police officer," he stated, eyeing Christopher as the Irishman planted his bum on the table next to him.

"So y'are," Christopher intoned. "But not much of one, hey?"

Will turned to face Emma. "You've stayed in my house and my wife's treated you like a family member." Bitterness edged his voice.

Emma shook her head. "I could say the same thing. But it's not a competition, Will, nothing gives you the right to sell someone's address for money. Nothing!"

Will shrugged. "This is over the top," he grumbled, confident that right was somehow on his side. "Let me call the station and my colleagues can find Rohan."

Christopher snorted. "They told her if she called the cops, she'd get her husband back in little pieces. You want that on your conscience as well?"

Will shook his head. "They were bluffing to scare her."

"Really?" Christopher took an aggressive step forward. "You wanna take that risk?"

"You can't touch me," Will said, his jaw working under his cheek. He sneered at the Irishman and Emma held her breath, wondering where the gentle Christian man she knew a few months ago had gone.

Christopher's reflexes proved lightning fast as he hit the back of Will's head, forcing his face into the wooden table. There was a dull thud and a cry and Will raised his head, blood oozing from his nose. "Oh, sorry," Christopher said. "What was that about me not being able to touch you?"

Another smack sent Will's face into the table again and Emma winced, the Irishman's behaviour going beyond her tame idea of revenge. Sickness engulfed her stomach and she squatted against the door to stave off the feeling. "Stop, Christopher, please stop."

Ray stood and walked over to Will, wrenching his head back using the man's mop of dark hair. It was as though Emma hadn't spoken. "What a shame, you broke your nose," he said and rammed Will's head back into the table.

Frightened, the policeman tried to stand and Ray blocked him, shoving him back into the seat. Will's speech seemed to gurgle from his lips and Emma groaned and knelt on the floor, her forehead touching the cold quarry tiles. "You can't do this," she gasped.

"She shouldn't be in here," Ray said, glancing across.

"Yep. You make her leave then," Christopher said. "Good luck with that."

Emma sat up and ran a clammy hand across her forehead. "Just tell them what they want to know, Will," she begged. "They can probably do this all night."

The policeman wiped a finger gingerly along the underside of his nose, his voice husky. "They haven't asked me anything yet."

"Oh, yeah!" Christopher let out a nasty laugh. "My bad. That attitude of yours distracted me."

"What do you want to know?" Defeat smothered Will's voice and he shifted in his chair. "I don't know what you want from me."

Ray scraped a chair across the tiles and sat it next to Will's, giving him no room for manoeuvre. Christopher stayed standing, flexing his knuckle joints until they cracked.

"You first, Sergeant," Christopher said, holding his hand out towards Ray, palm upwards.

Ray shook his head. "Oh, no, Flight Lieutenant, after you."

Will braced himself and closed his eyes, waiting for another blow to fall. Emma gave him points for stoicism and something extra for courage in the face of uncertainty.

"I want to know everything in wonderful detail," Christopher said. "I want to know who, when, why, what and how. If I suspect you're withholding information or outright lying, I'll let you know." He lifted his trouser leg and withdrew a spiteful looking knife from a sheath around his shin. The blade flicked outwards in a smooth movement and Emma held her breath.

"You won't get away with this," Will said, the last words shrouded in a cough.

"I thought that too," Christopher agreed, drawing the knife across his trousers to clean it, one side and then the other. He smirked. "But after the fifth time, I stopped worrying."

Will's face paled and Emma felt a wave of pity. She wanted to stick up for him, reassure him her presence guaranteed he wouldn't be buried in a deep hole in the woods at the back of her property. But part of her wasn't sure that was true and it was the same fraction of her soul which ached for her husband. Christopher put his shoe up on the corner of Will's chair and leaned an elbow across his thigh. The knife glinted in the overhead bulb. "From the beginning then, mate," he said, his voice coaxing and gentle.

Will glanced at Emma and his face crinkled with worry lines as she caught his eye. She knelt up on the cold tiles, one hand on her stomach and her eyes red. She saw him wince and he lowered his eyes to the table. "It started the night Allaine and I went into town with Rohan and Emma after New Year."

Christopher raised an eyebrow at Emma and she nodded. "That was the day after Alanya's funeral. Allaine and I thought it might distract Rohan for a few hours and stop him fretting."

Will waited for her to finish and continued. "I went to the bar to buy a round of drinks and this guy recommended one of the light beers instead of my lager. I tried it and it tasted good, so we got chatting. He said he was from London way and I mentioned I was stationed there before I married Allaine." Will looked hopefully towards the door, blood running over his top lip and dripping down his shirt. His wife didn't return, despite his obvious need of her support.

He sighed. "He watched us playing pool and walked into the gents' toilet behind me."

Ray raised his eyebrows at Christopher and Will blanched at the unspoken accusation. "No way! Don't even go there."

Christopher grinned. "So you chatted like old buddies over the urinal?" he asked, wrinkling his nose. "How sweet."

Will inhaled a ragged breath, self-preservation keeping him from tangling with the duo further. "Something like that. He asked about Rohan's accent and I said I thought he was Russian. That was all. He left and I didn't see him again for a couple of days."

"What then?" Ray asked, drumming his fingers on the table with impatience.

Will spread his hands, seeming surprised at the blood streaks covering his fingers. "I left work one night and nipped into town. Allaine asked me to pick up some bits at the supermarket. When I came out, he was standing by my car. He asked me outright for Rohan's address and I told him to clear off."

"Then?" Christopher wiped the blade edge along his thumb, careful not to depress the skin. Emma held her breath.

"Then he was everywhere I went. If I went for a run, he showed up and ran next to me. When I went to the garage to fill the car, there he was. Outside work, on the street, it didn't seem to matter. It was like he'd cloned himself and knew exactly where I'd be."

"Did he touch you?" Christopher asked and Will blanched.

"No!" His aggression hiked. "I told you; it was nothing like that."

"Did he touch you as in, did he slap you on the shoulder, shake your hand, give you your coat?" Ray asked, speaking as though Will was thick.

Will shook his head and then stopped the repetitive movement, his eyes growing wary. "Yes. I left my phone on the counter and he picked it up and handed it to me."

Christopher shot a look at Ray and the other man nodded. "Where's your phone now?" he asked.

"If he's got it on him, we just walked them right to our door," Ray hissed and Emma tensed, a detached bystander in a surreal farce.

"It's at home," Will said. "I didn't have time to get it." He rubbed at a spot on his cheek and jerked his head towards Emma.

The action started his nose running again. "She slapped me and Allaine wanted me to leave right then. I forgot it."

Christopher relaxed but pressed for the rest of the details. "So he probably tagged your phone or the case it's in. Do you carry it when you run?"

Will nodded his head, keeping the motion shallow. His face looked grey and Emma worried about brain haemorrhages and manslaughter or murder charges and bodies hidden on her property.

"He tagged you and the rest was easy," Ray said. He looked up at Christopher. "Do we kill the signal or let them think he's still at home?"

"Leave it for now," Christopher said. "It's an opportunity for fun later." He smacked his lips as though the thought of violence satisfied him like a filling portion of his favourite food.

Ray shook his head. "He won't be monitoring it now. He got what he wanted. Best to smash it."

"You're not smashing my phone!" Will snapped and Christopher sneered.

"Maybe I'll smash you instead," he said.

Emma shuddered and found herself praying to God for Rohan's safety. She wanted him back and promised herself she'd never rebel or give him trouble again. Never. As long as he returned to her.

"So he wore you down?" Christopher picked up the interrogation. "When did he give you the money?"

Will sighed. "He must've seen me admiring a mate's car outside the station. Next time he met me, he talked about seeing a newer model in a garage in Leicester. It was stupid, but I said I couldn't afford it. He got to me and it was hard staying focussed around him when he went on and on all the time. It was like having a wasp in my face and it didn't matter where I went, he was always there."

"Was he there when you were with Allaine?" Christopher asked and Will nodded.

"A few times. We took Kaylee for a walk around Welland Park and I saw him following. He has this way of making it look natural and it started to freak me out. The relief when I gave in and took the money was overwhelming but then I realised what I'd done. I tried to get rid of the cash by buying the car but Allaine knew something was up and I had to tell her."

"So, it never occurred to you to call in the police?" Christopher demanded, his tone illustrating the poignancy of his question. "Yet, you think Emma should have done that when Rohan was snatched off a street in broad daylight and his kidnappers warned her not to."

"I don't know," Will sighed. "I don't know anything anymore. Probably not, no."

"He freaked you out, but ya didn't think about what it might do to Emma's family once you'd sent him their way?"

"Just to the old house," Will asserted. "I didn't send them here."

"Rohan still owns that house!" Emma exclaimed. "Until last week his brother and family were living there."

Will had the decency to look ashamed.

"How did he give you the money?" Ray asked, still tapping his impatient beat on the table.

"In a brown envelope." Will's voice lowered, dripping thick with an ugly kind of shame. "Dirty money."

"You said it." Christopher sounded almost cheerful. "Now, I want to know what this guy looks like and how I can find him."

Will swallowed. "London accent, average build, nothing remarkable."

"White, black, Asian, Oriental? Come on, man, you're a cop, aren't ya?" Christopher pressed.

"He just looked average, like anyone else. I don't think I'd recognise him again if I saw him."

"It has to be one of the men from the sandwich shop." Emma stood up, wobbling on her feet. "The one I stuck the plastic fork into did most of the talking. He had a big fat chin, I remember. It was the only thing, apart from the length of his hair, which made him stand out from his partner, otherwise they looked like clones."

"I only saw one guy." Will sounded sorry. "But it wasn't him. I'd have noticed distinctive features. I should've stuck a fork in him," he mused. "Would have saved myself a whole heap of misery."

"And us," Emma said, her eyes hard. "They stopped us on the street and held a gun to my husband's side. They were going to take me too." Her chin wobbled. "Rohan asked them not to."

Christopher shoved Will in the chest. "So, how come this tiny lass managed to stick a plastic fork into a guy's leg and bite his finger half off, when all you did was get upset, take a wad of cash from a stranger and sell out a mate?"

Will looked ashamed. "I'm sorry," he said. "I'm truly sorry."

Ray stood up and leaned against the Aga, his face pensive. "Now we just need to work out if this is the same guy who followed you in the tube station, or whether the two groups are separate."

Emma closed her eyes and raked through her memory to the dash from one tube train to another. She glanced around in her mind's eye, seeing only strangers in her recollection. "No. I'd never seen those men before they approached us in the cafe. I thought when Rohan mentioned a tail, it was the chap opposite who hated us whispering and being intimate but he said no, it was the guy with the umbrella."

"Did you see him?" Christopher asked, his voice soft. "You're doing great, Em. Try to remember."

"No." Emma exhaled. "I looked around but saw no one unusual. Rohan moved us so fast, I didn't get a chance to see who we ran from."

Ray stood up and stepped behind Will. Emma watched the policeman's eyes widen in fear. He ran a hand beneath his nose and examined the blood which attached to the hairs. "Ok," Ray said, running his tongue over his bottom lip. "So, Rohan saw a man who followed him and Emma from King's Cross?" Christopher nodded and glanced at Emma. "He diverted them to a different station and wound up at their London house later than planned."

"We used a taxi," Emma offered. "The driver's a friend of Ro's." She clambered to her feet and moved around the edge of the room towards the sink, grasping a glass from the draining board and filling it with cold water. She laid it down with a clatter and gripped the edge of the Belfast sink, wondering if the old furnishings had ever witnessed anything so bizarre in their hundreds of years of existence. Christopher sidled across and lifted her ponytail with one hand, rubbing her shoulders with the other. Emma smiled in thanks and listened to Ray process his thoughts out loud. Ray used his index finger as a pointer, digging the air in front of him.

"What if the tail at the station was the same guy? We had blokes like him in the army. Grey men, we called them. They slipped through life unnoticed and it was impossible to remember particular features or characteristics afterwards. That's their skill set, blending and becoming invisible. It starts naturally, like that well behaved kid in school who never gets into trouble but doesn't stand out like a high achiever. If he was that kinda guy, it would explain why Emma didn't notice him at the station and this idiot can't give a description."

"Unless this idiot's lyin'," Christopher said, his voice sounding dangerous as he slipped a protective arm around Emma.

"I'm not lying!" Will stressed. His lips turned down in a fed up expression. "I've got nothing left to gain and everything to lose." He closed his eyes and exhaled in defeat.

"Rohan would notice him because he's trained to," Ray said, resuming a neat circle of pacing behind Will's chair. He stopped and nudged the back of Will's head. "Why did you tell the guy Rohan's old address?"

"I felt bad," Will replied. "It was a half-truth because Rohan still owns the house on Newcombe Street. The guy said he had something for him and I figured he'd leave it there and Rohan would pick it up. When nothing happened within a few days and the guy disappeared, I figured it was nothing."

"Nothing?" Ray said. "What was the value of nothing?"

"Five grand," Will said, shame edging his voice into sharp tones.

Ray raised his eyebrows at Christopher and shook his head in disgust. "Well mate, I hope it was worth it."

Christopher exhaled. "If he visited the house and didn't get to do what he came for, he would've gone straight back to where he made the five grand investment and either demanded his money back, or done some damage."

"Which means he did it," Ray said. "He got what he came for."

"But Rohan doesn't live there," Christopher said. "So that doesn't work."

"What if he knocked on the door and met Sergei," Emma said. "He speaks very little English and two weeks ago, he lived in that house with his wife and baby. They have the same eye colour and some similarities because they're brothers, so it's possible the guy thought he'd lucked out."

"But what would he do there?" Ray demanded. "Would he ask for Rohan?"

"Na." Christopher shook his head. "Few people know Rohan's real name in London and you said he was a Londoner, didn't ya?" He directed his question at Will and the policeman nodded.

"Yeah. He said he worked in banking or stockbroking, something like that. I worked in Brixton twenty years ago and he knew it like a man who'd walked the streets."

"Or drove a taxi," Emma mused.

"What?" Ray stopped his pacing and stared at Emma. "What do you mean?"

"Just something Rohan said about his friend," she replied. "They have to learn The Knowledge to drive taxi cabs and know every suburb of London to get a green badge. Then they can drive a hackney carriage."

Ray shook his head as though to clear it. "Red herring," he said. "I don't wanna go off at a tangent. Not while I'm getting somewhere." He paced again, waving his hands like a preacher. "So the grey man did exactly what he came to do. So why was he waiting at King's Cross for Rohan? He must've known he'd show up then, which suggests he knew about the dinner engagement. Why not go straight there? Hell, why not just show up at his office?"

"Maybe he did," Emma said. "Perhaps Maureen wouldn't let him in."

Ray's brow knitted at the mention of Rohan's fierce assistant but Christopher gave a slow nod. "Yeah. He thinks something's happened like he wanted it to, but there's been no result. He goes to the office and Maureen fobs him off so he waits to see Rohan."

"Ro said something weird," Emma commented, glancing sideways at Christopher. He rubbed his fingers along her shoulder with an absent minded action, stopping as she spoke, his face questioning. "We stood outside the hotel where the event was happening and I asked if we should be more careful in case the man was watching. He said he didn't mind the man knowing where he worked but he didn't need to know where he lived."

"Exact words, Em," Christopher said, turning her to face him.

She closed her eyes and listened to her husband's soft drawl in her head, repeating them out loud. "*I don't care if he sees me attend work functions but there's no need for him to know where I live when I'm here.*" Emma repeated the words. "Yeah, that's what he said." She sighed with tiredness. "Have you heard from Frederik yet?"

"No." Christopher looked sorry as he said the word but excitement sparkled in his brown irises. "So the guy knows where he works, but not where his London house is." Christopher tapped his foot on the floor. "Which might imply the guy also knew where Rohan's Harborough house was."

"Or where he thought it was," Ray added.

Emma groaned. "This won't bring back Rohan! And it doesn't tell us who the other men were, the ones who took him off the street." Her distress returned as the difficult riddle baffled her and Christopher put his arm around her and pulled her in close.

"It's ok, Em. Everything's a process, sweetheart. We've gotta work this stuff out. Why don't you go and have a cuddle with your wee man and let us sort things?"

Chapter 31

Emma woke up fully dressed in Nicky's bed, his head heavy on her upper arm. Her legs felt cold and her body shook with the shock of being woken from a deep sleep.

"Em." The voice sounded hushed as a hand moved from her arm to her hand. "It's Christopher. I need you to get up."

"Is it Rohan?" she asked, her breathing laboured.

"Shhhh." Christopher put a finger over her lips and Emma saw the shape of his head jerk towards Nicky. She extracted herself from the sleeping child and padded downstairs behind the Irishman, accepting his helping hand at the bottom of the stairs.

A council of war awaited her in the warm kitchen, the Aga cranked up to full heat. Allaine clattered over by the kettle, her back turned towards the room. Will sat in the same seat, crusted blood covering his chin and the back of his hand. His expression was one of exhaustion and misery as though he'd given up on life.

"Have a seat," Ray said with a smile. "We've got an idea and we need you."

Emma sighed and hefted herself into the seat. "I thought you'd found Rohan," she said, sulking. Worry returned to her face and Will couldn't meet her eyes. The kitchen clock declared it was eight thirty, twelve hours since the men snatched Rohan. "Have you heard from Frederik?" she asked, sounding hopeful.

"Rohan's not at the Falkirk house," Ray said, glancing across at the Irishman. "But he's been there. They found his mobile phone in a downstairs toilet."

Emma watched as Christopher shook his head, the movement so slight she almost missed it. "Is he alive though?" she asked and Ray nodded.

"We're assuming so."

Ray's pause told her more than she wanted to know and Emma bit back further questions about his possible state, comforted by the assurance he was alive. "What do you want from me?" she asked, focussing on Christopher.

"We're going to Newcombe Street," he replied, "and we need your help."

"This is stupid!" Will blustered. "She's a pregnant woman. I'll come with you. Don't make her go."

Christopher leaned in close to the side of Will's head. "I'd feel safer with the pregnant woman, if it's all right with you. I know I can trust her."

Will shook his head and looked at Emma. "I've said I'm sorry. At least let me help somehow. Please?" He glanced across at Allaine's back and winced.

"Stay here and protect my son." Emma stared at him until he looked away. "If you let me down, I'll go straight to the cops and tell them what you did." Emma didn't blink as she delivered her final message. "If Rohan doesn't come home, that will be the least of your problems."

Allaine gasped and spewed hot water over the counter. "Emma, don't say something you'll regret!" Her eyes widened in horror and Emma hardened her resolve against her gentle Christian friend.

"Then pray," she said, her voice soft. "Pray for Rohan and make sure he comes home, otherwise we'll both be widows."

Allaine nodded and her already reddened eyes glittered with tears. She turned back towards the rear window, watching their reflections as three of the adults left the room, her roiling emotions denying her the courage to face the one who remained.

Emma's car slid through the automatic gates and sped up on the main road heading north towards Market Harborough. She leaned forward between the front seats and addressed Ray and Christopher. "If the man found Rohan in the pub, why didn't he follow him home?"

"Because he didn't actually want to run into Rohan. He needed to leave something at his place of residence, something that might incriminate him if discovered by someone else; someone investigating, perhaps. And even better would be to hide false evidence at two of his homes. There would be no getting out of that."

Emma's eyes widened. "Maureen said she thought Rohan was being framed. So that makes sense."

"Aye." Christopher turned into Newcombe Street and travelled along for a hundred metres, turning left into the lane which ran behind the houses. "And I think Rohan knew what was goin' on and he's already removed whatever was delivered here. With any luck, he's hidden it somewhere safe or destroyed it."

"So why are we looking?" Emma asked, casting her eyes around in fear and Christopher put full beam on the headlights of her car and bounced along in the darkness.

"I just need to be sure," Christopher whispered. "Rohan was here when Sergei left, wasn't he?"

"He took them to the airport," Emma replied. "Sergei's wife cleaned the house and Rohan brought the bedding back to Wingate Hall to wash. I didn't see it; he did it himself."

Christopher parked the car outside the rear gates and put the handbrake on. He turned to Emma in the back seat. "You stay here, sweetheart. Ray will check the garden and I'll turn lights on in the house. If the grey man's come back to Harborough, it's likely he's watching this house."

"But he'll know Rohan's been snatched," Emma said, avoiding the word kidnap through a desire not to throw up in the back of her own car. "He knows Ro's not here."

"I think it's two different groups," Christopher said. "We both do. We think the grey man's planted evidence but needs Rohan to be in the same place as it. That hasn't happened so far and he's getting desperate."

"Has Rohan got nothing in his own name?" Ray hissed and Christopher snorted.

"A marriage licence," he said with a smirk. "He's spent the last five years not wanting to be obvious. Reckon he did a good job."

"But what about Wingate Hall?" Emma asked. "Wouldn't the man realise he actually lives there with me?"

"Rohan comes and goes, Em. I suspect the guy's targeting Rodney Harrington, so he's got no idea Rohan's married. You could be a recent girlfriend. The grey man needs to conclude his job tonight or he'll start poking around and come much too close to home. We're gonna give him a helping hand." He turned to Emma. "Stay here, Em. The windows on this have a better tint than the Mercedes. Squat down behind the seats and keep real quiet."

Emma nodded and scooted into the small space behind Ray's chair. She groaned as her belly wouldn't quite fit. Ray shoved his seat forward and she plopped into the gap with an unladylike grunt. "I'm fine, I'm fine," she reassured the men.

Ray and Christopher exited the vehicle and unlocked the rear gates, leaving them wide open. Of similar height and build to Rohan, Christopher pushed down the hood of his sweatshirt and Emma gasped at the mop of blonde hair covering his dark locks. The men strode away with Ray's voice cutting into the night but Christopher stayed silent, unable to mimic Rohan's accent. Emma leaned down and pressed her lips against the tiny microphone which Christopher attached to her sweater before they left Wingate Hall. "Rohan's hair doesn't stick up like a scarecrow's!" she whispered.

"He's got bed head," came the reply, sounding in Emma's head as though Christopher leaned over her shoulder and brushed his lips to her ear. She pinched her nose and mouth to muffle the squeak and worked on slowing her breathing.

Twenty minutes later she was about to stretch out her legs in protest and demand to be taken home when a dark shape moved past the rear window. She shoved her fingers harder into the chocolate brown mittens and pushed her face into her knees, obscuring the skin colours beneath the fabric of her black hood. The car rocked gently as someone leaned against it and a padded coat brushed against the paintwork with a quiet shushing sound. The intruder checked the rear and front seats before moving across the gravel and Emma listened as the noise changed from the grit outside the gates to the larger stones inside. "He's here!" she hissed into the microphone and heard Christopher's immediate reply.

"It's ok, sweetheart. Sit tight. I've got the TV playing in Ro's old room but we're outside. Radio silence until I say otherwise."

Emma swallowed. She wanted Rohan with a desperate ache, but terror overrode bravery and she cowered in the vehicle as an unknown menace trespassed on her husband's property. She heard and saw nothing, not daring to peek over the back of the seat in case she came face to face with the man. Her window tints worked well, but a pink upturned face in a darkened car would be obvious to anyone looking in. Emma held her position for another twenty minutes before hearing the sound of footsteps crunching back across the gravel. The dark shape slipped past, not bothering to check the car. Ten minutes later, Ray and Christopher returned, slithering into the vehicle with the minimum of sound. They were back out on the road before they fastened seatbelts and behaved as normal passengers.

"Flick that switch so the interior light comes on when we open the doors," Christopher ordered and Ray reached above the centre console and set it back to how it was before.

"Is he following?" Emma asked as she settled in the seat and rubbed the blood back into her limbs.

"Na," Ray replied, half turning. "He's gone off happy. I thought about getting rid of him on a permanent basis but then the idiot made a phone call and let someone know the target was home and the package on board. He's a private detective, Emma, just a paid guy a bit cleverer than the average. It's about the investigation. That's at the centre of all this. Someone wants Rohan to go down hard and fast and they're makin' sure it happens."

Chapter 32

♥

"Why did Rohan travel to the Falkirk house?" Emma asked as Christopher sped the Girly Car through the centre of Market Harborough. He slowed down for an oncoming police car and she saw his sneer in the rear view mirror.

"Dunno, sweetheart," he said, sounding tired. "The tracker must've been in his phone and he left it in a downstairs toilet. Maybe he hoped we'd send Frederik and the boys after him."

"I thought the place was a ruin after the fire," Emma mused. "I saw a news item on the internet a few days after it happened."

Christopher snorted. "Nah! Don't believe everything you read or see on a news channel. I flooded it first, remember, then the gas canister blew up. Everything was soaked by then. Part of it was destroyed but Rohan's been renovating it ever since." Christopher screwed his head around to grin at Emma, a cheeky expression which forced her lips upwards a fraction. "I thought I'd seen him angry until the day that gas canister exploded and the house went up like a firework. I think he bought it to surprise you; he'd only owned it a few weeks."

"I'm certainly surprised," she replied, her voice droll. "I wonder whose name that's in."

Christopher laughed. "Dat's my girl," he chortled, his Irish brogue comforting in the darkness of the town.

"I think you need to ring Maureen," Emma said as Ray used the remote control to open the gates of Wingate Hall. "She needs to know what we've found out so far."

"Aye, I'll do that," Christopher replied. "She's a good woman is our Maureen."

"Does she know Jed and Stephanie are heading her way tomorrow?"

Christopher turned around again, his brow furrowed. "Today, Em. She already sent them packing first thing this morning. She said they're getting desperate."

"Oh yeah. Sorry. I've lost a whole day," Emma sighed. "They'll go back again and break in now they know the master key doesn't work."

"And Maureen will be waiting for them," Christopher said with a smirk. "All dat woman needs is a good book and her knitting and she'll wait all night for their sorry asses."

"But how will she defend herself?" Emma sat up straight. "Rohan said she was past retirement age."

"Ach, she'll be fine," Christopher reassured her. "She's fit as a flea and I wouldn't wanna cross her, not when she's brandishin' a pair of knitting needles. I told her not to drop any stitches; she's knitting me an Aran jumper with all the swirly patterns and everything." He looked thrilled at the prospect and patted his chest in anticipation.

"I'd love an Aran jumper," Ray interjected. "Do ya think she'd knit me one?"

"Not like mine!" Christopher sounded indignant. "She can knit you a different one. It's got to be a different colour and a different pattern."

Emma closed her eyes and smiled in the darkness at the thought of Ray and Christopher wearing twin jumpers. She wanted to share the joke with Rohan and his absence seemed even more intense in that moment. Her breath caught in her chest as Christopher slammed on the brakes. A deer lolloped across the driveway and out onto the lawn, towing two tiny replicas behind it. "Geez!" he exclaimed.

"What's this?" Ray bent forward and grappled by his feet. He held up some papers and peered at them in the dim light. "They shifted out from under the seat as you braked. Rohan's? Are these whatever the guy planted?"

Emma felt the heavy sensation in the pit of her stomach and unclipped her seatbelt, launching herself forward in a single movement. She snatched the papers from Ray's fingers, leaving a corner of one sheet still in his grip. "They're mine!" she snapped, her voice wavering. "I put them there in London."

"I didn't see you." Christopher's tone grew insistent.

"You went into a garage. They're mine," Emma repeated.

"Let me see," Christopher asked, holding out his hand. Emma slumped back in her seat and clutched the papers to her breast.

"No. It's nothing to do with you."

"But it might help Rohan," Christopher said, meeting her eyes with suspicion. "Just give them here."

"No!" Emma shouted. "He doesn't even know about these." Her voice broke as her brain reminded her he might never see them. "I'll show them to him when he gets home." She hiccoughed in misery and Christopher shrugged and turned back to the steering wheel, driving the car the rest of the way up to the house.

"Is there anything else we can do tonight?" Emma asked, her tone heavy. She gripped the papers in one hand and tore off her boots with the other. The image she caught of herself in the lobby mirror looked small and grey faced, tired beyond the point of exhaustion and as miserable as she'd ever been.

"I don't think so," Christopher replied. He jerked his head towards Ray. "See what Allaine and her idiot husband have been up to. Make sure he didn't make any calls. Then we need to sleep. He doesn't leave tonight so you and I will take turns watching him."

"I'll go first," Ray said, lifting his finger as though claiming his slot. He patted his pocket. "Get some shut-eye and I'll text you when it's time to change."

"Ok." Christopher pushed Emma up the stairs to the landing and stroked her hair back from her face. "A shower will make you feel better," he said, his voice soft and tender. "Then you need to sleep. You look done in."

Emma nodded and walked to her bedroom, shutting herself in the ensuite bathroom. She leaned against it, not surprised to hear Christopher moving around in her bedroom shutting curtains, the floorboards giving away his location. In the shower she pressed her face against the cold tiles and wished herself back in time, desperate to rewind the clock and refuse the walk to the cafe, leaving the Clareville Street house only to hop into the taxi home. She sniffed back tears as the water pounded the back of her neck, remembering Rohan's words. *"They want to talk, not fight."* He'd also told her he knew them. Emma ran her hands through her hair, pushing back the water and shoving away desperation and misery. He went with them willingly as though resignation and not fear was his motivation. He'd made sure she was safe and then left. Emma assumed at the time; he'd left to keep her safe but hindsight pictured something different in her mind. The men planned to take Rohan anyway, he just made sure she didn't have to go. It seemed too big a leap to be about preserving at least one parent for Nicky. The men knew Rohan but not Emma. It was possible he wanted to keep it that way.

Emma went round and round the problem with no logical solution. She stuffed the papers into the bathroom cupboard, hiding them behind a jumbo bottle of conditioner and then stumbled into the bedroom wearing a towel over her head and another wrapped around her body. The bed looked so soft and comfortable, she sat down on the squashy mattress to catch her breath and woke up five hours later.

Emma sensed someone's presence in the room as she stirred and froze. The drawn curtains threw the room into pitch darkness and

Emma stilled, waiting for her senses to wake enough to assist her. He cleared his throat and spoke to her. "Em, I know yer awake. We've somethin' to tell yer, sweetheart." Christopher sounded nervous.

Emma sat up. Her damp towel stuck to some parts of her body and neglected others. She hauled it out from beneath her in the darkness and re-wrapped it around her. "What?"

"There's someone downstairs to see you," he said.

"Rohan?" She flew across the room dragging the towel and smashed and grabbed clothing from the antique dresser unit.

"No," Christopher replied after a silence. "But you need to come."

Fear snaked dread fingers around her heart as Emma pulled the sweater over her head, ignoring the need for a bra. The sweat pants stuck to her clammy skin and she yanked them up with shaking fingers. Her bare feet slapped against the floorboards as they crept past Nicky's room and headed down the main staircase to the ground floor.

Emma blinked against the light in the kitchen and entered a room filled with people. Allaine made tea in a pot on the draining board, her posture and position the same as it had been hours ago. She didn't look like she'd even attempted to sleep. Christopher nudged Emma in the back and closed the door, leading her forward to sit in a kitchen chair. Ray leaned with his back against the work top, arms folded and his face set in severe lines. Will slumped in a kitchen chair, his face grey with tiredness. He avoided Emma's eye and as she cast around, she realised with a jolt that most of the room's occupants did too. Except one.

"Hello again, Emma," Frederik said in his quiet, commanding voice. Emma swallowed as Farrell pushed his wet nose into her palm as though offering comfort for whatever loomed.

"Mrs Andreyev." The man next to him nodded and Emma stiffened, recognising his eyes and the slight Yorkshire accent.

"You drugged me," she said in accusation. "Last time we met, you stuck a needle in my neck. I'm pregnant."

The man who she met previously wearing camouflage combat gear and wearing a balaclava smirked. "I don't think it causes that," he answered and then glanced at the look of horror on Christopher's face. "Sorry."

"How's Susan?" Emma asked, referring to Frederik's wife, who she'd known since her university days. Susan and her guide dog, Jay were the bright spots in Emma's sadness soaked life back in Aberystwyth.

"Fine, thanks." Frederik smiled, a veiled, polite motion of the lips and Emma's brain sought inaner questions she could ask to delay the inevitable.

"Just tell her," Allaine said, her voice dull. She moved behind Emma's chair and rested her hands on her friend's shoulders. Emma held her breath.

"The boys and I went to the Falkirk house," Frederik began. "We found a phone in a downstairs toilet at the back of the house which we believe to be Rohan's. The tracker inside was turned off. Only he knew the tracker was there for emergencies and only he knew the code to deactivate it."

"So what are you saying?" Emma demanded. "He didn't want you to follow him, so what?"

Frederik glanced at Christopher and the Irishman slipped into the chair next to Emma, leaning forward and laying his hand over hers. "A body's been found outside the gates of the house. Frederik and his team intercepted an emergency call on their way down the motorway."

"And?" Emma gritted her teeth and looked at Frederik.

"The description fits Rohan," he replied, looking as though he'd rather sit in a vat of maggots at that moment. "We tried to go back but within minutes the place was cordoned off by the local cops. Whoever did it made it look like a hit and run."

Emma shook her head and clutched her stomach. Her child, awake and kicking stilled under the pressure from her hand and then rebelled, administering a decent prod to her palm. "It's not Rohan," Emma asserted. "He's not dead."

Will tipped his body forward and laid his head in his arms and sighed, putting guilt and regret into the sound. Emma worked her jaw, fighting the urge to clamber over the table and hit him until he lay unconscious and then carry on hitting him for the satisfaction. "I'm so sorry." He looked broken and Emma felt Allaine's fingers tighten against her collar bone.

"Em, I know it's hard to take in," Christopher said, his voice soft and placatory. "Frederik's guys saw nobody on the property but it's possible they were seen. Those guys said if you called in the cops, they'd send Rohan back in pieces. It sounds like they made good on their promise."

Emma shook her head and shrugged off Christopher's light touch on her hands and Allaine's futile shoulder massage. She stood, eyeing everyone in the room in turn. "Nobody got what they wanted, did they?" Her voice sounded acerbic in the tense airspace with only the dull thunk of the ticking clock as background noise. She jabbed a finger at Will, seeing him raise his head from his arms. "You did this!" she snapped, rising from her seat.

"No, he didn't, Em. We believe this was someone else; perhaps the men who took him from you."

Her eyes locked on Christopher's and she injected her rejection of him into his soul through the open chasm between them. "You'll never get me or my children, so if this was down to you, I'll kill you myself."

Emma shoved her chair backwards, catching Allaine on the shins. She felt sorry but didn't know how to say the words as she rushed from the room, flinging the door wide so it clanged against the surface behind it. Her bare feet slipped and slid on the cold tiles to the stairs where she tripped and lay sprawling face down before hauling herself upright. Christopher called from behind her and Emma ran harder, mounting the staircase like a maniac and flinging herself around the corner. At Nicky's bedroom door she slid to a halt, her hand half raised towards his door handle. She wanted to feel his soft arms around her neck and sniff his hair which smelled so much like his father's, but stopped herself. Waking a small boy in the middle of the night to tell him everyone believed his hero was dead seemed the epitome of cruelty. At the sound of Christopher taking the stairs three at a time, Emma launched herself into her bedroom and closed the door, locking it behind her. Knowing the Irishman's propensity for breaking into places, she jammed a chair under the handle and hurled herself onto the four poster bed, muffling her cries with Rohan's pillow.

Chapter 33

❤

Emma sobbed until the pillow lay saturated in her arms and exhaustion sent her into a fitful doze. She dreamed of Rohan in psychedelic memories where nothing seemed real. In one dream, she kneeled over a boy much bigger than her and watched as her fists pounded his face into a pulp. Her hands seemed tiny and when she stopped to look at the blood-spattered fingers, the face morphed into Rohan's. "No!" she moaned and woke herself up, searching the bed for his smashed form only to find herself alone.

"What's the matter, Mummy?" Nicky's voice sounded nearby and Emma raised her head and shook it, not wanting to sink into another, worse dream in which she harmed her own son. "Mum?"

Emma pushed herself up and squeaked in alarm as her son's face poked over the side of the bed. His blue eyes sparkled and his white blond hair looked slick to his head, a neat parting on one side. "I glued my hair down," he said, his tone matter-of-fact. "I want it to lay flat like Daddy's."

Emma swallowed and remembered the horror of Frederik's visit and the news he travelled to convey, shaking her head to dislodge the rising grief. "Oh, Nicky," she gasped, raising a hand to her mouth. "I need to tell you something about Daddy."

To her surprise, he shook his head. "No fanks. I know what them people in the kitchen are sayin' and it's rubbish. My dad's not dead."

Emma's eyes widened. "They told you? How could they do that?" Her voice rose at the end of her sentence and Nicky glanced back towards the bedroom door and flapped his hands.

"Shush! They'll hear. Harley Man's sittin' on the floor outside the door, Mum! Don't be yellin' and stuff! If I thought you was a girly-girl, I would've gone by meself." He put his hands on his hips and she noticed he was fully dressed and wearing shoes. "Get a grip!" he said, sounding like his father. "Let's do this!"

"Do what, baby?" Emma pleaded, reducing her voice to a low hush. She glanced towards the bedroom door and stilled at the sight of the chair still leaned up against the door handle. "How did you get in?"

Nicky patted down a spike of blonde hair which stood to attention on the crown of his head. As soon as he let go it sprang back up like an antenna. "Secret passages," he said. "I watched Harley Man."

"Christopher uses the secret passages?" Emma swallowed. "Does he come in here?" Images flitted through her brain which she'd rather the Irishman hadn't witnessed and anger sparked in her chest at the indignity. "Because I'll bloody kill him!"

"Shhhh!" Nicky raised a finger to his lips again and glanced at the door. "I'm not takin' you if you won't behave!" he said, posturing like a school teacher and wagging his index finger at her. "No, he doesn't know bout that passage. Only I knows bout that passage."

Emma shook her head and swung her legs over the side of the bed. "Where are we going?" she asked, the sudden activity making her feel wired.

"Get proper clothes on," Nicky whispered, pointing at the thin sweater which revealed Emma's lack of a bra. "You need trainers on your feet, not loud shoes."

Emma nodded and scooted around the room in silence, slipping her arms from the sweater long enough to stuff a bra underneath and then snatching up a jacket. She pointed towards the bathroom but Nicky's eyes widened in horror and he shook his head, denying the opportunity for her to use the toilet. Emma bit her lip looking scandalised and grabbed trainers from her side of the bed, slipping her feet into them and doing up the laces. She shoved Anton's fire engine into her pocket like a talisman. "Ready," she hissed. "Where are we going?"

"Out of 'ere," Nicky whispered back. "But you gotta be good. No squeakin' and stuff."

Emma nodded and followed her son into the adjacent dressing room. "Oh, just wait a minute," he hissed, stepping softly into the bedroom. Emma raised an eyebrow when he returned and he put his lips against her ear. "I moved the chair and unlocked the door. Harley Man will think we slipped past him." He grinned. "I wish I could see that."

Nicky lifted one of Rohan's work shirts and she noticed a dark opening in the wall behind the shelving. Nicky pulled and the opening widened, shoving a whole wall of clothing into Emma's face. She fought shirts and ties, pressing forwards behind her son's tiny trainers before emerging in a pitch black corridor. "I'm just shuttin' it," Nicky said, squeezing back past Emma's legs. The dim light of the bedroom disappeared by stages as he did something and the wall panel slipped back into place with the faintest of clicks.

"It's dark; I can't see," Emma hissed, feeling cold stone beneath her outstretched hands.

"Shhh!" Nicky said again. A click released a beam of yellow light and Emma glanced down at the Action Man head torch in Nicky's small hand. He lifted the light to shine on her face and Emma closed her eyes and turned away as he slipped the band over his stiff hair. "You gotta be quiet," Nicky said, his face earnest. "Otherwise people hear you through the walls. Farrell always hears me."

Emma breathed out a sigh of recognition, thinking of all the times the dog had stared at a blank wall and barked or wagged his tail. Kaylee believed the dog could see angels but Nicky's revelation seemed more likely. "You're so in trouble," she mouthed and her son smirked.

He beckoned with his hand and led Emma forwards, encouraging her to rest her hand on his shoulder like a blind person. She resisted at first but as the flooring grew more and more rubbled, found she needed to trust her child's judgement. The passage veered sharp right and Emma ran into Nicky's back as he stopped in front of a blank wall. He crouched near the ground and she watched as he pushed his finger through what looked like solid concrete between the bricks. With no noise at all, the whole wall moved inwards and Nicky slipped past, stopping to wait for his mother. "Don't touch in here!" he insisted, pushing the panel of brick back into place. Emma reached out, her fingers looking for explanations where her brain failed. The wall felt like any other as it closed behind them. Nicky pulled her hand away from the stone and put it back on his shoulder. "This is Daddy's play room," he whispered and narrowed his eyes at her, reiterating his instruction not to touch.

Weapons lined every available piece of wall space in the slender room which the toy torch lit up. It wasn't much wider than her shoulders and the weaponry made walking forwards difficult. She turned sideways and passed, holding her breath at the sheer killing power housed in one place, only metres from her pillow. She shook her head, astounded at her husband's deviance. No more secrets, he'd promised. "No more secrets, my ass," Emma muttered, rewarded with a glare from her miniature guide.

After a few more tentative steps, Emma felt Nicky tug on her jacket and drag her face down to meet his. "We're going between the upstairs floor and the downstairs ceiling in a minute," he whispered, his breath caressing her cheek. "It's a squeezy space so be slow and very careful otherwise people think you're a rat," he stressed.

Emma mouthed the word *rat* and Nicky nodded as the light went on in her eyes. She shook her head in wonder and totted up the cost of two separate exterminators in the last month; neither of whom managed to stop the odd scratching sounds when the house was at its quietest. "Does Daddy know about all the tunnels?" Emma asked in a hushed voice and Nicky shook his head.

"Daddy knows about this one and Harley Man knows about some of the other ones." He grinned, a spooky, eerie look in the up light from the torch. "But I know bout all the ones."

Emma nodded and watched as Nicky moved around the armoury with caution, motioning to her to stand still. He pulled a small purse from his trouser pocket and extracted something sharp, digging it into a slot on the wall beneath a rack of terrifying looking guns. A panel slid back, revealing a space the width of an air duct at floor level and Emma's heart clenched. Nicky stood up and tugged on her jacket again, bringing her face close so he could whisper. "This one shuts itself," he said. "So I'll go first and you follow. Take your shoes off and tie the laces round your neck, otherwise you'll make scratching sounds on the ceiling."

Emma watched as he took his own advice, knotting the laces before slinging the shoes around his neck. She copied, hating the feel of the cold floor beneath her socks. With a confident thumbs up, the six-year-old boy climbed into the gap behind the weapons of mass destruction and disappeared from view.

Chapter 34

♥

The lack of disturbance made during their progress surprised Emma. A plain wooden surface helped her knees slip along, a sound which could be attributed to the tiresome spring winds outside if anyone downstairs heard. The passage went on for metres in a straight line and she followed the glow ahead of her as Nicky's head torch lit up the space before him. After five minutes of non-stop crawling, Nicky stopped, squirming so he could face Emma and blinding her with the torch. He mouthed something which Emma missed and pointed at the floor beneath him. "Down?" she mimicked and he nodded.

A panel in front of the child slipped away, revealing a rickety ladder and another dark hole which disappeared vertically downwards. Emma held her breath and ran a hand over her face, feeling grittiness from her fingers. She wondered how many hundreds of years of dust she'd slithered through and shuddered at the thought of the overhead cobwebs which might have seated themselves like a crown on her dark curls. Praying the spiders hadn't been home at the time, Emma watched the top of Nicky's head disappear and the glow from his head torch point upwards at the beamed ceiling of the passage. As her eyes slid right, she met the long pointed legs of a spider dangling a few inches from her nose and exhaled, swiping at her face and head in a flurry of activity. Nicky's head bobbed up over the lip of the hole and beckoned her, his tiny features screwed up in annoyance. "You're rubbish at this!" he hissed.

Emma spun around and tried not to kick Nicky's bobbing head as she pushed her feet into the hole. The ladder felt less fragile as her fingers clutched it and she descended, struggling in her socks against thin metal rungs. A clunk sounded as the trainers slung around her neck whacked the lip of the hole and she froze in place, waiting for the beginnings of hurried alarm. When she tried to peer downwards at her son, her eyes smarted from the brightness of the torchlight and black spots popped in front of her eyes as she struggled to fix on the rungs. "I'm never bringing you again!" Nicky whispered and continued his descent into oblivion.

When Emma's feet touched the solidity of ground level, she resisted the temptation to whoop for joy. Instead, she peeked at the soles of her white socks and screwed her face up at the blackness of them in the torchlight. "Where now?" she asked. It seemed inappropriate to refer to him as 'baby' when he'd morphed into a daring explorer before her eyes. "Can I put my shoes on?" Her voice echoed and she clapped a hand over her mouth. "Sorry," she whispered.

"No shoes yet. We go that way and then that way," Nicky mouthed, letting only a little sound carry. "Just follow me. We're in the walls underneath the downstairs hallway."

Emma rolled her eyes and padded after him. The space felt narrow and her shoulders brushed the walls either side of her, forcing her to move like a crab. What it lacked in width, it compensated in height and she was relieved to walk upright. Nicky strode ahead making no sound and she followed, eager to stay close to the light. Hearing sounds above, she stopped and strained to hear more. Allaine's voice came to her through the thick wall overhead. "I don't know if we can go back," she said, sadness in her tone. "I thought we were good people, Will. We pray, we go to church and if someone told me last week I'd discover you'd taken a bribe, I'd have called them a liar."

"It wasn't a bribe, Alli!"

Emma heard the scrape of a chair and held her breath as Nicky's lit face bobbed back towards her. She put her finger over her lips. He nodded and paused, his brow knitted.

"And that's our problem," Allaine replied, her voice sounding right above Emma's head. "You're a serving police officer and someone paid you for information relating to a member of the public. It's a bribe and until you acknowledge that, I've got nothing to say to you."

Another chair slid back on the floor. "He asked for a friend's address, Alli, a friend! Not just a member of the public. I didn't have to do anything dishonest to get it and it's nothing to do with my role as a police officer."

"It's everything to do with your job, Will. A man's dead because of what you did! I don't understand why you can't see it. Everything I believed about you is ruined." Allaine choked back a sob. "You're a liar, Will, a greedy liar. You hated how Emma bought your car for cash and came into money after having nothing. It was all fine while you could feel sorry for her and play act as Nicky's father figure, but now she's settled and happy with money in the bank; you're jealous. It's warped you, Will. I feel shocked at what you've done."

Emma held her breath and stared down at the circle of light Nicky's head torch shone on the stone wall in front of them. She felt his little hand slither into hers and squeezed.

The slam of the kitchen door overhead made them both jump and duck as dust trickled through the beams. Emma bit her lip and closed her eyes, not wanting to inhale and end up sneezing. She'd assumed Will and Allaine were alone by the conversation, but the steady voice of Ray spoke into the silence. "Christopher said you can leave. If you report anything you've heard or seen, your commanding officer will get a very interesting summary of your activities with regards to taking a bribe from a known criminal and supplying confidential information in your role as a police officer."

Emma heard Will scoff and wanted to burst through the floorboards and hurt him. "You've got no evidence at all!" he sneered. "He wouldn't believe you."

Footsteps trod across the floor and Emma saw dust puff through a vent in the wall next to her face. Ray's voice sounded muffled and growly as it carried down. "You're messing with the wrong people, mate. You think they can't hack into the police system and leave a trace of you in places you shouldn't be looking? That'll be child's play for them. They could show evidence of you hacking into the Chief Constable's personal laptop if they wanted; these guys are good. I suggest you heed my warning, mate. You probably thought you were so clever accepting the money in a brown envelope in the middle of a public car park but it turned out to be one of your less genius moves." Silence and then Ray's voice came again, laughter in the tone. "Next time you pass the back of the Baptist Church, look up. Christopher downloaded the footage from that camera this morning. He's got you on tape as you take your payoff and by the time he's finished, he'll show you up as more than just a little bent. You'll be so covered in conspiracy theories and blackmail, you'll be able to use that double sided tongue of yours to lick yer own boots."

The kitchen door opened overhead and closed. Nicky blinded Emma with the torch again as he looked up at her. "I knowed he was jealous," he whispered. "I'm glad Harley Man beat him up."

"You heard that?" Emma exhaled in horror, trying not to squeak. "But you were with Allaine."

The torch light bobbed left and right. "Nobody can't stop you going to the toilet when you say you need a poo," he said with conviction. "Mrs Clark said no to Mo once and he pooped his trousers. That's what people's scared of; trouser poops." He set off back down the passage, dragging Emma along by the hand. She lagged, remembering another time when needing the bathroom proved fortuitous. Whilst being held hostage in the Falkirk mansion, Emma pleaded desperation and Christopher was sent with her. He'd snagged a screw driver to defend them with and broke the toilet cistern, flooding the upper levels and causing mayhem with the water and electrical wires. While it was the exploding gas canister which wrecked the house, Christopher's idea had proved a good one. Rohan knew the story and hope burgeoned in Emma's heart. There had to be a reason he'd left his phone in the toilet.

Tears pricked in her eyes as she contemplated the body outside the gates of the mansion. She focussed on her footing, working hard not to conjure images of Rohan's bashed and bleeding body lying in a road. Nicky stopped and Emma gasped, running into the back of him again. "Dad's not dead," he said, as though reading her mind. Emma closed her eyes and prayed he wasn't. "He can't be," Nicky whispered. "I can still feel him here." He let go of her hand and touched his chest. "I always knowed he was here and he still is. He's not dead."

Emma sighed as the child snatched up her fingers and led on, twisting this way and that in the bowels of the house. Nicky reached the age of six without ever meeting his father and Emma felt guilty about all the times she'd dodged his questions, fulfilling the role of mum and dad to the best of her ability. Yet Nicky knew without being told that Rohan had fathered him, picking up the slack on some ethereal cord which connected them as though they'd known each other a lifetime. He'd known and so had Rohan.

"Butler's pantry," Nicky hissed, pointing at a wooden panel to the right as he swung round a corner. "Put your trainers on, we might have to run. Harley Man uses this all the time because it forks off towards the folly." He waited as Emma shoved her feet into her shoes and laced them. Nicky pushed his onto his feet and tightened them in half the time. "Ready?" he asked and she nodded.

He set off at a cracking pace, moving through a tunnel which bowed down into the earth. The small light from his head torch dimmed as the battery complained and Emma inhaled loudly as it winked out altogether. "Sokay, Mummy," Nicky said, reaching backwards for her hand. "I've done it heaps of times." He led her on with confidence and Emma tried to relax, stopping herself from looking over her shoulder and losing her footing.

"Where are we?" she asked as Nicky pushed against a loose stone and what appeared to be a dead end rolled outwards into sunlight.

"The old chapel," her son replied. "Isn't it pretty?"

Emma looked around her at the tenth century church which Lord Ayers had locked before she was born because of the expense of the work required to mend the ailing roof. Pigeons chuffed and cooed above in rafters covered in bird muck and dust and the stained glass windows looked out of place, like pearls in a pig sty. "I've only seen it from outside," she said. "It's beautiful."

"I come here lots," Nicky said, climbing up into the pulpit. "It's my thinking space."

Emma stared at him aghast. "When? I always know where you are and you're not here."

"Yeah, I am," he said. "There's a passage from my room and from Lady Celia's old room. I like the one from the sitting room best though. It was mean of Daddy to close it up. It takes me longer to go upstairs and crawl through the house."

"I don't understand." Emma scratched her head and wrinkled her nose at the dust which fell down and the sneeze she'd held onto for half an hour erupted like a steam vent.

"I don't really watch TV, Mum," Nicky said, emerging from the pulpit with a rucksack. "I pretend I'm watching it and then when you come looking for me, I come downstairs saying I needed the toilet and you don't question it."

"But how do you get here and back so fast?" Emma asked. Nicky grinned and pulled his skateboard from the steps up to the pulpit. Emma rolled her eyes. "You're not in the basement making that noise at all, are you? The rumbling I can hear is underground, in the tunnels."

Nicky giggled. "Yep." He froze at the sound of a vehicle tooting in the distance and hefted the rucksack onto his slender shoulders. "That's our ride. Come on." He fitted a massive brown key into the door and slid it open, locking it up as Emma walked out into the early morning sunshine.

"Where did you get that?" she demanded and Nicky giggled.

"Freda," he said, taking her hand. "Come on, Mummy, be quick."

Emma stumbled after her son as he headed for the southern perimeter of the property and watched the back of his dust covered hair as it lifted as a single unit in the breeze. "What about the dust?" she called, puffing after him. "How do you get it off?"

"Play clothes," Nicky shot back over his shoulders. "And a hat. I keep them in the passage from my wardrobe."

Emma shook her head and followed her son through the woods, wondering at how devious he'd become. He enjoyed a whole other life she knew nothing about. Nicky continued ahead as Emma slowed to a stop and bent in half puffing, hands on her knees to help her breathe. When the child ran back for her, his Action Man camouflage rucksack bouncing in time to his steps, he found her in a paroxysm of parental agony. "I'm a rubbish mother," she groaned. "Utterly useless."

"Na, you're not." He patted her on the back. "I'm my father's son."

Chapter 35

♥

Nicky slowed to a fast walk through the thicker part of the woods, glancing over his shoulder at regular intervals. Emma sloped along next to him, her feet wooden and uncooperative against half buried tree roots and jagged rocks. "I don't think I know you at all," she sighed. "Where's my cute six-year-old son gone?"

"I'm still here." He elbowed her in the hip. "But it's my job to take care of you. Always. Uncle Anton told me that over and over again. Once, when he drove me to McDonald's for a burger when you got that chest infection and couldn't come out in the cold, he told me all about Wingate Hall and the secret passages."

"Did he?" Emma closed her eyes against the memory of Anton's laughing eyes and gentle smile. A tree root snagged her foot and she opened them in a hurry, stabilising herself against a tree. "You never said."

Nicky shrugged. "No need, was there? But when you took me there the first time, I thought he'd be waiting for me and he wasn't. It made me sad to think he died without showing me."

Emma's brow knitted and she forced the words out, talk of Anton making her chest hurt. "When you're sneaking around in the passages, you don't go into the one behind our room, do you?" His blank look forced her to expand on her fear. "When mummies and daddies are in bed, they sometimes have special cuddles."

"I don't go in Daddy's playroom." Nicky interrupted her. "He asked me not to. He said he'd be cross and that he'd know because he's got things in there which would tell him. Once I thought I'd have a little peek and when I climbed through the passage he was waiting for me."

"What did he do?" Emma asked. She stopped again, her breath coming in heaves.

"He said he'd tell you and you'd have a discussion about whether I could go in them at all."

Emma snorted. "A discussion! I'd board the damn things up, so you'd need a bulldozer to get back in!"

Nicky nodded for emphasis. "Yeah, Daddy mentioned that."

Emma stopped at the sight of something red being flapped up ahead and a voice came to her on the breeze. "Coo-ee!"

Nicky picked up the pace and headed towards the flapping object. Emma burst out of the trees behind him and gaped in surprise at Freda, flapping a large pair of red knickers through a hole in the wire fence. "Hello, Lady Freda," Nicky called and stopped short of the boundary, dropping into a majestic bow.

"Hulloooo, Lord Nikolai," she responded in a put on posh voice and bent her knees into an impressive curtsey. The fart which Emma heard, wafted away on the fresh breeze and she observed as the old lady passed her son a key and withdrew the underwear from the fence, shoving the knickers into her coat pocket. Nicky unlocked the padlock on the wide perimeter gates and passed through, beckoning to Emma to follow. Emma swallowed her bewilderment, opting to let the pint-sized commander push her around some more, following Nicky out and waiting while the padlock was reattached. "High five, LN," Freda intoned, slapping Nicky's outstretched palm.

"Mission accomplished, LF," he replied with a smirk. "Did you bring the getaway car?"

"I certainly did," she replied and stood back to wave her arms at the rust heap stationed behind her.

"Oh." Nicky looked disappointed at the dilapidated Datsun Cherry leaned on the grass verge at the side of the lane. As he stared, the rear bumper headed south and touched the ground on one side.

"Not again!" Freda complained and popped the boot. She fiddled around inside and threaded knitting wool around the bumper, tying it back up.

"Never mind." Nicky tried to sound upbeat and Emma figured he'd expected a getaway car that at least looked driveable. No. That wasn't his objection. "I would've liked a go on your scooter but I don't think Mummy could run behind. She looks a bit knackered."

"I think so too, darling." Freda winked at Emma and to her shame, the single act of solidarity unpicked her and left her feeling inside out.

"They said Rohan's dead," Emma managed, running a hand over her face and heaving in a huge breath.

"I know, I know," Freda replied. She hurried over and wrapped Emma in a burly embrace, bustling her over to the car. "But we know your handsome Russian better than that, don't we, dear? Let's get back to mine and have a cup of tea."

"Farrell!" Nicky's shout made Emma jump back in alarm. The black dog hurtled out of the woods and dashed across the grass barking. "I'm not leaving him."

Emma opened her mouth to speak, the effort wasted as the boy and old lady reopened the padlock and let the spaniel out. He bounded into the car as though it was a normal activity.

"In we get," Freda said, striding over to the vehicle. She opened the driver's door and sat down, disappearing into the worn seat so only the top of her head showed over the steering wheel. "Everyone else in the back," she called as the car belched out a cloud of acrid black smoke. "You'll need to bob down as we go through Great Arden village, otherwise you'll draw attention to us."

"Of course we will," Emma sighed, searching around for seat belts. Their absence set the car's age at some time prior to the legislation and the almighty backfire suggested pre-war. Emma sank into the seat and felt the springs digging into her bottom with gusto, every time the vehicle dived over a bump in the lane. Nicky pushed Farrell into the foot well and then cuddled up to his mother, shoving a dirty thumb into his mouth and relinquishing responsibility back to its proper quarter.

Chapter 36

♥

"We're here!" Freda's singsong voice carried into the back seat as she squinted at her passengers. Emma lifted a tired head and sighed, wiping dribble from the side of her mouth. The horrendous journey along rural lanes pushed the final limits of her daring. Sleeping her way into death along with her son and favourite dog seemed the better option.

"Where's here?" Emma asked, sitting up despite the crick in her neck. Nicky stirred next to her, looking groggy as he hauled himself upright. The dog bounded onto the back seat and stuck his wet, sticky nose in Nicky's ear and licked.

"At my house," Freda said, exiting the vehicle after several failed attempts at pushing herself upright. Emma looked around in confusion at the village pub and the neat village green which stretched out a few hundred metres away. "Oh, not my apartment," she said in dismissal. "My country house. My John bought it when we got married and we always intended to come back here at the end of our ministry. After John died I let the tenant stay a little longer, but it's still mine."

"What're we doing here?" Emma asked, wondering if that were the better question.

"Hiding," Freda said and slammed the car door. The wing mirror bowed in response, pointing its reflective self at the grass.

"Lord Nikolai rang me early this morning and said you needed help. We had our escape plan ready, so we put it into action."

"Lord Nikolai and I have things to discuss," Emma bit back, clambering from the vehicle. The dog headed into an open gateway and cocked his leg on a giant lupin. Emma cringed. Freda moved around the vehicle locking each door in turn, in the absence of such modernisation as central locking. Emma shook her head and wondered whether to mention she'd left the driver's window wide open.

"Come on, cup of tea time," Freda intoned and followed the dog. She waited for Emma and Nicky to catch up and then slammed a huge wooden gate closed on the street, latching it behind her. She beetled up a path which took a meandering route around a pretty cottage garden and covered twice as much ground as necessary before disgorging them on a wide front porch. "Welcome to my house," Freda said, grinning with such largesse, it drew a smile even from Emma.

The furniture looked aged but comfortable and Emma kicked her trainers off inside the front door. Nicky followed suit and they both looked at their filthy socks and removed them too. Emma headed for a squashy armchair and paused, eyeing the unfortunate stain in the seat. Freda squeaked at her from the kitchen. "Don't sit there, dear. Mr Lambert died there and I haven't had time to wash the seat covers."

Emma leapt back as though shot, covering her hand with her mouth. "When did that happen?" she asked, listening to Freda's clanking noises in the kitchen.

"A year ago last Christmas," Freda replied. "He had a heart attack and I think a little bit of wee came out."

Nicky dissolved into giggles and collapsed onto the sofa. Emma glared at him and wondered who'd died on that. He shot up with sudden urgency, his eyes wide with recollection. "School," he said. "I need you to tell them I won't be in today."

Emma gulped, imagining the conversation in which she told the school secretary her husband was missing, presumed dead. She dumped herself onto the sofa next to Nicky and put her head in her hands. "What do I say?" she asked.

"I'll do it." Freda bustled over with a tray of bone china cups on saucers and a tea pot balanced on the edge. She laid it on an ancient coffee table and stepped back. "But as it's only seven-thirty in the morning, I'll wait awhile."

"No!" Nicky bounced up again. "Do it now. There's a line for bent trees and you won't have to talk to anyone."

"What?" Freda pulled her spectacles down her nose and peered over them at the child. "Bent trees?"

"Oh, absentees," Emma said, looking up at her son. "That's a good idea." She looked across at Freda. "Can you do it and say he's your grandson? They'll recognise my voice and it's the first place the others will look."

"Righto," Freda said and pulled out her flashy iPhone. "I should have the number on here somewhere; I'm sure I've rung you at work before."

"I'll do it," Nicky groaned. He held out his hand and fiddled around on the screen, handing it back as a green telephone made connecting sounds. Freda waited through the options and pressed the three instead of the one.

"Oops, sorry," she said to the automated machine in the secretary's office. "I wanted someone else but you'll do. Nikolai Andreyev won't be in school today." Her eyes widened and she drew a blank, having failed to prepare an excuse.

"Me dad's not dead," Nicky said, puckering his lips in protest. "Don't tell 'em that."

"He, er, he er...puked up on the dog," Freda concluded and hung up. Emma lay her head back against the fusty sofa as Nicky helped Freda call back. "It's Freda Ayers," she said, "reporting that Nikolai won't be in school today because I forgot to say who I was."

"Bloody hell!" Emma closed her eyes.

Nicky sniggered and Emma opened one eye. "You're funny," Nicky chortled. "Mum stinks. Can she have a bath?"

Emma looked down at her filthy pants and dusty sweater. "Sorry," she said and stood up, hearing a spring doink in the sofa as she removed her weight.

"What a wonderful idea," Freda remarked, bristling towards the back of the house. "Did you bring spare clothes for her?"

"Yep." Nicky pulled the rucksack from his skinny shoulders and disgorged a pair of tiny shorts and a tee shirt. Long knee-length socks followed and a pair of black sports shoes.

"Oh, I love the Beatnik look," Freda commented as Emma stared in dismay at her son's odd ensemble.

"Well," he shrugged, "if I bringed anyfink else, you'd have missed it."

Emma looked at the summer clothes piled up on the floor, already a season too small for him. She shook her head and focussed on a yellow nicotine stain on the ceiling.

"Here's some clothes for you." Nicky looked thrilled with his choice as he yanked out a pair of lycra exercise leggings which Emma misplaced weeks ago. She peered at them in surprise.

"There they are," she said, smiling through the realisation they would probably give her unborn baby elastic marks around the forehead. A disgustingly grey pair of ancient knickers followed the lycra and then to Emma's horror, out pinged a sexy bra she'd bought as a surprise for Rohan. Bright red with the itchiest lace she'd ever endured, it twanged from the rucksack and hit Nicky straight in the left eye. But for the tears it induced, Emma would have been grateful for his temporary blindness.

Emma left Freda dealing with her son and feeding him brown liquid from a tumbler which bore a horrible resemblance to Bourbon. Deciding a good wash and dressing like a hooker would somehow make her feel better, Emma stumbled down to the bathroom at the back of the house and watched grey water gush into a bath stained with debatable yellow water marks.

"I'm all better now," Nicky sniffed, wandering into the bathroom and wiping his face on Emma's shoulder as she bent over the side of the tub. She kissed his upturned face, noting he smelled like a brewery and mentally blaming Freda for any future bouts of alcoholism. "Your bra just whacked me in the eye." He pulled his lower lid down and flashed her a red eye which a zombie might be proud of. "Freda put stuff in it," he said, blinking his eyes and creating a furious strobe effect for himself. "Now my lashes is sticking together."

"Yep, Bourbon will do that to a dude," Emma sighed, running her hand across the top of his head. "What did you glue your hair down with?"

Nicky smiled up at her, his baby teeth glinting in the light through the bathroom window. The tap spluttered, stalled and then dumped various shades of brown water into the bath. Emma wrinkled her nose and reached for a tub of bath salts, sprinkling in enough to make the water turn green instead. "It looks like a swamp," Nicky said and wiped his nose on the back of his hand. "I did it with some stuff of Ray's," he said. "I found it in the stables."

Emma's eyes widened and she said nothing, not wanting to rain a skinhead cut on the little boy's parade. "You were very brave and clever this morning," she whispered. "But why did we need to run away?"

Nicky examined her as though she resembled a specimen in a petri dish. He huffed and puffed like an old maid; a lot like Freda, Emma realised. "Because they was talkin' like Daddy's already dead. But he isn't. I know he isn't."

"But they weren't going to hurt us," Emma said. "They're our friends, Christopher and Ray and Allaine."

"Will isn't!" Nicky spat, saving her the trouble of an explanation. "He's a double agent. I don't like him anymore."

"Oh, Nicky." Emma sought to soothe him, caressing his cheek and avoiding the shiny hair. "Grown up stuff is hard sometimes."

"Those two soldier men left in the night. They said he was dead. Harley Man said he didn't believe it. I love Harley Man."

"But why Freda and why here?" Emma asked, leaning forwards and cutting off the water. The tap ceased spurting and settled into a warm dribble.

Nicky cocked his head to one side and attempted a wink which contorted his whole face and involved most of the muscles in his body. "Remember when you and Daddy had a big argument a few weeks ago and he ran away?"

"He didn't run away," Emma said, feeling the colour flush up her neckline and into her hair. "He lived somewhere else for a while so we could sort things out."

"So he could get you jewellery," Nicky said, referring to the wedding band on her ring finger engraved with a Russian promise.

"No, not exactly," Emma said, struggling to right his topsy turvy world. "We needed time apart to get our heads straight. What's this about?"

"Where did he go?" Nicky demanded.

Emma paled, the high colour disappearing as fast as it arrived, pushed back into her blood vessels in reverse order. "Er..." Emma swallowed, praying her son knew nothing of his abusive, psychotic grandmother. "An apartment on Northampton Road."

"No, he didn't," Nicky chirped. "He went to Freda. She told me. They watched black and white movies and he kissed the old ladies back to life."

"Ohhhh." The child's skewed logic struck home and the jigsaw fell into place. "So, you think if he went to Freda before, he'll go to her for help again?"

"Yeah," Nicky replied, rubbing his cheek against her shoulder. "Can I have your bath after you if it doesn't stink too bad?"

Chapter 37

♥

"Christopher will find us here eventually," Emma sighed, sipping tea from the china cup. The slinky red bra itched up a storm on her right breast, which was the only one still able to fit in it properly. Pregnancy seemed to have taken the left one by storm, much to her husband's delight.

"I doubt it; he knows nothing about my John. Is that Rohan's sweater?" Freda asked, watching as Emma clutched at the fabric and lifted the hem to her nose.

"Yeah. I'm not sure why Nicky packed this."

"Aren't you?" Freda's eyes channelled wisdom as she nibbled on a ginger nut biscuit.

Emma allowed the small smile and pulled Freda's attention elsewhere. "Why are you driving a car? I thought they refused to renew your licence. That's why you bought the scooter."

Freda waved her free hand and made a noise of dismissal. "Pfshaw! What will they do to me, Emma? Lock me up? I doubt it. I'm ninety. Nobody wants my death on their watch. I'm at the stage where I can pretty much do as I wish."

Emma sighed. "What happens now?"

"We wait," Freda said. "The police haven't knocked on your door looking for the widow of a dead man so perhaps they won't. I find it hard to believe your husband would stand still while someone drove a car at him. It's not the first time this has happened, is it?"

Emma's brows knitted in confusion. "What do you mean? Rohan's never been run over. Blown up, stabbed and shot at, but not run over."

"But a man died outside the gates of your house a few weeks ago, didn't he? It seems someone has an interesting way of getting rid of people."

"The Chinaman," Emma breathed. "You're right. We assumed Mikhail killed him to stop the Triads warning Rohan about him, but what if it's someone else?" Her enthusiasm dried up. "They might get rid of my husband the same way." Her chest tightened and Freda's head shake in her peripheral vision made her look up.

"That crazy Russian of yours is on my prayer list every morning and the Good Lord hasn't told me to take him off yet." She stood and hovered for a moment, waiting for the bones in her spine to straighten as much as they were going to. "There's cash in the kitchen and a village shop across the road. I've left a spare key with the money. If nosey Laurel serves you, say you're my guests. I often spend the weekend here so it's nothing unusual. I'll take the car back to Mabel Lafferty before she realises it's missing. If the horny Irishman comes looking for me, I'll deny, deny, deny." Freda smiled and gripped Emma's shoulder in her arthritic hand. "We'll be back at work next week and all this will be over."

Emma's smile looked more wistful than positive and she forced a nod. Freda started the car with an enormous backfire which sent birds skittering out of the nearby trees and into the cloudy sky. The sun winked on and then ran behind a cloud, not wanting to observe the elderly woman's suicide ride. Nicky's footsteps padded down the stairs, thud, thud, thud. He appeared in the lounge rubbing his eyes, his shorts pulled tight around his crotch. "Can I 'ave a squeeze?" he asked, sounding more little boy than superhero. Emma held her arms out and he stumbled across to the sofa, planting his face in her lap. "Oh, fank you," he sighed.

The bath hadn't quite removed the glue and Nicky's hair stuck up in the centre like a mohawk. Emma touched one of the prongs and winced at the stickiness. "What would you like for breakfast?" she said, her tone soothing.

"Chips," Nicky replied, his voice muffled in Emma's lycra pants. She shifted in her seat to avoid the seam which was intent on shoving itself into her delicate places and the boy stood up. "Yeah, chips, please."

"You'll be lucky," Emma mused. "There's a village shop I think and that's all."

"And a school," Nicky asserted. "Mr Dalton bringed us 'ere to thrash them at tag rugby."

Emma cringed. "Oh. A school means a truant officer and you're meant to be sick. I think the cops pick up truants too."

"Sick boys can't 'ave chips, can they?" Nicky looked disappointed.

"Not really."

"I'll stay here, then," Nicky said, flopping onto the sofa and sinking in up to his hips. "Let Farrell in and he'll protect me against the baddies."

Emma shook her head. "I'm not sure, baby. You're six." She looked away at the incongruity of her statement.

Nicky raised his eyebrows. "I was raised in drug town, Mummy and I've been running around the inside of our house for months without burning it down or ruinin' anyfink. I can probably sit here for five minutes while you get me chips."

Emma sighed and pulled on the spare shoes which tumbled from Nicky's cavernous rucksack. "I'm sure there won't be hot chips anywhere in this smudge on the map," she grumbled. Hefting the rucksack back upright, Emma saw a glint of metal in the bottom. She reached her hand in and pulled out Rohan's phone. "Nicky!" She spun round, giving herself whip-lash. "Where did you get this?"

He paled on the sofa and waved his arm at the French doors. "Please can you let the dog in?"

"You'll need more than the dog's protection!" Emma raised her voice. "How did you get this?"

Her son looked shifty and hopped up to open the door. Farrell slunk in and flopped to the carpet next to Nicky's legs. The child pursed his lips and used his wiles to invoke sympathy. "It's Daddy's. They don't get to keep what's Daddy's. He's not dead, Mummy, I promise. Harley Man wanted to do stuff to the phone and Daddy will need it when he gets home."

The child's earnest belief in his father turned her chest inside out so that her heart felt naked and unguarded. She nodded, not knowing what to say, figuring Christopher wanted to hack into it to find evidence of where Rohan might have gone. Gulping back misery, Emma zeroed in on Nicky's use of the nickname, Harley Man. "You don't need to call him that anymore," she said, fondling the phone in her fingers. "You know he's Christopher Dolan, now?"

Nicky shrugged, his blue-eyed gaze never leaving the phone. "I knowed him my whole life as Harley Man. I don't want him to be Christopher because Christopher doesn't look out for me like Harley Man used to." The child looked sad, his gaze straying to the stained 1960s carpet. "I liked him more when he was a figtree of my magination."

"You've got me," Emma whispered. "You've always had me."

"Yes, for the lovin' stuff but Daddy does the takin' care. Harley Man used to do the takin' care but I don't want 'im to now. I want Daddy." Nicky's eyes narrowed. "I think Harley Man loves you a little bit." He pursed his lips and frowned.

"Chips, then?" Emma stuffed her feet into the shoes, in and out through a giant hole in the front. She sighed, remembering why she threw them out in the first place. "I hope I don't see anyone I know," she muttered. "I look like a poor, fat hooker."

"Na, you look bootiful," Nicky replied with a pout. "Chips."

"Chips," Emma sighed. She laid the phone black screen down on the table, figuring there wasn't much Nicky could do with a dead cell phone. "Lock the door after me," she warned. "And don't come out for anything."

"Ok."

The doors clicked shut and Emma heard the key turn in the lock with a grinding sound. Nicky swished the curtains across the glass like the wily child he'd turned out to be and Emma trudged along the winding path towards the gate, with Freda's cash loan in her hand.

Chapter 38

♥

Great Arden didn't seem all that great in stature although it might have been a great place to live. The main buildings gathered around the wide village green like mothers around someone else's ugly baby; sympathetic but reluctant to get involved. A road ran between houses and grass, the greenery encroaching on the concrete through cracks and pockets of damp mud. Freda's little oasis of sanity from the rat race snuggled in a small side street and Emma grinned at the wide tyre marks in the verge showing frequent visits. Freda often complained about the residents of the old peoples' apartments and probably stole a car and backfired her way up to the cottage a few times a week. Emma pondered what it must feel like to live such a vital and energetic life, only to have a doctor tell her she couldn't live alone where she wanted to, or get there how she pleased.

Emma crossed the road and headed for the village green, spotting a shop sign swaying outside a building diagonally opposite. "I know they won't have chips," she muttered to herself, hiding behind a century old oak tree to yank her pants out of her bum. Her toes peeked out of the left shoe and Rohan's heavy sweatshirt barely masked the fact that one boob had forced its way out of the lacy bra before she'd even closed the gate. A bell jangled over the front door as Emma entered, dragging her back at least sixty years in history and the interior channelled 1950s like a rite of passage. A small mouse-like woman peered from behind a counter covered in newspapers and tugged bifocal glasses down her nose.

"Can I help you?" she asked, staring at Emma as though she were a new species.

"I'm just staying here for a few days," Emma replied. "I wondered where to buy things."

The woman jerked her head back as though poked in the eye. "We probably don't have the kind of things you want," she said, sounding affronted. "You need to drive into Harborough for that!"

Emma's eyes widened, wondering what 'that' could be and contemplated searching the town for some if she ever went back. She cast her eye over the upside down newspaper headline, seeing the word, 'Missing' in capital letters and pointed at it. "Can't I buy a paper?" she asked.

"I suppose so!" the woman grumbled and pressed buttons on an old-fashioned cash register. The drawer shot out as she prodded the final key and hit herself in the left breast. "Oof," she said, "that'll be one pound fifty, thanks. And we don't want your sort round here!"

Emma stared at the price label being stuck to the other newspapers with a device in the woman's hand, seeing the ninety pence label on their covers. She considered challenging her and then thought better of it. A packet of salt and vinegar crisps lurked in front of the counter amidst an array of other flavours and Emma snagged a packet, hoping her precocious son would accept them in lieu of hot chips.

"Them's two quid," the woman snapped and held out her hand. Emma held her gaze, recognising something familiar in the set of the jaw and shape of the shoulders. Without meaning to, she curled her top lip backwards in a snarl of distaste and the woman's eyes widened. "Let's call it two fifty for cash," she said, wiggling her fingers. Emma placed the five pound note into the hand and accepted the change, counting it and forcing the woman to wait.

"Thanks," she said, her voice hostile and walked towards the back of the shop. The newspaper, crisps and cash took some sorting before she could spare a hand to open the shop door. She wasn't yet ready when it opened with a click, heading towards her face at speed. Emma jumped back and dropped the crisps, bending to retrieve them as the newcomer entered.

"Oh. It's you!"

Emma rose with a sinking feeling in her gut as she recognised the pointy red shoes with the gold rims parked neatly before her. She raised her head and met the gaze of Clarissa Jameson-Arden, chairwoman of the board of governors for Nicky's school and Emma's ultimate employer. "Hello," Emma said with forced politeness and put her hand on the door handle.

"What are you doing here?" the woman snapped, standing her ground and blocking the swing of the door.

"Just visiting a friend," Emma responded, keeping her tone light.

"What friend?" Clarissa snapped, her eyes widening in horror. "You can't have any friends here."

"Oh, sorry. I didn't realise it was against the rules," Emma returned and pulled on the door handle. A flash of anger consumed her and she turned, glaring into the older woman's face. "And leave my son alone. If you attempt to take him anywhere again, I'll go to the police."

Clarissa gaped. "I thought he'd look great in our publicity for the celebration."

Emma shook her head and leaned closer, letting go of the door handle. "We both know that isn't true. I'm sorry your brother died in the church and we both know it was because he tried to make the plaque disappear. I haven't made my research into the Jameson family public, although it's out there for anyone else to find and if you come near me or Nicky again, I'll have a chat to the same radio journalist who seemed very interested in why everyone believed the school was five years younger than it is." Emma's eyes narrowed in threat. "So don't push me."

Clarissa shifted out of the way with great reluctance and allowed Emma to pass. The sinking feeling followed her out of the door and onto the pavement outside. Without checking, it stood to reason Clarissa would attempt to stalk Emma home, if only to chastise the person giving her house room. She moved away from the shop front and leaned against the brick wall to the side.

"You all right there, lass?" a voice asked and Emma jumped and peered towards it. An elderly man perched on a bench to her right, swaddled in blankets and wearing a flat cap and tartan scarf.

"Yes thanks," she lied.

"Well, yer face is sayin' reet different," he wheezed, chuckling to himself. "Mebbe thee should let it know."

Emma laughed and nodded. "I should, shouldn't I?"

"Is it that Jameson woman?" he enquired, a knowing look in his rheumy blue eyes.

"Yeah." Emma nodded and glanced back towards the door. "It's clearly her town and she doesn't want me in it."

"Snot eer town!" the old man said with indignation in his crinkly face. "Bloody upstart!"

"I meant Harborough," Emma sighed. "Probably Leicestershire or perhaps not restricted to or exclusive of the Midlands."

The old man cackled and slapped his knee through the blankets. "I like you," he said. "What yer doin' here lass?"

"Looking for a bit of peace," Emma said with honesty. "I'm staying over there." She pointed towards Freda's house and the old man nodded.

"I hear ya, lass," he said. "Sit ye here with me." He patted the bench with mittened hands and Emma obeyed after a nervous glance over at Freda's gate.

"My son wanted hot chips for breakfast," she confided, jiggling the crisp packet. "I think these'll have to do."

"He can 'ave 'ot chips," the old man replied. "Sally's bakery on yonder corner does 'ot chips for the younguns to take on't bus in the mornin's."

"Really?" Emma sounded relieved and planted her feet ready to stand. The old man patted her leg.

"Sit 'ere a minute," he said and Emma heard the authority in his tone.

As she made the decision to obey him, the shop door jangled again and Clarissa stomped out, her expensive coat swishing against slender calves. She marched over to the red pillar box and shoved an envelope into the slot. "Where are you staying?" she demanded, narrowing her eyes and addressing Emma with her hands on her hips.

Emma wavered between being honest and telling her to mind her own business, but the elderly man cut in for her. "She's stayin' with me, yer nosy old witch," he said, jabbing pointed mitten fingers in Clarissa's direction. "So get back in yer hoity toity castle and carry on workin' on yer spells. I'm sure if you work 'ard enough you'll find one to turn that frog face into summat decent."

Clarissa's mouth opened and closed but nothing made it from her brain to her lips. She turned around and whirled away towards a white two-storied house surrounded by rose bushes and an immaculate picket fence. Emma turned to the man, amusement on her face. "Thank you," she said with a giggle. Her expression grew serious. "But what will she do to you?"

The old man cackled. "Nothin' lass. She wouldn't dare."

"If you're sure," she said, sounding doubtful. "But she's the chairwoman of the board at the school I work at. She lives to make trouble for people."

"Nay, lass!" The old man's laugh was punctuated by a throaty cough. "I changed that bairn's nappy when she was a snot nosed toddler. Er's just waitin' fer me to die because she thinks she's collectin'." He tapped the side of his nose with his finger. "But she ain't. The whole lot's goin' to the hospice people so she can get stuffed."

"Why would she think she's getting your money?" Emma asked, confusion in her eyes.

The old man laughed and held out a mittened hand. "Bob Arden," he said, bowing his head on a scrawny, frail neck. "She's my daughter-in-law." He jerked his head backwards towards the shop. "And 'er in there's another of 'em. They're like an infection in this county, them Jamesons."

"Ohhhh." Emma winced. "Commiserations?" she said, her face unsure. The old man chortled and shook his head.

"Our Freda always has interestin' visitors," he grinned. "Glad ter meet yer lass. And good luck."

Emma nodded and stared at the folded newspaper in her hand. The 'missing' headline slithered open to reveal a cute picture of a dog and she sighed. Nothing to do with Rohan.

"You want that?" Bob asked, jerking his head towards the newspaper and Emma shook her head and handed it over.

Bob Arden pointed out the bakery at the end of the street facing the village green and gave Emma a beatific smile filled with his own teeth. "John Ayers was my best friend in school," he said, a wistful smile on his face. "T'was bad what happened to him, getting his face all shot up like that, but our Freda still loved 'im. She's a great lass that one. If I could move by meself, I'd 'ave a pop at 'er but I think she'd probably send me early to me grave." He gave a raucous laugh and Emma giggled.

"I'll tell her she has an admirer," she promised and he chuckled.

"Ah, she do know already, lass," he said.

Emma planted a kiss on his cold cheek and squeezed the frail fingers beneath the mittens. She waved at the end of the street and hurried towards the tantalising scent of hot food. Inside Sally's Bakery the cabinets held a feast for eyes and stomach and Emma emerged with pies, sausage rolls and a paper bag filled with steaming hot chips. Bob Arden was gone from the bench and Emma jogged past, hearing the flop of her loose sole on the ground.

She struggled through the garden gate and knocked on the French door with her elbow. "It's Mummy, Nicky. I've got chips!"

The dog barked as the boy whipped back the curtains with glee in his face. "You found some!" he exclaimed, standing on tip toes to open the door. "You were ages."

"I had to hunt for them," Emma said. "I hope you're hungry."

"Kinda," Nicky admitted, poking a finger in the chip bag and wrinkling his nose. "Me and Farrell ate some cold pop tarts while you were out."

Emma glanced down at the dog, spotting a blob of red jam on his right eyebrow. "Why did you do that? I thought you wanted chips."

Nicky patted her thigh and looked guilty. "I didn't think you'd find any," he admitted. "I just wanted you to be long enough for me to do this." He held up Rohan's expensive phone and Emma gasped at the lit screen, unlocked with the icons showing in neat order.

"What did you do?" She panicked, shoving the bags of food onto the coffee table. The dog made a lurch for a sausage roll poking out of the packaging and Emma held him off with her leg outstretched. "You've activated the tracker. You'll bring them straight here!"

Chapter 39

♥

Nicky pushed chips between his lips, the heat burning his tongue. His other hand lifted one from the packet and Emma heard the snap of the dog's jaws under the table. "Farrell, go!" She pushed the dog's rear end with her shoe and sent him to lie next to the French doors. "You're a rubbish guard dog!" she complained. "You're a disgrace to the doggie community."

Nicky giggled and pushed another chip into the slot in his face. "Chips for breakfast is quite nice," he commented. "Better than cold pop tarts." He glanced at the dog. "Farrell sicked his up on the kitchen floor."

"Oh, great!" Emma sighed. She pushed her half eaten sausage roll away.

"About the phone," Nicky began, sounding six going on sixty. "It's like this; Daddy turned the tracker off, see." He held it up and pointed at an icon on the screen leaving a greasy finger mark. "It's not like the other bugs and stuff he uses, it's just GPS." He pressed the icon and the screen changed to show a login box needing a password. "If I put the password in, I can turn it on."

"Don't!" Emma said. "Unless you want the others to turn up and drag us home."

"Harley Man wants to marry you," Nicky said, his voice turning sullen. "That's why he wants us home."

"No he doesn't," Emma argued. "I'm already married; he knows that."

"Yeah, but if Dad's out of the way, he could marry you then."

Emma shook her head. "I wouldn't marry anyone else, Nicky. I love Daddy and that's all there is to it."

Nicky smiled. "Good girl," he said as though he'd assumed the role of parent. "I won't put the password in then."

"You don't know it," Emma said with a smile.

"Do," Nicky replied, his face becoming coy. "I pretend I'm sleeping on his knee and Daddy does stuff on his phone and his laptop. I can see the numbers and I just love numbers." He rolled his eyes like a connoisseur and Emma shook her head.

"Nicky, who are you?" she sighed.

"My father's son," he said with pride. "I'm gonna be a British spy when I grow up and play the stock market to make my fortune. Dad's already showed me how to work the blue chip companies to make money; he's gonna show me some other ones next holidays. He might let me put pocket money on one, he said. Then we can watch it go up and down."

Emma groaned and put her head in her hands. "What was the password for the phone then, clever clogs?" she asked.

Nicky smiled. "It's, 'I love Emma Andreyev,' translated into Russian and then hexadecimal."

Emma opened her mouth and then closed it again. "That's nice," she managed. "I don't even know what hexadecimal is."

Nicky looked at her with exaggerated sympathy. "It's ok, Mummy. Me and Daddy do; so you don't really need to."

"Great. I'll just stick to cooking and cleaning, shall I?" Emma regretted the sarcasm in her voice but her son seemed oblivious.

"That would be very helpful, thanks," he said and pushed another chip into his open mouth.

"So, what's on Dad's phone then," she asked. "How can we use it to help us find him?"

"We don't need to," Nicky said.

Emma stood up and began pacing. Farrell danced to her side and matched her stride for stride until Emma fell over him. "This is messed up," she complained, stress eating into the last of her nerves. "I've just escaped from my own home, leaving people I thought were my friends, led by a child who knows hexadecimal and tells me everything will be ok." She put her head in her hands and closed her eyes, falling over the dog again. "Sit down, Farrell!" she shouted.

The dog sat right in front of her and Emma pitched over the top of him and into the chair of death and wee. She leapt up at speed and the dog slunk back over to the French doors looking disgusted.

"Settle down, dorogaya," Nicky said, sounding like his father. Emma's eyes filled with tears and she scrubbed them with her fists, feeling a gnawing grief biting at her innards as though eating her from the inside out. The half a sausage roll roiled in her guts and she slumped into the folds of the sofa in defeat.

"Why don't we need to find Dad?" Emma asked. "Is this you guessing or do you have evidence?"

"This." Nicky turned the screen towards her and Emma squinted. He relented and got off his chair, padding across the carpet in his socks with his knobbly knees on show under the too-short-shorts. Emma held the screen up to her face, seeing words but not able to take them in.

"I don't get it," she said. "It's just numbers."

"No, it isn't," Nicky said. He went back to the table and dragged a sheet of paper from under the newspaper. What Emma mistook for crude line drawings morphed into words in front of her eyes. "It's from a Google Document which is held in the Cloud," Nicky began.

"Bleh, blah, bleh," Emma replied, shaking her head in confusion. "I have no idea what any of that is."

Nicky turned the screen off and put his hands on his hips, the phone resting against his shorts as he postured in front of her. "It's a document in the sky that other people can share. Dad's left us a message on one, but nobody else can read it unless they know how we speak to each other. He translates into Russian and then converts it to hexadecimal language, but when you turn it back again you get the words."

"And that's a message?" Emma asked. "And you can read it?"

Nicky smiled. "Course. Me and Daddy play this game all the time. Don't you remember when he got furious because of something I did and we had to have a private talk?" Nicky punctuated his sentence with imaginary speech marks drawn in the air around the word 'talk'.

"Yeah," Emma said. "He thought you'd sworn at him."

"I did, but it was an accident. I got the Russian bit wrong and called him a 'shithead' in hexacimal. He wasn't happy with me but we worked it out and he showed me where I went wrong."

"When do you do this stuff?" Emma demanded. "I'm always with you." She ran her hands through her hair in frustration, smelling Freda's fruity shampoo.

"You do sleep quite a lot," Nicky said, sounding apologetic. "When you've had my sister, you'll be back to normal." He sounded regretful and Emma pouted.

"Charming," she retorted. "Sorry to spoil all your fun when I give birth. And it might not be a girl."

"It's a Stephanie. Do you want to know the message?" Nicky looked coy. He pursed his lips and stood with one foot on the other.

"Not really," Emma said, sarcasm dripping from her tone.

Nicky smirked and held the phone away from her as she reached for it. "You won't understand it." He pushed the piece of paper in her face and chewed his bottom lip as though seeking her approval for a special work of crayony art.

'Tell Mama I'm fine. Don't look for me.'

Emma looked at Nicky, aghast. "He wrote this on his phone?"

Nicky shook his head. "No, in the Clouds, but that's how we talk. He must have guessed I'd log on to a computer to check our special document. He knowed I'd look here because that's the game!" The child grew frustrated and stamped his foot. "I knowed you wouldn't get it!" His voice degenerated into a whine and Emma held her arms out.

"I'm sorry, baby," she soothed, kissing his sticky hair. "You're a clever boy and I'm so impressed with you."

"Fanks, Mummy," he replied, smugness returning. "Are you tired, because I'm very tired."

Emma stroked his forehead and wiped her hand on the lycra pants. "I am. I could sleep here."

Nicky reached up and kissed the underside of her chin. "Why don't we go upstairs and sleep on the bed?" he asked. "Do cuddling together; bestest cuddling like our favourite?"

"What's the bed like?" Emma winced, imagining Mr Lambert's left over bedding.

"It's ok," Nicky reassured her. "Freda put clean sheets in the spare room and we can take Farrell with us."

Emma conceded and dragged her feet up the narrow stairs to a pretty room overlooking the front of the house and sprawling cottage garden. She sank onto the bed and then bounced up again as the pants attacked her bum. "I have to take these off," she groaned, yanking them over her feet. "They're killing me."

"Me an all," Nicky giggled, hauling off his shorts. "My packing sucks."

Emma lay down, relieved to smell floral washing powder on the pillow and not festering old man. She turned on her side in the double bed with Nicky laid on his back behind her. Feeling the bed move, she screwed her head around, finding her son messing with the phone. "What're you doing?" she demanded, sitting up.

Nicky waved a charger cable in her face. "It wasn't off, Mummy, it'd runned out of battery. I'm fillin' it up again in case we need it."

Emma laid back down with a sigh. She heard a beep and sat up again. "You're doing more than charging it, you little monkey! What else are you up to?"

Her son grinned, the image of his missing father. "I just sent Daddy a message," he replied, looking smug. "I deleted his message, so it's now empty and got rid of the editing history."

"Why would you do that?" Emma panicked. She couldn't read the hexadecimal, but knowing Rohan's last words were recoverable somehow comforted her. Losing them seemed like losing him.

Nicky rolled his eyes around his head until Emma thought they might detach themselves. "I'm protecting us," he said, his tone indignant. "That message was for us, not hackers. Next time Daddy logs on, he'll see it's gone and know someone's read it. He'll know it was me."

"How?" Emma turned onto her side to face her son.

"I wrote 'shithead' in hexadecimal," he snorted. He laughed until his face turned pale and the combination of cold pop tart and chips threatened to put in a reappearance. Emma chastised him like she felt she should and then cuddled him into her chest, ignoring the prickly lace. She pulled a blanket over them both and plunged into an exhausted sleep, dreaming of absolutely nothing.

Chapter 40

The vibration woke Emma from a deep, groggy sleep, starting and stopping and then beginning again. She squeezed her eyes shut tight and imagined the bus parking outside would eventually leave, so she could pitch back into sleep again, but it wasn't to be.

"Hello." Nicky's voice brought her to the surface and she sat up, rubbing her eyes and lurching for her son. He put one finger in his ear and hopped off the bed, standing in the far corner of the room out of reach. "This is Nikolai Andreyev," he said. "Who's this?"

With an expletive not fit for childish ears, Emma held her hand out for Rohan's phone, the scowl on her face brooking no disobedience. With great reluctance, Nicky slapped it into her palm and flopped across the bottom of the bed, burying his tired face in Farrell's shaggy rough.

"Hello?" Emma sounded puffed and rubbed her eyes, seeking a state of hurried competence to deal with the caller seeking her missing husband.

"Is that Emma?" the voice asked and she groaned with relief.

"Hi, Maureen. I'm so glad you've called." Emma swung her feet off the bed, nudging the dog which had made himself far too comfortable next to the footboard. "Have you heard from Rohan?"

"No." Maureen's tone sounded anxious. "Can you talk or should I call back?"

"I'm good." Emma stood up and stretched using one arm, heading for the small staircase down into the kitchen. "I've left the house for a few days. I'm somewhere safe."

"Where's Rohan?" Maureen asked, annoyance creeping into her voice. "He knew the auditors from the disciplinary panel were due; he had notice weeks ago. He should be here."

"Christopher said he'd spoken to you," Emma said, watching her footing on the rickety stairs. "Two men took Rohan off the street yesterday morning after we saw Jed and Stephanie trying to break into the office the night before."

"And he's not back yet?" Maureen sounded surprised, as though it was usual for Rohan to be stuffed into cars at gunpoint and show up the next day for work.

"No." Worry seeped into Emma's tone. "What should I do? Do I need to speak to these auditors or the police? The men said not to, but I don't have much choice."

"No, stay out of it," Maureen warned. She sighed and Emma tuned in to the worry coming out of the phone. "We got rid of The Actuary's communications so there was only one big box left of things which could be taken the wrong way. The digital stuff gets purged straight away. I took the box home and made David carry it down to the air raid shelter."

"You have an air raid shelter?" Emma asked, her archivist's fascination distracting her.

"Yes," Maureen replied. "And a husband who doesn't like the spiders in it. It's well hidden in the back garden. We didn't even know it was there for the first four years, so a group of nosy panel members wouldn't find it even if they did knock on my front door."

"Do they do that?" Emma thought about Wingate Hall and the array of possible hiding places Rohan may have used.

"No," Maureen said, sounding confident. "Unless it's a serious fraud issue and then the police get involved. They still won't find my bunker unless by some horrible fluke."

"What about computers and all that digital traceability?" Emma asked, filling the kettle one handed and putting it on to boil. The gas stove lit first time as Emma pressed the ignition for the electrical spark and she waited for Maureen's answer.

"We're not amateurs," the woman said. "We've been at this game a very long time, love. Give us some credit."

"Ok, sorry. The thing is, Jed and Stephanie wanted to plant documents on you or Rohan, which would make him appear involved in a transaction that had already happened and is on the auditor's radar. Yet Christopher said there's something big coming. What do you make of that? I think there's two things in play here. One man spent time in Harborough trying to find out where Rohan lived and it's possible he planted something at the old house which I still need to find. Rohan didn't seem to care that he knew about Newcombe Street or followed us to the hotel for the work dinner, but he didn't want him to have the Clareville Street address. The men who snatched him weren't far away from the London house, so I'm thinking they're a totally different group. What do you think?"

"I think it's a bloody big mess and the auditor is due in half an hour," Maureen replied. "I can say Rohan's been called away this time but I can't keep doing it. She'll want to see all documents and correspondence relating to that report he did and I'll have to let her."

"So, it is a woman who's coming then?" Emma said. "Christopher implied the woman had a liking for Rohan."

Maureen snorted. "I don't think so, love! She's married to Lord Fincham and retires at the end of this year. From the looks that Irishman was giving you at the dinner, I don't think he's happy with you and Rohan being together. Watch your back."

"Christopher had this phone for a couple of hours after Frederik dropped it off." Emma pulled it away from her face and peered at it before putting it back to her ear. "Do you think he could've bugged it?"

There was a short pause as Maureen thought for a moment. "Did he expect to lose it straight away or did he think he'd have longer to hack into it?"

"Longer." Emma sounded definite. "My son stole it and he wouldn't have expected that."

"Then I very much doubt it," Maureen said. "Given a decent amount of time, he probably would have, but Rohan has apps on that phone which would find them anyway. Is it the one with the black case or the blue?"

Emma pulled it away from her face again and held it up to the light. "Blue. Navy blue. I haven't seen this one before."

"Then guard it with your life," Maureen advised. "And yes, that one definitely has something on it to counteract any kind of bug or tracker apart from the GPS one which Rohan built in himself for emergencies. Don't turn that one on. It's probably the one Hack locked on to in the first place so leave it off."

"Ok." Emma sighed. "I'm not sure what we can do at the moment."

"Oh, I'm not just going to sit here," Maureen said, bristling at any suggestion of complacency. "As soon as Lady Fincham gets here, I've got a little gift for her."

"What?" Emma asked, not sure if she wanted to know.

"I've got a lovely DVD of those two downstairs trying to break into this office, plus their whole conversation on audio. If there's something going on, I'm sending her in their direction. I've also got all of Rohan's reports ready in a file. I typed them myself and he's been over and over them and can't find anything wrong. That means whatever he submitted was ok, or it's been substituted."

Emma ran a shaking hand across her forehead. "I think Rohan knew about whatever Jed and Stephanie were cooking up. It's the bigger thing which is coming that bothers me."

"Well, Rohan's not here to see it at the moment." Maureen sounded thoughtful. "So at least they won't be pushing that his way too."

Emma nodded and sank into the sofa cushions. "Yeah, you're right. He's not here." The tension in her neck began to dissipate and for a moment she felt gratitude towards whoever had wiped her husband temporarily out of the game. "Let me know how you get on with the audit lady."

"Are you sure you don't know where he is?" Maureen asked and her tone made Emma want to tell the truth.

"I know he's ok," she replied. "He's communicated with our son but asked that we didn't try to find him."

"Well, let's assume he knows what he's doing," Maureen humphed. "To be fair, he usually does."

"Ok, so we do nothing for now, then?"

"You can do what you like," Maureen sighed. "I've got an auditor to appease; she'll be expecting a tall, handsome Russian and instead she's got an English midget."

Emma snuffed out a laugh and then pursed her lips. "Maureen, please don't tell Christopher we've heard from Rohan. He thinks Rohan's dead. The police found a body outside the house Rohan was taken to."

"It won't be Rohan," she asserted. Her assurance comforted Emma. "Ok, talk later." Maureen disconnected the call.

The clock above the fireplace chimed midday as Emma slouched on the sofa and allowed herself to be sucked into daytime television. The mindless chat show helped to move the day from morning into afternoon and she forced herself to relax, stroking a finger across her stomach where the baby danced a jig in the beginnings of hob-nailed boots. The national news contained an item about a body found outside the Falkirk manor house and Emma crouched by the TV to study views of the crime scene flashed across the screen by eager media keen for a scoop. The camera panned to a single black shoe abandoned next to a pool of blood on the road. Emma heaved out a sigh at the sight of it.

Rohan wouldn't fit his good foot in it, let alone the fractionally bigger prosthesis.

The clatter of the back gate sent her to her feet, casting around for somewhere to hide. The door curtains blocked out the view of the garden but anyone pressing their face against the side windows would see inside. Emma dodged behind the armchair and then realised the TV would give her away. She bolted out to flick off the ancient contraption using a button on its side and then squeezed herself into the gap. She breathed out through her lips and tried to control her frightened panting, waiting for the newcomer to either knock on the door or break the window.

The handle rattled and Emma pressed her fingers over her lips, hoping Nicky or the dog didn't wake and launch themselves down the stairs and into danger. Something slammed against the door at the same time as the dog barked upstairs. Emma heard a squeak as the French door opened into the lounge and deciding the element of surprise was best, popped up from behind the armchair like a jack-in-the-box screaming, "Don't hurt us!"

Freda howled and dropped the bag of groceries. Oranges shot off in every direction and she narrowly gripped the carton of milk, letting the door keys spew to the ground as a less messy alternative. Farrell rushed down the stairs barking in anger and disappointed to see Freda, changed direction and chased an orange until his claws and teeth splatted it onto the skirting board.

"I'm hungry." Nicky appeared at the bottom of the stairs rubbing his eyes.

Freda bustled into the kitchen and deposited the milk on the side. She shrugged off her coat and ruffled Nicky's blond hair on her way back to shove the coat over the newel post. "I'll make fruit salad," she declared. "If you rescue the rest of the food from the dog."

"I'm so sorry!" Emma's hands shook as she braced herself on the back of the armchair. "I thought you might be coming to kill us."

Freda emerged from the kitchen with a furrowed brow at the same time as Nicky turned with the squished orange in his hand. "What did you say?" Freda asked.

Nicky's face crumpled and he dropped the orange with a splat onto the carpet. The dog fell upon it again, alternately licking the mess and rubbing his face on the carpet, making a whooshing, snorting noise. "I don't wanna die!" Nicky wailed and Emma regretted her unfortunate moment of verbal diarrhoea.

"Not really," she said, holding her arms out to her distraught son. "I exaggerated, it's ok."

Nicky pushed his face into her stomach and wiped his sticky hands on the back of her sweater. Freda cocked her head like a bird and Emma shrugged and looked apologetic. The old woman shook her head at Emma's attempts to dismiss her terror, not fooled for a minute. "Come on young man!" she barked. "There's fruit to peel and chop if you want this salad before next week. I've also bought cream for you to whip, although Mummy probably just did that for us."

Nicky heaved out a sigh and followed Freda into the kitchen, standing on a chair to peel and chop at her direction. Freda stood over him while he wielded the sharper implements, taking over when he got bored. "You can go into the garden with Farrell if you like," Freda said. "But don't go out of the gate."

Emma sat up straight and peered into the garden and then back at her friend. Freda shrugged. "The fence is over five feet tall," she hissed, "and the gate's a bugger to open. Nobody can see into the garden so he'll be fine getting some fresh air."

Feeling nervous, Emma sat by the French doors and watched her son dance around the garden with the dog, playing a game which involved running behind trees and bushes and jumping out with an imaginary gun held out in front of him. The dog went along with it for the pure pleasure of being with his favourite playmate, satiating his boredom by watering the flowers and sniffing the ground for something far more interesting than the bouncing, three-foot assassin accompanying him. Emma watched as Nicky disappeared and then reappeared in a nauseating step routine which made her eyes woppy. "He's full of beans," she remarked, smiling as Freda pushed the finished fruit salad into the fridge and sat on the sofa, wiping her arthritic hands on a pinafore tied around her waist.

"Get up off the floor," Freda implored her, patting the sofa cushion next to her. "You'll get too big soon to do that."

Emma crawled to the sofa and up onto the squashy seat, turning her body so she could watch Nicky's antics. "I'm a bit stuck," she said with a sigh.

Freda peered at her. "But you only just sat down, dear," she said, shoving her fingers under Emma's thigh.

"I meant with life," Emma replied, laughing. "I don't know where to go from here."

"Ah." Freda nodded. "I see. You're welcome to stay as long as you like."

"Thank you." Emma smiled and squeezed Freda's fingers. She jerked her head towards the garden where Nicky rolled around on the ground having apparently been shot by Farrell. "But I don't think I can contain him indefinitely. He's an Andreyev and they're not known for sitting still."

"Such a pity," Freda said with a wink. "Although life would be jolly dull."

"I spoke to Rohan's assistant." Emma flicked at a peeling label on the leg of the lycra pants. "Rohan had an appointment with an investigator at his office this morning, to go over his reports."

"Oh." Freda pursed her lips and winced. "Will that count against him?"

"I don't know. Maureen's handling it at the moment. She's got footage of a man and woman trying to break into Rohan's office late at night and the audio of their conversation. But something doesn't add up."

"Are they the people who took him?" Freda asked. She bent forward and examined a ladder in the knee-high stockings, yanking them up and watching as they puddled round her ankles again. "Elastic's gone," she muttered to herself.

"Nobody knows. I think it's a whole other group of people but I have no proof. Unless I can call the police, I'm stuck here wondering if Rohan's ok. He told Nicky he was, but what if they've hurt or killed him since then?" Emma worried at her thumb nail, processing her dilemma. She glanced across as Nicky hopped out from behind a tree and shot at the dog with pretend bullets. The impact of the fake back blast seemed to have induced a heart attack and he collapsed in a blackberry bush, leaping up at speed and examining the spindly legs poking out of his shorts. "I could ask Nicky to log in to the Google Doc thingy," she mused. "But I suspect Rohan sent the message before he left his phone at the Falkirk house and disappeared. I don't want to start Nicky on a track of hourly checking, just in case Christopher somehow latches onto that phone."

The phone in question vibrated, making Emma jump and Freda ping her stocking elastic. It shuddered itself off the arm of the chair and shivered around on the stained cushion. Emma leapt up and answered it. "Hello."

"You won't believe this!" Maureen sounded wired. "She was a nice lady; the panel member. It's nothing to do with any of the other actuaries in the building. A client of Rohan's made a complaint about him. Only him! Listen to this." Papers shuffled and Emma waited for Maureen to continue. "The insurance underwriter, Wright Holdings Ltd claims that a reasonable actuary would have deemed it within the scope of his objective that the treatment of the data should be documented on the file and the fact of the action and the quantum should have been made available to, and explained to, the Trustees of Wright Holdings Ltd prior to the making of their business critical decision."

Emma heard a sound like a trumpet blast and waited until Maureen finished blowing her nose. "Gosh. They don't believe in using commas do they?" she remarked, understanding none of it.

Maureen ignored her interruption. "And the other thing this company claims is that the actuary did not reference the liability profile and the average duration of the liabilities in his advice on setting discount rates and inflation." There was silence.

"I'm hoping you don't expect me to understand a word of that," Emma said into the airwaves.

Maureen snorted like an angry bull. "I showed Lady Fincham everything she needed to see. It's all there in black and white. Rohan explained his whole process on paper and I've got a letter from the company thanking him for the trouble he took travelling to bloody Glasgow to speak to the trustees! And she was scratching her head looking at the beautiful document he provided showing the average duration of the liabilities and a whole commentary on how that might affect both discount rates and inflation. I knew he'd done nothing wrong!"

"So did you give her a copy of Jed and Stephanie trying to break in?" Emma asked.

"What was the point?" Maureen snapped. "She went off to make her recommendations to the panel but I don't understand what's going on."

Emma's head whirled with the information overload. "Leave it with me," she said. "I need to pay a visit to Newcombe Street."

Chapter 41

♥

"This is an absolutely terrible idea," Emma said, wincing as the car backfired before shuddering to a halt. "Will's further up the street and if he sees us, I have no idea what will happen next."

"Hurry and get the gate undone," Freda urged, pulling her snood around her head until her eyes bulged. Emma shook her head at the debatable disguise, wondering where the elderly ghost of the Virgin Mary fitted with breaking and entering. "If anyone comes I'll pretend I've had a heart attack."

Nicky giggled and patted Freda's thigh. "And I can jump up and down on your chest, can't I?"

"No!" both women bit in horror.

"With my hands!" he reassured them. "Not my feet."

The huge drive gate slid open and the three sleuths slipped through the gap. Emma closed it behind her and engaged the deadlock.

"Cool!" Nicky exclaimed. "I love this garden." He skipped off towards the apple tree and began to climb.

"Fantastic!" Emma grumbled. "He lives in a ninth century manor house with acres of space and he wants suburbia."

"Don't be like that," Freda chastised her. "You were grateful enough to be here once."

"I was." Emma stopped on the pretty gravel path through the orchard and stared up at the white house, feeling a flush of pleasure mixed with misery. "Compared to where I came from it was palatial. But every day felt like an agony of waiting; either for Rohan to realise Nicky was his son and throw us out, or his dreaded girlfriend to throw me out instead."

"Yes, well, you can't hold him responsible for any of that now, can you?" Freda raised her eyebrows at Emma and she shook her head at the disguise.

"Please take the snood off. I think you're more noticeable wearing a pink burka than you are as a little old lady."

"It's not a burka, it's a niqab," Freda protested. "My eyes aren't covered."

"It's a pink, woolly scarf sewn up at the back!" Emma grunted. "Pink-clad burglars aren't in vogue right now." She pushed her key into the back door and turned it, hearing a satisfying click. "Wait until I deactivate the alarm," she said.

Emma ran for the key pad in the front lobby and stopped the threatening beeps while Freda nosed in the pantry. "We could take some of these supplies up to the house," she said. Her eyes flashed with excitement. "What fun. I'm hiding fugitives."

"We're not fugitives and it's a rubbish hiding place. You forgot the presence of Clarissa Jameson-Arden."

"Oh, her!" Freda spat. "She's not talking to me. Not since the radio announcer called me Lady Freda Ayers. I wish I'd seen her face turn the colour of a mulberry." She sighed. "I'll have to be satisfied with Pauline Carmichael's description at the Church morning tea last Friday. I thought my heart might give out."

"From shock or fear?" Emma asked, her eyes raking surfaces for something strange.

"From laughing," Freda said, sounding indignant. "What a way to go. If I'd dropped dead then I would've been remembered forever. Instead, I just wet myself."

Emma opened her mouth and then closed it again. "Help me search the rooms for something which looks wrong; a parcel, letter, something random that shouldn't be here."

"But dear, you came here on a covert visit with the boys, didn't you? Wouldn't they have searched for it?"

Emma nodded. "Yes, but they didn't live here. I'll know it when I see it."

Freda poked around the downstairs rooms while Emma searched upstairs. Each room tugged her heartstrings while metaphorically kicking her in the head. The house represented both the best of times and the worst. In Rohan's former bachelor haunt, Emma stopped and sat on the bed. Her sister-in-law had cleaned the house, leaving the bedding by the front door for Rohan to collect and folding the duvet and stacking it at the bottom of the bed. "Where would I put a late delivery?" Emma asked herself. "I'm getting my family ready to go back to Russia and someone comes to the door. If I didn't lay it on the lobby dresser or in the kitchen, where would it be?"

Emma checked her old bedroom at the front of the house, finding it just as she left it. Freda called from the bottom of the stairs, her voice wavering as she declared the downstairs devoid of anything unusual. "Shall I come up?" she asked and Emma heard the clop of her skate shoes on the bottom step.

"No, don't worry," Emma called back. "There's nothing here; I'm done."

She moved into Nicky's old bedroom and without her son's endless array of homemade toys, the room looked bare. Sticking her head into the room across the hall, Emma halted, noticing the dents in the carpet where the borrowed cot stood, holding Sergei's baby boy. Venturing further into the room, she sucked in a breath at the sight of a brown envelope on the dresser, the address label sporting a thin veneer of dust. The name of Rodney Harrington graced a typed label and Emma felt reluctant to touch it, suspicious of its contents.

"I've found it!" Emma shouted, her heart pounding in her chest. "It was here all the time. I can't believe Christopher and Ray didn't find it. And what about Rohan? Surely he checked the house after Sergei left."

Freda's surprising speed alarmed Emma as the old lady barrelled into the back of her. "What's in it?" she demanded.

"No idea," Emma hissed, "and we're not opening it. What if there's a tracker inside or something chemical?"

"Damn! Good point," Freda answered. She pulled a pair of woolly gloves from her pocket and slipped them over her gnarled fingers. "I'll pick it up with these," she said.

"What then?" Emma asked. "Inside that envelope is something which will destroy my husband."

Freda tapped the side of her nose with one hand whilst gripping the brown envelope in the other. "Nothing good comes in brown envelopes," she said with appropriate drama.

They carried the envelope downstairs, Emma walking with care in front of the old lady who clumped down behind her regardless. Nicky still ran around the garden with the dog, giggling and getting muddy.

The wood burner in the lounge obliged with the right degree of enthusiasm as Emma lit the ready kindle and watched the flames begin. Freda chucked in a plastic milk carton from the recycling bin and Emma shrieked as the plastic melted onto the wood below and the flames bit in a frenzied inferno. "Why did you do that?" she complained, closing the door against the acrid, black smoke. "Are you trying to warn the street we're doing something illegal?"

Freda shrugged with dismissal and opened the door while Emma held her nose. She flipped the envelope into the fire and the women crouched and watched as the excitable flames licked around the edges before consuming it in a giant, hungry gulp. "It's just papers," Freda whispered, as though their actions might have incited some ethereal revenge.

"Of course it's papers," Emma replied, keeping her voice low. "Incriminating papers which someone paid a stranger to plant. He went to an awful lot of trouble to do this, so it has to be really, really bad."

"Oh, look," Freda remarked, pointing towards the fire. A logo showed beneath the brown envelope as the paper curled. A woman sat within a circle, coins tumbling around her. The spear in her right hand was offset by the leafy branch in her left and Emma peered at the cross of St. George adorning what looked like a circular shield to her right. "That's the Bank of England logo," Freda said with a shrug. "I think we just torched your husband's tax returns."

"Really?" Emma looked doubtful but Freda nodded.

"Yep. Whatever it was, we're in the clear. That thing's not gonna climb out of there in a hurry."

Emma chewed her lips and settled herself in an armchair, feeling the tension ebb out of her chest. "Let's wait here until it's gone," she pleaded. "I need to make sure the fire's out before we leave. Only then can I be sure the threat's gone."

Freda settled on the sofa opposite and looked at the fire with genuine longing. "Ok," she agreed. "I love a good fire." Her eyes roved the lounge with its minimalist decorations with a sense of disappointment. "What else can we burn?"

Chapter 42

♥

"I should go home and face the music," Emma said, sitting on the sofa back at Freda's house in Great Arden. "They're probably going frantic. I'm forcing myself to trust that Rohan's ok so I'll use my energies to think up a suitable punishment for when he does wander home like nothing's wrong."

"You do that." Freda smiled at her with a knowing look in her eyes. "But you won't follow through, so why waste your energy.

Emma pouted and knew the old lady spoke sense.

"Wait until tomorrow," Freda suggested. "You're safe here and it gives you a chance to rest up and relax. Nobody will think to look for you here."

"Except Clarissa Jameson-Arden," Emma grumbled. "I can't believe I ran into her."

"Inevitable, I'm afraid," Freda answered. "She thinks she owns this village."

"Her father-in-law thinks differently." Emma narrowed her eyes at Freda. "He's cute and he's got the hots for you."

Freda giggled and put her fingers over her lips, simpering like a sixteen-year-old. "Such a sweet man. He proposed to me at school on my sixth birthday," she said.

"Don't you want a little extra happiness?" Emma asked, her tone thoughtful.

Freda shook her head with emphasis. "Can you imagine being with someone other than your husband?"

"No." Emma punctuated the single word with a sigh. "I was willing to settle for Christopher when I truly believed there was no chance with Rohan. But it didn't feel right. He's exciting and dangerous but when it came down to it, he wasn't Ro."

"It's the same for me," Freda conceded. "Perfection comes once in a lifetime and once we've had it, we're grateful to live on our memories."

"One more night," Emma said. "Then we'll go home."

She stayed two more nights in total before the effort of washing her knickers by hand and drying them on the radiator drove her crazy. Emma climbed into the ancient Datsun and allowed Freda to take her home. Nicky bounced into the seat next to her, balancing on a cushion. "I've enjoyed our holiday," he said with enthusiasm. "Can we do it again?"

"Yes!" Freda cried. "It's been wonderful."

Emma clutched her son as they lurched through the village and made it onto the country roads. She leaned forward and spoke into Freda's left ear as they took a corner too fast and Nicky slid onto the floor giggling. "Just drop us back at the gate," Emma yelled over the sound of the engine. "We might be able to sneak back through the passages."

"Don't be ridiculous!" Freda screeched back. "Walk back in like you own it."

"I do own it," Emma repeated, pushing herself back into her seat. Nicky rolled around in the foot well with the dog and Emma prayed they didn't meet a police car as Freda careened around corners on the wrong side of the road. "I'm a responsible parent, I'm a responsible parent," Emma repeated, out loud for her own benefit, closing her eyes against the greenery which fled past the windows.

"Code!" Freda yelled as they skidded to a halt in front of the keypad for the gates to Wingate Hall.

Nicky recited the numbers as Emma gripped the seat and dug her fingers into a hole in the worn leather. She hadn't opened her eyes since the last village which whipped past like a slice of bread in a blender. The gates slid open before her, the brass plate declaring the house name obliterated by Verdigris. Freda kangarooed the vehicle up the gravel driveway and finished with a handbrake turn in front of the house. "Weeeeee!" Nicky screamed from the foot well, giggling as the dog scrabbled on top of him.

As soon as the doors opened, boy and dog headed onto the lawn to continue their excited rolling. Ray dashed through the front door, his face ashen and his lips drawn into a straight line. "Where the bloody hell have you been?" he demanded, as though Emma was a recalcitrant daughter who'd shinned down a drainpipe and enjoyed a forbidden night on the town. Every footstep wrought another foul swearword from his lips and Emma shrank back against the car in fear. Freda took a fighting stance in front of Emma, protecting her from the angry man who powered down the front steps, three at a time. She held her tiny fists up in front of her face like a miniature boxer, lurching at the fresh air before her nose. Realising Freda had her eyes closed, Emma groaned as her self-appointed bodyguard failed at the first test.

"Are you all right?" Ray circumnavigated the flailing pensioner whose blows rained on his shoulders like hail stones. He reached out for Emma and then dropped his hands to his sides. "I could strangle you right now," he shouted across the metre between them. He turned in anger as Freda wobbled on one foot to kick him in the calves, almost overbalancing herself. "Bloody hell, woman!" he yelled. "What are you trying to do?"

"Defend my friend's honour!" Freda postured, inserting herself between Emma and Ray and squishing Emma back against the car.

Ray held his arms out by his sides and shook his head in dismay. "I'm a medic!" he squeaked. "I want to check her over, not molest her."

"Did you ask her permission?" Freda demanded. "No, I heard nothing of the sort. Get out of the way so we can go inside."

Ray stepped back, gaping like a fish as Freda called Nicky and the dog to heel. "Get your bag from the car," she snapped at the boy and he obeyed, hauling the rucksack onto his slender shoulders and trotting after her like an obedient puppy.

Emma yawned as she entered the house, feeling it wrap around her shoulders with a soporific sense of peace. Allaine met her in the hallway, her eyes demanding explanation while her lips remained sealed.

"We gave you until today and then I was calling the police," Ray asserted, slamming the front door so the glass rattled in its frame. Emma glared at him, reminding him of his role as the hired help and he held his ground against her irritation with a look of determined pique. "Don't you look at me like that!" He wagged his finger at her and Emma pursed her lips in defiance. "How the hell did you get out of that room?"

"I wasn't aware I was a prisoner," Emma replied, her tone curt. "Put your stuff in the laundry," she told Nicky, watching as he soaked up the terrible atmosphere like a sponge. "I'll sort it out later."

The child looked to Emma for reassurance and then bounded upstairs, leaving Farrell at the bottom still wagging his tail and waiting with great expectation for his master's return. "I'm going for a shower," Emma stated, fondling Anton's fire engine in her pocket. "I just need some space."

Chapter 43

♥

"Mrs Andreyev." The man stepped in front of Emma as she emerged from the apartment building, and she clutched her purse to her chest. His lip seemed to curl as he said her surname. A flock of sparrows took flight from the tree outside the sliding doors and she started and turned, narrowing her eyes at the sight of the man who'd called her name.

"Yes?" she replied, waiting as he strode towards her.

"A moment of your time," he asked, holding his hand out in front of him as though to allay her fears. Tall, with a frame which age had done little to attack, the man towered over her. Switched on blue eyes blinked from beneath white hair which had escaped from its backward brushing and his smile showed a set of neat, even teeth. "Sorry to bother you," he said and his English accent sounded fresh out of a posh private school. Emma dated his age around sixty and something about him seemed familiar.

"Ok," she said. "But I need to fetch my son."

The man's brow knitted and he licked his lips as though unsure where to begin. "I understand you were related to Alanya Andreyev," he began and Emma closed her eyes and shook her head.

"Harrington," she corrected him. "Her first husband died and she married my father. His name was Harrington."

"Oh. My apologies." He looked confused. "So, you're not Rohan Andreyev's wife?"

Emma gnawed on the inside of her cheek and felt irritation grow. Her lips parted as she formed the sentence which would tell a stranger that she'd married her step brother, but she closed them again. "I don't think that's any of your business." Her hostile tone made the blue eyes widen and the man took a step forward, apologising with what appeared to be genuine regret. "I'm terribly sorry. It wasn't my intention to pry. I'm friends with Freda and knew Alanya through the book club here. Alanya gave me something for safekeeping and I wondered when would be a good time to return it." He took a step back and raised his hands again. "No matter. We'll talk another time when you're not in so much of a rush." Nodding, the tall man turned and strode away, waiting for a fraction of a second so that the sliding doors could give him access. He stood back to let an elderly woman negotiate the gap on a zimmer frame and nodded to her with regal finesse. Despite his age, he moved with grace like a swan, cutting through the distance with determination.

"Like an old fashioned prince," Emma muttered to herself. She followed the path onto the main road and walked through the park, wondering what damaging message Alanya might have left her poor son. She toyed with the urge to forget the conversation, but knew Rohan would be upset.

Sunshine speckled the green grass of the park and Emma chose to walk through it, deviating from her usual stroll beneath the huge oak trees. The ultra-violet rays caressed her dark hair and sapped her energy at the same time as infusing her with the vitamin D she craved. It seemed like an unfair swap and she reached the back gate to Little Arden School feeling drained. Allaine met her at the step up into the playground. "You look tired," her friend said and Emma experienced a spark of irritation.

"I'm fine."

"You didn't have to come out," Allaine continued. "I told you I'd get Nicky and bring him home with me."

"Home to mine or to yours?" Emma asked, regretting her question as Allaine paled.

"I wondered if it would be ok to stay at yours for a few more days. You can say if it's not." She chewed her bottom lip and closed her eyes against ready tears.

"Of course it's fine," Emma relented. She watched as Allaine struggled to hold in her misery. "Have you had another argument with Will?"

"No. I haven't seen him." Allaine pursed her lips and pushed out a breath. "You didn't come home after work." Allaine's eyes looked wide in her pale face. "You're sick of me, aren't you?"

"No, silly! I went to see Freda. She didn't feel great yesterday, so I popped round and found her surrounded by casseroles and baking. It's just a bad cold and she swears she'll be fine by the end of the week."

"That's good." Allaine heaved out a breath and the smile she forced onto her face looked weak. "I bought food so I'll make tea for us all tonight. You put your feet up; you look done in."

"Thanks." Emma smiled, trying to look grateful. "I just met a man who wanted to tell me something. I feel like I know him." Her brow knitted with worry and confusion.

"About Rohan?" Allaine whispered and Emma shrugged.

"It's fine," she said with a sigh. "It probably means nothing. He didn't even give me his name."

The children bounced out of class, delighted that Kaylee could stay longer. They skipped off towards the park holding hands and making plans for illegal midnight feasts and dare devil skateboard tricks in the basement. Neither woman revisited the issues in front of them and sat on a bench to watch the children play on the swings.

"I wish I could have a couple of hours of being six again," Allaine sighed.

"No thanks," Emma replied. "I'd have to go back to my mother dying and Daddy wheeling in Alanya Harrington as the wicked step mother. It was probably the worst year of my life."

"Sorry," Allaine sounded glum. "I didn't mean really go back in time. I meant having a couple of hours with a six-year old's cares and worries."

"Instead of your own?" Emma asked and Allaine nodded.

"Yeah, I could do with an hour of running around like a maniac, getting hot and sweaty and hungry, then having someone take care of sorting me out. It sounds like bliss."

"Let's do it then," Emma said, standing. She left Nicky's book bag and PE kit on the park bench and strolled over to the playground.

"Hey, Mummy!" Nicky squealed as his legs swung into the air. "Look at me!"

"I see you, baby," Emma laughed. "Can me and Allaine have a go?"

Nicky's jaw dropped as he processed the request and the other children around them stilled in their play. "Ok." He hopped off the swing, hauling his trousers up as they threatened to plunge around his knees. Small eager hands stopped the swing mid wobble and helped Emma into its plastic bucket seat.

"Gosh!" Emma exclaimed. "In my day we sat on a piece of wood, not a bum shaped plastic chair. Where're the cushions?"

"Silly Mummy." Nicky laughed and waited until she settled. Then he scurried behind her and shoved her in the small of her back. Emma lifted her feet and closed her eyes, allowing the easy motion and the pull of gravity to drag her into the past.

In her mind's eye, Rohan's hands clasped her around the waist as they shared a swing, putting off the awful journey home. She remembered her scuffed shoes from yet another fight with Clarence Clutterbuck and Rohan's busted lip dripped blood onto his school shirt. Alanya lost it that night, hitting Emma so hard with the wooden spoon that she snapped its head clean off. When Rohan stepped in to ward his mother off, putting his fifteen-year-old body between the women, he'd earned himself a thorough belting with one of Emma's father's old leather straps. Emma remembered Rohan's face as she cowered in the corner of the kitchen and Alanya lashed at him like a mad woman. He stood there like a prisoner of war as she lashed, stoic and brave, his face still and his jaw gritted. Emma never loved him more.

"Higher, Mummy?" Nicky giggled and Emma shook her head, enjoying the gentle pitch and toss of the movement.

"No, this is perfect," she said, her voice dreamy.

Emma achieved a higher altitude than Allaine with the help of Nicky's arm muscles but the women called it evens. She felt wobbly exiting the swing. "My car's outside Freda's apartment," she said. "I'll meet you at Wingate Hall."

"Can I ride with Kaylee?" Nicky pleaded, his eyes round like saucers.

"I've got a spare booster seat," Allaine said, so eager it made Emma wince.

"I don't blame you, Allaine," Emma whispered, covering her mouth with her hand. "You don't have to make up for what Will did."

Allaine stared at the floor, her cheeks flushing pink with shame and embarrassment. "I feel responsible," she hissed back. "I don't know how to make it right with you."

"Then don't." Emma reached for her friend and drew her into a hug, feeling Allaine shivering in her arms. "I still love you," she whispered. "Nothing changes that." Emma heard Allaine sniff and sought to distract the children. "Group hug!" she called and Nicky and Kaylee latched onto their legs, giggling.

"Are you sad, Mummy?" Kaylee's small voice came from somewhere near Emma's hip and she felt Allaine stiffen.

Emma gave her a fortifying squeeze and answered for her. "A bit," she said. "I think she needs a daughter cuddle and lots of help to get home and making some tea."

"Can I see Lady Freda?" Nicky asked and Emma released Allaine and shook her head.

"No, Lord Nikolai," she said with a grin. "Get home and get tea cooking. Freda's got the raging sneezies and it's not pleasant. You don't want to see her wielding tissues with a nose like Rudolf the Red-Nosed Reindeer."

The children giggled and Allaine frowned and jerked her head towards Emma's small bump. "Should you be around her?" she asked, her voice quiet.

"It's fine," Emma said. She leaned closer to Allaine. "It's not that bad really."

The children skipped through the trees with Allaine, heading back to the car on the other side of the park. Emma turned and walked back to Northampton Road and Freda's apartment. The warden smiled and waved from her office as Emma navigated the lounge and headed to the lift, passing a group of senior citizens re-enacting a scene from Anthony and Cleopatra, the Shakespearean version rather than the Carry On rendition. She paused for a second, curiosity piquing at the sight of a pair of stockinged feet poking out of the rug and four old men in the process of rolling up their geriatric Cleopatra. Emma caught the eye of the warden and pointed, sending the woman scurrying out into the public area in horror. The lift doors opened, affording Emma an escape to the sounds of the warden's loud admonishment. "I didn't realise you meant to act it out too!" she wailed. "You don't have to deliver poor Mrs Nordstrom in the rug. Anthony's wheelchair is right here. You might've tipped him out"

Emma alighted on the second floor with a smirk and entered Freda's apartment with a brief knock on the unlocked door. "I'm back," she called, hopping around to unzip her boots. "Allaine took the children home, so I came back for the car. I thought I'd see if you needed anything else before I head after them. You're missing a right treat downstairs. Poor Mr Blythe is playing Anthony and the others have rolled up Norma in the rug from in front of the fire. I don't know how they thought they would manage to lift her between them. The warden's having a fit and Mr Blythe is sitting there smirking at the whole thing!"

Emma poked her head into the bedroom and saw the covers pulled back and Freda's slippers gone from their position under the bed. "Why are you out of bed?" she said, turning and tramping along the passage way towards the lounge and kitchen. "I'd have got you a drink."

"Yes, but you couldn't wee for me," Freda said, a smirk playing on her lips.

Emma stared at the sight of the tall stranger and he stood at her entry, bowing in that same, graceful way. Emma's eyes darted from Freda to him and back again, something important nagging at her subconscious. With the stranger's attention on Emma, Freda used the distraction to remove her hair net and flip out all five of her hair rollers, flicking them onto the floor next to her seat. She primped and fluffed her hair and even managed to drag out a lipstick from her knitting bag, which she hastily applied as the man focussed his energy on Emma.

"I'm glad you're here," Emma said to the man. "It saves me asking Freda questions about you which you can answer for yourself."

"For once, I know nothing," Freda said with a giggle. "I only know Mr Wright from our fortnightly book club." She reached into her nightie and stuffed her breasts back into their proper slots one at a time while the stranger stared at Emma with a curious mix of emotions on his face. Emma closed her eyes as Freda's left boob did a hurried exit-stage-left through the arm hole of her nightie and she fought to contain it with the determination of a bull wrangler. "I'll make tea," Freda said, staring down at her chest in dismay as the unruly breasts disappeared south towards her waist again. "I might get dressed first though." She shimmied from the room with her back to the stranger, muttering to Emma as she passed, "Bloody Norma Nordstrom knew I wanted to be rolled in the rug. Gah, she's off my Christmas card list now!"

"Sit, Mrs Andreyev." The tall man sank into an armchair in front of the sliding doors, the light from behind him coming across the balcony and setting his white hair on fire. He held his hand out to indicate his vacated spot on the sofa and Emma sat with great reluctance.

"Why do I suspect I'm not going to like what I hear?" she asked.

He smiled, a familiar expression that tugged at something deep in Emma's soul, clamouring for recognition. "Because I'm told you're a realist," he replied.

"Who are you?" A wave of confusion began in the pit of her stomach and worked its way up into her throat.

The man half stood and held out his hand. "Winston Wright," he said. "It's nice to meet you."

Chapter 44

E mma yanked her hand back and stood, in one fluid motion. "Where's my husband?"

The man smiled, self-assured and confident of his status as the Alpha male. "All in good time," he said.

"Fine!" Emma stood. "I'll just call the cops." She reached for Freda's phone on the sideboard and the man stayed seated, watching her with apparent calm. The handset appeared dead and Emma bashed the dashboard a few times, panic rising into her heart.

"Don't be silly, Emma." Freda appeared behind her dangling the cord. "I've unplugged it from the wall in the hallway. Listen to what the man has to say and then we'll make decisions about what needs to happen. Rohan's one of his clients."

"He made the complaint about Rohan!" Emma squeaked. "Maybe he's the one holding him prisoner." She gripped her stomach as the child elbowed her in the bladder and Freda and Winston Wright exchanged looks.

"I hope that's not true," Freda warned him. "I have access to weapons, Mr Wright and I know how to use them all."

"Sit, please," Winston said, ignoring Freda and taking Emma's arm to lead her to the sofa. "Call the police if you wish, but first, let me speak."

"You owe him that, Emma," Freda said, cocking her head to one side. "He was Alanya's last victim. At least hear him out. If he's not the lovely man from our book club, I'll hit him with the rolling pin while you sit on him. But first, I'll make some tea."

Emma sat on the cushion and listened to Freda bustling around in the kitchen with kettle and china cups. A spoon skittered across the work surface, breaking the silence with its high, metallic ring. The man said nothing, watching Emma with piercing intensity and she began to join the dots of her jumbled puzzle, slotting things into place. Winston watched with an expression of pride. "He said you were a smart girl," he breathed as Emma's eyes widened. "You're smart and beautiful and I didn't expect him to be right on both counts." Winston settled back in his armchair, long legs bent at the knees and his ankles crossed.

"You said Alanya gave you something for me," Emma said, her voice sullen in the quiet room. "What is it?"

Winston sat forward, leaning his elbows on his knees. His blue eyes sparkled. "She did. I have a story to tell first," he replied. Emma's nose wrinkled, but the man persevered, ignoring her unpleasant sneer. "I met a most talented and beautiful ballerina when I was a much younger man and attended a performance at the Bolshoi Theatre in Moscow. She was stunning with white blonde hair and the bluest eyes I'd ever seen. She danced like a sprite and captivated my attention. I was a rich businessman and that fact gained me access to most of the things I wished to acquire. In a poverty stricken Soviet Union where scientists were reduced to washing dishes to pay for bread, money was king. Alanya Romanov fell into the category of conquests and whilst she was innocent and sincere, I looked upon her as another trinket in my treasure box. We began a romance and she became pregnant."

"That's awful!" Emma put her hand over her mouth and shrank back from the man. "Why are you telling me this?"

"Because it was Alanya's wish for you to understand," he said, his voice gentle despite the callousness of his tale. "I don't care if you hate me, but try not to be too harsh on her." Winston resettled himself and licked his lips before continuing. "Alanya disclosed her pregnancy and asked for help. Russian officials were in the process of asset stripping to cope with their growing debt and the need to provide aid to silence the masses. The KGB proved instrumental in that task. More of my associates began to disappear and I was keen not to join them in the labour camps of Siberia or buried in an unmarked grave. I arranged a fake British passport for myself and Alanya, intending to take her with me when I left."

Emma shook her head. "You expect me to believe that you moved from love rat to hero in how long? A week, month, year?"

Winston cocked his head and stared at Emma. "My relationship with Alanya began in 1980 and I defected in 1988, by which time we were very much more than casual lovers." The vibrant blue eyes narrowed and stared into Emma's soul. She swallowed, shifting in her seat at the intensity of the stare and knowing exactly who Winston Wright was.

"Alanya did not arrive at the agreed place and I left without her, not realising she collapsed and went to the hospital. Once I reached Britain, I sent word to her but the Iron Curtain sealed closed behind me and she never received it. Alone and pregnant, knowing her dancing days would soon be over, she formed an alliance with Davidov Andreyev and they married. I did not see Alanya for another six years when quite by chance she attended a political luncheon hosted by a friend of mine in London. Her husband was a diplomat working with the Russian Embassy and I was eager to hear news of my child. The first time I met my son, he was almost six years old. He looked me up and down as though I represented some complicated mathematical problem and it became my personal mission to ensure that I made up for the missing six years of parenting he'd endured."

"He had a father!" Emma said. "A father, two brothers and a sister!"

Winston Wright nodded. "He did. Although only one younger brother believed living at the time. I flushed money into my son's education with tutoring behind the scenes and he visited me in Scotland at decent intervals as though I was a distant uncle taking an interest. Davidov Andreyev ploughed on with his political ambitions and Alanya followed behind, riddled with gratitude for his rescue of her in her hour of need. He was a good man by all accounts and continued the pretence of parenthood until the day he died."

Winston's eyes narrowed and he shook his head. "Alanya disappeared. Gone, just like that. It took me five years to find her by which time my son had reached fourteen. Another man replaced me in his affections and it proved an impossible task to win him back." Winston pointed with a slender finger at the centre of Emma's chest and she felt the atmosphere shift, even from her safe distance. "I observed him with you and knew it wouldn't end well. I forbade him from entering into a relationship with you, so imagine my dismay when I discovered he'd disobeyed. He swore he loved you and I had no choice but to warn his mother. Alanya reacted badly and I've had time to regret the course of action she took in bullying such a young, motherless girl. When Rodney Harrington died I offered Alanya marriage and she refused. Something had changed in her by then, some dark, latent spirit peered through her eyes and to my shame, I concentrated on my own son, securing his education and teaching him the skills he would require in business. His school telephoned me on the day he was scheduled to sit the Oxbridge exam which would guarantee him a place at either Oxford or Cambridge University. He hadn't turned up."

Emma nodded. "He enlisted in the army," she said. "I remember the upset."

Winston shook his head. "My beautiful, clever son; cannon fodder for the British army; that same nation which unpicked mine with a gold nibbed pen and a dirty thank you." Hatred poured from his voice. "I've never been so angry or disappointed."

Emma shook her head to clear the haze as Freda laid a tea tray between them on the coffee table. "Tell me where my husband is!"

Emma snapped, her patience at an end. Her brown eyes blazed with fury. "I don't want to listen to this rubbish. I want my husband."

Winston put his hand out for the tea which Freda poured, but Emma stood and backed away. "I'm calling the cops," she said. "You're holding him against his will and you can't do that."

Winston sipped too hot tea and blinked several times in surprise. "I'm certainly not holding him against his will," he said, his voice calm. "He's not happy with me, but he could leave any time."

"Why doesn't he then?" Emma shouted. She balled her fists in front of her. "Why isn't he here?" Her hand strayed to her stomach again as fear budded like a rose in her chest. "I need him," she said, willing her voice not to break.

"The Financial Reporting Council and Scotland Yard's Serious Fraud Office is bearing down on your building, even as we speak." Winston stirred sugar into his tea and sipped again, nodding in satisfaction. "It's in my son's best interests to not be there when they arrive."

"Why?" Emma backed up until her bum touched the sideboard and she heard the china inside rattle.

Winston placed his cup in its saucer with care. "Because the actuaries who rent the office space in the same building have been playing a dangerous game. They've systematically defrauded millions of pounds from unsuspecting businesses who relied on their figures to make bad decisions."

Emma pictured Jed Smith and the noxious Stephanie and shrugged. "So? There are good actuaries and bad ones, just like any profession."

Freda looked at Winston for clarification and Emma waited while he bit into a cookie from a side plate next to him. He took his time, enjoying the attention and Emma took a step forward, barely resisting the urge to slap the biscuit from his hand. Freda got there first, snatching it with expert reflexes and leaving the man staring at his empty fingers. "You asked to speak to my friend, not torture her! Now tell her what she wants to know and then leave her alone, you young gigolo, you!"

Emma opened her mouth and closed it again, staring at the white haired pensioner in surprise. But with more than two decades between Winston and Freda, the description was perfectly logical to her. Winston Wright sat back in the chair and stared at his empty fingers in disappointment. "The other actuarial firm in the building is owned by a large corporate which specialises in buying up struggling companies and ripping the guts out of them. They liquidate, strip the assets and sell them off to the competition."

"But that's illegal." Emma took a step forward and Winston nodded and held out his hand for the cookie.

"Exactly. And a little chat with the Serious Fraud Office let them know where to look a few months ago. The trickiest part was keeping my son out of it. As one of his clients it was a simple matter to lodge a complaint to the Council and let them investigate. I knew they'd turn his documentation inside out and he'd be exonerated before the real trouble started."

"Did he know it was you?" Emma asked, remembering how perplexed Rohan was and hoping he hadn't drawn her into another pretence. "I was worried sick!"

Winston chuckled and accepted the cookie, nibbling on a rounded edge with a look of glee on his face. "He didn't know what it was about until my men paid him a visit which I believe you witnessed. Then he was angry, but not unamenable to the prospect of disappearing for a while."

"Did your men pay the friend in Harborough for his address and follow us through London?" Emma asked, her tone accusing.

"No." Winston's eyes narrowed and his white brows formed a single line across his forehead. "My men think it was a crappy investigator employed by the corporate attempting to frame my son for their own ends. It would've made a neat conclusion for them to shift the blame away from their own puppets."

"Why do you do that?" Emma demanded, putting her hands on her hips.

"Do what?" Freda swivelled her head around to stare at Emma in confusion. "What do you mean?"

Emma stared at Winston Wright through eyes filled with determination and anger. "*He* knows."

Winston smiled and wagged his finger at Emma. "You really are sharp, devotchka," he said, struggling to contain his mirth.

"I don't get it." Freda creaked forwards and tugged up her falling stocking.

"You haven't said my husband's name yet. So, say it!" Emma gritted her teeth. "Say your son's name."

Winston sat up and folded his arms. "Алексей Oskar? Is that what you wish to hear, young lady? Alexei; that is my son's name."

Emma balled her fists. "He's Rohan," she said, her voice a low hiss. "Rohan Andreyev. Say his real name!" Maureen's warning about not speaking to Myles Oskar came too late to save her.

"I will not. But no matter." Winston stood, towering over her and Freda. "He came to me when the army returned him broken and ruined. Our relationship is strong."

Emma's eyes widened as the plummy English veneer faded and she caught the cadence of a Slav accent lurking in the background. Winston leaned in towards her face and his voice was a low whisper. "I will defend Alexei to the death and you do well to remember that, Emma Harrington. Lately he's attracted too much attention with his antics and I find your presence makes him sloppy. I've disposed of both potential problems the same way; the first outside your pile of bricks and the other outside his. He has two identities and always has, one the Russian of his mother and the stand-in father she produced and the other; my gift to him." He reached the door before Emma remembered his promise and stopped him, her voice straining with emotion.

"What did Alanya leave with you for safekeeping?" she asked. "What was it?"

Winston stopped and turned, putting a hand into his inside pocket. Freda's eyes grew wide and she reached for a sharp knife sitting on the nearby kitchen counter and hid it behind her back. "She wanted you to have this," he said. "I don't know what it is, but she wanted you to have it."

"When did she give it to you?" Emma spat. "In prison?"

Winston snorted with disdain. "No, Mrs Andreyev." He said her surname with a look of arrogant disgust on his lips. "I didn't visit her there; I was busy recovering in hospital from the mysterious dose of poison she fed me the last time I saw her. She handed it to me then, just before dessert."

Emma took the envelope without touching his fingers and held her breath until the front door clicked behind him. Then she exhaled. Freda gripped Emma's upper arm and gave it a shake. "I'm sorry. I didn't know he was fake. I should've guessed he wasn't reading the books but turning up to the club to make trouble. What a mean man; poor Rohan to have him as a father. What's in the envelope, dear? Open it."

Emma ripped open the envelope and pulled out a photocopy of the documents she'd found in her father's wooden box. Alanya's final blow was the knowledge contained in the damaging paperwork. Freda's face tried to peer over the top, raking the words with her rheumy eyes. "What is it?" she demanded. "Is it a sorry letter for the misery she caused you?"

Emma swallowed and her eyes filled with tears. "No, Freda. I can't believe I fell for that rubbish she fed me, pretending she loved me but I'd rejected her. None of it was true." She ran a shaking hand through her hair, finding it difficult to keep still. She sped to the kitchen and yanked open a drawer. Freda shrieked as Emma lit a match and set fire to the papers, burning them in the sink.

"The smoke alarm!" the old lady yelled, hauling open the patio doors onto the deck and waving her arms around.

"I hate her," Emma sobbed. "I bloody hate her."

The offending papers burned in the sink as black smoke kissed a pyre of misery. Emma slid down the cupboard and sank onto her bottom, screwing herself into a ball and burying her face in her knees.

Chapter 45

A cruel wind whipped up Freda's tweed skirt as over two hundred frail and elderly folk milled about on the pavement outside the apartment block. Traffic heated up on Northampton Road as rush hour approached and sensible people dashed home before the roads clogged. "You don't have to stay," Freda said, hugging herself and drawing the crinkly emergency blanket around herself. She looked like a thin, silver chocolate bar in sparkly wrapping and the blanket made rustling noises as she moved. It was echoed by the other two hundred crackling around the shoulders of the residents as they waited for the all clear.

Emma shook her head, her eyes puffy from crying. "I'll take the blame and pay for the fire vehicles. It was my fault."

Freda squeezed her icy arm and shook her head. "Do you want me to ask the paramedics for a blanket for you? You didn't grab your coat." At Emma's silence, Freda lifted a corner of hers and shrouded them both, putting her frail arm around Emma's shoulder. "I'm so sorry for letting that awful man near you," she sighed. "I had no idea he wasn't who he pretended to be. Gosh, I nearly let him roll me in the rug last Wednesday!" She shot a sideways look at Emma, guilt sparkling her rheumy blue eyes. "Apart from the rotten first meeting with your father-in-law, I know there's something else wrong. I wish you'd tell me what it is. What were the papers, dear?"

Emma's chest heaved and she swallowed, unable to answer. Her eyes filled with tears again and she shuffled her feet as though desperate to bolt, but reluctant to barrel over the sweet old lady who gripped her shoulder for dear life. "I just want Rohan," she managed through her tears. "Why did you let that nasty old man speak to me?"

"He visited Alanya." Freda's face crumpled with the weight of guilt. "I thought he'd be able to give you some answers. I'm sorry."

Emma nodded and let Freda grip her cold hand. "It's fine," she said, brushing away fallen tears and turning her face away from the group. "Forget it."

"It's a false alarm; you can all go back inside now!" the fire chief shouted, standing on a car bumper and using his gloved hands to amplify his voice. The multitudes drifted back inside like a reverse tide and the warden helped them in, casting frightened glances back towards the amassed testosterone in fire suits.

"Will it be expensive?" she called over her shoulder.

"No, it's fine; no charge," the fire chief shouted back and gave her a half salute. The warden heaved a visible sigh of relief and helped a lady indoors in a wheelchair.

Emma watched as the chief made a bee line for her and Freda, readying herself to face his wrath and wondering why he didn't do it in front of the warden. She stiffened her upper body and tried not to look so pitiful and broken. The man was in his thirties, dark haired and handsome and Emma had a moment of appreciation as he strutted towards them with purpose. Freda jabbed Emma in the ribs. "Say nothing," she hissed.

"Hey, Aunty Freda," the chief said, his smile widening to a grin. "How are ya?"

"Good thanks, Andrew," she replied, placing a butter-wouldn't-melt look on her face. The fire chief bent to kiss her cheek and Freda's face crinkled with pleasure. She tugged his arm and tightened her grip on Emma. "This is my favourite niece's little boy," she said, giving Emma a wink. "He knows what a silly old lady I am, don't you Andrew?"

The fire chief looked from one to the other and his brow furrowed. "You know what I'm gonna say, don't you?"

Freda widened her eyes. "No, dear."

The fire chief sighed. "The smoke alarm which triggered the call is based in your kitchen, Aunty. What were you doing?"

Emma swallowed and opened her mouth, lurching sideways as Freda wobbled. It took a moment for Emma to realise that the old lady was standing on one leg, trying to kick her shin. A mixture of horror and indignation overrode her need for confession. Freda covered her imbalance by holding the back of her hand to her forehead. "Oh, I've come over all faint."

The emergency blanket slid to the floor of the car park as the handsome fire chief bent his knees and scooped up the old woman, hoisting her up against his chest. A look of pure delight filled Freda's face. As the fireman headed towards the front doors, Emma held back, desperate to end her dreadful afternoon with an immediate escape. She groaned as the man swung his body around half way across the car park and Freda spoke from his embrace. "Come on, Emma. Andrew and his men are coming in for afternoon tea." She grinned and her top set of dentures came loose and crashed down on the bottom ones.

Emma shook her head. "No, thanks. I need to get home." She backed away, wishing a hole would open up in the ground and suck her in. While she felt responsible enough for the evacuation to confess her part in it, entertaining a few truckloads of handsome firemen with her eyes like peeled onions was worse than any possible punishment.

"Come on, dear." Freda's beckoning finger forced Emma to cross the distance between them and follow the fireman's neat backside through the foyer, into the lift and up to Freda's floor. The wily old lady pointed to the hearthrug on her ride through the sitting area. "Much better than a roll in a rug," she mouthed to Emma. They overtook several of the shambling mounds of woolly jumpers and baggy trousers pushing zimmers or wielding sticks and arrived at Freda's front door in record time.

Emma dodged the fireman as he struggled to detach Freda from his chest and plant her in a chair. She seemed quite happy to cling around his neck like a monkey, her grip proving surprisingly difficult to release. While he struggled, Emma inspected the sink, relieved to see only the water splashes where she'd flushed the last of the ash down the plug hole as Freda argued with the warden about not wanting to go outside in the cold. Emma had sighed at the sight of the warden's face as Freda declared she'd rather die in a burning building than stand in the same car park as Norma Nordstrom.

"It's all fine in here," she said, working on a look of innocence and cracking open the kitchen window.

The fireman's face creased into a grin as he managed to flip Freda onto her back on the sofa where she lay flailing like a turtle. "Only because one of you flushed the evidence," he said, his face serious. Emma swallowed and opened her mouth to confess.

"She knows nothing," Freda shouted, righting herself and hauling her skirt back over her knees. "I wanted you to meet my friend, Emma," she said, distracting the fireman. "I rarely get to see you nowadays and I wanted your approval."

"What for? Are you marrying her?" Andrew asked, going up in Emma's estimation for his ability to induce humour under stress. He winked at Emma and she smiled, feeling a jerk on her heart strings as she recognised that same x-factor which Christopher Dolan exhibited.

"No!" Freda chortled, covering her mouth with her palm to stop her teeth flying out. "But I wouldn't mind pairing you off with Emma."

Emma exhaled, wondering at what point her marriage to Rohan had ceased to matter to Freda. Andrew saved her the bother of retorting. "Well, you don't have to burn your flat down to achieve it. At least this is better than last time." He glanced across at Emma. "Last week she got some poor old bloke's electric wheelchair stuck at the top of the fire escape and the week before that she used a blow torch to brown off a dessert and melted a plastic bread board in the communal room."

Freda looked proud of her achievements, patting the man's hand and peering into the hallway. "Where are your friends?" she said, fluttering her eyelids and affecting a pout.

"Downstairs waiting for me," he said, kissing her lightly on the cheek. "The trucks from Northampton are out on a call and we're on standby. If you've got any more of those nice chocolate chip cookies, I'll take them out for the guys. I'm sure they'll appreciate them."

Freda scooted into the kitchen and Emma listened to a lid being prised from a metal tin. An awkward silence engulfed the lounge as the fireman eyed Emma with something like interest. "Would you be interested in dinner?" he asked.

Emma swallowed and shook her head. "I'm a lesbian; sorry to mislead you. Freda can't get over it."

The man pulled a face and Emma felt pleased to read it as disappointment. "Never mind then," he said. "You're better than the last few she's lined up for me. One of them carried her own defibrillator and Aunty swore blind she'd go the distance."

"She just wants everyone to have what she did with John Ayers," Emma said, keeping her voice low.

The fireman nodded and smiled at the sight of Freda standing on the cookie tin to get it closed. "She's an accident waiting to happen," he groaned and made his farewells, depositing Freda on the floor and snatching up the cookie tin. "Cheers Aunty," he called as he closed the front door behind him and Emma listened to heavy, asbestos lined boots clumping along the hallway towards the lifts.

Freda emerged from the kitchen looking disappointed. "Oh, I felt sure he'd go for you," she said, wrinkling her nose.

"Thanks!" Emma snapped. "Everyone else thinks Rohan's dead but I at least hoped you believed me."

"Oh, I think he's alive and well and holed up somewhere, just like his father said he was," Freda replied. "But that doesn't make him any good for you. That family's brought nothing but misery to you, Emma. Perhaps it's time to think of yourself and your children."

Emma channelled the betrayal through her eyes, putting her hands on her hips and regaining some of her fire. "What happened to the sanctity of marriage? You're the Christian here and yet you're telling me to get rid of my husband!"

Freda smiled, the wily look established back in her face. "No, dear. I'm telling you to choose. Get on with your marriage and dump the past, or leave. Those are your choices and they're very clear."

Emma held her breath. "There's no way you could've read those papers; not that quickly."

Freda blinked and pulled her glasses down further on her nose, peering over them. "I saw enough," she said in a whisper. "School teachers learn to read at speed. Upside down is my speciality."

Emma nodded. "I just need to talk to Rohan," she said, pleading.

"They can't always make it better, Emma," Freda said and her voice held the wisdom of bitter experience. "We demand it of them, but we can't complain when they're unable to deliver."

"I know," Emma replied. "I'm aware he can't sort this out, but I still need to hear myself say the words." Her chin wobbled with the effort of not crying and she closed her eyes against swirling emotions which made her chest wall feel lined with brick.

"Oh, dear, dear, dear," Freda sighed, rubbing her gnarled hand up and down Emma's forearm. "People tell me the world's more messed up than it used to be but I often find that hard to believe. You've only got to look in the bible to see what a disappointment the human race has been right from the start. Adam and Eve messed it up within the first generation and it was downhill from then on." She smiled at Emma and something of her former beauty crossed through as her noble heritage shone in her eyes. "Your Russian will turn up soon," she said. "And when he does, promise me you'll sit down and have a good hard look at where you're headed. You're both building on sand, Emma. If someone doesn't get the drill out and start making decent foundations soon, you'll both be washed away."

Emma nodded, coupling it with a shrug. "But where do we start?"

"At the beginning," Freda answered. "Like any good love story. It's like making cookies, Emma. You mix the butter, sugar and flour and it tastes good. If it doesn't stop tasting delicious when someone tells you the flour was really salt and the butter was candle wax, then all you've done is discovered a new cookie recipe. Rohan's the same person you believed him to be last week or this morning, so if you still love him and he still loves you, why sue the baker?"

Emma breathed out a laugh. "I'm sure your brain's gone and we're the fools for not noticing," she said with a smile. She snatched her coat from the sofa and rolled her eyes as Freda smirked. "And what's with being so desperate to pair off that poor fireman, anyway?"

"His mother's frantic," Freda said, padding after her to the front door. "She thinks he's gay."

"He's not!" Emma snorted. "He's disillusioned with women and at a guess, needs time to heal from something painful. Leave him alone, poor guy. He needs to find his own Mrs Right." The expression reminded her of Rohan's father and she paused, the haunted look returning. Her voice sounded wistful as she turned to leave and wrapped her arms around Freda. "At least I know what name the Falkirk house is in now," she said, walking out into the corridor and heading for the lifts. "Alexei Oskar," she murmured, trying the name on her tongue and feeling a resonance she hadn't expected.

Chapter 46

♥

Christopher sat on the front steps with his knees apart, examining the ground beneath his shoes. He seemed set on his task until Emma ground her car through the gravel and pulled up next to him. The Irishman took a slow, lazy drag on the cigarette between his fingers and blew out a line of smoke, his dark eyes smouldering and sexy. "I thought you gave up." Emma slammed the car door and locked it, glancing at Allaine's truck parked further along. She was so eager to please Emma; she'd left her the spot right in front of the main steps.

"I've given up a lot of things in my time," Christopher mused. He took a longer drag and let the smoke roll around in his mouth before exhaling. He flicked ash from the end of the cigarette, making the action look seductive. "But some things are harder to give up than others."

Emma nodded and left him to his regrets, climbing the steps next to him. As she levelled, he stuck out an arm almost tripping her and jerked his head towards the step. "Sit down," he commanded.

"I don't want to," she said, chewing her lower lip and ignoring the slow drawling accent which made her want to do whatever he ordered. "You're meant to have left on today, remember?"

"Aye, well, I don't care what you want," he said and pulled on her lower leg. "So, sit yerself down."

Emma heaved out a grumble of protest and allowed herself to collapse onto the cold stone next to Christopher. She left an appropriate distance between them and saw the look of pain on his face. "Rohan's not dead," she said, listening to the sound of crows cawing in the paddock nearest the house. The cacophony of noise amped up the pressure in her head and she closed her eyes to negate its effect on her vision. "He communicated with Nicky."

"Why'd you run?" he asked, hurt in his brown eyes. "I told you I'd take care of yous and yer ran."

Emma shook her head. "Nicky overheard you say it and it's not what he wanted. It's not what either of us want. I can't seem to get through to you that it's Rohan or nobody; it always has been."

Christopher shook his head. "The night I waited on the tables at the actuaries' dinner, I had seven phone numbers pushed into my back pocket before I'd finished serving the entrée." He took another drag of his cigarette and blew the smoke away from Emma. "The only person in the room I wanted, didn't even look my way." Christopher pulled a strand of tobacco away from his lower lip and stared at it on his finger as though waiting for it to wiggle away. When it didn't, he wiped it on his jeans.

Emma smiled and thumped him on the shoulder. "Maureen's already got your phone number, Irish. I think she's waiting for you to call her."

Christopher didn't laugh, his dark hair flipping into his eyes and a rash of stubble gracing his chin. In the glare of the porch light he could've been a model posing for some photo shoot dedicated to handsome but ruthless sex symbols. "I told you I loved you and you ran away from me." He flicked the cigarette butt onto the step and crushed it under his shoe. "I've never told anyone I loved them before."

"Sorry," Emma breathed. "I don't know what to tell you. You feel like a brother to me, a bloody gorgeous brother, but in that category."

Christopher raised his eyebrows. "Well, Rohan was yer brother so there's hope for me yet."

Emma opened her mouth in horror and elbowed him. "Don't be cruel; I don't make a habit of hypothetical incest!"

He laughed then and shook his head. "I don't know what you want from me, Em. I don't want to be here hanging around yer feet like a bloody spaniel but I can't seem to leave either. I tried and it hurt like hell."

"Oh, Christopher Dolan," Emma sighed and ruffled his hair. "You're a complete conundrum."

Christopher pursed his lips, revealing attractive dimples buried in the designer stubble. He kept his head down but Emma sensed him rallying as his humour returned and he gave it one last try. "If Rohan doesn't come back by de end of de month," he said, his accent exaggerated on purpose. "Would ya consider shaggin' another brother?"

Emma inhaled and raised her hand to slap him, but Christopher's reflexes were far quicker. He jumped to his feet and skipped away down the stairs and headed to Emma's car. As he unlocked it and put the driver's seat back to accommodate his long legs, Emma grappled in her pockets realising he'd snagged the keys while she was distracted. He blew her a kiss as her car revved and spun in a neat circle, disappearing through the stable yard and heading for the folly a few miles across the bumpy lane, headlights bouncing against the darkening landscape.

Chapter 47

♥

He limped up the driveway four days later as though he'd never been away; the gate sliding closed behind him.

Emma knew he'd return as soon as the news broke that Scotland Yard had raided a building in London, believed to be the offices of a firm engaged in a financial fraud of epic proportions. The newsreader on the teatime broadcast stood outside the familiar brick building with her microphone, burbling away with her accounts of hearsay and speculation as Emma watched police officers carry out computers and boxes filled with records and files.

"The pensions underwriter for Andover Finance toppled yesterday bringing the pound crashing to its knees on the stock market. A series of questionable decisions by the trustees last year led to a hostile takeover by a finance company. Several leaked documents found their way into the possession of the Serious Fraud Office at the start of the year and the subsequent investigation began. A covert operation was mounted, indicating the scale of the fraud which is thought to stretch across three continents." A gust of wind fluffed the woman's hair and Emma saw her wince with vain discomfort and worry about how she might appear to the British public, as they gorged on their dinners across the nation and took little notice.

With courage and a valiant flick of her hair which sent her blond curls across her lips like a moustache, the newsreader continued her on-the-spot report as Jed Smith appeared in the background, sandwiched between two police officers wearing body armour. "A sting carried out this morning placed the culprits in custody, although Scotland Yard is not commenting at this time. A press conference is set for later on this evening and we'll be back with you then." The woman smiled as her hair swiped mahogany lipstick across her cheek and the producers cut back to the newsroom, where talking heads dissected the crisis.

Emma sat on the window seat in the sitting room, watching her husband's steady progress along the half mile hike, thinking of all the dedicated men and women whose pension contributions amounted to a big fat nothing through another's greed. Rohan limped up the driveway with his hands stuffed deep in his pockets. He looked more cross than tired; a bear kept in a small cage for far too long. She knew she should run to meet him, playing the dutiful wife and calling his name from the top step, but anger stopped her. He'd left her to fend for herself in a strange metropolis and even though her rational mind knew he couldn't help it; anger dictated he should have done something.

Chewing her lip, Emma pondered another problem as Rohan's pronounced limp twisted his body with each tired step. He struggled that way when exhausted and she felt a modicum of compassion spark into her chest, dulling the anger. But which name should she call him if she met him on the front steps? Rohan or Alexei? Clearly he answered to both. Her own agonies mirrored his, something she'd struggled with for the last week and she'd gotten no closer to discovering her own equilibrium than she suspected her husband had; even though he'd enjoyed far longer to get used to his multiple identities.

She intercepted Rohan on the front steps, watching as he rounded the bend at the top of the driveway and walked towards her. He took his hands from his pockets and studied her face, looking for some extreme of emotion which he would be forced to deal with. Emma's silence made him more unsettled than tears. "Hey," he said, standing at the bottom of the stairs, legs splayed and hands behind his back as though on parade. Only the slightest list to his right gave away the unlikelihood that would ever happen again.

"Hey." Emma folded her legs and sat on the top step, reminiscent of her conversation with Christopher a few nights ago in the same spot. She examined a hole in the toe of her sock as Rohan observed her with his clear blue eyes. Her husband chewed his bottom lip and Emma felt her baby move within its safe confines as she acknowledged the swell of love for her husband. The urge to skip down the steps into his arms took the place of awkwardness, but Emma's natural stubborn streak kept it in check. "You look tired," she said, running her heel over a nugget of gravel. "Did he make you walk home?"

Rohan wrinkled his nose and ran a hand over his beard and up through his hair. "Nyet. They dropped me at the gate." He looked back towards the main road in the distance where a car sat outside the gates, puffs of white exhaust fumes leaking from its rear. He lifted his left hand and offered a rude gesture to the man leaning against the bonnet and Emma watched the driver climb back into the vehicle and reverse out onto the road. Rohan returned his gaze to Emma, fixing his expression from scorn to apprehension. "How have you been?" he asked, his brow knitting for a fraction of a second before he resumed control again. It was as though a mask slipped before being shifted back in place.

"Good." Emma nodded. "Nicky and I had a few days away from here but we've been fine." She ran a hand over her belly. "The baby's kicking heaps, especially in the evenings."

Rohan's face creased into a smile and his eyes softened. "I want to feel that," he said. His lips twitched at the corners and he heaved out a sigh. "I've missed you, Mrs Andreyev."

"Then why did you let them take you?" Emma gritted her teeth, needing to ask.

Rohan shook his head and set his jaw, disbelief in his eyes. "Because your safety means more to me than my own. You're my wife, Emma, but you also make beautiful leverage."

Emma nodded and forced a smile onto her lips, wondering if she'd ever feel quite the same way about the name on her marriage certificate again.

Chapter 48

♥

Emma sat on the closed lid of the toilet and watched as Rohan moved around the bathroom naked. He braced his hands on the side of the shower and hopped over the sill, heading towards the plastic stool in the corner and sitting with an uncharacteristic heaviness. Reaching forward, he flicked on the water, braving the cold dousing in favour of a dry surface to move across. He growled under the freezing water but the greyness of his pallor began to wane. As the water heated, he leaned forward and adjusted it.

"We should install a wet room," Emma said, her tone conversational but her mind racing. "Do you think that's possible up here?"

Rohan shrugged, his voice echoing in the glass cubicle. "Probably not. We could do it downstairs."

"But then you'd need to either put your leg back on or use your crutches to get up to the bedroom," she replied, the impracticality irritating her.

"Chto?" Rohan said, spluttering in the spray as he shampooed his blond hair and pushed his head under the water.

"Nothing," Emma sighed. She watched him reach for the shower gel and miss, stretching his arm out further and tipping the plastic stool. Regret pricked at her heart for moving it after her own shower as though some part of her subconscious believed in his death.

She stood, stripping off her clothes in a frenzy of fumbling and hearing the sweat pants tear at the waist. Emma entered the shower naked and winced against the hot spray which covered her in seconds. Rohan looked up in surprise and despite the extreme tiredness in the set of his body, his eyes glinted with interest. Emma opened his left hand revealing the squirt of shower gel he'd managed to snag, running her fingers over the calloused palm and transferring the scented soap to her hand. "Who hurt you?"

Vibrant blue eyes stared up at her as she massaged Rohan's shoulders and leaned over to soap his back, feeling his hands grip her around the hips and his soft kisses dust her ribs. The corded muscle still ridged under her fingers but he felt thinner, less healthy and robust. Black bruises dotted Rohan's spine and the line of blood she'd spotted on his shirt came from a long scratch running from the back of his neck to his shoulder blade. The skin opened as her palms moved across it and she heard him hiss with pain as the soap entered the wound. "Sorry." Emma bent and scooped up the plastic jug under the stool, turning to fill it with water.

"No matter." Rohan's fingers caressed the swell of his unborn child, revelling in her pregnancy with a primeval joy in the tilt of his lips. "It was a familiar enemy, Emma."

"Your father? His name's not Winston Wright, is it?"

Rohan shook his head, his eyes widening in surprise. "It's best you know nothing, Emma. Promise you'll never speak to him again!" His fingers dug into her waist until she moved to release the pressure and Rohan bowed his head and rested his cheek against her hip.

"I won't willingly, I promise." Emma tipped the warm liquid along the line of the cut, flushing out the soap and sighing with relief at how pink and clean it looked as the water ran clear. "I remembered you visiting him as a teenager but only after he said." She swallowed. "You were always so quiet but after you'd been away, you were withdrawn in a different way."

Rohan's beard growth felt scratchy against Emma's skin as he busied himself with kissing her sensitive ribs and stomach and she reached for the shower gel again, washing his chest and tangling her finger ends in the downy blonde hair across his muscles. "You need a shave," she whispered, smoothing her palms up his neck to his chin and then caressing his cheeks. "I want my husband back."

Rohan smirked and his lips quirked upwards. "I'm here, dorogaya," he whispered. His arms snaked around her waist and he pulled her onto his knee, supporting her weight on his strong left leg.

"Are you?" she questioned, cocking her head on one side. "I don't know that you've ever been really here." She wanted to utter his other name, Alexei Oskar, but it caught in her chest and refused to be spoken. Instinct told her Rohan would not react well to hearing it from her lips. She searched his blue eyes, seeking revelation in their azure depths and knowing she would find only painful bedrock at the bottom. She saw his hand move higher in her peripheral vision, recognising the unmistakable line across his wrist from something sharp and metallic which had bitten into his flesh and left a spiteful welt. Her stomach quailed at the thought of Rohan kept prisoner and beaten, played with like any other captive held by sadists. It seemed so unlike everything she knew of him; the questions rolled through her mind unanswered but the look in his eyes made her suppress them for his good.

With a hand behind the back of her neck and water dripping from Emma's long dark curls, Rohan pulled her face to his, inhaling in shock as their joined mouths filled with water from the jet. Emma reached backwards and shoved the handle, shutting off the water and the distraction and stealing her husband back from Myles Oskar, using a weapon the severe man would never understand; love instead of violence.

Chapter 49

♥

The rhythmic movement of Rohan's fingers over the soft skin of Emma's bare shoulder created a soporific effect. She shifted closer to his body and pushed her nose into his armpit, inhaling the clean male scent of him in the big bed. He squirmed and she opened her eyes and sought his face in the darkness. "What?"

"I cracked a rib," he said. "I hate those guys; always have."

"Sorry," Emma whispered and relinquished some of her monkey grip on his torso. She took back the leg which crossed over him, her inner thigh resting over his and then changed her mind and put it back, desperate not to let him completely go. "I missed you," she said.

She heard him sniff in the darkness and kissed the pectoral muscle nearest her face. "Da. It's been a long week," he sighed.

"How did you cope with knowing your father wasn't Davidov Andreyev?" The question loaded itself up with emotion and Emma expected Rohan to rebuff her. It was late and tiredness coursed through his voice.

"Don't think I have," he said. "I liked my father. Perhaps parenthood is more than just biology."

"Do you feel him?" Emma tapped Rohan's sternum. "Your real father, do you feel him? Here."

Rohan sighed. "I don't know, devotchka. The father who meant most to me was Rodney Harrington. He spoke to me like an equal and took time to show and explain how to be an Englishman." Emma felt his neck tense as he frowned. "I grieve for him more than for a papa I rarely saw or one I do not know or understand."

"Nicky says he feels a connection to you in his chest," Emma whispered. "He knew you weren't dead." Her eyes wandered across to her dressing table where the red fire engine sat next to her hairbrush. Her idea of family connection had taken a beating in recent days.

Rohan nodded. "I feel that link as well. But it began when I met him; until then it wasn't there."

"Winston Wright said he gave you another nationality. He sounded quite proud."

Rohan's body shuddered with laughter and Emma lifted her head from his chest to peer at him, confusion on her face. "He's Serbian," he snorted. "If I try to use the citizenship he bestowed upon me, I'd be arrested in every airport in Europe. He's so out of touch, he thinks a Serbian passport is a ticket to liberty and respect."

Emma laid her head back on his chest and knitted her brow. Serbian was the one nationality she hadn't expected but the proud tilt of Winston's jaw and the distinct Roman nose gave him away. Rohan was a younger, fitter Slavic version with all of Alanya's grace and poise. Emma left the subject, sensing his displeasure with it.

"Do you know what happened in your office building?" she asked. "It's been all over the news. I didn't know if you'd seen any TV in Falkirk."

"Da." Rohan nodded. "I won't keep my business address there after this. It's best not to be associated with what went on. I think you should sell your interest in the building." He squeezed her and Emma snuffed out a laugh.

"Ok," she said. "Can you handle it for me?"

"If you insist," Rohan replied. "And yes, I watched TV in Falkirk. He kept me in the gatehouse at the entrance to the property. It was the furthest place he could take me at short notice without questions and it has enough room to land a helicopter."

"Could you not get away?" Emma asked. "I thought you could get out of anywhere."

"Da, I can," Rohan agreed. "But he knows about you now. Nothing is worth the risk to you and my children. It's in his interests to keep me alive and working as an actuary. It's part of his plan. I knew you'd be safe as long as I behaved, but I didn't expect him to seek you out and speak to you." Rohan sighed.

Emma shuddered as her mind strayed to the sinister Winston Wright and felt grieved that Rohan's sacrifice was for nothing. The man knew her, knew where to find and could access her or Nicky whenever he chose. Emma pushed the frightening thoughts away. "Why did you draw us to Falkirk? Why not just leave us hanging?"

Rohan turned to face her, his eyes filled with confusion. "I didn't draw you to Falkirk; that was the last thing I wanted."

"But you left your phone in the bathroom with the tracker on. Then someone killed the tracker and we thought you'd died or something."

Rohan shook his head. "Nyet. I'd never do that. Why draw the people I love into danger?"

Emma leaned up on one elbow. "But I've got your phone. You sent Nicky a message on a Google Doc saying you were ok."

"I wrote that when they let me use a garage restroom; for him to access on any device from anywhere." Rohan's eyes looked troubled. Then his expression fell into misery. "They confiscated the phone after a call from my father, realising I had two. Who retrieved the phone?"

"Frederik," Emma said. "What's wrong? And why didn't he check the gatehouse? That was remiss of him."

Rohan swallowed. "I'm not sure. I didn't see or hear them so I'm guessing they approached the house from the rear to avoid the builders. The gates are locked as it's a hard hat area while they demolish the damaged rooms and rebuild. It would be tactical to approach through the forest from the private lane. That's also sealed to the public but he'd get in without difficulty.. I'll speak with Frederik tomorrow. Why draw him up there? I fear my father's closing the parts of my life he can't control. Mikhail kept his influence at bay, but not anymore."

Emma settled back on his shoulder as he laid down, his mind working beneath a look of neutrality. She tried to engage with him again, to understand some small part of the last week. "What was the big thing the actuaries at the dinner had in play? The thing Christopher heard them plotting?"

Rohan shifted under her, tightening his grip around Emma's body. "They had an actuary in the Bank of England helping their cause," he replied. "That was the ultimate coup."

"Why did your father think you might be implicated?"

"Why wouldn't I be?" Rohan answered. "I work in the same building and the two companies often collaborate. When Jed Smith heard I was being investigated, he manoeuvred to dump some of his evidence on me. The examination by the FRC exonerated rather than implicated me and he foolishly didn't realise the main investigation had been going on for a while under his nose. He was the main investigation, not me."

"Did you know about it?" Emma asked and Rohan's head shifted the pillow as he nodded.

"Da, I knew one of the investigators."

"Really?" Emma sounded surprised. "But you seemed to be so lax about everything, so casual."

"I have nothing to hide. But an investigation of that magnitude would've suspended all my business activity and damaged the reputation of Rodney Harrington Actuarial Services indefinitely. It still may, just by association. If I removed myself from the building and declined further offers from them to provide a second opinion, I risked drawing attention to the investigation. No good actuary refuses work from a known source and they would've wondered why. I was asked to maintain a working relationship with them and that's what I did."

"Who told you about the investigation?" Emma asked, prodding Rohan in the ribs and then remembering his pain as he winced and moved away enough to chastise her.

"I sat next to the lead investigator at the dinner," Rohan said, grunting. "Please don't do that; it hurts."

"You reported Jed and Stephanie, didn't you?" Emma asked. "It was you."

Rohan's smile confirmed her suspicions. "I knew it was someone in their company but believed they were too stupid to follow through."

"You weren't wrong there." Emma rolled her eyes in the dim light. "But the investigators would never think you were involved, not if you were the whistle blower."

"Da, but my foolish father didn't know that." Rohan used the English term for his parent and Emma noticed the difference, the word sounding harsher than its Russian counterpart.

"Why did you pay the doorman?" Emma asked.

Rohan raised an eyebrow in surprise. "Very observant, Emma. I made sure we arrived on time and nobody followed us to the event. Therefore I knew the real fraudster would attend. The doorman was primed to let me know if anyone asked about me using either of my names. He sent one of the staff to speak to me at the bar and identified Jed Smith, who arrived after us, although his fake drunkenness intentionally suggested otherwise. The doorman confirmed I was there and Jed headed straight for us."

"You're a head taller than most of the people in that room. He didn't need to ask anyone."

"Da, but he's lazy and stupid. He wouldn't know whether to stay in the foyer or venture into the main room. He couldn't go in and out; it would look too obvious. A smart man would've figured it out but not Jed."

"Sorry. So you had everyone running around like headless chickens while you sat calmly and talked numbers all night to the undercover investigator."

"Da," Rohan said, rubbing at the space under his armpit. "He's a friend from university."

"So Winston Wright didn't need to strong arm you out of the way?"

"Nyet," Rohan replied. "I was angry when he reported me but couldn't tell him I would be ok. He wouldn't have listened to me anyway. He always knows best. His intention was to get my licence temporarily suspended and when that didn't happen, he panicked."

"Did you know it was him from the start?" Emma asked. "Is that why you weren't worried?"

Rohan kissed her temple. "Nyet, dorogaya. I didn't worry because I knew I wasn't guilty. The initial complaint was anonymous but in order for me to prove my defence, I needed to know which documents the complaint related to. I don't think he thought that would happen."

"So it was all just about money?" she sighed, her tone heavy. "Was Jed cleverer than you suspected?"

"Well, the Bank of England scam was a good one," Rohan admitted. "Having someone inside to pull the right strings and move suspicion around when people asked questions was ingenious. But it wasn't Jed Smith's idea, devotchka. This is way beyond his capabilities. My guess is that he got sucked in when someone uncovered a minor misdeed on his part; probably due to sloppiness rather than intentional deception."

"Blackmail?"

"Da," Rohan confirmed. "Has to be."

Emma nodded, her hair feeling tight against his chest and she inhaled, unhappiness in every pore. The memory of the smouldering documents bearing the Bank of England crest made her heave a sigh of relief. She wrinkled her brow. "Winston

Wright knows about this house, doesn't he? Your father killed the Chinaman at the gate. Why?"

"An overzealous sense of protectiveness, he would have me believe," Rohan replied, his voice betraying a tiredness which leaked from his bones. "He got some of his goons to follow me before Christmas and when I spent time here, he guessed I'd involved myself with you and did some digging. It didn't take long to discover your identity or our connection. Our brief separation confused him but by then his men had already killed The Contessa's messenger. My father knew about my issues with the Triads but I doubt his command was given without an ulterior motive."

"He wouldn't snatch Nicky would he?" Emma asked, her voice tight with worry.

"Nyet," Rohan replied, the answer given with an ease and speed which offered comfort. He snorted with laughter. "My natural inquisitive nature and need to uncover every last detail drove him crazy; Nicky would send him self-checking into a psychiatric unit."

Emma smiled until she remembered the other mysterious death, the man killed in a hit and run outside the Falkirk house. "He said he took care of both problems. Who was the second man? Frederik heard on the radio that his description fitted you, but his feet were way smaller."

"No, idea," Rohan said. He winced. "And not much chance of clarity now."

Emma sighed but any sense of peace remained blocked by the other thing on her mind. "Rohan," she whispered, the burden in her heart too heavy not to release and share the weight. "Are you too tired to deal with something for me?"

"Never," he said, grunting as he turned towards her. "I'm not too tired to listen to you." He drew back his top lip in a wistful smile as his fingers ran up her neck and cradled her cheek. "What's wrong, devotchka?"

She swallowed, her mouth dry and her pulse quickening. "I looked in the bureau in the London house and found a box in a hidden drawer. I have a memory of my dad showing me the same box as a little girl and knowing there was something he needed to say. Inside the box were papers." Her voice caught and Rohan stroked her cheek, brushing away falling tears as they tumbled over the bridge of her nose and plopped onto the pillow between them.

"Tell me," he whispered.

Emma's chest locked and went into a painful spasm, leaving her gasping for breath as the full awfulness of the revelation hit her like a train. She couldn't speak; the memory of her parents' short but gentle love overriding everything else. Emma cried, a series of undignified squeaks and hiccoughs through which Rohan held her until the worst was over. She laid in his arms as the involuntary shaking and jarring of her lungs subsided to isolated jerks of her body and she forced away the images of their kind, grateful faces. "They adopted me," she whispered, her voice rising and falling without control. "I found my birth certificate in the box with the adoption paperwork."

She heard Rohan tut and exhale, the stroking of the back of her head resuming in long, gentle movements infused with sympathy and compassion. Emma sniffed, her chest burning with the pressure of keeping it in. "I have an older brother," she said, her sentence punctuated by a jerk from her chest. "They adopted him out first but the couple wouldn't take me."

"Why?" Rohan asked, disbelief in his voice.

"The paperwork says I was sick," she whispered. "What could've been wrong with me, Ro? What if it was bad and I've still got it?"

Rohan kissed her hot forehead and soothed her with his hands. "You're perfect," he breathed. "It would've been nothing; don't do this to yourself, Em."

"But my own parents didn't want me and nor did the ones who took my brother." The hysteria leaked back into her voice. "And then your mother hated me." The tears began again and Rohan crushed her to his chest, her face and hair damp. "Remember what she always called me? Kukushka. It means cuckoo and we thought it was after that Russian film but it wasn't. Do you see now? She knew I was a cuckoo she'd got lumbered with."

"Emma, stop!" he ordered, his voice harsh. "Don't go down that ulitsa. It's a road to nowhere but sadness."

Emma wrestled her hands free and heard her husband hiss with pain, forcing herself to relax against his grip. "But what will I do?" she begged. "Who am I?"

Rohan put his hands either side of her face and pressed his lips to her forehead. "You're the very capable mother of Nikolai Andreyev and the beautiful wife of Rohan Andreyev. My brother adored you enough to employ a man to watch over you in my negligence and left his entire fortune in your hands. You are who you are, devotchka. You're ours and we love you."

Emma nodded and pushed her face into Rohan's neck, hating the hitch of her chest which revealed her misery, even as she fought to suppress it. The ache began and spread out in a knot of pain as though something had been torn from her being. Somewhere in the world a man of twenty-six shared her DNA, pulling and tugging on the link as he went about his business, perhaps oblivious to her existence.

Or not.

The next novel in this series is
The Heart of The Actuary.

The Heart of The Actuary

♥

Sample Chapter

Emma Andreyev clutched her daughter tighter, fearing her trembling hands might drop the tiny body to smash on the hard floor. "I need to fetch my son from school." A mistimed swallow cut her sentence in half.

"Then you'd better organise something." The security guard folded his arms and spread his legs, the stance intended to intimidate Emma. "Because the cops are on their way. This store doesn't tolerate thieving, lady."

Humiliation sent an unhealthy flush spreading from her chest to the roots of her hair. She'd stolen nothing since the sandwich which fed her starving belly on her sixteenth birthday. The sympathetic shop owner caught her and compounded her shame by offering her a chocolate bar to add to her meagre meal. The items clung like ash to her throat, and she vowed to starve in the future.

Her gaze flicked to the doorway and the guard turned his body to study whatever caught her interest. He shifted enough to block the open door, and the flash of determination in his gimlet eyes removed it as a viable escape. Emma backed up further in the tiny office. Her spine hit a filing cabinet and the dull clang sent papers spewing sideways from an unwieldy pile teetering behind her head. They floated to the brown carpet like flakes of snow. The scent of cheese and onion crisps wafted around the room as a haze. Stephie murmured and bumped her forehead against Emma's shoulder. Dread filled her heart, and she cringed as her breasts tingled and then ached in a simultaneous warning. Feed time.

The two security guards had approached her as she exited the store. At first, she hadn't acknowledged their shouts, her mind occupied with her next task. Emma had bought the craft items required to turn her son into a book character overnight, the plan both genius and achievable. She'd intended to feed her daughter in the car park before fetching Nicky from school. When the guards took her by surprise in the blinding sunlight, all common sense deserted her. She allowed them to cup their palms beneath her elbows and frog march her through the aisles. Other customers turned to stare, and shock struck her dumb.

"You won't let me check your bags, but the cops will make you." The security guard postured, a wide grin splitting his face almost in half. Enjoyment flickered behind his muddy brown irises. His shirt buttons strained against a torso which arced from his collar to his waistband. He formed a human grenade stuffed into a uniform. "You're the second one today." He rocked back and forth on his heels as though expecting Emma to congratulate him. She pressed her spine against the filing cabinet and it tipped enough to hit the wall. Stephie grumbled again, bopping Emma's ear with her tiny head. Panic heightened the blue buzz in Emma's ears and prevented her from rational thought.

"I need to sit down," she rasped. She blew out a breath between pursed lips. "I don't feel well."

"She doesn't look good, Pete." The guard's sidekick stepped through the office door in time to hear Emma's plea. The antithesis of his colleague, he walked on beanstalk legs and his wrist bones protruded from the cuffs of his sleeve. "You need to let her sit down. The cop earlier said you can't be mean to them."

With a grunt of irritation, the overweight guard shoved a chair towards Emma. Its wheels splayed beneath it as it juddered across the worn carpet. Emma stared at it for a moment before sinking into the blue fabric. She rested her shopping bag on the floor between her feet, wincing as her handbag plunged south from her shoulder and landed on top of it. An unhealthy clunk told her it squashed one of the craft items. She prayed it wasn't the paint.

A vibration from the phone in her pocket acted as a starter motor. Emma shifted Stephie to lie with her head in the crook of her elbow and gazed down at her baby daughter. The child blinked her long lashes, wide blue eyes peering out at her from a state of perpetual curiosity. Her crown bounced against Emma's arm as she swivelled to drink in as much of the scene as her brain could process. Her gaze settled on the two guards and she frowned. At not yet six weeks old, her eye muscles and developing retinas would only discern the blurry shapes in the distance. But Emma's reaction to them communicated fear.

Stephie's rosebud lips parted in a wail and her forehead creased. Emma groaned in misery as her body responded and the pads in her bra soaked up the first of her milk leakage. She looked up at the guards. "I need to feed my baby." Panic added a note of aggression to her tone, galvanised by Stephie's discomfort. "Get out."

The heavier guard glanced at his colleague and rolled his eyes. Then he scowled. "No way, lady."

Stephie squirmed in her arms and drew her legs into her chest. Turning her face towards Emma, she scented the milk and urgency infused her cry. Responsibility and hormones cauterised the vying emotions of humiliation and fear. The child's needs dominated everything, and Emma slipped her hand into her blouse and released the catch on her maternity bra.

The security guard's eyes bulged like boiled eggs as Emma's knuckles showed through the fabric. He saw no flesh, but his brain ran riot with ideas and suggestions. She pushed Stephie inside her oversize blouse and winced as her daughter latched on to her nipple. Her toes curled in her plimsolls with the effect of the first strong sucks. The child quieted, her tiny fingers fretting at Emma's blouse as she got busy filling her stomach.

Maternal instincts lit a fire in Emma's belly, and rational thought returned. In a pretence of shifting position on the chair, she slipped her right hand into the pocket of her sweatpants and caressed the hard edges of her phone. The skinny guard nudged his colleague. "We should give her some privacy, Pete. She might report us for human rights or something."

"I won't do that." Emma's voice sounded stronger. Her phone buzzed against her fingers. "But you will be sorry." She pressed the longest button on the right of the screen. Three presses in quick succession. The action seemed to suck the energy and life from her. Putting her faith in someone else to bring rescue and consolation presented a risk. She tried not to consider what might happen if no one came. Because he would this time. He would come for her.

Dear Reader

♥

I would love it if you could leave a review at your usual retailer.

I find the opinions of readers helpful and constructive. Reviews are the Holy Grail to an author as they cause our work to sink or swim. It is the bench mark for other readers and can determine whether our work will be successful and reach many or none. It doesn't have to be an essay or a literary criticism. A few words about what you liked would be most appreciated.

The shortest review I ever received for my work was, *'Great,'* accompanied by five stars, and the longest was a whole video from a gorgeous woman in the USA. My favourite to date has to be the lady who said, *'I read until my eyes fell out.'* I keep looking at that one because it makes me laugh.

You can review on my website, ktbowes.com.

Or go to the book's buy page where you can follow through to your own retailer and leave a review for me.

And hey, let me know when you've done it at admin@ktbowes.com

I'd love to hear from you.

About the Author

K T Bowes is a bestselling teen and women's author. Her novel, *A Trail of Lies*, was the winner of the genre award for Author's Cave in 2014.

Phoenix Du Rose was considered for the prestigious Ngaio Marsh awards for 2021 and *Her Quiet Legacy* in 2022.

K T Bowes is an Englishwoman in exile in New Zealand, swapping rugged cosmopolitan for mountain ranges and terrifying rivers. She loves Māori culture and has learned to weave flax using traditional methods. Her other passion is Rongoa Māori, which involves creating medicines from native plants. She is a student of Te Reo Māori.

You can find her hanging out on social media in the following places.

Check in and say hello. Maybe suggest she gets back to writing and stops watching cat videos.

FACEBOOK
https://www.facebook.com/NZauthorKTBowes/

INSTAGRAM
https://www.instagram.com/k_t_bowes

A Trail of Lies
Gone Phishing

Escaping the Back Country NZ Series:
Pirongia's Secret
Deleilah

Standalone novels:
Artifact
Demons on Her Shoulder
All Saints
Her Quiet Legacy

Humorous Cozy Mystery Series from New Zealand
Dead Straight
Bad Hair Day
Side Parting